Wilder Hearts

JUDY DUARTE
KAREN ROSE SMITH
RAEANNE THAYNE

MILLS & BOON

First published in Great Britain 2013
by Mills & Boon, an imprint of Harlequin (UK) Limited,
Eton House, 18-24 Paradise Road, Richmond, Surrey TW9 1SR

WILDER HEARTS © by Harlequin Enterprises II B.V./S.à.r.l 2013

Once Upon a Pregnancy, Her Mr Right? and *A Merger...or Marriage?* were published in Great Britain by Harlequin (UK) Limited.

Once Upon a Pregnancy © Harlequin Books S.A. 2008
Her Mr Right? © Harlequin Books S.A. 2008
A Merger...or Marriage? © Harlequin Books S.A. 2008

Special thanks and acknowledgement are given to Judy Duarte, Karen Rose Smith and RaeAnne Thayne for their contribution to THE WILDER FAMILY miniseries.

ISBN: 978 0 263 90551 9
ebook ISBN: 978 1 472 00124 5

05-0413

Printed and bound in Spain
by Blackprint CPI, Barcelona

ONCE UPON A
PREGNANCY

BY
JUDY DUARTE

Judy Duarte always knew there was a book inside her, but since English was her least favorite subject in school, she never considered herself a writer. An avid reader who enjoys a happy ending, Judy couldn't shake the dream of creating a book of her own.

Her dream became a reality in March of 2002, when Mills & Boon® Cherish™ released her first book, *Cowboy Courage*. Since then, she has sold nineteen more novels.

Her stories have touched the hearts of readers around the world. And in July of 2005, Judy won a prestigious Readers' Choice Award for *The Rich Man's Son*.

Judy makes her home near the beach in Southern California. When she's not cooped up in her writing cave, she's spending time with her somewhat enormous, but delightfully close family.

To the authors who worked with me on this series—
Marie Ferrarella, Mary J. Forbes, Teresa Southwick,
Karen Rose Smith and RaeAnne Thayne.

Thank you for making this book fun to write.

Chapter One

Simone Garner studied the home pregnancy test kit sitting on the white tile countertop in her bathroom and waited as one long second stretched into another.

She was thirty-seven years old and a nurse at Walnut River General Hospital, so she certainly should have known better than to let something like this happen.

But...she *had* let it happen, and there was no one to blame but herself.

Two months ago, at a cocktail party Dr. Peter Wilder hosted to celebrate the rechristening of the hospital library in honor of his late father, a waiter holding a tray of champagne approached Simone and offered her a glass.

A teetotaler by nature, she nearly declined, but the festive mood had been contagious.

At first, the champagne hadn't done much for her

except to tickle her nose and throat, but she'd soon acquired a taste for it, as well as a mind-numbing buzz.

So when Mike O'Rourke, an attractive medic she'd known for a while, volunteered to drive her home, she'd agreed. Then, while he opened the door to let her into his Jeep, she'd let him kiss her.

Or maybe she'd been the instigator.

Looking back, she wasn't entirely sure who'd actually made the first move. All she knew was that the star-spinning, knee-weakening kiss had happened.

After they arrived at her place, she should have thanked him for the ride and let it go at that, but for some reason, she felt compelled to invite him in. She'd given him a tour of the house she'd remodeled, then turned on her new stereo system and played a soft, suggestive love song.

"Do you want to dance?"

Her boldness had been so out of character that, in retrospect, she'd blamed her newfound self-confidence on the alcohol, as well as the sleek black cocktail dress she'd purchased for the occasion and the cute but impractical heels she'd probably only wear once.

With her senses still reeling from both the champagne and Mike's charm, Simone had slipped into his embrace, quickly relishing his musky, mountain-fresh scent and the faint bristle of his cheek against hers.

They'd swayed to the soul-stirring melody, hearts beating and bodies moving as one—until she'd stumbled.

She'd grabbed on to Mike for balance, and they'd shared a laugh, followed by a heated look, a lingering touch.

One thing had led to another, and they'd kissed again.

Oh, Lordy, how they'd kissed.

Then, for some crazy reason—the heat of the moment, she supposed—she'd led him to her bedroom.

Waking up in Mike's arms and then sending him on his way would have been a lot easier to do if their love-making had only been so-so. In that case, he would have understood why she'd ended things.

But the entire experience had been off the charts.

And now she feared that if great sex had anything to do with sperm motility or fertility, she'd be having septuplets.

Oh, God, no. *Please,* no.

Just the thought of what a pink dot on the testing apparatus meant made her nauseous, even though she'd already had the dry heaves earlier this morning.

At first, she'd told herself that stress from work had caused her period to be delayed. After all, there had been some allegations of insurance fraud at Walnut River General, and the timing couldn't be worse, with the hospital in danger of being taken over by Northeastern HealthCare.

And to top it off, someone was leaking financial information and other sensitive data to the conglomerate, putting the hospital at a significant disadvantage for negotiations.

But Simone hadn't been able to explain away her symptoms any longer. So she got up from her seat on the commode and stood before the test, while her future and the pale yellow walls of the small bathroom seemed to close in on her.

No pink dot yet, though.

Maybe it *had* been stress. Maybe her conscience and

her imagination had become a tag team and were really doing a number on her, punishing her for allowing herself one little sexual fantasy.

After all, she and Mike had used condoms, but, looking back, she had to admit they'd gotten a little careless with their use as the night wore on.

She blew out a sigh, then glanced at her wristwatch, realizing it was silly to second-guess the test results when she'd know for sure in a few more minutes.

Nevertheless, she wasn't the kind of woman she'd pretended to be and couldn't help feeling foolish for her lack of self-control.

Over the past five weeks, she'd rationalized about what she'd done at least a hundred times, telling herself she was a healthy woman with sexual needs that hadn't been satisfied in a long time. And that she couldn't help having a one-night stand with the dark-haired paramedic who was too sexy for his own good—or rather, for *her* own good.

But Mike O'Rourke was five years her junior. And he deserved a girl his own age, a younger woman who shared his white-picket-fence dreams.

Now, here Simone was, facing the reality of her champagne-induced mistake.

If her suspicion was right, if she was pregnant, she would make an appointment with Mark Kipper, one of the doctors in the Walnut River OB/GYN Medical Group. She was determined to do whatever it took to make sure the child was as healthy as possible.

A thump sounded against the door, followed by a bark and a whine.

"Hold on, Woofer," she told the big, clumsy mutt

who demanded her time when she was home. "I'll be out in a minute."

Each day after a trying but satisfying shift at the hospital, she went home and was met at the gate by the ugly but lovable dog she'd adopted through an animal-rescue group.

Finding Woofer and bringing him home had been a fluke that had proven to be a blessing for both woman and dog, even if there were times she missed her privacy and freedom.

But at least she could put Woofer out in the backyard to entertain himself with butterflies and chew toys while she was at work. She certainly couldn't do that with a baby.

Simone took a good hard look at the testing apparatus that held the answer to the question that had been haunting her since the morning she'd awakened in Mike's arms.

As a mental clock ticktocked in her brain, she watched the little pink dot grow darker by the moment. Then she blew out a ragged sigh of resignation.

She *was* pregnant.

With Mike O'Rourke's baby.

What the hell was she going to do?

There was no telling how the handsome paramedic was going to feel about this. She suspected the news might blow that crush to kingdom come—a good thing, actually. But still, Simone was in no hurry to tell him.

"Ar-oof." Woofer's tail thump, thump, thumped against the door. "Ar-oof, ar-oof."

That darn dog could be such a baby sometimes.

In fact, he was the only baby a woman like Simone ought to have. Which was why there was only one option for her to consider...adoption.

As she watched the dot turn a deeper shade of pink, her uneasiness grew by leaps and bounds.

Mike wanted more out of their professional relationship than friendship, and ever since they'd made love, he'd been even more determined than ever to be a part of her life.

If he weren't such a nice guy, if he didn't make her laugh like no one else could, she would have given him the cold shoulder and completely shut him out until he saw reason and left her alone.

It was a ploy she had perfected in the past, an easy ruse that had come with the old baggage she carried from childhood.

But she'd never been able to fully shoot an icy glare at Mike. He'd just been too sweet, too charming.

Another thump sounded on the bathroom door, followed by a loud bark. "Okay, Woofer. We'll take a walk. Just give me a—"

The doorbell rang, and Woofer took off, howling up a storm, his paws clomping across the hardwood floor of the small, cozy house.

"Oh, great," she muttered, assuming a neighbor or possibly a salesman was at the door. "I'm coming!"

She left the pregnancy test in the bathroom, its pink dot shining like a beacon, and headed for the entry, where she would have to run interference between the person knocking and her four-legged roommate.

Woofer might look and sound like one heck of a guard dog, when in truth, he was a real softie. If confronted with a burglar, he'd probably knock him to the floor and lick him to death.

When she reached the door and peered through the

peephole at the man on the front porch, instant recognition caused her heart to drop to the pit of her stomach.

There stood Mike O'Rourke, as big and gorgeous as you please. He wore a pair of faded Levi's, a navy-blue T-shirt that displayed a white Walnut River Fire Department logo across his chest and a heart-stopping grin.

In his hands, he held a cardboard box.

What was *he* doing here?

"Just a minute." She grabbed Woofer's collar and pulled him back so she could get a hold of the knob. Hopefully, the screen door would prevent the dog from dive-bombing Mike and knocking him on his butt, which more than one E.R. nurse had admired behind his back—a butt that Simone had learned was even more noteworthy bare.

She swung open the wooden door, leaving the screen to separate them.

Mike, with his black hair stylishly mussed and his green eyes sparkling, shifted the box he held from one side to the other. "I brought you something. Can you put Woofer in the backyard for a couple of minutes?"

He'd brought her something?

Well, it certainly wasn't flowers. Or chocolate, which seemed like the kind of romantic gift he might offer her.

"Give me a minute, will you?" She grabbed Woofer by the collar again. "I'll be right back." Then she led the dog to the kitchen and opened the back door, encouraging him to romp in the yard.

But Woofer wasn't happy about missing the excitement of having a guest, and Simone, on the other hand, wasn't all that thrilled about having Mike O'Rourke stop by, especially today.

Of course, she supposed it wouldn't hurt to sit outside with Mike on the front porch for a little while and chat.

But when she heard the hinges of the screen door creak open, followed by footsteps on the hardwood floor, her senses reeled and her tummy took a tumble.

She didn't need to consult a psychologist or social worker to figure out why.

Not with that home pregnancy test propped up on her bathroom counter, the results as obvious as a pink neon sign.

Mike couldn't imagine that Simone had expected him to stand on the stoop like a pizza deliveryman. And although she hadn't exactly invited him into the house, she was putting Woofer in the backyard, and she'd said she would be right back.

So he'd entered the living room, took a seat on the pale green sofa and waited for her to return.

Actually, what he'd brought her wasn't exactly a gift—unless she wanted to keep it, which, he guessed, would be okay.

He glanced down at the cardboard box with the airholes he'd poked in the lid. He was in a bind, and the first person he'd thought about was Simone, who had a soft spot for animals.

After all, she'd not only opened her heart and home to Woofer, a brown, mop-haired dog who stood a slam-dunk chance to win an ugly-pet contest, but she also treated him as though he had a pedigree and was destined for nobility.

The night Mike had driven Simone home from the cocktail party, she'd invited him in and introduced him to the oversize, gangly mutt that couldn't walk across the floor without his hind end doing a hokeypokey shake to the right.

"That's got to be the ugliest dog I've ever seen," Mike had said.

"I know," she'd responded with a pride-tinged voice. "That's exactly why I adopted him. He needed a home more than any of the other dogs. Besides, he's a real sweetheart."

At that point, Simone had turned to Woofer and given him a big hug, which had caused the hem of her dress to hike up and reveal a lovely expanse of her upper thigh.

A smile had stretched across Mike's face, but not just because of the sexy flash of skin. It was the glimpse he'd gotten of the *real* Simone Garner that evening that had turned his heart on end. A fun-loving, brown-haired beauty that the no-nonsense nurse kept locked away.

Most of the medical staff at Walnut River General, as well as a lot of the guys at the department, thought Simone was cold and distant, but Mike knew the dedicated E.R. nurse better than anyone and saw things in her no one else did.

Sure, she could be aloof at times, but Mike suspected she'd been hurt by someone in the past—and badly. He also believed that if anyone could help her heal and forget about the pain, it was him.

When he first met her a few years ago, it was on a professional level. He and his partner had brought in a teenage girl who'd been the victim of a hit-and-run. The seriously injured teen had been in severe pain and was screaming for her mom, who'd yet to be identified or notified.

Simone had begun talking softly to her at first,

soothing the teen's fears, while doing her job and getting a name and number for the mother.

Mike had walked away from the E.R. that night with a great deal of respect for her. Respect had given way to admiration, and over the course of the year, Mike had taken a long, hard fall for her.

There'd even been a time or two when he'd caught her looking at him, passion clearly brewing in those soulful brown eyes. A guy didn't misread something like that.

Yet even though he knew she felt something for him too, she'd turned down each of his attempts to date her.

Then came the cocktail party that Dr. Peter Wilder had hosted.

Simone had been a warm and sexy woman that night, her walls and her legion of defense mechanisms down for the count.

But she'd soon grown distant, claiming it had all been a mistake and referring to what they'd experienced as a one-night stand.

As soft footsteps sounded, he glanced up and smiled.

But she didn't return the friendly greeting. Instead, she seemed nervous, agitated and slightly unbalanced.

Of course, she'd been acting that way around him ever since they'd slept together. So maybe he shouldn't read too much into it.

She nodded at the box he held. "What do you have in there?"

He untucked the lid and pulled out a sleepy puppy, its black-and-white coat soft and curly. It didn't take a blood test to determine that it had various quantities of cocker spaniel, poodle and terrier DNA.

"Oh my gosh. He's darling." Simone started toward

Mike, then stiffened and froze. "Wait a minute. You said you brought me something. I hope you're not thinking that I'd consider taking in another dog."

"Well, I didn't exactly plan to give little Wags to you permanently, but he and I really do need your help."

She tilted her head slightly to the side. "What's going on?"

He held the puppy close, and it nuzzled against him, then gave him a lick. "I was out jogging yesterday and found this poor little guy wandering on the dirt trail near the river. He's too young to be alone like that. And since we weren't near any neighborhoods, it was obvious that he'd been abandoned. So I couldn't just leave him there."

Her stance softened—just a bit.

"I ended my run right there, then took him home. I even checked with the animal shelter, but so far, no one has reported him missing."

She looked at the puppy, which was squirming to get down and start checking out its new surroundings.

"Poor little guy." Simone reached out and scratched its head. "I wonder who would abandon him like that."

"That's why I decided to keep him," Mike admitted.

She looked up and caught his gaze. "Then why is he *here?*"

"Because right now, I'm sharing a house with Leif, and when I took Wags home, I found out that Leif is allergic to pet dander. So if I'm going to keep him, I'll have to find another place to live sooner than I anticipated. I'll also need someone to keep him for me until then."

"And that someone is *me?*" She stroked one of the puppy's ears.

Good, she was beginning to warm and, hopefully, to bond. "Leif's sister is a real estate agent, and she's going to search the MLS listing for something in my price range."

Of course, even if the agent found something that Mike liked, escrows took time. So he was hoping Simone wouldn't mind puppy-sitting for quite a while.

"Here." Mike handed Wags to Simone. "What do you think? My options are limited, and I can't just dump him at a pet-boarding place when he's so young."

Okay, so that wasn't entirely true. Mike did have other options. He could find the puppy another home, maybe with one of the firefighters at the department. Surely someone would want him. After all, a puppy as cute as Wags stood a heck of a lot better chance at being adopted than Woofer. But there was no need to mention that to Simone. Not when Mike was hoping she'd take the fluffy, black-and-white pup and allow him to visit her regularly.

Wags gave Simone a wet, loving lick on the chin, softening her even more.

"All right," she finally said. "He can stay. But only until you find another place. I have no idea how Woofer is going to feel about having him here, and I could be making a big mistake."

"You said Woofer doesn't even know that he's a dog," Mike said. "He thinks he's human. And all kids need a pet. Woofer will probably love having this little guy to pal around with."

"I hope so."

Mike *knew* so. Finding Wags hadn't been an accident. Fate had stepped in to give him and Simone another helping hand.

"Where are his things?" Simone asked.

"His *things?*"

"You know, puppy food, toys…"

Simone's pretty brown eyes grew large and luminous. "All you brought is a puppy and an empty cardboard box?"

Oops. He'd been in such a hurry to bring Wags to Simone that he hadn't thought about her not having everything the puppy would need. Last night, he'd knotted up an old sock for him to chew on, although he'd left it at home. And then he'd fed him some leftover steak that had been chopped up. This morning, he'd given Wags scrambled eggs and bacon. So it wasn't as if he'd neglected to take care of him. But a shopping trip was definitely in order.

He could do it on his own, but maybe it would be in his best interests to feign ignorance. "I'll be happy to purchase whatever he needs, but you'd better come with me. I'm not sure what to buy."

She looked at him in disbelief, and he suspected she might decline to go with him.

But then again, fate seemed to be working in his favor when she handed Wags back to him. "All right. You take the puppy to the car and I'll meet you there."

"What are you going to do?"

"I need to go to the bathroom and grab my purse."

"Your purse is in the bathroom?"

She shot him a frown that suggested she didn't find his joke funny. "Just give me a minute, will you?"

Sure. He'd give her all the time she needed.

At thirty-two, he was ready to get married. And if it took her a bit longer to get used to the idea, then so be it.

Her arguments would soon go by the wayside.

So what if she was older than he was? Or if she wasn't used to big, happy families?

And so what if she wasn't ready to settle down?

Mike was a focused competitor and believed that there wasn't anything he couldn't do or have—once he set his mind to it.

And he'd set his mind—and his heart—on Simone.

Chapter Two

Simone handed little Wags back to Mike. She hoped and prayed he wouldn't ask to use her bathroom before she got rid of the testing apparatus. If he did, she'd have to race him there.

She crossed her arms and waited for him to head for his Jeep, yet he merely stood in the living room, studying her with expressive green eyes and a dimpled grin.

"I really appreciate this," he said.

She supposed he did, but she wasn't keen on taking care of Wags for him, no matter how cute either Mike or the puppy was.

Nor was she up for a shopping trip.

But agreeing to go with him seemed to be the quickest way to get him out of her house. And the sooner he went outside, the better.

"I won't be long," she said. "You can even go out to the car and start the engine, if you'd like to."

"That's all right. I'll just wait for you here." Mike glanced at Wags. "We don't mind, do we, buddy?"

The longer her one-night lover remained in her house, the more uneasy she became.

She doubted that he suspected anything, though.

How could he?

"Okay," she finally said. Then she turned and hurried to the bathroom, where she locked herself inside.

With her secret safe for the time being, she rested her back against the door and blew out a ragged sigh. Then, feeling only slightly relieved, she quickly scooped up the plastic apparatus that still displayed evidence of the baby they'd created and shoved it into the back of the cupboard, behind a stack of towels.

As soon as she returned home, and Mike was no longer around, she would double-bag the test kit in two plastic grocery sacks and throw it away.

Of course, she'd have to level with him sometime and tell him she was pregnant, but she was still processing the news herself.

So, some other day, when the time was right, she'd let him know that it was her problem, not his. And that she wouldn't need anything from him. She would also tell him she'd decided to give up the baby for adoption, which was the best thing she could do for everyone involved, especially her child.

Adoption was the decision she'd wished her mother had made when she'd been pregnant with Simone. Instead, her mom had botched up the whole mother/daughter thing, something that continued to plague them both to this day.

Simone flushed the toilet, just to make Mike think she'd had the usual reasons for locking herself in the bathroom, then washed her hands and dried them on a white, fluffy towel reserved for guests.

Not that she and Woofer had many of them.

Dr. Ella Wilder stopped by sometimes. So did Isobel Suarez, the hospital social worker who'd become a friend.

Of course, Mike was here now—and waiting for her.

She looked in the mirror, caught the frumpy, pale image looking back at her.

Her hair, which had been put into a just-hanging-out-at-home ponytail earlier, had come loose. And she wasn't wearing any makeup whatsoever.

Dressed in her favorite pair of well-worn jeans and a Rosie the Riveter T-shirt, she was a mind-boggling contrast to the chic, sexy woman who'd invited Mike into her house and into her bed five weeks ago.

But she didn't feel like putting on makeup or a happy face. Nor did she want to draw attention to herself in a feminine sense.

After all, look what had happened when she'd dressed up for that cocktail party and had pretended to be someone she wasn't.

But she couldn't very well go out looking like a total frump, although she wouldn't change her clothes. How could she when she wore a shirt with Rosie the Riveter rolling up a sleeve and proclaiming, "We can do it!"

So trying to draw upon Rosie's confidence and determination, she removed the rubber band and ran a brush through her hair, leaving it down. Then she dug into her makeup drawer and pulled out a tube of lipstick. But after taking off the cap, she paused.

She really didn't want Mike to think she was getting dolled up for his benefit. Of course, the sexy paramedic didn't need that kind of encouragement.

The first time he'd come on to her—more than a year ago—had been in the hospital doctors' lounge, where she'd been pouring herself a cup of overbrewed coffee. She was wearing a pair of blue scrubs and was close to finishing up a long, grueling twelve-hour shift.

"Hey," he'd said. "I've got tickets to a concert at the Stardust Theater on Thursday. And I've asked around. We're both off that night."

She'd caught him looking at her several times in the past, and the intensity in his gaze had always spiked her pulse. Mike O'Rourke was a handsome man, and any woman would be flattered to know she'd caught his eye.

But Simone hadn't expected his interest in her to take a romantic turn, and her senses had reeled.

"I...uh...I've already got plans," she'd lied, scrambling to come up with an excuse.

And she'd been putting him off ever since, even though he told her he was prepared to wait until she was ready to give "them" a try.

He'd never been pushy, but now that they'd slept together, his determination seemed to have grown stronger.

So she re-capped the lipstick without using it and put it away. Then she slid the bathroom drawer shut and headed to her bedroom for her purse and a light sweater—just in case. The New England weather was always a bit unpredictable in April, although the past few days had been remarkably pleasant.

When she returned to the living room, Mike was standing by the door, ready to go.

He held Wags in the crook of his arm and opened the door for her with his free hand. Then he waited on the sidewalk while she made sure Woofer had fresh water and locked up the house.

"Where do you suggest we go to find dog supplies?" he asked.

"There's a pet store on Lexington, across from Prudy's Menu. It's called Tails a Waggin', and they'll have everything we'll need."

"All right. I know where that is." He opened the passenger door of his Jeep Wrangler, and after she climbed into the seat, he handed Wags to her. "He hates that box if he's awake. Why don't you hold him."

Simone took the squirming pup. She had to admit, it was a cute little thing. But she needed another dog around the house like she needed a hole in the head, and she couldn't help wondering what she'd gotten herself into.

Wasn't her life going to be complicated enough for the next seven or eight months?

"Thanks for coming with me," he said. "I don't want to forget anything."

"No problem," she said, although she wasn't being entirely truthful.

She really wasn't in the mood to go anywhere. Not when she had a stack of laundry to do at home. She'd also planned to clean out the refrigerator and wash the windows, chores she saved for her day off. And she'd told Woofer she would take him for a long walk this afternoon.

Not that the dog would hold her to it, she supposed. But some things easily became habits that were hard to break.

And speaking of habits, she couldn't even imagine

the effect a new puppy was going to have on her normal routine.

Of course, a baby would really shake things up.

Thank goodness she knew better than to open herself up to that.

Mike backed his Jeep out of Simone's driveway and drove through Riverdale, an older part of town, where the houses near the river had been built in the 1940s. With only a few exceptions, the yards and structures had been kept up throughout the years.

"I've always liked this neighborhood," he said, thinking it had a Norman Rockwell appeal.

"Me, too." Simone glanced out the window, as though appreciating the maples, sycamores and the occasional hemlock that shaded the sidewalks and the street on which she lived.

When Mike and his brothers were in high school, they'd worked summers for their uncle, who was a building contractor. As a result, each of the boys could do just about anything—electrical, plumbing, drywall, painting—skills that could turn an old house into something special.

A lot of people might prefer to buy newer homes, but Mike was drawn to the quaint, nostalgic ambience of this particular neighborhood. In fact, he'd told his Realtor that he was looking for a fixer-upper but wouldn't mind purchasing anything in Riverdale, should one of the properties become available.

"Did you have to do a lot of work after you moved in?" he asked, thinking about the cozy, two-bedroom brick structure she'd purchased.

"Yes, but it was actually fun to roll up my sleeves and watch things change before my eyes. I even took some of those home-improvement classes they offer at Hadley's Hardware Store. I couldn't afford to do everything at once, but I started by working on one room at a time. The first thing I did was to tear up the carpeting and refinish the original hardwood flooring. Then I painted."

Overall, he had to say he liked what she'd done to the place, although his focus had been on more than beige walls and white crown molding the night he'd taken her home.

In fact, as they'd left the cocktail party, he'd stolen a kiss while the two of them stood next to his Jeep, and his hormones hadn't given him or his brain cells a free moment until dawn.

He'd known their lovemaking would be good, but it had been better than either of them could have imagined, and they'd awakened like a pair of spoons, completely spent and sated.

Yet one night hadn't been enough.

He slid a sidelong glance across the seat and saw that she was staring straight ahead and biting her bottom lip. Then she glanced at him, lips parting.

Had her thoughts gone in a sexual direction, too? Was she thinking about the pleasure they'd given each other in the antique bed in her candlelit room?

He suspected so, because her words seemed to have dissipated in the cab of the Jeep.

But he didn't let the silence get to him. "I told Karen, Leif's sister, that I'd be interested in buying something in this part of town, especially if it needed some work."

She tucked a strand of hair behind her ear. "I'll keep

my eyes and ears open. Mark Griffith, who lives with his wife and son on Ash, might have to be transferred to another office out of state. If so, he might be interested in selling."

"That would work out great for me." Since Simone didn't comment either way about the possibility of them being neighbors, he let it drop.

Minutes later, he pulled the Jeep into a parking spot on Lexington, two spaces down from the pet shop, and turned off the ignition.

"How'd you know about this place?" he asked.

"Originally, Ella Wilder mentioned it to me."

"She has animals?"

"Yes, a cat named Molly. She found the poor little thing injured and lying on the side of the road. A lot of people might have put her to sleep since she lost a leg, but Ella nursed her back to health."

Mike never figured the young orthopedic surgeon as an animal lover, but then again, he hadn't suspected Simone to be one, either. Not until he'd seen her with Woofer.

"One day, after shopping, I stopped at Prudy's Menu to place a take-home order, and I noticed it across the street. Ella had said it was a mom-and-pop–type store and that it could almost be entertaining at times. So I decided to check it out. And that's the day I met Woofer."

"You've gotta be kidding. I thought pet stores only sold animals with pedigrees."

"Actually, the Baxters allow several different pet-rescue organizations to hold adoption days at the store on weekends. And that's exactly what was going on the first time I stopped in to visit."

"Wait a minute." Mike slid her a crooked grin. "You

mean that you make a point of visiting the pet store even when you don't have anything to buy?"

"Yes, I do that every once in a while. Millie and Fred Baxter are nice people. I first met them a year or so ago when Fred was brought into the E.R. after suffering chest pains."

"Oh, yeah?"

Simone had always told him that she tried not to get attached to her patients, which is why she enjoyed working in the E.R. Most of the patients were just passing through. But obviously, she got attached to some of them.

"Fred had suffered a major heart attack," she said.

"Obviously, he pulled through."

Simone nodded. "Millie was trying to be tough for his sake, but I could see the fear in her eyes. They were pretty young to be going through something like that, and for some reason, I was drawn to her. So when I was off duty that evening, I picked up a cup of coffee in the doctors' lounge, then offered it to her. I sat with her for a few minutes, and we started chatting."

Mike had seen Simone with her patients, and while she was good to all of them when they were in her care, she was able to detach when they were either admitted or discharged.

And she didn't normally spend her free time visiting with them.

"What was so special about Millie?" he asked. There had to have been something that appealed to Simone, and he was curious to know what it was. To know what drew her to certain people.

Simone shrugged, then focused her attention on the

puppy in her lap, her thoughts appearing to drift somewhere else.

When she glanced up, her gaze snagged his, tugging at his heart in that way only Simone could do. "I'm really not a romantic person, so you'll probably think this is weird coming from me, but I think Fred and Millie are soul mates—if there is such a thing."

There was. Mike suspected he and Simone were, too, but she hadn't quite figured it out yet.

"Anyway," Simone continued, "Millie was worried about losing Fred, which was understandable. But she mentioned they'd been trying to…" Simone paused and glanced out the passenger side of the window, as though distracted and drifting off topic.

"Trying to *what?*" Mike asked, steering her back to the conversation they'd been having.

She cleared her throat. "They'd been trying to have a baby for years and had finally given up. In vitro and other expensive fertility treatments are out of the question, since they're new business owners and have poured their savings into the store. They'd just started the adoption process when Fred was brought into the E.R. However, Millie realized that his heart condition might make it more difficult for them to adopt."

Again, Simone glanced out into the distance, but Mike could see the cogs turning, her mind drifting, and he wished she'd share those thoughts with him.

He couldn't imagine his future without kids. He adored his nieces and nephews and looked forward to the day he could give them a couple of cousins to play with.

She obviously felt badly that Millie couldn't have the family she'd dreamed of. Maybe that was because

Simone harbored some secret maternal urges, too. And if so, that would play right into Mike's hands.

Unless, of course, Simone had reason to believe that she couldn't have children. Maybe that's why she took such a strong stance against marriage or even a relationship.

"Adopting a child is a good option," Mike said, just in case he'd touched on a sore subject. He wanted her to know that he'd be okay if she was infertile—disappointed, but okay. "And there's always a need for good foster parents. So even if a person can't have kids of their own, there are plenty of opportunities to be parents."

"Yes, you're right." Her voice came out soft, burdened. "Millie's the kind of woman who would make a great mother. And if I were a kid, I would have loved to have someone like her adopt me."

One night at the hospital, he'd mentioned that he came from a big family and that he hoped to have a few children of his own someday. She admitted to being an only child and said she wasn't big on kids.

But that couldn't be true. She was terrific with the pediatric patients who came in to the E.R.

"You know," Mike said, "not being able to have children wouldn't be the end of the world."

"You're right. And honestly, Millie was far more concerned about losing Fred than her chance at adopting a baby. She loves him more than anything in the world and is glad to have him for as long as possible. She's also resigned to the fact that their pets will be the only children they have." Simone unhooked her seat belt, handed Wags to Mike and reached for the door handle. "Come on, I'll introduce you to one of the nicest couples in Walnut River."

* * *

Millie Baxter, a tall, slender blonde in her late thirties, broke into a smile that lit up the room when she spotted Simone enter the pet shop.

"Well, if it isn't my favorite nurse." She left her position near the cash register and greeted Simone at the door with a warm hug.

The Baxters tried hard to remember the names of not only their customers, but also their customers' pets, but they didn't offer hugs to just anyone.

"Where's Woofer?" Millie asked.

"He's at home and not all that happy about it. But he'd really be pouting if he knew where I was. He loves coming here with me to shop, although part of the reason is because of those meaty treats you always give him." Simone turned to Mike and introduced him to Millie, calling him her friend and mentioning that he was a paramedic.

"And who is this sweet little guy?" Millie asked, zeroing in on the puppy in Mike's arms.

"His name is Wags," Mike said, "and he's going to stay with Simone until I find another place to live."

"I'll bet Woofer loves *you*," Millie said to the dog.

"They haven't met yet," Simone said. "And I'm not sure how Woofer is going to feel about sharing my time or having a houseguest."

"Just take it slow and easy when you introduce them. There's always a bit of an adjustment period, but I'm sure they'll be the best of friends before you know it." Millie looked at Mike. "Would you like me to hold Wags for you while you shop?"

"Thanks. I have a feeling we'll be needing both

hands." Mike passed the puppy to Millie. "So, if you'll excuse me, I'd better get a cart."

"Where's Fred?" Simone asked. She hoped he was feeling okay and hadn't stayed home.

"Helen Walters purchased a new aquarium for her nephew, so he drove over to the boy's house to help them set it up. He's been gone quite a while, so I expect him back soon."

The Baxters were very generous with their time and their expertise, so going the extra mile wasn't surprising.

"That was sweet of Fred to help."

"Aw, you know how Fred is." Millie smiled, eyes crinkling. "If there's anything he likes more than animals it's kids."

"Okay," Mike said upon his return with a cart. "Where do we find the dog supplies?"

"They're on aisle one." Simone pointed to the right. "I'll show you."

As they strode through the small but well-stocked and -organized shop, Simone pointed to the basset hound snoozing on a blue pad by the cash register. She noticed that he was wearing the usual bandanna around his neck. It was red this time, although the color and print usually varied from day to day.

"That's Popeye Baxter," Simone told Mike. "He comes to work with Fred and Millie each day and is practically a fixture around here."

"Lucky dog."

"Yes, he certainly is. The Baxters own quite a few pets." All of which they referred to as "the kids."

"Are the other animals here at the store?"

"Most of them are. Tina the cat is usually playing on

a carpet-covered climbing structure in the kitty section. And Herb the parrot is perched in the bird aisle."

Mike scanned the interior of the pet store. "I can see why you like to stop in and visit."

"Can you?" she asked. She'd always thought animal lovers were a bit…over the top. But that was until she met the Baxters—and adopted Woofer. The big, goofy dog had really grown on her. She suspected that was because she and the mutt had a lot in common.

"Honey," a man's voice rang out. "I'm back."

"That's Fred." Simone nodded to the short, heavyset man who'd entered the store through the back door. "I'll introduce you after we finish stocking up on supplies."

Ten minutes later, they'd filled the cart with a doggie bed, chew toys, puppy food, a pet carrier, leash and collar.

"Hey, wait." Mike threw in a bulky piece of knotted rope and a rawhide bone. "We don't want Woofer feeling left out."

She figured the toys would all become community property eventually. "You don't need to worry about Woofer."

"Maybe not, but my sister Kari just had her second baby—a boy. And she bought a doll and a toy stroller for his big sister. She didn't want her little girl to be jealous of the new baby."

See? Simone knew nothing about that sort of thing, which was another reason she would make a lousy mother, if given the chance.

"You know," Mike said as they approached the checkout counter, "speaking of kids, this kind of feels like we're preparing a doggie nursery."

The hint of a chuckle tickled the tone of his voice,

but Simone didn't find anything warm or amusing in the words.

They *weren't* co–dog owners.

And there wasn't anything parental about their relationship, even though a child they'd created was growing in Simone's womb.

A sense of uneasiness settled over her as she thought of giving up the baby. But the child deserved a loving home with two parents, a couple who would lovingly prepare a nursery in anticipation of the child they'd always wanted. And she tamped down the momentary discomfort.

Simone glanced at Millie and recognized a soulful longing that whisked across her face, a momentary stab of grief.

It wasn't likely that Millie and Fred would ever have the chance to decorate a nursery. And the shame of it all was that they'd make great parents. If given the opportunity, they'd welcome a new baby…

Simone's musing took an interesting turn.

Maybe Fred and Millie would want her baby.

Wouldn't it be easier to give the child to people she knew? A couple she trusted?

It was certainly something to consider. And she hoped that Mike would see the wisdom in it—when the time came to tell him that during their one night together they conceived a baby.

She sure hoped he wouldn't give her a hard time about the decision she'd made.

Still, her tummy tossed and turned.

What if Mike didn't agree? What if he didn't let up on her and tried to push her into something she knew was wrong—at least, for her?

"That will be a hundred and twenty-seven dollars and sixteen cents," Millie said, drawing Simone from her musing.

Mike whipped out his credit card in a blur. Or so it seemed.

Simone blinked, feeling a bit dizzy and light-headed.

Whew. All she needed to do was to pass out. The dedicated paramedic and the dutiful suitor in Mike would have a field day with that.

Uh-oh.

A buzz filled her ears, and she reached for Mike's arm, felt the bulge of muscle tense.

He turned and caught her eye, his smile morphing into a frown. "What's the matter?"

"I…" Damn. She didn't want to tell him. But if she didn't, he was going to figure it out all by himself. "I think I'm going to…"

Her knees buckled before she could finish the thought.

Chapter Three

Mike caught Simone in his arms just before she crumpled to the pet-shop floor.

As much as he wanted to hold her close, to cling to the citrusy scent of her bath soap and shampoo, he gently laid her down and knelt beside her. He might be medically trained and competent in an emergency, but he wasn't at all prepared for Simone's collapse.

"Oh my gosh," Millie said, hurrying around the counter to see what was going on. "Is she okay? What happened?"

Mike didn't know for sure. "I think she fainted."

Simone's vulnerability damn near sent him reeling, and he took her hand, checking her pulse while assessing her respiration. He placed a hand on her forehead to gauge her temperature and found it cool, so she didn't have a fever.

Her lashes, dark and lush against the skin that had gone pale, fluttered ever so slightly.

"Fred!" Millie called. "Come quick!"

Simone lifted her lids, blinking them a couple of times until her eyes searched Mike's face, as though she was trying to focus.

When she tried to sit up, he stopped her. "Just lie still for a minute or two."

"Okay." She drew in a shaky breath, then slowly blew it out.

"How are you feeling?" Mike ran his knuckles along her cheek—God, he'd missed touching her.

"A little light-headed and buzzy, but nothing hurts."

Again, she began to fold up into a sit. And this time, he placed his hands on her shoulders and gently held her down. "I'm calling the shots, and you need to lie still a little longer."

She offered him a wry smile. "I thought paramedics were supposed to yield to the nursing staff."

"Yeah, well, not when the nurse is incapacitated." He tried to shrug off his concern, but couldn't. What the hell had happened? And why?

Damn. He wanted to do so much more than tell her to stay put and to remain quiet, but she was conscious. And he couldn't find any of her vitals out of whack. So he relied on his training to tell him she was okay when his heart was telling him to call 911 and ask for backup.

Deciding upon a compromise, he said, "As soon as you feel up to moving, I'll take you to the hospital and get you checked out."

"No, that's not necessary. I'll be okay." She closed

her eyes, but only for a moment. "This isn't serious, Mike. Besides, it was my own fault."

"What do you mean?"

"I haven't eaten anything since yesterday at lunch, and I really should have grabbed a snack on our way out the door."

He hoped she wasn't dieting; she didn't need to lose weight. She was in *great* shape. And even if she *could* stand to lose a couple of pounds, she ought to know that starvation wasn't the way to go.

"I got a little light-headed and—" she shrugged her shoulders "—I passed out."

She could say *that* again.

He watched the color slowly creep back into her face. "Why haven't you been eating?"

"I was tired when I got home from work last night and decided to stretch out on the sofa and watch a little television before fixing dinner. The next thing I knew, it was morning." She slowly sat up and leaned her back against the counter. "And when I woke up, I... Well, I just got busy. That's all."

And then he'd dragged her shopping for pet supplies. Great.

By this time, Fred Baxter came running to their side, his breathing heavy and more labored than a short, indoor jog should have caused. "Oh my goodness! *Simone.* What happened?"

"I fainted," she said. "I'm sure it was caused by low blood sugar."

"I've got some orange juice in the back room," Millie said. "And a granola bar."

"That would help." Simone slowly sat up, then ran a hand through her hair. "Thank you."

As Millie hurried through the store, Mike said, "You're going to need to eat more than juice and a snack. I'll take you across the street to the deli so you can order lunch."

And for once, when it came to Simone, he wasn't going to sit back and let her call the shots.

Minutes after Fred had loaded their purchases into Mike's Jeep and returned the key, Simone allowed Mike to lead her across the street to Prudy's Menu. The small bakery/deli specialized in scrumptious desserts, gourmet coffees and teas, as well as homemade breads, soups and sandwiches.

They sat at one of the green bistro tables that graced the street-front patio of the eatery. An umbrella shaded them and their place settings from the dappled sunlight that filtered through the leaves of several old maples that grew along Lexington Avenue.

The waitress had just given them water and taken their orders.

"Are you feeling better now?" Mike asked.

"I'm still a little shaky, but it's passing." Simone offered him a smile she hoped was convincing.

She wasn't used to being coddled or taken care of. Even as a kid, when she'd actually been sick, she'd had to fend for herself. So she'd gotten accustomed to being alone when she was under the weather and, to be honest, actually preferred it that way. For a woman who dispensed endless doses of TLC for a living, she was uneasy being on the receiving end.

Of course, now that she'd had a granola bar to eat and some juice to sip, she was almost back to normal—at least, physically. Emotionally, not so much. The news of her pregnancy was still a little unsettling.

Giving the baby up might not be easy, but it would be for the best.

"Are you too cold?" he asked. "Or too warm? We can go back inside if you'd be more comfortable."

She reached across the table and placed her hand over the top of his. "I'm *fine*. And I'll be even better when the waitress brings my soup. Besides, we have to sit outside because of Wags."

"You're right, but I'll bet Millie and Fred would have watched the puppy for us."

Simone peered under the table, where Wags was tethered to a chair leg by a new red collar and leash. He was so content to be greedily chomping on a little rawhide bone that he didn't even glance up at her. "Look how happy he is."

Mike's gaze remained on her. "If it gets too warm for you out here, if the sun is too bright, let me know and I'll take him across the street so we can go inside."

"The temperature is perfect. And besides, the fresh air will help clear my head." She offered him another don't-worry-about-me smile, then scanned the small patio, where only one other group of diners—an elderly man and two women—sat.

There hadn't been many people wanting to eat outdoors during the winter months, so it was nice to see the weather changing. And while she knew a cold spell could still strike at any time, she preferred to think that spring was here to stay.

Apparently, Belle, Prudy's daughter who was now running the eatery, agreed, because there were several pots of red geraniums gracing the patio that hadn't been there the last time Simone had stopped in for a bite to eat.

When the waitress brought their lunch—a turkey sandwich and vegetable soup for her and a pastrami on rye for Mike—Simone dug in.

The fainting spell was probably a combination of pregnancy hormones as well as a low blood sugar level from not eating, but she would talk to the doctor to make sure. There was no reason to take any unnecessary chances or to jeopardize the baby's health. From now on, she would put the child's best interests above her own.

Simone didn't need a psychiatric evaluation to tell her the baby would be much better off with another mom. She'd wished a hundred times over that her mother would have had the courage to do the right thing when faced with an unwanted, unplanned pregnancy. Susan Garner would have done herself and Simone a huge favor by signing over maternal rights at birth, but that hadn't happened.

And now, ironically, Simone was faced with the same decision. And while that decision might have come quickly, it wasn't being made easily.

Would the baby look like Mike, with his black hair and green eyes? Or would it look more like her?

She could hardly imagine.

Had her mother been faced with those same questions when she'd been pregnant?

Maybe even more so, under the circumstances. And

she suspected that when handed a baby who favored her father, Susan Garner had recoiled emotionally.

Genetics could be a real bitch sometimes.

When Simone had taken her second bite of the sandwich, she glanced up to catch Mike studying her. His hair, as black as a young raven's wing, was spiked in a style that suited him. And his eyes, as green as a blade of new grass, were intense and quick.

He was of medium height, but there was nothing average or run-of-the-mill about him.

Their gazes locked, as they sometimes did, with a bond of friendship and professional respect.

So there was a bit of sexual attraction, too. But she knew better than to latch onto something as fleeting as that and glanced back at her food.

"Maybe you ought to see your doctor and have your glucose level checked," he said.

"Don't worry. Now that I'm eating, I feel much better."

"Okay, but promise me you'll make an appointment with the doctor anyway."

Simone placed her half-eaten sandwich on the plate, then picked up her soupspoon. "All right. I'll do that as soon as I get home."

It was a promise she meant to keep, but she wouldn't call Dr. Grayson, her general practitioner. Instead, she would contact Dr. Kipper's office and schedule her first obstetrical appointment.

Of course, at thirty-seven, it was a little embarrassing to be unmarried and expecting a baby, but at least something good would come of it—especially if she could set up a private adoption with Millie and Fred.

Yes, she understood that Fred had some serious

health issues, but he was a wonderful man. Her baby would be lucky to have a daddy like him.

"Okay," Mike said, "you're probably right."

She glanced up from her nearly empty bowl, knowing that she hadn't been thinking out loud, but having the strangest feeling that he'd been privy to her musing. "Right about what?"

"You're wolfing down your food as though you hadn't eaten in ages."

"I told you that I hadn't. Didn't you believe me?"

"You've never lied to me, so I guess I have no reason not to."

Would his worry increase if he knew she was pregnant?

Once Mike had implied that she would make the perfect wife. And he'd made no secret that he was ready to settle down and start a family.

She sure hoped he wouldn't give her a hard time about the decision she'd made. Surely he'd see the wisdom in it.

And if he didn't?

She could recite a list of reasons why it was the perfect decision—for both of them.

First, there was the age difference. And she wasn't just talking chronologically. Simone had always been older than her years, even as a child; she'd had to be.

Secondly, his upbringing had been so completely different from hers that the two of them had very little in common. Mike had tons of stories he could relate about his childhood, memories that always brought a smile to his face. And on the other hand...well, hers were better left unsaid.

In addition, Mike had been born into a big, happy

family. And Simone—an only child and a loner by nature—wasn't comfortable in a crowd, especially when there were expectations of intimacy.

The one and only serious boyfriend she'd had in college had referred to her as an ice queen.

At the time, she'd laughed it off, but the words had hurt since they'd held a ring of truth. And while she preferred to think of herself as having intimacy issues, it hadn't taken a major in psychology to connect the dots and realize that it was a miracle she'd become the woman she was.

So what if she'd avoided having a relationship with another man after that?

She might not be able to pin her hopes and dreams on having a typical home and family, but she was happy with herself—and with her life.

Eventually, Mike would realize that she'd done them both a favor by refusing to let him get tied down with a woman he would soon grow unhappy with.

She looked up from her meal, saw him relishing his pastrami on rye as though he didn't have a problem in the world.

And he didn't.

The pregnancy dilemma and possible solutions were hers.

Still, a wave of nausea rolled across her stomach, something that she believed had more of an emotional cause than hormonal.

She pushed her empty soup bowl aside.

What if Mike didn't agree with her decision to put the baby up for adoption? What if he didn't let up on her about wanting some kind of commitment?

She didn't want to jeopardize her friendship with Mike; she truly liked the handsome paramedic.

But if worst came to worst, she would be forced to shut him out of her life—permanently.

As Simone led Mike along the sidewalk to her front door, Woofer howled at the side gate, welcoming her home.

"Hey, buddy," Mike said. "We've got a surprise for you."

"It'll be a surprise, all right." Simone glanced at the puppy in her arms. "I'm not sure how he's going to feel about having Wags as a houseguest."

"He'll adjust," Mike said.

Simone let them into the house, then went to the back door to greet Woofer.

Mike hadn't given it much thought before, but he now realized that if the big dog didn't take to the puppy, he'd be in a bind. Of course, Woofer didn't seem to have a mean bone in his body, so maybe he was being overly concerned.

He took a seat on the sofa and waited for Simone to return. He could hear the click of the lock as she opened the door and let in the dog.

"Ar-oof, ar-oof." Woofer's tail thumped against something in the kitchen, and his claws scratched against the floor.

Since Simone didn't immediately return, Mike figured she was trying to calm Woofer down in the other room before allowing him into the front of the house.

Maybe bringing the puppy here hadn't been such a good idea after all.

Mike looked at Wags and whispered, "If she wouldn't have fainted earlier this morning, I wouldn't feel so uneasy about this now."

Of course, Simone had seemed fine during lunch and on the way back home.

Moments later, Simone led Woofer into the living room, and when the happy-go-lucky mutt spotted Mike, he padded across the hardwood floor to greet him. But he froze in his tracks the moment he saw the puppy and made a growl-like grunt.

Mike put Wags on the floor, and the pup began to check out his surroundings, oblivious to Woofer. That is, until Woofer decided to investigate the new arrival.

After ten minutes, several barks, a few whines and a whole lot of sniffing, the dogs began to tolerate each other.

"What do you think?" Mike asked.

"I think I need to have my head examined for agreeing to look after Wags. These two are going to need a human chaperone."

"Our work schedules ought to overlap some, so I can stop by and look after them when you're not home. At least, some of the time. I have to leave for work pretty soon, but since your shift doesn't start until tomorrow, it ought to be okay."

For a moment, she seemed to ponder his suggestion to share the burden of both dogs, then she shrugged. "Let's just take things one day at a time. I'll take the first watch this evening. And we'll see how it goes."

"Okay."

While the dogs continued to check each other out, the humans seemed to be tiptoeing around their thoughts and feelings. At least, Mike was.

Simone had once said that she couldn't figure out what a guy like him saw in her. But the answer was a no-brainer to Mike.

He'd witnessed the compassion that drove her and made her one of the best nurses on staff at Walnut River General. And he'd seen the emotion that pooled under her cool surface.

No, there weren't many women like Simone Garner in this world, and the rest seemed to fall short, at least in Mike's eyes.

He glanced at his watch. "I guess I'd better take off. I really appreciate this."

"You're going to definitely owe me a huge favor after this." Her eyes, as warm and sweet as a melted puddle of milk chocolate, glistened.

"You're right." And he'd be happy to come up with ways to repay her, although he figured she still needed more time. So he stood and let her walk him to the front door.

"How about a thank-you dinner at Rafael's on Saturday night?" he asked. "Maybe you can wear that little black dress that looked dynamite on you."

She crossed her arms. "I'm afraid that dress and Rafael's would be a little too romantic for me."

"Listen." Mike placed his index finger under her chin and tilted her face to his. "I'm not sure why you're fighting your feelings for me."

"We've talked about this several times, and if you think about it, you'll realize my answers have always been consistent."

"Well, you're *not* too old for me. And I have no problem if we don't socialize very much. I've learned what a nice quiet evening at home can be like, and you won't find any argument from me." He tossed her a boyish grin. "I'd agree to another sleepover anytime."

She shifted her weight to one foot, and her cheeks flushed. An emotional reaction to either the memory or the reminder, he suspected.

"As nice as it was, it was a one-night stand," she said.

"No way, honey. I'm not sure how many of those you've had, but I can tell you from experience that first-time lovers don't get in tune with each other's bodies that way."

"Okay, I admit it was good. Great, even. But a relationship between us will never work. I'm not family material, and you grew up like one of the Waltons."

So Mike was one of five kids, and Simone didn't have siblings. He couldn't see a problem in that. Couples compromised all the time, learning to respect each other's differences. Hell, his father had been raised Catholic, and his mom had been Protestant through and through. They hadn't let it stand in their way, so he couldn't buy *that* excuse.

"Do you think about it at all?" he asked. "The night we spent together?"

She didn't answer, but he saw the struggle in her eyes. The fight between heart and mind. At least, he could swear that's what he kept seeing in her. Normally, he knew how to cut bait and run when a woman wasn't interested.

But his gut told him Simone was different. She wasn't being coy or shy. Neither was she playing games.

She wanted him as badly as he wanted her. And there was only one reason she'd fight the feeling.

"Someone in the past hurt you, Simone." His words seemed to strike some tender spot in her heart—God, he sure hoped they had, that he'd finally gotten to the bottom of whatever was standing between them.

As he studied her troubled expression, he realized his words had hit the mark.

"I'm not going to pry and dig for the truth," he added. "But I can see it in your eyes. You're afraid to let go and love me. But the feelings are there, brewing under the surface."

"That's not love, it's lust," she said, her voice husky with it.

"There's that, too." He was tempted to kiss her, long and deep and thorough, but he wasn't at all ready to start something he couldn't finish. Not when he had a shift starting soon. "But I'm serious about giving you the time you need."

Then he reached for the doorknob to let himself out.

"You're right," she finally admitted.

He turned, his gaze snagging hers. "Right about what?"

"About me being hurt in the past, about me being afraid to get close to people. But those scars are deep and permanent."

"Then you can't blame me for wanting to be the guy who makes them disappear."

They stood like that for a while, a man and a woman teetering on an emotional precipice that someone else had created.

He was sorely tempted to brush a kiss across her lips, to taunt her with memories of the sexual pleasure they'd found in each other's arms more than a month ago. But instead, he kissed her forehead, much like his mother used to do to him and his siblings when they'd scraped an elbow or stubbed a toe.

"I'll call you in the morning," he said before letting himself out and closing the door behind him.

Time, he figured, was his best ally. He knew her scars were deep. He just hoped they weren't as permanent as she wanted him to believe.

Chapter Four

Woofer found his new playmate entertaining, but when he grew tired of the puppy's games and wanted to rest, little Wags was still going strong.

There'd been a few growls and yips and whines at first, but as the day wore on, the dogs grew more and more comfortable with each other.

So far, so good, Simone thought as she locked up the house and turned off the porch light.

Woofer usually slept in her bedroom each night, but since Wags wasn't housebroken yet, she decided to put them both in the kitchen. One of the purchases Mike had made was a portable gate Millie Baxter had said might come in handy for separating the two, if it became necessary, and Simone had put it to good use several times.

Neither Wags nor Woofer was happy about being contained, and she hoped they would adjust soon.

After taking a nice long shower, she put on a flannel nightgown and pulled down the covers to her bed. The faint scent of laundry detergent and fabric softener reminded her the sheets were clean and fresh.

As she climbed onto the mattress and fluffed her pillow, it was the first real moment she'd had to relax all day, the first time she'd had a chance to ponder something other than dogs.

And that something was Mike.

Do you ever think about the night we spent together? he'd asked.

Of course she did. How could she not?

She'd never let down her defenses like that before. But there were several reasons she had.

She'd felt unusually pretty the night of Dr. Wilder's cocktail party.

Dressed in a sexy dress and heels while holding the flute of bubbly had also made her feel elegant and sophisticated—a nice change for a woman who spent her workday wearing scrubs and her time off in an oversize shirt and a pair of comfy sweats or well-worn jeans.

As luck would have it, the conscientious waiter kept refilling her glass until she'd had a mind-numbing buzz, which had made the night seem surreal.

And as enchanting as a fairy tale.

Just seeing the way Mike had looked at her was enough to make her lose her head and pretend to be someone else.

And as he'd taken her hand and led her from the party and out of Peter's house, she'd wondered if the night air would have the same effect on her as the clock striking midnight had on Cinderella.

But it hadn't.

Overhead, the wintry sky was adorned with a million twinkling stars. And all around them, crystal flakes glistened on the banks of fresh-fallen snow.

When they'd reached Mike's Jeep, he'd drawn her into his embrace. Then he'd tilted her chin and lowered his mouth to hers. She should have stopped it right there, but her pulse and her hormones had been pumping like a runaway steam engine, and she'd been lost in the magic of the heated moment.

The first tentative touch of his lips to hers had quickly intensified into a mind-spinning, knee-weakening kiss.

If she closed her eyes, she could imagine it still, the way his tongue had swept into her mouth, stealing her senses and making her ache for more.

Her physical reaction, which had bordered on wild and wicked, at least for someone as staid and conservative as she was, had merely been a result of lust and alcohol.

Still, whether she liked admitting it or not, something deep inside her was moved by Mike's charm and flattered by his crush on her. So when he'd driven her home, she'd thrown caution to the wind and continued to play the role of a princess at the ball. And for the next few hours, she'd pretended to be a woman who always wore her hair swept up in a classic twist, someone who actually belonged in a sexy dress and spiked heels.

But it wasn't a game she would continue to play. Not with a guy like Mike, who wanted so much more than a one-night fling. And not when the kind of commitment he wanted would lead to love and marriage, which was more than Simone could—or would—give to anyone.

Too bad she hadn't been able to get Mike to believe that.

Yet, in part, she could understand why.

On the night they'd made love, she hadn't had any of her usual intimacy issues, so the sex had been incredible.

In fact, they'd made love until they'd run out of condoms, and she'd lost count of the climaxes she'd had.

But as the morning sun began to peer through the slats of the miniblinds, Simone had awakened, the sheets tangled at their feet and the scent of lovemaking in the air.

Dawn had brought forth a sobering reality, just as the gong sounding midnight had broken the spell cast on Cinderella.

Simone could no longer keep up the pretense in the light of day, so she'd slipped out of bed, grabbed a robe and found an excuse to send Mike on his way.

She just wished she could do the same thing with the memory of their romantic bedroom antics.

A sharp, whining cry tore through the house, and Simone threw off the covers and jumped out of bed.

Poor little Wags.

What in the world had Woofer done to him?

When she reached the kitchen, Wags had stopped his cries and sat next to Woofer at the gate, their tails swishing across the linoleum floor as though the whining had been a ploy to draw her back to them.

Nevertheless, she picked up Wags and looked him over carefully.

There wasn't any sign of blood.

"Darn you guys," she uttered.

If Mike had been home, she would have called and insisted he come pick up Wags. But he was on duty tonight.

And she was stuck until his shift ended.

* * *

At seven-fifteen the next morning, Simone finally climbed out of bed and, while exhausted, gave up any hope of getting a solid block of sleep. Thanks to the dogs, who'd whined and begged to be allowed to run free in the house all night, she'd slept fitfully. And since Wags wasn't housebroken, she'd had to make repeated trips outside.

The trouble was, she hadn't made it two feet out of her bedroom when she was laid low by a wave of nausea, followed by an annoying case of the dry heaves.

Being pregnant wasn't any fun at all, and she wanted to blame Mike, the stars or just plain bad luck, but the only one responsible was the pale, red-eyed, wild-haired woman staring back at her in the bathroom mirror.

After washing her face with cool water, she'd taken the dogs out to the backyard. Now she stood in the middle of the dew-drenched lawn in her pale green bathrobe and a pair of fuzzy pink slippers that had seen better days. She watched Woofer, who was—*hopefully*—teaching Wags what he should be doing outdoors and not inside on the kitchen floor.

The sky was overcast, and a wintry chill that had been absent yesterday urged her to slide her hands into the pockets of her robe.

She didn't want to be outside; she wanted to go back to bed.

God, what was she going to do?

She had to go to work this afternoon and had planned to leave Wags and Woofer in the yard alone, but they still needed supervision.

Mike wouldn't get off until six this evening, so she

was stuck without any chance of taking a nap before her shift started. That is, unless she found someone else to puppy-sit.

Think, she told herself. There had to be someone she could call.

Oh, wait.

Talk about lightbulb moments.

Maybe Millie would take Wags and keep him at Tails a Waggin' today. Then Simone could get some sleep before she had to work.

"Come on, you guys." She turned and headed up the back steps to the service porch, the dogs on her heels. She was going to call Mike at the station and tell him he could pick up Wags at the pet store when he got off work.

Once inside the house, she grabbed the phone book and looked for the number, then placed a call to the Walnut River Fire Department.

Woofer, who couldn't have gotten much sleep either, curled up at her feet, while Wags took off, exploring the part of the house that had been off limits to him all night.

Someone grabbed the phone on the second ring. "Fire department."

She didn't recognize the man who'd answered, but supposed it didn't matter. "This is Simone Garner. Is Mike O'Rourke available?"

"He sure is. I'll get him for you."

She was placed on hold for a moment or two, until a familiar voice came over the line.

"Hey, Simone. How's it going?" His tone was light and upbeat.

Hers, unfortunately, was *not*. "This isn't going to work, Mike."

"What's the matter?"

"The *dogs*. I didn't get any sleep last night. I'm going to have to ask Millie Baxter if she'll look after Wags so I can get some rest before I have to go to the hospital. And I hope she'll say yes. If so, can you pick him up at Tails a Waggin'?"

"Sure."

"You'll have to watch them tonight. Woofer isn't always happy about sharing his territory with a pesky pup, so sometimes they'll have to be separated." She glanced up long enough to see that Wags had returned, carrying something in his mouth.

When he growled as though he'd captured a pint-size prowler and was going to shake the life out of it, she took a closer look at what he'd locked his teeth onto.

Her shoe!

"Oh, no!" She dropped the phone on the counter and hurried toward Wags, who had chomped down on one of the brand-new black heels that she'd spent entirely too much money on.

But the moment Wags saw her coming, he dashed off, taking the shoe with him.

She'd probably never have reason to wear it again anyway, but that wasn't the point. "Come back here with that! You're going to ruin it."

As Wags ran through the house, dodging her at every turn, she swore under her breath.

Now this *was* something she could blame on Mike.

Mike gripped the receiver and strained to hear what was going on at Simone's house.

"Honey?" The endearment slipped out before he

could catch himself, and when there was no response from her, he blew out a sigh of relief.

What in the hell was going on over there?

He could hear her yelling at Wags, who'd undoubtedly taken something of value.

"No, Wags. No!" she said. "Bad dog."

He heard the approaching footsteps as she returned to the phone.

When she got back on the line, he asked, "What happened?"

"Wags chewed up my brand-new shoe."

Uh-oh. The puppy was going to wear out his welcome, if he hadn't done so already.

Maybe Mike had better find him a home with one of the guys in the department who had a family. He'd have to ask around.

"I'm really sorry about the shoe, Simone. I'll buy you another pair."

"You don't have to do that. I probably wouldn't have worn them again anyway. It's just that…that…" She sniffled, then broke into tears.

Damn. Simone *never* cried. At least, not out loud or in front of anyone. He'd seen emotion well in her eyes, but she'd always managed to hold it back. So what was with the tears?

Maybe it was that time of the month.

Of course, it could be something else. A buildup of some kind of stress, and Wags had been the last straw.

Either way, Mike had dumped the puppy on her, and the timing had been bad. Talk about guilt trips.

"I'm really sorry for the trouble I put you through, Simone."

"You'd *better* be sorry." She sniffled again, the words practically drowning in her throat. "See what happens when I don't get my rest? I fall apart."

"Aw, don't do that…"

As much as he dreaded the sound of her crying, a part of him liked to see the emotional side of her; it was so rare that anyone did.

Again she sniffled, and he wished he was there to put an arm around her, to let her lean on him.

"I can't handle this two nights in a row, Mike."

And he couldn't handle her tears—at least, not at a distance.

"I'll take care of everything," he said, not sure that he could. "If you drive to the pet store and ask Millie to look after Wags, I'll pick him up there when I get off duty. Then, if you don't mind, I'll sleep on your couch and take care of the dogs for you tonight. And when you get home from work, you can go into your bedroom, close the door and get a full night's sleep."

It was a last-ditch effort to pull things back together, and he really expected her to say no, to suggest he and Wags find somewhere else to hang their hats.

But she surprised him. "Okay. But if *that* doesn't work, you'll have to figure out something else."

Nice save. "Okay. Will do."

"I'll leave a key under the potted plant on my porch."

A grin tugged at his lips. He'd been hoping she would give him a key to her place, although he had to admit, these weren't quite the circumstances he'd had in mind.

But hey. He wouldn't complain.

A selfish side of him wanted to hold on to every little inch Simone gave him.

* * *

Later that afternoon, while seated at the desk at the nurses' station and reading the doctor's orders on one of the patient files, Simone yawned, wishing she could curl up in a corner and take another nap.

Bless Millie for keeping Wags earlier today.

Upon returning home from the pet store, Simone had slept for several hours, then showered and got ready for work.

So why was she still so tired?

The only explanation was pregnancy hormones, which meant she'd have to get used to feeling sluggish.

She glanced at the clock displayed on the wall that was directly across from the nurses' desk: 8:34.

It had been fairly quiet this evening, just the typical Wednesday-night complaints. They'd treated a toddler with a case of croup, a woman with a sliced finger that required sutures and a teenager whose intestinal flu had left him dehydrated.

Currently, they were examining a child with a broken thumb, as well as a middle-aged woman who'd fallen off a scooter and presented with a nasty scrape on her knee and a sprained wrist.

Just steps away, Dr. Ella Wilder was making notes in the injured woman's chart.

At twenty-nine, Ella was one of the youngest doctors on staff. She was also one of the most attractive.

Her hair, dark brown and straight, was cut in a neat bob that reminded Simone of the style worn by flappers in the Roaring Twenties. It suited her.

And so did her chosen profession.

Ella Wilder had come from a long line of doctors.

Her father, Dr. James Wilder, had been chief of staff before his recent death. Her oldest brother, Peter, an internist, was the acting chief of staff until a replacement could be found. Another brother, David, a renowned plastic surgeon who'd been living in Los Angeles, had just relocated here in Walnut River, where he would open a practice.

Only Anna, Ella's adopted older sister, had opted for a different career path.

From what Simone had gathered, the two sisters had been close growing up, but there was a strain between Anna and all of her siblings now.

Simone, an only child, didn't understand family dynamics, nor did she try to. Suffice it to say, she found it best to keep her nose to herself and just do her job.

Still, Simone liked Ella, a young woman who'd recently completed her residency in orthopedics at Boston Mass and now worked at Walnut River General. Simone wouldn't exactly say they were close, since she didn't warm to many people, but there was something about Ella that Simone admired.

"Dr. Wilder," Simone said to the orthopedist, "when you have a moment, Dr. Fitzgerald would like you to take a look at some X-rays. Jeffrey Colwell, the little red-haired boy in 4-A, broke his thumb and, apparently, knocked the growth plate out of whack."

"All right. I'm almost finished here."

Unable to help herself, Simone yawned again, and Ella chuckled.

Simone felt a little guilty. She prided herself on not missing work more than a handful of days in the last fifteen years, but maybe she should have called in sick today.

"I'm afraid I didn't get much sleep last night," she admitted.

Ella slid a glance her way and smiled. "I hope you had a good reason for staying awake—like a special man in your life. Maybe a handsome paramedic."

There was a glow to Ella these days, which was undoubtedly due to the "special man" in her own life, J. D. Sumner, who had recently resigned from his position with Northeastern HealthCare, the conglomerate hoping to take over Walnut River General.

But Ella was jumping to a conclusion Simone didn't want anyone to make.

"I hate to blow your theory to smithereens," Simone said, "but my *special someone* is a puppy."

"Oh, really?" Ella closed the file in which she'd been writing. "You adopted another dog, a playmate for Woofer?"

"No. I'm puppy-sitting for Mike O'Rourke."

Ella's grin broadened, and her eyes glimmered. "I was wondering how you two were doing. That guy is crazy about you."

The day after Peter's cocktail party, while talking privately to Ella, Simone had let it slip that she and Mike had slept together. After all, Ella had seen the two of them locked in a heated kiss beside Mike's Jeep the night before.

Simone couldn't blame Ella for wondering, but not everyone was destined for a romantic happy ending.

"Mike's a wonderful man," Simone admitted. "And he'll be a great catch for some lucky woman. But I'm a loner, and I always have been."

Hooking up with anyone, even a female roommate, would be tough on Simone, who'd grown comfortable with the peace and quiet at home. Of course, having an additional dog around was going to push her comfort level to the limit, but Mike was supposed to be looking for a place that would allow him to keep Wags. So, hopefully, her life would be back on track soon.

"You'll have to forgive me for wishing it had been the man keeping you awake instead of his dog."

Simone yawned again. "And you'll have to excuse me. Boy, what I wouldn't give to go home early and call it a night."

"Give me a moment to check that X-ray of Jeffrey's thumb," Ella said, "then you can join me for a cup of coffee in the doctors' lounge."

"All right." Simone doubted that the caffeine would be good for the baby, but she also needed to be able to function while at work. She wasn't going to get off until eleven. Maybe half a cup would be okay.

Fifteen minutes later, as Jeffrey and his mother prepared to head home with his hand stabilized in a cast, Ella returned. "Come on. Let's take a quick break before we get another rush."

After letting the E.R. resident and a fellow nurse know where she could be found, Simone joined Ella in the employee lounge, where they poured two cups of coffee and took a seat at the table.

"I've been off for a couple of days," Simone said. "So fill me in. What's the latest news about Northeastern HealthCare?"

The question shouldn't have surprised Ella. After all, it was on everyone's mind.

The threatened NHC takeover had many of the medical staff up in arms. The hospital had a reputation of providing the human touch and the kind of medical treatment patients deserved, while NHC was known in the industry for focusing on the bottom line at the expense of patient care.

"Well," Ella said, taking a sip of her coffee, "the attorney general's office has decided to investigate the claims of insurance fraud."

Simone had known that the state examiner's office claimed that the hospital was keeping patients longer than necessary and billing for treatment that wasn't given. She blew out a sigh. "I know we tend to keep patients longer than the average, but that's because we don't want to rush them out of the hospital too soon. I can't believe there's anything fraudulent going on here."

"I can't, either," Ella said. "But I don't like what a charge like that means in regard to an NHC takeover."

"Neither do I." Simone rested her cup on the table, yet held it in both hands. "If the hospital is found to be at fault, profits will go down and we'll have problems operating. Then NHC can swoop in like a superhero and save the hospital's reputation by including it in their 'family.'"

"Exactly." Ella glanced at her watch. "Where did the last hour go? I need to call it a day. I've been here since early this morning."

"You've got to be tired, too," Simone said. "Maybe you shouldn't have had the coffee."

"It's definitely been a long shift, which is the reason I wanted a bit of caffeine." Ella smiled, her eyes glimmering and her cheeks taking on a pretty flush. "J.D. has been staying with his dad since he quit NHC, but today we started living together, and we're having a celebratory dinner as soon as I get home."

The couple had been seeing a lot of each other for the past two months, and apparently things had gotten serious. Ella's happiness was impossible to ignore.

"Congratulations," Simone said. "Is he taking you out?"

"No, we're eating in. In fact, he's cooking and even has a bottle of champagne chilling. Apparently, I'm in for a romantic evening." She grinned. "So I need to get out of here."

Simone could understand why. "Have a wonderful night."

"Thanks. I intend to."

Simone's thoughts drifted to the man who was waiting at her house.

Of course, it wasn't the same.

Even if Mike thought that it should be.

Chapter Five

Mike, whose primary motivation for being at Simone's house *wasn't* because of the dogs, had gone grocery shopping when he'd gotten off work. And now that Simone was due home within minutes, he had a late-night snack ready for her.

He'd prepared a platter of cheese, crackers and fresh fruit for them to munch on, and if she was really hungry, he had all the fixings for a Dagwood-style sandwich.

Now all he had to do was wait.

Ever since he'd picked up Wags from the pet shop, where the puppy had been harassing Popeye Baxter all day rather than Woofer, the little guy had been playing hard. And now both dogs were resting near the hearth, where a steady flame licked the logs Mike had just added to the fire.

Simone's little house looked especially warm and

cozy tonight. The candles he'd lit and placed on the fireplace mantel gave it a romantic glow.

In truth, Mike hoped Simone liked the idea of coming
home to a guy who loved her, a guy who knew what she
needed without being asked.

As a car sounded outside, alerting him to her
arrival, he met her at the door. Wags, apparently, was
too tuckered out to even care that someone had
entered, and Woofer merely raised his head and
assured himself that Simone was home and that all
was now well in his world.

"Good evening," Mike said as Simone hung up her
jacket on a hook by the door.

Even after a tiring shift at work and wearing a pair
of blue scrubs, she was an attractive woman who could
turn his heart on end with a smile.

She scanned the small living room, took in the sight
of the fresh flowers he'd placed on the coffee table.
"What's that?"

"A peace offering," Mike said. "From Wags. He may
not look very contrite at the moment, but he's very sorry
for being such a pain in the butt last night."

A smile stretched across Simone's face, but he
couldn't help noting the hint of crescent shadows under
her eyes. He suspected they looked worse in the warm
glow from the flickering candles.

He didn't mention how worn and tired she appeared,
though. But he would do whatever he could to see that
she got plenty of sleep tonight.

"If you're hungry, I have something for you to eat.
And if not, I'll put it in the fridge."

"Thanks," she said. "That was sweet. A little snack

sounds good. If I don't keep something in my stomach, I get…"

"You get what?"

She gave a half shrug. "I get a little shaky. No big deal."

"You need to have that blood test. Did you call your doctor like you said you would?"

"Yes. And I have an appointment next week."

"Good."

Mike went into the kitchen and brought out a tray bearing the cheese, crackers and fruit platter, as well as a bottle of merlot, a corkscrew and two goblets. "I also thought a little wine before bed might help you unwind and fall asleep easier."

"I'd better pass on the wine, but there's some apple juice in the refrigerator. That sounds a lot better to me."

Was she afraid of the effect alcohol might have on her? That it might lower her inhibitions like last time they'd spent the evening together? That she might let down her guard and allow herself to feel again?

If so, he hoped she didn't think he was trying to ply her with wine. He'd only meant to set a romantic ambience, not get her into bed. The next time they made love, he wanted her to be completely sober and still willing. And, more important, he didn't want her to have any regrets in the morning.

"Look at this cheese plate." A smile that reached her soulful brown eyes sent his pulse topsy-turvy. "Have the guys down at the department been reading magazines on entertaining? This is pretty, as well as appetizing."

"Actually, a lady Leif has been dating invited a few of us over to watch the game and she set out a tray like this. It was pretty cool, and I thought you'd agree." He shrugged, cheeks warming. He hoped she didn't think he'd gone over the top.

"It's a nice touch," she said. "No one has ever prepared anything special for me."

Someone ought to.

And often.

"Then you're welcome."

As Mike turned to get the juice for her, she stopped him. "I'll get it. Why don't you have a seat and unwind. I took care of the dogs yesterday, so I know how tiring that can be."

"Actually," Mike said, glancing to the hearth where the canines lay side by side, "they weren't that bad tonight."

He'd taken them out in the backyard and thrown a ball to them until they were both worn-out and ready to settle down.

While Simone was in the kitchen, Mike poured a glass of wine for himself.

She'd just returned and settled into a comfortable position on the couch when her phone rang.

"Uh-oh." She furrowed her brow as she turned and reached for the telephone that rested on the lamp table. "I don't know who it could be at this hour."

"A woman called earlier," he said, "but she wouldn't leave her name. I told her you wouldn't get home until after eleven."

Mike watched as Simone snagged the receiver and answered on the second ring.

"Hello?" The furrow in her brow grew deeper. "Yes, it is."

He wasn't sure what was going on, but he listened to

her side of the conversation. It obviously wasn't a wrong number, but who the hell called people after eleven o'clock at night?

"That's too bad. No, I didn't know." She raked a hand through her hair, as though forgetting she wore it held back in a clip. Then she stood. "Would you please give me your number. I'd like to have it in case I need to speak to you later."

She made her way to the small rolltop desk against the wall and pulled out the top drawer. She fumbled inside until she withdrew a notepad and pen. Then she made a note.

"Thank you. I'll…uh…call her first thing in the morning."

Mike tensed, his senses on alert. Just from listening to Simone's side of the conversation, the news sounded serious.

She cleared her throat. "Yes, well…I don't know why she didn't call me, either."

When she hung up the phone, she remained standing, her back to him. She'd always carried herself with strength and pride, but her shoulders slumped and she blew out a heavy sigh.

Mike put down his glass and made his way toward her. "Is everything okay, honey?"

Damn, there went the endearment again. But this time, he wasn't sorry he'd let it slip out. Not when he sensed she needed some tenderness.

"I…uh…yeah. I'm fine." She turned to him, her eyes red and welling with tears. "It's just…well, my mom found a lump in her breast last week. But for some reason, she didn't want to bother me with the news.

That was a friend of hers who took it upon herself to call and let me know. She figured, even if my mom and I weren't close, that I was a nurse and could answer some of her questions and put her at ease."

Mike slid his arms around her, and she leaned into his embrace, resting her head against his chest.

He held her for a while, providing her with all he had to offer. His sympathy, his heart.

Finally, as she drew away, her gaze caught his, and he saw the pain inside. The grief.

What did one say to a woman who'd just learned of her mother's frightening discovery?

"That's just like my mom," Simone said, tears spilling from her eyes.

"What do you mean?"

She wiped the moisture from her cheeks and sniffed. "Needless to say, I'm concerned about her health and sorry she's struggling with all that lump could mean, but this is the kind of thing a mother should share with her daughter, whether she's a nurse or not. And it hurts to be reminded of just how lousy our relationship is. Especially if her condition proves to be life-threatening and I stand to lose her without ever having the kind of bond other mothers and daughters have."

Mike didn't know what to say, what to do. He couldn't get a handle on how a woman might feel upon finding a lump in her breast. Nor did he have any idea what that woman's daughter might be going through.

He figured they'd both be scared, anxious.

A simple, well-meant "I'm sorry" slid out. Yet it seemed so…inadequate.

"I'm sorry, too. And not just because of the news. I'm used to having my mom shut me out. She's been doing that to me for years. But I got the feeling that her friend thought I was too busy to be bothered. And that's simply not true."

"I know it isn't." If anyone had a heart for a person who was ill or hurting, it was Simone. And Mike was sorry that she and her mom were not close.

Maybe, in its own way, a diagnosis like this might draw the two of them together again. He hoped so; he couldn't imagine what his life would be like without the love and support of his family.

A shank of glossy hair had fallen from the clip Simone wore; now the strands hung along her cheek. Mike brushed them aside. "If you need anything, if your mom needs anything, you can count on me for help."

"Thanks."

"That's what friends…and lovers are for." As he brushed a kiss across her forehead, she gripped his waist as though hanging on to him, to everything his offer held.

When her lips parted, tempting him to place his mouth on hers, he was lost in a whirl of desire. He half expected her to push him away, but she slipped her arms around his neck and drew him closer instead.

It had been so long…

Too long.

The kiss deepened, and their tongues mated, sweeping and swirling in sleek, hot need. He couldn't get enough of her taste, of her touch, of her scent. And he held her tight, yearning to make them one.

Still, he wouldn't push. Wouldn't make the first move toward the bedroom. He'd been serious when he'd vowed that the next time they made love it would be at Simone's invitation, and she wouldn't need even a drop of alcohol to influence her decision.

As his hormones pumped, as his blood pounded in need, he reined in his desire to the point he thought he might die. And when she placed her hands on his chest and pushed him away, he thought he surely would.

"I'm sorry, Mike. But I can't. I just can't do this."

Oh, she *could*. And she *had*. But he knew better than to argue.

She unclipped the barrette in her hair, then combed her fingers through the strands. "I'm not the kind of woman who wants or needs a man in my life."

"You may not *want* one. But you definitely *need* one." And Mike was the man she needed most.

His suspicion that she'd been hurt in the past only deepened now.

She strode back to the coffee table and picked at a clump of grapes he'd placed next to the slices of cheese. "In the three or so years you've known me, how many times have you seen me with a man—romantically speaking? How many times have I actually gone out on a date?"

"That's not healthy," he said.

"I'm not very good at relationships, so it's easier this way."

He couldn't buy that. Still, it had been five or six weeks since the two of them had slept together. But he had no idea how long it had been for her prior to that.

Too long, he suspected. The last guy she'd been involved with must have done a real number on her self-esteem.

"Can't you be content to let us just be friends?"

God only knew how long he could keep this up. His hope was that she'd give in to her true feelings before he grew tired of waiting.

Damn. He was only human.

"I'll take whatever you can give me," he said.

At least that was his plan for now.

The next morning, Simone woke to the sounds of dogs barking. She rolled over in bed, raised up on an elbow and peered through the curtains. In the backyard, Mike was playing ball with Wags and Woofer, who obviously hadn't learned the rules of Fetch.

But she had to give Mike credit for trying to teach them how to bring the little rubber ball back to him and not keep it as a well-earned prize.

What was she going to do about that man?

If she believed in the power of true love, if she believed that she could become involved in any kind of lasting relationship, she would definitely consider making Mike a part of her life.

But she knew her own flaws, as well as her strengths.

When Cynthia Pryor, her mom's neighbor, had called last night to inform Simone of something another mother would have disclosed on her own, she'd been completely taken aback. Not just by the terrible news, but by the blatant reminder that she and her mom had never been close, that they never would be.

And thanks to their dysfunctional relationship, Simone would never be able to create a warm, loving family of her own.

After the call, when Mike had held her, when he'd

kissed her, she'd wanted so badly to accept all that he'd been willing to give her.

But how could she when she knew she'd always hold back? When she knew she'd always retreat to that special place in her mind where no one could ever hurt her again?

As she climbed from bed, another bout of morning sickness struck with a vengeance, and she hurried to the bathroom. When it was all over—God, she hated being sick—she washed her face, returned to the bedroom and sat on the edge of mattress. Then she dialed her mother's house.

After the third ring, a click sounded. Simone opened her mouth to respond, but when the canned voice of her mom's answering machine began its recitation, she blew out a ragged sigh instead.

"You have reached 518–555–2467. I can't come to the phone right now, but if you leave your name and number, I'll return your call at my earliest convenience."

Simone cleared her throat. "Hi, Mom. It's me. I just wanted to touch base and see how you've been. Please give me a call when you can. It's—" she glanced at the clock on the bureau "—it's ten-fifteen on Thursday. I have to go into work this afternoon around three, but I should be close to home until then. I love you."

As she hung up the phone, she realized that she always ended her calls that way. *I love you.*

But did she?

Did that little girl inside of her still exist? The one who'd desperately wanted to hear those three little words repeated and know, without a doubt, that her mother truly meant them?

No. That lonely child had faded into the past when

Simone hit high school, where she learned that she could get the affirmation, respect and attention she craved from her teachers. So, as a result, she studied hard and excelled—especially in science.

At one time, she'd actually thought about going to medical school, but the cost was prohibitive, especially without any family support. So she'd settled for nursing school, where she graduated at the top of her class.

Fifteen years ago, she landed a job at Walnut River General and worked on any floor she was assigned. But she soon found her real calling in the emergency room, where she gained the respect of patients, coworkers and administrators alike.

One nice thing about the E.R. was that Simone could become personally involved with the patients for a few hours, then was able to back off as they either went home or were sent to other floors in the hospital.

Yes, she'd overcome a lot in the past thirty-seven years, but she still found it difficult to actually connect with people.

When the rubber ball Mike and the dogs had been playing with hit the side of the house, the wooden window frame and the glass shook and shuddered.

Simone peered out into the yard to see what was going on outside.

Through the pane of glass separating them, Mike caught her gaze, smiled and shrugged at the same time. Then he mouthed, "I'm sorry."

She was sorry, too. Sorry that she couldn't pin her heart and her dreams on Mike O'Rourke. That she couldn't create something she'd never had.

Once upon a time, she'd hoped and prayed to have

what other children had been blessed with, but that dream had faded along with that little brown-haired girl who used to cry herself to sleep each night.

The child whose mother had looked at her newborn for the very first time and determined that she was unlovable.

Mike had found his true calling when he'd pursued EMT training at the local junior college.

In fact, he loved everything about his job—the adrenaline rush, the satisfaction of saving a life.

Sure, there were times when it was tough, times when he came upon an accident victim too late to be of any help.

He didn't like having to look into the eyes of a victim's family and tell them there was nothing left to do but to call the coroner. But he accepted that as part of life, as part of his job.

Tonight, just after eight o'clock, he and Leif were sitting around the television at the station with several other guys when the next call came in, and the men all sprung into action.

Four and a half minutes later, they arrived at the scene of a car accident that had occurred when a seventy-six-year-old woman ran a stop sign at the intersection of Lexington and Pine, broadsiding a vehicle driven by a sixteen-year-old boy.

The teenager in a white Honda Accord had suffered a possible skull fracture, lacerations to the face and a broken collarbone.

The elderly woman had been hurt, too. But Mike suspected she might have had a seizure or ministroke while behind the wheel, which had probably caused the accident. They wouldn't know for sure until she was examined at the hospital.

Eight minutes after the arrival of the paramedics on the scene, both victims were loaded in the ambulance and en route to Walnut River General.

As Leif and Mike monitored the vitals of the victims, the flashing red lights and siren alerted the other cars on the road to pull over and let the emergency vehicle pass.

Simone was working tonight, and Mike hoped that after the patients were stabilized he'd have a chance to see her, to talk to her.

After passing both the teenager and the woman to the E.R. staff, Mike and Leif stopped by the nurses' desk to complete the necessary paperwork.

"Hey," Leif said, nodding toward an open doorway, where Simone stood at the bedside of a young girl who had a gash in her leg. "If you're both working, who's looking after the dogs?"

"We decided to leave them alone tonight and hope for the best." Mike glanced up from the form he'd signed. "I sure hope they don't disturb her neighbors. They get a little loud and rambunctious sometimes."

The radio squawked, and Leif responded, alerting dispatch that the medics were available again. When he'd done so, he excused himself. "I'm going to get a soda. Want me to get you one?"

"No, I'm fine."

As Leif walked away, Mike took the time to study Simone, to watch her interact with a frightened little girl he guessed to be about six or seven years old.

Simone took a disposable glove from a box, blew into the opening to create a balloon, then knotted the end.

The fingers stood straight up, resembling either a rooster's comb or a kid's Mohawk. Then she took a black pen and drew a pair of eyes above the thumb and a mouth below it.

The result brought forth a smile on the child's face, providing some relief from her pain and fear.

Why couldn't Simone see in herself what he saw in her—the compassion, the dedication, the heart of a woman who truly cared?

A woman who would make a great wife and mother.

In the past, Mike had sowed his share of wild oats. But as family holidays came and went, each one growing bigger with another new in-law or the birth of a baby, he'd begun to feel a growing urge to find a mate, settle down and create a home and family of his own.

Simone was a challenge, though.

As she returned to the desk where Mike continued to stand, she tossed a pretty smile his way. "Wags and Woofer must be doing okay. Otherwise, I suspect Mrs. McAllister, the woman who lives next door to me, would have called to complain by now."

"I knew they'd eventually learn how to get along." He'd taken that same stance with Simone, hoping that she'd get used to having him around, that she'd let down her guard and quit fighting her feelings for him.

"Did you ever get ahold of your mother?" he asked. "How's she doing?"

Simone's movements slowed to a snail's pace. "I'm afraid I really don't know. We've been playing phone tag."

"I'm sorry to hear that."

Simone gave a half shrug. "Actually, that's par for the course."

"Because you're both so busy?" Mike had a brother who worked odd hours and was hard to find at home.

"My mom and I never seem to connect." She crossed her arms and shifted her weight to one hip.

"Maybe you ought to try and talk to her again this evening," he suggested, "when you get a break."

"We'll see."

"I guess you'll want to call her when you can have some privacy."

Simone scanned the E.R.

Looking to see who was listening? he wondered.

She uncrossed her arms and straightened, distancing herself from the conversation. "I'm probably the last one on earth she really wants to hear from. So I'm going to let her call me if and when she's ready."

Mike watched as Simone returned to her young patient, the rubber soles of her shoes squeaking upon the tile. He'd suspected that the person who'd hurt her had been a man. That the wrongs she'd suffered and her subsequent pain might be something he could heal and rectify.

But maybe he'd been wrong.

Chapter Six

Three days later, Mike was still coming by the house to watch the dogs whenever he could, and Simone continued to drop off Wags at the Baxters' store when she didn't want to leave the dogs alone.

"I feel like a real parent," he'd told her earlier as he prepared to leave for his next shift at the station.

She'd imagined him as a father, too—to *real* children; not the kind with four paws and fur.

"This isn't the same," she'd responded, wanting to change the subject to one that wasn't so...so steeped in truth.

Something warm and tender had simmered in his gaze, something that threatened to not only pull her in, but to drag her through a rush of emotion.

"I can't help wondering what our kids would look like," he'd said, "if you and I were to have them."

The statement had nearly knocked her to the floor, and she'd struggled to recover.

Ever since learning that she was pregnant, she'd been thinking a lot about the baby they'd created and had tried to imagine whether it was a girl or a boy. But she couldn't allow herself to focus on the child being theirs—or even his. Instead, she'd forced herself to think about the joy the baby would bring to its new parents, a couple who'd been hoping and praying for a child to love.

A couple like Fred and Millie.

"You'll make a fabulous father," she'd told him. "But I'm not the maternal type. Trust me on that, okay?"

He'd cupped her face with both hands. "And I say that you *are*."

For a long, heart-stopping moment, she'd wanted to believe him—for his sake.

And for the child's.

But she knew things Mike didn't. Things that would make him change his mind.

"You're going to be late," she'd told him, trying to shoo him out the door before she was forced to tell him the truth sooner than she was ready to do so.

Now she'd just parked in front of Tails a Waggin'.

"Here we are," she told Wags as she reached for the handle of his carrier and took him inside the pet shop.

Simone had called the store earlier, and Millie had agreed to take Wags home for the night. Although Simone was feeling better about leaving the dogs alone, she didn't like the idea of Wags being unsupervised inside the house. Not when he chewed everything in sight and still wasn't housebroken.

She could, of course, leave the dogs outside, but there

was a biting chill in the air, and dark clouds had gathered on the horizon. Because of the threatening weather, they couldn't stay in the yard tonight. But if Wags stayed with Millie, Woofer could be left in the house alone.

"Look who's here," Millie said to Popeye Baxter, who wore a yellow bandanna around his neck and sat next to the register. "Your little friend is back."

Simone watched as Popeye perked up in response to the news, and a smile crept across her face. Woofer was still getting used to having Wags around, so it was nice to think that Popeye found him entertaining.

"I sure appreciate you taking Wags for me," Simone said. "And hopefully, I won't need to impose on you too many more times. Mike is hoping to find a place, and his real estate agent called about a house that sounds promising. She's going to show it to him on his next day off."

"Fred and I don't mind watching Wags." Millie took the dog carrier from Simone and set it on the counter. Then she unhooked the latch, swung open the little door and reached inside. "Are the dogs getting along any better yet?"

"With each other? Yes. But when I got in last night, there was a note left on my door by the woman who lives next door. Apparently, they were barking and making an awful racket while I was gone."

"That's too bad," Millie said. "You don't want to upset your neighbors."

Simone didn't like to be kept awake by someone else's noise, either. She also tried to be considerate of the people who lived near her.

"Life is so much nicer when everyone in the neighborhood is on friendly terms," Millie added, giving

Wags a cuddle before setting him down on the floor so he could play.

It's not that Simone really cared about maintaining any kind of relationship with those who lived near her. She waved to a couple of people when she saw them in their yards or on the street, but for the most part, she kept to herself.

When at home, she preferred her privacy and wasn't interested in community gossip. Neither did she want just anyone to pop in unexpectedly for a leisurely cup of coffee and a chat.

Fortunately, her neighbors seemed to have read into her let's-not-get-too-chummy expressions and gave her plenty of space.

She couldn't say the same for Mike, though. He hadn't seemed to read anything into her words or her demeanor. She supposed it was flattering that he'd stuck it out so far, but he had more faith in her than she had in herself.

If she were to let his charm go to her head and allow something to develop between them, she would be crushed when it ended, just as she had been when Tom Nichols said he couldn't deal with a cold and unfeeling lover.

And if Mike made the same claim, it would be devastating since she cared more for Mike than she had for Tom.

A *lot* more.

Mike was a better man all the way around. And he was proving to be a good friend, too.

So why exchange their friendship for a temporary affair? It didn't make sense, especially when she had very few friends in her life.

"I'm really going to miss Wags when you quit bringing him by," Millie said. "He's such a sweetheart."

"He has his naughty moments, too. You ought to see the shoe he destroyed, the puddles he made on the hardwood floor and the fringe on the throw rug he chewed."

"Aw, you can't get mad at Wags for that," Millie said. "He's still a baby."

"I know. I try to keep that in mind." Simone tucked a strand of hair behind her ear. "By the way, speaking of babies, how's the adoption search coming along? Are you having any luck?"

"I'm afraid not." Millie scanned the store, as though searching for someone who might be eavesdropping.

Fred maybe?

Another customer?

"We were turned down again. And a couple of weeks ago, after another..." She blew out a sigh. "Well, let's call it another monthly disappointment. Anyway, Fred, bless his heart, took me for a long drive. We ended up at Crescent Lake, where we found a nice little spot and had a picnic—just the two of us. Then we prayed together, telling God how badly we wanted a child, but agreeing to abide by his will. If he wants us to have a baby, he'll provide one for us. And if not?" Millie smiled warmly. "Fred and I have complete peace about whatever happens."

Que sera, sera, Simone thought. What will be, will be.

"It won't be the end of the world if we don't have children," Millie said. "After all, there aren't too many couples who have what Fred and I've been blessed with. We have a loving, marital bond. We're business partners, too, and the very best of friends. A child would merely be frosting on a cake that is moist and rich in and of itself."

Simone wasn't a religious person. After all, she'd prayed countless times that her mother would love her when she'd been a little girl. And it just hadn't happened.

Who knew why some kids were conceived in love and others weren't. Why some were born into loving arms and others into a cold environment.

Or why some women could accept the love offered them when others were afraid to.

Either way, a relationship like the one Fred and Millie shared was rare in this day and age. The Baxters were fortunate.

And if they had a baby, it would be lucky, too.

Yet Simone admired their resolve to give up their dream of having a child of their own and to trust that things would work out—one way or another.

Still, she couldn't help thinking that her baby might be destined to be the frosting on the Baxter's cake.

Late that afternoon, while raindrops danced upon the hospital windows, Simone sat across from Isobel Suarez in the hospital cafeteria, where they'd each set down a tray carrying a cup of soup and a half sandwich.

Isobel, an attractive woman in her mid-thirties, with curly auburn hair and a ready smile, always had a kind word or a bit of wisdom to share. But then again, that shouldn't be a surprise. Isobel was also the hospital social worker, a job she'd had for the past ten years.

From the first day they'd met, Simone had found Isobel different from the others and easy to talk to. So gradually, she'd begun to open up to someone for the first time in her life.

Simone had eventually admitted why she and her

mother had never been close, a shameful secret Simone had stumbled upon by accident but had never discussed with anyone else.

At first, Simone had feared that Isobel might try to psychoanalyze her, but that hadn't been the case. Isobel knew how to be a true friend without letting her training and her degree get in the way.

"Can I share something with you?" Simone asked.

"Sure."

"In *confidence*," Simone added.

"Of course." Isobel laid down her spoon and pushed her cup of soup aside. "This sounds serious."

"It is." For a moment, Simone sat on her secret, clung to it, but she felt safe with Isobel. Still, the words came out softly, tentatively. "I'm…pregnant."

Isobel picked up her napkin and blotted her lips. "How do you feel about that?"

"Flabbergasted. Overwhelmed. Foolish. Afraid. Awestruck." Simone shrugged. "I think that about covers it."

Isobel placed her elbows on the table and leaned forward slightly. "What are you going to do?"

"Give the baby up for adoption."

"And the father will be okay with that?"

Simone's thoughts drifted to Mike, to the young paramedic who seemed to think she'd make a good wife and mother. The guy who had a slew of nieces and nephews and would love to have a kid of his own someday.

"I haven't told him about it yet," she admitted, "but when I do, I hope he'll eventually be able to see the wisdom in my decision."

Actually, she was afraid Mike would react positively

to the news. And that he'd try to talk her into marrying him and keeping the baby.

But what would he say when she was forced to level with him about the past, about her shortcomings?

The emotional scars that she carried would cause him to resent her someday.

Hadn't Simone come to resent her mother for the same reason?

She'd tried to tell Mike that he was barking up the wrong tree when it came to a long-term commitment. But he seemed to think that, with time, everything would work out between them.

Simone knew better, though. And she suspected that, as a social worker, her friend would agree with her.

"Is there any chance that you and the father might want to raise this child together?" Isobel asked.

"No. In spite of an age difference, our family backgrounds are completely opposite. So nothing lasting could ever come of a relationship with him."

Besides, Mike wanted so much more than Simone could give him.

"Sometimes opposites not only attract, but bring out the best in each other," Isobel said.

Simone reached across the table and placed her hand over her friend's. "I've told you about some of the pain I went through as a child, but I held back on the worst of it."

"You're a strong, dependable and resilient woman, Simone. It seems to me that you've overcome the emotional obstacles you faced."

Some of them, she supposed. "But I never learned the emotional skills needed to parent. Not by example, anyway. And for that reason, I'm afraid I'll fail the baby just as badly as my mother failed me."

Isobel's gaze snagged Simone's, soothing her in a pool of compassion and understanding.

Over the years, Simone may have shared certain details about past events with Isobel, but she'd never revealed the depth of her feelings, her fears.

"Adoption is best for everyone involved." The words came out sure, steady. Yet for a moment, something waffled inside. Something she couldn't quite put her finger on.

"You've got time to let your options simmer for a while," Isobel said. "And, after you do, I'm sure you'll make the right decision—whatever that might be."

"Thanks." Simone withdrew her hand and leaned back in her seat.

"There's something else you should keep in mind," Isobel added. "Just because you had a bad role model doesn't mean you're going to make the same mistakes. I happen to believe you'd make a wonderful mother someday—to this baby or to another."

Unfortunately, Simone didn't share the same faith or the same vision that Mike and Isobel had.

"Thanks for the vote of confidence, but I can't even begin to think of myself as a mom. Not with the mothering I had." Simone chuffed. "And even now, our mother/daughter relationship is limited to Christmas cards and an occasional phone call."

Isobel didn't comment. Other than sympathize, what could she say?

Of course, maybe she was thinking about how close she'd been to her own mother and how tough it had been to lose her. From what Simone had gathered, Isobel had moved in with her dad after her mom passed away. The two were very close.

Simone could hardly imagine a relationship like that. She reached for the cellophane-wrapped packet of crackers that had come with her soup. "My mom recently found a lump in her breast, and even though I've tried to contact her several times and left messages, she won't return my calls. She's completely shut me out."

"Fear of breast cancer can blindside a woman." Isobel took a sip of water. "I'm not trying to make excuses for the mistakes your mom made when you were growing up, but she may find it difficult to talk to anyone right now. You might need to be patient with her."

"You've got a point."

They returned to their meal, but Simone focused on the saltines she'd unwrapped. Looking right through the little squares as she pondered the only real option she had.

"How do you feel about open adoptions?" she asked Isobel. "Do they work? Would it be difficult watching a child grow up in someone else's home if everyone knows each other?"

"It depends upon the people involved. In my experience, open adoptions work out beautifully if the biological and the adoptive parents are able to put the child's best interests ahead of their own."

"I've got a couple in mind," Simone said. "But you're right. There's time for me to think things through. And if I should decide not to give the baby to someone I know, I'd like you to recommend a good agency that will help me find just the right parents."

"No problem. Tomorrow, when I have a chance, I'll

give you the names of several organizations I've worked with in the past."

Simone ought to feel relieved, yet handing over her child to strangers made her uneasy, too.

But how could she even consider dumping all her personal baggage on a poor defenseless baby?

Besides, even with the few friendships she had—Isobel and, more recently, Ella—she always held back—just as she feared she would do with a baby.

On top of that, children needed a primary caregiver, someone they could trust to see to all their needs, physical as well as emotional. They needed someone to kiss their owies and to make them cookies. Someone to tuck them in at night.

How could Simone give up her job to be a stay-at-home mom?

She loved everything about being an E.R. nurse—the pressure of being in a life-or-death situation, the competent and dedicated medical staff with whom she worked, the patients who rushed in with complaints and symptoms that were sometimes hard to diagnose.

Why, she even loved the hours she kept, never complaining about a night shift or two.

No, her life wasn't conducive to motherhood.

And she was a fool on those rare occasions when she allowed herself to think otherwise.

Nearly a week later, after Ella Wilder had treated a teenage boy who fell off a skateboard and broke his arm, Simone took the orthopedic surgeon aside. "There's a cake in the solarium to celebrate Dr. Randall's being hired as the new chief of staff."

Owen Randall was a cardiac surgeon who'd suffered a serious hand injury and could no longer perform the operations for which he was trained. But that didn't mean he wouldn't make a top-notch chief of staff.

Although he'd been hired from the outside and not from within, those who'd already met the man had talked about being impressed with his professionalism, as well as his people skills.

"Peter's very happy to be back in private practice," Ella said.

"I'm sure he is." With a new lady in his life—Bethany Holloway, a hospital board member—and a wedding on the horizon, Peter was undoubtedly glad to pass the baton to someone else and get back to his patients.

"Dr. Randall is in the solarium, as we speak," Simone said. "He's making himself accessible to the entire staff. He's also serving cake, which is chocolate, by the way."

Ella smiled. "My favorite. All right, let's stop by and congratulate our new boss."

The solarium was located on the first floor and looked out onto the hospital gardens, which had just begun to bloom with various displays of red, yellow and pink buds.

In the center of the room, Owen Randall, a stocky, fifty-something man with thinning silver hair, met Ella and Simone with a smile. He introduced himself, then handed them each a slice of cake. As he did so, the tip of his bright yellow-and-green tie dragged across the white, butter-cream frosting.

"Oops. Would you look at that?" His jovial chuckle reverberated in the lounge. "Another tie bites the dust."

The ability to laugh at himself was a good sign, Simone decided. It would make working under him much easier.

They made small talk with Dr. Randall, who seemed to be a friendly sort.

Simone wondered if he'd do as well in the chief-of-staff position as the late Dr. James Wilder had. She hoped so. James had been a well-liked and respected physician who'd put quality patient care above all else.

Since Ella and Simone were both on duty, they excused themselves, then carried their cake back to the nurses' station.

"There sure are a lot of changes going on around here," Ella said as she took a seat behind the desk.

"I know. I wonder if we'll have cake again on Saturday, when Henry Weisfield officially steps down as the hospital administrator."

"It's possible." Ella dug her fork into her slice of the chocolaty concoction and took a bite, obviously relishing the sweet taste. "You know, J.D. applied for Henry's job and..." She leaned in closer to Simone and lowered her voice. "From what we understand, he's being seriously considered for the position."

"I'd heard that," Simone said. "With J.D.'s business skills, I'm sure his chances of landing the administrator's job are excellent."

"I've certainly got my fingers crossed," Ella said.

"I'll bet they are." Simone glanced at Ella, only to see she had indeed crossed the fingers on both hands, one of which—her left—sported a sparkling diamond ring.

"Well, I'll be darned. You're engaged."

Ella beamed. "As of last night."

"Congratulations."

"Thanks." Ella took another bite of cake, seeming to enjoy every morsel.

Under usual circumstances, Simone would be doing the same. But the sugary taste wasn't sitting too well, and she didn't want to push herself or her sensitive stomach by eating any more than she already had.

"How goes the puppy-sitting?" Ella asked.

"So far, so good. Mike helps out a lot. But I'll be glad when he finds a place of his own soon."

"That's too bad. I was hoping that the two of you would hook up."

"Mike is, too." And while Simone had begun to think his feelings for her might be genuine, she just couldn't trust herself to be the kind of wife he expected and deserved.

"It doesn't surprise me that Mike is wishing for more. The guy's definitely in love." Ella scooped a dab of frosting from the top of her cake and popped it into her mouth. "And you're not going to be able to convince me that lust has anything to do with the way that man looks at you."

Okay, so Simone had to admit that she'd seen the way Mike looked at her, too. And that it didn't appear that he was only interested in sex.

But how long would his affection and loving glances last?

When would he look beyond her facade and see her for what she really was?

For a moment, Simone was tempted to tell Ella about the pregnancy, about her decision to give the baby up for adoption. After all, assuming she was able to carry the baby to term, it would be public knowledge soon enough.

She bit her tongue instead.

One emotional revelation like that was a record for Simone.

But two disclosures in less than a week?

No way.

The next person she told about her pregnancy would be the baby's father, but she just couldn't bring herself to tell him yet.

Simone may have reached a decision she could live with, but she didn't have a clue how to drop the bomb on Mike.

Chapter Seven

Late Thursday morning, after Mike met with Leif's sister and looked at a three-story Victorian-style home on Maple, he stopped by the New England Ranch Market. The trendy grocery store, a favorite of the locals, offered farm-fresh eggs, organic vegetables and an old-fashioned butcher shop that cut meat to order.

While pushing his cart through the aisles, he picked up a couple of chicken breasts, some red potatoes, fixings for a salad and the special ingredients needed for his killer vinaigrette dressing. Then, before heading to the checkout line, he stopped by the bakery section and picked up a lemon meringue pie—his favorite.

The guys in the department took turns with kitchen duty, and Mike, who'd had no experience cooking at all when he'd first been hired, had to ask his mom to teach him how to prepare some of his favorite family meals.

He'd even picked up a few culinary tricks from some of his coworkers and, while not what you'd call a pro, he knew how to fix a decent spread.

Now, as he climbed from his Jeep Wrangler, Woofer barked at the fence. Mike had a feeling it was more of a "Welcome back" than a "Don't even think about trespassing" announcement. Either way, little Wags followed suit.

It was kind of cool that the puppy had the watchdog lessons down pat. Too bad he wasn't doing as well when it came to getting housebroken.

Once on Simone's front porch, Mike shuffled the two grocery bags he held in his arms so he could ring the bell. He hoped Simone was okay with what he planned to do.

He had a key, so he could let himself in, but Simone wasn't working today, and he didn't want to overstep his boundaries.

She answered the door in her robe. Her hair was wrapped in a white towel turban, her scent powdery fresh with a hint of shampoo, soap and a citrusy body lotion that he'd grown accustomed to.

Damn, she sure smelled good.

But it had to be nearly noon. The times he'd spent the night on her sofa, she'd always showered first thing.

"Did you just wake up?" he asked.

"I wasn't feeling…" She cleared her throat. "Well, I woke up tired, so since I'm off today, I decided to go back to bed."

"Are you okay?" he asked, remembering that she was supposed to be going to the doctor. When was her appointment? What would the blood work show?

"I'm fine." She offered him a smile. "It's amazing what a little nap will do."

"Can I come in?"

"Oh. Sorry." She stepped aside so he could enter, then nodded at the bags he held in his arms. "What's that?"

"It's our dinner. I'm going to cook for you."

"You really don't have to." She tightened the sash of her robe—one that had faded from use and bore a light scent of detergent, giving it the fragrance of home and hearth. "I'll just fix myself a sandwich."

"Not tonight. We've got something to celebrate."

Her brow furrowed. "What are we celebrating?"

A sense of pride settled in his chest, a tinge of excitement. "I just made an offer on a house."

"No kidding?" She followed him into the kitchen. "Where's it located?"

"In Riverdale. Leif's sister knew I was looking for something that needed a little work, and as soon as she snagged the listing, she gave me a call. I met her first thing this morning, and she was right. It's just what I was looking for. So she wrote up my offer."

"That was certainly fast," Simone said. "It took me weeks to decide upon this place. I had to hire someone to come out and inspect it for me so that I could make sure it didn't have any unexpected problems."

Mike placed the bags on the countertop and began to remove the items he'd purchased. "I called my brother Aaron, and he stopped by to give me his opinion. But he agreed, the house needs a lot of work, but it's nothing major."

"Congratulations. I guess that *is* something to celebrate."

"Thanks. It's possible they won't accept my offer, but Karen feels pretty confident they'll be willing to negotiate." He removed the chicken breasts that had been wrapped in butcher paper and placed the package in her fridge, next to a gallon of milk.

That big plastic jug seemed like a pretty large amount for a single woman to purchase for herself. Maybe she was getting used to having Mike around.

He sure hoped so.

"Tell me about the house," she said.

"It's the old Dennison place. I'm not sure if you remember, but three or four weeks ago, Ethel Dennison fell and broke her hip. Leif and I got the call and transported her to the E.R. I think you were on duty that night, but you were working with someone else at the time."

Simone remembered the elderly woman who'd come in that night. "Ethel is a nice lady. I felt badly that she'd gotten hurt and that she would probably have to go into a convalescent home while she recuperated."

"Her only child, a daughter, lives in Ohio and insisted that it was time Ethel moved in with her."

"It's too bad she had to give up her home, but it's nice that she gets to be with her family."

"Yes, it is," he said. "Being with loved ones beats the heck out of going into a long-term-care facility."

Yes, it did. But just thinking about Mrs. Dennison and her plight brought a question to mind.

If something happened to Simone's mother, would she invite the woman to move in with her?

Sheesh. How far did one's obligation go to a biological relative who acted more like a stranger?

Did it go beyond those occasional phone calls and Christmas dinners eaten in silence?

The only thing that made her feel slightly better about envisioning the scenario was the fact that even if Simone were to make an offer like that, her mom probably wouldn't want to live with her.

"If they accept my price, Karen is going to ask them if I can rent the house from them until the close of escrow. And if they agree, Wags and I will be out of your hair in no time at all." Mike tossed her a boyish grin. "So you see? Now you have good reason to celebrate, too."

How could she say no to that?

Yet, for some reason, she didn't feel particularly relieved about having her home to herself again.

"So," Mike said, "now that I'm here, I'll take the dogs for a walk. I thought maybe Woofer would show Wags how it's done."

"That would be nice."

"You can walk with us, if you like. Or if you have any errands to run, go ahead. I'll take them by myself."

Actually, Simone had an appointment for a pedicure later this afternoon. And she wanted to pick up a new pair of nursing shoes, too. She also needed to replace her iron. Yesterday, before work, she'd been pressing a pair of scrubs when Wags got his head stuck behind the lamp table. She'd rushed to help him, tripped over the cord and knocked the iron onto the floor, breaking off the little spout that provided steam.

"Are you sure you don't mind going alone?" she asked.

"Not at all. Take the day off, go shopping, have lunch with a friend. Whatever."

His grin caused her heart to flip-flop, and for the

briefest moment, she had the urge to tell him no, that she'd rather stick close to home and hang out with him and the dogs.

But how lame was that?

Taking a walk and spending the day with Mike might be counterproductive to everything she'd been trying to tell him.

That he couldn't expect anything other than friendship from her.

It was late in the afternoon when Simone returned from her errands, but she didn't find Mike or the dogs inside the house.

She did see signs in the kitchen that he'd started dinner. A covered pot sat on the stove, and a bottle of red wine rested on the counter, uncorked and breathing.

She heard a noise outside, made her way to the back door and glanced out the small window. She spotted him standing on the patio and firing up the grill, the dog and the puppy sitting on their haunches beside him.

Rather than let him know she was home, she stood there a moment, enjoying the sight of man and beast and nature.

Or rather, just the man.

Mike's efforts at the barbecue had caused a hank of raven-black hair to fall across his brow. The intensity in his expression as he stoked the fire was enough to captivate her, to make her think of a Scottish laird on a windswept moor.

If Simone believed in miracles, if she believed that he might be right about...

But she couldn't. Her mother had slowly whittled

away at her self-esteem and her ability to trust anyone with her true emotions.

Instead, she tore her attention away from Mike, fearing that, if he caught her eye, the attraction she just couldn't seem to kick would be too obvious. And if that happened, she could end up encouraging him to think the two of them could live happily ever after, rather than convince him they wouldn't.

After putting away the items she'd purchased while shopping—a pair of scrubs to go along with the nursing shoes, as well as an iron and a few other household cleaning products—she went into the kitchen and announced, "Hey, I'm back."

For a moment, her words had a honey-I'm-home ring to them, and she almost forgot that, when it came to love, she was a nonbeliever. At least, when it came to her and that particular emotion, she was.

Maybe she'd be better off coming clean with Mike about her past. About her irreparable scars. Then, when she finally leveled with him about the baby, he'd be more inclined to understand why she felt the way she did.

The door swung open, and Mike strode inside, as charming and hunky as ever. "Hey, beautiful. How was your day?"

Darn him. She almost felt pretty when she was with him. Even in a pair of jeans and a plain white cotton blouse.

She conjured a smile and lifted her right foot, which was wearing bright pink nail polish and a turquoise flip-flop. "It was great. I had a pedicure. See?"

His mouth quirked in a boyish grin that nearly buckled her knees. "Your toes look great. So does the rest of you."

Oh, yeah. She'd gotten a haircut while she was at the salon. She supposed she couldn't blame him for noticing. She usually wore it pulled back, out of her face.

"I like it down and curled under like that."

Yeah. Well… "Thanks." She combed her fingers through the strands, feeling them sluice along her hands, and struggled to find something else to say to that.

A change of topic would be good about now.

"What's for dinner?" she asked.

"Barbecued chicken, seasoned red potatoes and a salad that'll have you begging for the secret recipe of my vinaigrette dressing. But I'll warn you right now. It'll be virtually impossible to get me to crack. No one has been able to pry it from my lips."

Her gaze drifted to his mouth, her thoughts to his kisses. No, no, no, she told herself. Not there. Not now.

"I like vinaigrette dressing," she said instead. "I can't wait to taste it."

He winked, and those kissable lips quirked up in a crooked grin.

She felt herself weakening, her thoughts flirting dangerously with memories of the past, of the night they'd made love until nearly dawn.

And that couldn't be good.

She struggled to find some generic words, something that would get their conversation and her thoughts back on track.

"What can I do to help?" she asked.

"I've got it all covered. So just come outside and watch me grill."

Okay. That was easy enough.

Once outdoors, he pulled up a patio chair, and she

took a seat. All the while, Woofer and Wags scrambled for her attention. The puppy jumped on her leg, and the dog nuzzled her hands, hoping for a scratch behind the ears.

"Hey, guys," Mike said to the dogs. "Give the lady a break."

She smiled, providing them each the attention they wanted. "It's kind of nice to know I was missed."

Mike had missed her, too. But he was glad she'd gotten out of the house and treated herself to a new hairstyle and a pedicure.

"Why don't you two go play," he told the dogs as he reached for the rubber ball he'd left on the porch railing a while back and hurled it to the back of the yard.

As the dogs raced to the corner of the fence, his words echoed the instructions his parents used to give him and the other children on nights the couple had sat down to watch a movie on television. Mike hadn't realized how difficult it must have been for his parents to juggle a love life around a houseful of rugrats, and his admiration for them grew.

"The dogs seem to be getting along much better now," Simone said.

"I agree. We should be able to start leaving them alone when we both have to work."

"Speaking of work," Simone said, "we had an interesting case the other night. A little boy found a stray bullet in his backyard and apparently decided to put it up his nose."

"Crazy kids. I've seen them put jelly beans and crayons up there. But a bullet? That must have been a bit tricky to get out."

They continued to talk about some of the interesting cases they'd had while working, as well as a couple of humorous situations they'd come across.

"My dad's birthday is Monday evening, so we're all going to get together at my parents' house. Sometimes, it's a bit of a zoo, but it's always entertaining. If you're free, I'd like you to go with me."

"Thanks, but I'll pass this time."

He nodded, focusing on the fact that she'd said *this time,* which implied she might be up for it in the future.

They made some more small talk, and before long, the chicken was done. After Mike placed it on a clean platter, they left the dogs in the yard to eat outside and went indoors to enjoy their own meal in the dining room.

Mike pulled out Simone's chair so she could sit down at the antique oak table. "I've got a bottle of merlot on the counter. If you give me a minute, I'll pour us each a glass."

"That's okay. I'd rather have water."

Was she still worried that the alcohol would lower her inhibitions and make her more susceptible to temptation? If so, she didn't need to be. He wasn't trying to go that route. He just wanted to set the mood and add a romantic touch.

He felt a bit funny drinking alone, but he didn't want the wine to go to waste. "I'll pour myself a glass, then. Do you want ice in your water?"

"Yes, please."

When he returned to the table, she seemed pensive, introspective. She bit down on her bottom lip, furrowed her brow and stared at her plate. He watched her for a while, intent upon keeping his mouth shut. But as they ate in silence, curiosity finally got the better of him.

"Who hurt you, Simone?"

She glanced up, her gaze snagging his. "What do you mean?"

"Who broke your heart? I get this feeling that a man did a real number on you, and you're not about to put yourself in that same position again."

She studied him for a moment, as though pondering what to say, what to reveal.

About the time he'd decided that she wasn't going to tell him, she said, "I dated this guy in college. I can't say that he did any real number on me. But he certainly made me aware of my deficiencies in a relationship."

Mike couldn't think of any flaws that she might have, other than refusing to let her feelings go and give love a chance. "The guy was a fool."

"No, Tom might have been brash and insensitive. But he pretty much got it right. He called me an ice queen, and it hurt—a lot. But I knew what he meant, and there wasn't anything I could do to change that."

"You weren't cold or unfeeling the night you and I slept together."

Her voice softened, even if her resolve didn't. "How about the next morning?"

Yeah. There was that.

She blotted her lips with a napkin, then pushed her plate aside. "I don't connect very well with people, Mike. I always hold back. And while I care about you— far more than is in my best interests—I can't give you and me the chance you want us to have."

"Why?" he asked, wanting to understand.

"Because my mother hated my father. Because she

never wanted me in the first place. Because she decided to be noble and carry me to term, which I appreciate, but she was hell-bent on keeping me when she should have given me to someone who would have loved me." Simone stood, picked up her plate, glass and silverware, then carried them into the kitchen, leaving Mike to second-guess what she'd just told him and to wonder what, if anything, she might have held back.

He, too, got to his feet and made his way to the kitchen with his own place setting.

"Hey," he said, sidling up to her as she filled the sink with hot, soapy water. "I didn't mean to pry."

She turned to face him. "I know. But it's best that you understand something. I didn't have the love that you had growing up. I'm not sure if you put any merit in child psychology, but I never bonded with my mom. I didn't learn to trust. Whenever I was hurt, no one gave a damn. So on the outside, I might look okay and act professionally. But on the inside, I'm scared and not so sure about things. And for that reason, I'm happier being alone."

Mike gently gripped her shoulders, the silky strands of her hair brushing against his knuckles. "You're a queen, but you're *not* made of ice. And I'll give you the time you need. Just don't shut me out because you have some wild-ass notion that you're looking out for *my* best interests."

Then he kissed her, long and hard and thorough.

Their tongues mated, their breaths mingled. Their hearts pounded out in need.

And when he was done, when there was a flush of arousal along her neck and chest, when her lips parted

and her eyes widened, he excused himself for the
evening and left her alone.

To think.

And, hopefully, to yearn for all that they could be
together.

Chapter Eight

On Monday, Simone was asked to work an early shift to cover for Maureen Wiggins, an E.R. nurse who'd called in sick because of food poisoning.

So far, the morning had been relatively quiet, so while she took a lunch break, she carried a fantasy novel into the solarium, where she planned to spend some quiet time reading.

The solarium was a convenient place to take a break—and a cheerful one. An abundance of windows provided sunlight, as well as a view of the garden and the various elms, oaks and maples that had been growing on the hospital grounds for nearly forty years.

For the first time since the winter months had stripped the bushes bare, the roses had begun to bloom in a colorful array of buds and blossoms.

Because of the solitude and the view, the solarium

had become Simone's favorite place to steal a little reading time and escape into another world. Once inside, she planned to find a little alcove of cushiony chairs and make herself comfortable for the next twenty minutes or so. She'd even set the alarm on her watch so that she'd know when to end her break.

As she'd hoped, the solarium was nearly empty, other than a man talking on his cell phone in the corner.

She'd no more than glanced his way when she recognized Dr. Peter Wilder. Now that he was back in private practice, she didn't see him as often.

At first, she planned to ignore him and go about her business. But when she sensed he was having what appeared to be a serious, personal conversation with someone, Simone decided that it might be best if she left the room and let him speak in private.

"You're wrong, Anna," he said.

Simone easily surmised he was talking to his adopted sister.

Years ago, when Anna was an infant, she'd been left at the hospital by an unknown woman and adopted by Peter's parents. According to what Simone had gathered over the years by comments made to her by both Ella and Peter, their father, the late James Wilder, spent years trying to prove the family's love to Anna, which only created a strain between her and his other children.

To make matters worse, Anna had taken a position with NHC, and her family loyalty was in question.

Simone supposed, in some instances, adoptions might not work out the way everyone intended them to. And she'd have to keep that in mind.

For the first time since learning she was pregnant, she

realized that giving up the baby might not be the slam-dunk solution she'd been hoping for. That there were a lot of factors to consider.

But she supposed parenting, in general, was a difficult job—and not one to be taken lightly.

Peter glanced up, and when their gazes connected, Simone whispered, "Sorry." She motioned that she would leave him in private, but he shook his head, indicating that she didn't need to go.

Unfortunately, she felt uncomfortable either way.

"All right, I'll let you go. But do me a favor. Just try to see the family's side in this situation." Peter's lips tensed, then he slowly folded up his cell phone, ending the call without saying goodbye.

"I didn't mean to interrupt," Simone said.

"You didn't. We were hanging up anyway. Anna had a meeting to attend, so she said she'd talk to me later." Peter blew out a heavy sigh. "But I'm not so sure she'll call back. I'm afraid my sister is so removed from my life that she doesn't understand why I'm against the NHC takeover."

"I'm sorry to hear that." Simone thought highly of all the Wilders, and she sensed that the rift between Anna and her siblings was becoming more and more serious.

"If you had walked in a few minutes sooner, you would have heard a few heated words. I tried to explain how my dad felt about this hospital, how Ella, David and I feel, but Anna... Well, she just doesn't get it. I'm afraid that conversation we just had might have made things worse."

"Do you want to talk about it?" Simone didn't usually open up to her coworkers about her personal concerns and issues, but sometimes they found it easy to share with her. She suspected that was because she never took part in gossip or betrayed a confidence.

"There's really nothing to say." Peter got to his feet. "We've got some upcoming family weddings on the horizon, including my own. But I'm not even sure if Anna plans to attend any of them."

"It's tough when there's a rift in a family." Even when it was only a family of two, like Simone and her mother.

"You're right." As Peter approached Simone and headed for the door, he said, "The solarium is all yours now."

"Thanks."

As he left the sunlit room, Simone no longer felt like reading. Instead, she strode toward one of the windows and peered into the garden, noting the colorful signs of spring and renewal, the shoots of new growth and colorful blooms.

Peter's trouble with Anna only reminded her of the relationship she had with her mother.

It had been nearly a week, and her mom still hadn't returned her last call. But what else was new?

If the two of them had a normal relationship—she let the fantasy briefly play out in her mind—Simone would have called her mother to tell her about the baby. And if things had been different between them, she might have even looked forward to being a mother herself.

And perhaps she wouldn't be the least bit apprehensive about creating a family with Mike.

That night when she got home from work, Simone picked up the telephone and dialed her mother's number one last time. It wasn't all that unusual to be playing telephone tag with the woman.

But this time, Susan Garner answered on the third ring. "Hello?"

"Hey, Mom. It's me."

"Hi, Simone. You finally caught me at home. I'm afraid that I've been in and out a lot. I meant to return your call."

That was questionable.

"How are you doing?" Simone asked, disregarding the excuse given. "Cynthia called last week and told me you'd discovered a lump in your breast. I…I've been worried. And I wondered if there was anything I could do. If there were any questions you had."

"It was a bit scary for a while, but they did a biopsy and it came back benign."

"Well, good. That's great. And I imagine it's a big relief for you."

"Yes, it was." Susan blew out a sigh. "I'm really sorry Cynthia called you and bothered you with that. If it would have been…more serious…I would have called myself."

Would she have?

Somehow, Simone didn't think so. It was almost as if the two had never lived together, as if once Simone turned eighteen and could legally fly the coop, Susan's maternal responsibilities—what few she'd actually assumed—had ended.

"Well, I'm glad it all turned out okay," Simone said.

"Yes, everything is fine."

But it really wasn't. Not this conversation, not their relationship.

"I guess I'd better let you go, Mom. Be sure to tell Cynthia hello for me."

"I will. Good night, Simone."

The line disconnected.

Simone supposed the news should have been comforting, but she wanted to scream in frustration.

Why couldn't her relationship with her mother have been…normal? Or even just moderately dysfunctional?

In spite of the years Simone had spent building up a durable, Teflon hide and telling herself it really didn't matter, the disappointment and pain she'd experienced as a child and had locked away as an adolescent began to flood her heart with regret, and tears welled in her eyes.

Damn those pregnancy hormones.

And damn the past.

Woofer barked, then headed for the door, just moments before the bell sounded.

Oh, *great.* Now what? Simone hated to bother answering, especially all weepy-eyed and splotchy-faced. But neither did she want to hole up inside the house and pretend she wasn't home.

So she answered, albeit reluctantly, and found Mike on her porch. She could have sworn he'd told her he had an O'Rourke-family birthday party to attend. He must have decided to stop by on his way.

"Oh, honey," he said, reaching for the knob of the screen door without waiting to be invited inside.

She supposed he'd gotten used to making himself comfortable at her house. And she must have gotten used to having him around, too, because she grabbed Woofer's collar and used her foot to keep Wags from dashing outside. Then she stepped out of the way to let Mike in.

He gave each dog a detached greeting while focusing his attention on her. "What's the matter?"

Oh, God. She hated to spill her guts. But maybe, if she did, it would eventually make him realize why she wasn't the motherly type. Why the whole idea of home and family scared the heck out of her.

When Simone admitted that she'd finally talked to her mother about the lump she'd found, Mike wrapped his arms around her, probably assuming her tears were caused by bad news. "I'm so sorry."

Instead of immediately correcting him, she accepted his embrace and allowed herself a moment to savor his musky scent, his warmth, his compassion.

"Actually," she finally said, slowing drawing away from his arms, "the lump was benign."

"So you're crying from relief?"

"Yes and no. It's kind of complicated. It also hurts that my mother refused to return my calls, saying she didn't want to bother me with her problem."

"Maybe she was trying to protect you."

"If it were anyone else's mom, I might accept that. But not when it's mine."

He took her by the hand and led her to the sofa. "Why don't you sit down and talk to me about it."

It didn't feel right having the ugliness out in the open, but maybe it would be therapeutic in a sense. So she took a seat and waited for him to join her.

"I told you some of it already," she said. "About how my mom was cold and unloving."

He nodded. "I figured you'd held something back. You always do. But you don't need to do that with me."

She hoped he was right. "I knew that other kids had parents who played games with them. Moms and dads who asked how their day at school went, who tucked them in at night and listened to their prayers. But I never experienced anything like that. And no matter how hard I tried, I couldn't seem to connect on any level with my mother."

He didn't comment; he just continued to listen as she vented—something she wasn't used to doing.

"When I was a kid, I would have to change the channel whenever *The Wonderful World of Disney* was on television. It was too sad. I'd see commercials about Disneyland or Walt Disney World, with happy, loving families having the time of their lives. But I never even went to an amusement park. No visits to the petting zoo, no pony rides. None of the usual family experiences."

"I'm sorry that your childhood was so lousy."

"Me, too," she said. "But don't get me wrong. I never went without the material things. There was plenty of food. And I had regular health checkups. But sometimes my mom would glare at me. Or strike me for no reason."

"You were physically abused, too?" he asked.

"It's not like I was beaten. But I learned to stay out of my mom's reach."

While Mike continued to hold her hand, he brushed his thumb across her skin, soothing her, comforting her with the simplest touch. And she couldn't help but accept all he offered.

"I have a great mom," he said. "And I can't even imagine what I would have done or who I would have become without her."

He still didn't know the worst of it, Simone realized. He didn't know why her relationship with her mother had been so bad. Or why it still was. And so she decided to tell him what she hadn't told anyone else.

"When I was in the seventh grade, my mom told me to clean out the garage. And while I was moving some things around, I found a box of old photos and a diary. I knew her journal contained her private thoughts and that I shouldn't read it. But I'd always wanted to know my mom better, to understand what made her tick."

"And did you?"

"Yes. The early pages revealed a much different person than the one I'd known. She'd grown up in the sixties and had been happy and carefree. She used to write poetry. I guess you could say that she was… normal."

"When did that change?"

"When she was seventeen. By the time I got to the end of the diary, to the place where she'd finally quit writing, it all fell into place." Simone's fingers tightened around Mike's hands, then she slowly loosened them. She wasn't sure whether she wanted to cling to his touch or pull away.

His grip tightened, making the decision easier for her.

"My mom was raped, and I was the result."

Mike didn't respond, and she struggled not to peer at his face, not to try and read something in his expression. She'd just revealed the fact that she'd been the product of a violent act, not a loving one.

"My mom actually knew the guy and had gone out with him," she added. "So it would be classified as a date rape now. But back in the late sixties, when it happened, she felt that it was all her fault. And because I look like my father…"

"Did you know him?" Mike asked.

"No." She paused, thinking it best to explain. "Well,

my mom never said that I resembled him, and I never asked. But I don't look at all like her, so I can't help believing that each time she looked at me she was reminded of him, of what he'd done to her. And for that reason, she inadvertently—and subconsciously—took her anger and resentment out on me."

"You have no idea how sorry I am. For you, of course. But for her, too."

"Needless to say, this isn't something I'm proud of. But it's had an adverse effect on any relationship I've had. And that's why having a husband and children scares me to death. I don't want to hurt the people who depend upon me the most."

He seemed to ponder her words and her concern for a moment, then slowly shook his head. "No, that's not going to happen. For the past couple of years, I've watched you with your patients, young and old. And I've even seen you interact with the dogs, even when they're misbehaving. You'd never hurt anyone, intentionally or otherwise."

"I wish I could believe you, Mike. But I'm damaged goods."

He cupped her cheek. "You'll never be able to convince me of that. It's simply not true. I'm in love with you, Simone. And that's not going to change."

She wanted to believe him—she really did. But she couldn't take the chance.

What if he was wrong? What if she couldn't bond with the baby she was carrying?

Simone sat in the Walnut River OB/GYN waiting room, thumbing through a magazine and listening for her name to be called. She'd had blood drawn earlier, as ordered, and had already discussed insurance and financial obligations.

Now she was waiting for her first exam.

Last night, Mike had stayed at her house until she'd chased him off, telling him not to be late to his father's birthday party. She could tell he was reluctant to leave her alone, but she'd insisted she was fine.

And she was. She'd been dealing with her mom and the past for years.

Several times over the course of his visit, she'd been tempted to tell him about the baby. But she'd decided to wait until after seeing Dr. Kipper. After all, other than a little morning sickness and an occasional bout of light-headedness, she still didn't *feel* pregnant. Shouldn't she wait for some kind of confirmation?

As she sat in the cheerful waiting room, with its cream-colored walls and the lavender- and green-stenciled border, she couldn't seem to focus on any of the colorful ads or articles in her magazine.

Instead, she checked out the other patients, most of whom were visibly pregnant.

A blonde with a belly the size of a watermelon sat across from her, and she imagined herself big with child, her hands resting on her womb. Maybe she'd feel a little bump move by—a hand or a foot.

The dark-haired new mother to her left held a sleeping newborn in her arms. And, for a moment, Simone envisioned herself bringing the baby to an after-delivery checkup.

The door swung open, and someone else—a redhead—entered. She was about six months along and had a toddler with her. An older woman was only steps behind, and Simone suspected it was the grandmother.

Pregnant women should have the love and support of their mothers, which was another reason why Simone couldn't imagine keeping her baby. The only person she had to rely on was herself. But that was her reality, and she'd learned to accept it.

She wished she could say that her revelation to Mike about the details surrounding her conception and her childhood had been therapeutic. In a way, she supposed it had been. At least it was out in the open now.

When the nurse, a fifty-something blonde with a warm smile, called Simone's name from the doorway, she stood, leaving the magazine on the table next to her, and let the matronly woman lead her toward the exam rooms.

They stopped by the scale, then went through the usual routine of taking her blood pressure and checking her pulse. After being given a plastic cup and pointed in the direction of the restroom, she provided them with a urine sample.

It was an interesting twist to be a patient rather than a medical professional for a change. And she wasn't sure that she liked it.

Next, she undressed and donned the backless hospital-style gown that everyone hated, then climbed up on the exam table. Fortunately, she didn't have to wait long for Dr. Kipper to come in, accompanied by the nurse.

"I've gone over the lab work," the tall, slender obstetrician said. "Everything looks good."

The following pelvic exam was also normal.

"Since you're over thirty-five," Dr. Kipper said as he reached for her hand and helped her to a sitting position on the table, "I'm going to suggest an amniocentesis at sixteen weeks."

He went on to explain the procedure and the risks, then answered all her questions.

She mentioned being light-headed a time or two and actually fainting once, although she hadn't eaten since the night before. He told her that it wasn't uncommon and suggested that she keep her blood sugar level steady by having more frequent and smaller meals. He also told her that a sudden change in blood pressure could also be the cause. And that she should change positions slowly.

"Let me know if the fainting or dizziness becomes frequent," he said.

"All right. I will."

He wrote something in her chart, then glanced up. "Are you taking any vitamins?"

"Just the generic variety I normally take."

He dug through the cupboard and found a couple of packets. "I've got a sample of the prenatal vitamins I'd like you to start taking instead. I've got them in either pink or blue. Do you have a preference?"

"No, it doesn't matter." Yet thoughts of pink had her thinking about sugar and spice and everything nice, while blue brought on a reminder of frogs, snails and puppy-dog tails.

Would Mike have a preference?

No, she snapped at herself. Don't even go there.

"I'd like to see you back in three weeks," Dr. Kipper said.

She nodded, feeling a bit robotic.

When the doctor and his nurse left her alone in the room, she removed the drafty gown and got dressed.

Next, she stopped at the checkout window, where she made a payment.

On the way out of the office, she spotted Millie seated in the waiting room, near a potted palm.

Millie looked up from the magazine she was reading, her gaze landing on Simone. "Hey! Fancy meeting you here."

Simone had thought the exact thing. And for a moment, she hoped that Millie was here for the same reason, that God had listened to her prayers, and she'd somehow become pregnant.

"How about that," Simone said.

Millie set the magazine in her lap. "I'm here for my yearly Pap smear. How about you?"

Simone didn't have the heart to tell her she was pregnant. And for more reasons than one.

If she miscarried, which was a possibility, especially in the first three months, and Millie was expecting to adopt the baby, it would be an unnecessary disappointment and heartbreak for her friend.

And secondly, she wasn't ready to let the cat out of the bag.

Or is it more than that? a small inner voice asked. *Are you trying to hold on to the baby, as well as the news?*

Simone quickly shook off the stray thought.

"Pap smears aren't something I look forward to, but they're very important," she told her friend, tottering on the truth and a lie of omission.

"I know." Millie scanned the room and zeroed in on a petite brunette who looked to be about nine months pregnant and ready to pop. When her gaze returned to Simone, her eyes glistened with unshed tears.

Simone's heart went out to the woman who would make a wonderful mother. Again she thought about giving her baby to Millie and Fred. If she were to do that, the child would undoubtedly grow up happy and loved.

Yet a sudden sense of uneasiness settled over her when she thought about handing over her child, a selfish response that left her with a nagging sense of guilt.

Simone didn't have any business even thinking about keeping the baby.

So what had caused the momentary change of heart?

Chapter Nine

Last week, Mike had invited Simone out to dinner to Rafael's, a classy restaurant in downtown Walnut River, complete with candles, white linen tablecloths and the best chef and service for miles around.

For a woman who'd never had a romantic bone in her body, she was sorely tempted to don that only-worn-once black dress she owned—or maybe buy a new one—and let him sweep her off to a dreamy dinner for two. She could almost imagine herself sitting across a candlelit table from the most handsome man in all of Walnut River, a young, dark-haired hunk who clearly had eyes for her.

Little by little, Mike had been whittling away at her resolve to remain single and unattached, which had protected her well over the years. And at times, she found herself leaning toward sentiment rather than wisdom.

So, she'd declined—with more reluctance than she cared to admit.

Then, on Tuesday, he'd suggested they each take some vacation time and go to Martha's Vineyard for a few days. He'd said he wanted to take her to the Cape before the tourist season kicked in.

She'd found the idea strangely appealing and the thought of the possible sleeping arrangements...intriguing.

But again she'd refused.

She didn't think it would be wise to leave the hospital when it looked as though the allegations of insurance fraud were being investigated. Nor did she know how long she could fight her attraction to a man whose perseverance was both frustrating and flattering.

And now, Mike stood on her front porch with a bouquet of roses in one hand and two white bags in the other. Apparently, he was at it again—trying to make more of their relationship than it really was.

Still, as much as she hated to admit it, she'd begun to enjoy Mike's company, so she invited him in.

The first thing he did, after handing her the flowers, was to kick off his shoes by the door. "If you'll put those roses in some water, I'll get everything set up."

"What do you mean?"

He tossed her a boyish grin that knocked her heart on end. "I'm setting the mood. Our food will taste better this way. We're going to sit on the floor and use chopsticks instead of forks."

She watched as he placed the bags that boasted the red pagoda logo of the Tokyo Palace on the coffee table.

Then he removed two cushions from the couch and set them on the floor.

Too cute, she thought, heading for the kitchen. And far too charming for his own good.

Hers, too, she realized. Sometimes, in spite of their opposing goals and dreams, she found herself weakening toward him and wondering, What if…

And not just sexually speaking.

While she stood at the sink and filled a vase with water, she glanced out into the yard, where Woofer and Wags lay in the shade of an elm tree. The dogs had grown comfortable with each other in the past week or so.

The same could be said for Simone and Mike, she supposed.

She had to admit that she admired his spirit, as well as his thoughtfulness, and a solid friendship was clearly developing.

Would that make telling him about the baby easier or more difficult?

She couldn't be sure.

Maybe she ought to just get it over with while they ate dinner—a game plan which seemed wise, especially after the dream she'd had last night. She'd awakened in the midst of it and found the image so unsettling that she'd climbed out of bed at 4:00 a.m. and put on a pot of water for a cup of tea.

In her dream, she'd held a baby girl, a sweet bundle of flannel and lace who'd had Mike's black hair and green eyes. The smiling cherub had settled comfortably in Simone's arm and turned a new mommy's heart inside out—until the helpless babe began to cry.

A sense of panic had settled in, waking Simone from her sleep.

She feared that dreams like that might start hounding her subconscious until she finally told Mike she was pregnant and was able to put it all behind her.

Mike might have taken her past in stride, but he couldn't convince her that she hadn't come away from it unscathed.

And although he wasn't worried about how she'd handle marriage and a family, she wasn't ready to gamble with a child's psyche.

Before the water threatened to spill out of the vase, she shut off the spigot. Next she cut off about an inch or so from the stems of the roses and arranged them carefully. When she carried the red buds back into the living room, Mike appeared to have everything planned just so.

"Do you care where I put these?" she asked.

"Not at all."

In that case, she placed them in the center of her antique china hutch, then took a seat on one of the sofa cushions Mike had placed on the floor and studied the Japanese feast he'd spread out on the coffee table. He'd picked up wontons, California roll, a variety of sashimi, miso soup, steamed rice and chicken teriyaki.

"It looks good," she said.

"Thanks. Why don't you take a seat while I get us something to drink."

"All right."

"What would you like?"

"Water sounds good to me."

When he returned from the kitchen with both glasses,

he placed one in front of her and the other on his side of the table. Then he took his seat.

"How about some sashimi?" he asked. "I've got ahi and salmon."

"I'll pass." She wasn't sure what the rules were on eating raw fish when a woman was pregnant, so until she had a chance to read up on it, she thought it was best to decline.

He took a sip of his ice water. "I stocked some beer and wine in the fridge last time I was here. But I decided not to offer you any. I didn't want you to think I was trying to ply you with alcohol."

"Why would I think that?" she asked.

"I don't know. Because I've offered you wine a couple of times. Of course, to be honest, I wouldn't mind seeing you loosen up some."

She bristled, sensing what he was about to say.

"You hold yourself back," he went on to explain. "And I understand why you do. But there was a warm glow about you on the night we attended Dr. Wilder's party, and you had a happy glimmer in your eyes."

"That's because I was tipsy." And she'd be darned if she'd let that happen again.

"No, I noticed it when you reached for your first glass of champagne. I'm not sure you'd even taken a sip, but either way, I saw a side of you I hadn't seen before, and it was nice."

"That side of me doesn't really exist."

"I disagree. I think you let that woman out of her cage every now and again."

For a moment, Simone was transported back to her college days. Back to when Tom broke up with her, saying pretty much the same thing. *You need to loosen up, Simone. You're strung too tight. You've built walls around yourself. And whenever anyone tries to get too close, you shut them out and turn on the deep freeze.*

Tom's words had stunned her to silence, and she'd felt herself recoil into an emotional fetal position, her heart frosting over and preparing for the worst.

Dammit. He'd slammed the palm of his hand down on the console of his car. *There you go again, Simone, shutting me out. You're an ice queen.*

Mike hadn't said those exact words, but his meaning was clear. And his thoughts had undoubtedly drifted in the same direction as Tom's had that long-ago day on the way home from the shore.

"Is something wrong?" Mike asked.

Yes, something was wrong. They'd created a child. A baby she couldn't keep. And she was going to have to level with him—*now.* While he was reminded of the woman she really was.

And who she wasn't.

Oh, God, she pleaded, hoping The Man Upstairs cared enough to listen to her these days, that he cared enough to help her get the words out and set things to rights. *I've got to tell him. And then I need to stand firm.*

She raked a hand through the strands of her hair, then blew out a ragged breath. "There's something you need to know."

Mike, who was fiddling with his chopsticks, placed them on his paper plate and gazed at her. "What's that?"

"I'm pregnant."

His brow twitched, and his jaw dropped. "You're kidding."

"Believe me, I may not have the best sense of humor in the world, but there's no way I'd joke about something like that."

"Is it mine?" His expression went from disbelief to *well-duh* in less than a millisecond. "Sorry. Of course it's mine. I didn't mean to... Wow."

Yeah. *Wow.*

"That's actually...cool," he finally said, his initial shock morphing into an easy grin. "It's a bit of a surprise, but I'm perfectly okay with it."

Simone wasn't sure what she'd been expecting him to say. Exactly that, she supposed.

But apparently, he hadn't been listening to her. Didn't he get it?

"Well, *I'm* not okay with it," she admitted. "And I think it's best for everyone involved if I give the baby up for adoption."

As Simone's cold hard solution hung in the air like the courthouse sentence of a convicted felon, Mike wanted to lash back, to argue. Yet he knew her well enough to keep his mouth shut and try to make some sense of this. To try to wrap his mind around it and form another game plan.

Damn.

Simone was pregnant.

With *his* baby.

For some crazy reason, he couldn't stop a goofy smile from curling the edges of his mouth.

Their lovemaking had created a child.

Mike adored his nieces and nephews—seven of them and still counting. How he'd like to see his own son or daughter join its cousins in a game of hide-and-seek or freeze tag.

His grin broadened—until the realization that she'd wanted to give up their kid shoved it aside.

Was she just trying to feel him out? To test his reaction?

Women did that sometimes.

"You know," he said, "I've never made any secret about my feelings for you. And while I wasn't in a big rush to get married or have kids, that's not something we ought to put off."

"And I've made no secret about my fears," she countered. "I'm not mommy material. Haven't you been listening to me?"

Yes, but he'd hoped to change her mind.

In fact, he still did. He just hadn't counted on something like this happening—at least not this soon. But just because the timing might make a pregnancy a bit inconvenient didn't mean the baby would be a complication.

Hell, Mike could see himself getting used to the idea in no time at all.

He picked up his chopsticks and began to eat, even though his appetite had fizzled in the pit of his stomach and he was merely poking at his chicken.

Hers must have done the same thing, because she picked at her food, too.

They ate in silence until he felt compelled to argue his case one more time. "You can't convince me that you don't have feelings for me, too."

"I told you that I do. And more than I should."

"Our lovemaking was off the charts," he added. "We couldn't be any more sexually compatible."

"I agree. But great sex isn't enough of a basis for marriage. Neither is parenthood."

What was up with her attitude about the baby?

Their baby.

She could have been blindsided by the news, he supposed. And didn't pregnant women's hormones play havoc with them? "All I'm saying is that we need to give ourselves some time to sort through this."

She pushed her plate aside, then dropped her used napkin on top. "Time isn't going to change anything. You're looking for Mrs. Right, and I'm clearly not that woman."

He tried to tell himself to go easy on her at a time like this. She'd told him about growing up with a mother who hadn't shown her any love. And on top of that, she had to be struggling with a multitude of changes in her body.

Maybe she was also considering all the obvious adjustments a baby—and a husband, if Mike had his way—would require her to make when it came to the life she'd created for herself.

But the news of her pregnancy, along with her thoughts of adoption, had unbalanced him.

"You know," she said, "I'm really tired and probably ought to turn in for the night."

Was she? Or was she just trying to get rid of him?

"Okay," he said. "I'll take off. I'm on duty tomorrow, too. But maybe we can talk more about this the next day."

"There's not much to say."

"Oh, I think there is." Yet something twisted in his gut, something that made him want to shove his plate aside, too.

Damn. Why was her first thought to give up their baby?

If she insisted, there was no way in hell that Mike would stand for it. And she had to have his agreement, didn't she?

All his carefully laid plans had begun to unravel at the edges.

Ever since the night of Dr. Wilder's party, he'd been telling her that he'd give her the time she needed. That she'd soon realize the two of them were made for each other. But if she didn't give him something to go on soon, he was going to back off. Hell, his ego, as strong and cocky as it sometimes was, couldn't take the constant brush-off.

She walked him to the door, and while he thought about kissing her senseless, he brushed his lips across her brow instead.

"Sleep tight," he said.

"You, too."

Yeah, right. He had a lot to think about, a lot to keep him awake.

He tried to remind himself how good sex had been. How hot their kisses were.

But Mike was only human.

And the truth was, his heart could only take so much.

The next morning, at the station, Mike watched a gin game that had grown pretty intense, but his mind was on the bombshell—actually two of them—he'd received the night before.

Simone was having his baby.

And she wanted to give it up.

At least, she hadn't decided upon an abortion, which made him feel better.

He understood that she might have wished her mother would have given her to parents who would have loved and appreciated her. But this was different.

Mike wanted the baby. And deep in his heart, he believed Simone wanted it, too.

Preferring to stew in his own thoughts and suffer alone, he got to his feet and walked out of the station.

When footsteps sounded behind him, he turned to see his partner, Leif Johnson, a stocky redhead with blue eyes and a quick wit.

Leif knew how Mike felt about Simone, but then again, a lot of people probably did. Mike never did try to hide his feelings.

Of course, that didn't mean he was the kind of man who kissed and told.

"Hey," Leif said. "You look like you're a million miles away."

"I guess I am."

"Would getting it off your chest help?"

Leif had known that Mike had taken Simone home after Dr. Wilder's party, but that's all he knew. Mike hadn't leveled with anyone about what he and Simone had shared that night. But now that Simone had him second-guessing himself and his feelings, he wasn't sure about anything anymore.

Mike leaned against the outside wall of the building and crossed his arms. "Do you remember when they christened the hospital library in honor of James Wilder? And the cocktail party Peter Wilder invited us to?"

"Yeah."

Normally, paramedics didn't get included in those kinds of hospital social events. But Mike and Leif had been on duty the night James Wilder suffered the fatal heart attack. And they'd tried valiantly—but unsuccessfully—to save his life. As a result, the two had been added to the guest list.

"I gave Simone a ride home that night," Mike said.

"Yeah, I remember." Leif smiled. "She looked like maybe she'd had a little too much to drink."

"Well, one thing led to another and…" Mike blew out a loaded sigh.

"No kidding?" Leif grinned, knowing how much Mike cared for Simone and immediately making the appropriate jump. "Are you two still seeing each other?"

"Not like that. She says she just wants to be friends."

"Hey, that's life. I've had my share of women tell me the same thing. That is, until Linda and I hooked up."

Leif was dating a kindergarten teacher he'd met when her class had come to the fire station for a field trip. Leif didn't kiss and tell, either, but Mike knew that they'd been sleeping together.

One morning about a month ago, Leif hadn't come home the night before. He'd apparently left his headlamps on and couldn't get his car to start. So he'd had to call Mike and ask for a ride to work.

Linda seemed like a nice woman, and Mike hoped they'd be happy.

"So what's the problem?" Leif asked. "Just cut bait and run."

"I would, but I can't help believing that Simone and I are meant for each other. But she's so…" Mike didn't want to go into too much personal detail. "So damn set in her ways."

Leif placed a hand on Mike's back. "I know it hurts,

man. But you can't chase after a woman who clearly isn't interested. There are stalking laws and all that."

Mike clucked his tongue. "I'm not a stalker. And I know when a woman isn't interested. If I truly believed it, I'd back way off."

"So she's given you reason to believe there's hope?"

"Yeah." She'd admitted that she cared for him. And he couldn't help believing her, especially when he remembered the way she'd looked at him when they'd made love—talk about someone wearing their heart on their sleeve.

At three in the morning, she'd lost that tipsy glow, and it had been replaced by something else. Something laden with an emotion a man couldn't mistake for friendship or simple desire.

But maybe he'd read her wrong.

Maybe she didn't have the right kind of feelings for him, and he'd been pushing her too hard.

"Chasing after her just isn't cool," Leif added. "It makes you look needy."

His partner had a point. Mike had made himself too available. It might be best if he backed off.

"Linda has a couple of friends. They're both single and hot. Without a doubt, either of them would drop everything to go out on a date with you."

The trouble was, Mike didn't want to go out with anyone other than Simone. And he sure as hell didn't want to go out with anyone when Simone was having his baby.

Damn.

His baby.

Their baby.

"What you need is a diversion," Leif said. "And have

I got the woman for you. Her name is Christy, and she's about five-two. She's a school librarian, but don't think that means she's prim and proper. She's bright, well read and funny."

Mike needed to get his mind off Simone, all right. But not by dating another woman. "I may back off with Simone. But I'm not ready to go out with anyone else."

"Why not?"

"It's complicated."

"Suit yourself," Leif said. "But promise me you'll stop pining for a woman who doesn't want you."

While Mike could see the value in that advice, he couldn't completely give up on Simone.

Not just yet.

But how could a woman be so stubborn?

Mike still hoped to change her mind, but he was beginning to have his doubts. He suspected that was why the seed of a plan B began to form. A plan that he'd implement if backed into a corner.

A move that could end any dream Mike had of him and Simone creating a family together.

Chapter Ten

After Mike left Simone's house, she'd cleaned up the dinner mess. It had been quick and easy; she'd just packed up the leftovers in plastic ware before refrigerating them, then thrown away the take-out bags and cartons.

But she suspected she'd made a mess out of her friendship with Mike. And if she chose to do something about that, it wouldn't be as easy to straighten up.

She'd shut him out by suggesting he go home, which she was prone to do whenever things got emotionally involved. But for once in her life, she hadn't been especially happy about being left alone.

After feeding the dogs and getting them situated in the kitchen for the night, she'd showered and put on her favorite pink flannel gown, then climbed into bed. The sheets had been laundered earlier that day, which, under normal conditions, meant she could expect a good night's sleep.

Instead, her mind refused to shut down and continued to go over their dinnertime conversation again and again. She'd kept trying to figure out a better way she could have handled it, but hadn't been able to.

Mike had a different spin on the pregnancy situation than she had. And he had a different solution, too.

Unfortunately, she'd had to work the next day, and as a result, had arrived at the hospital a bit distracted by lack of sleep and thoughts of Mike and the baby. Of course, she'd tried to shake them off the best that she could.

Now she sat behind the desk at the nurses' station in the E.R., reading the orders one of the residents had written on a patient's chart.

There'd been a traffic accident on the interstate about an hour earlier, and a seventeen-year-old passenger in one of the cars had been sent to X-ray with a possible broken arm and collarbone.

"Is that the Stephens chart?" Ella asked.

"Yes, it is." Simone handed her the paperwork, pleased Ella had been the orthopedic surgeon who'd been called in to treat the teen's injury.

Ella looked the chart over, then asked, "When is he due back from radiology?"

"It shouldn't be much longer."

Ella nodded. When she finished perusing the chart, she glanced across the desk at Simone. "Did you hear that the state attorney general's office is sending an investigator to do a preliminary investigation about possible insurance fraud?"

"When?"

"Within the next few days, I've heard." Ella set the chart aside.

"I don't like the sound of that."

"Neither do I."

"It's so unfair," Simone added. "Walnut River General might keep its patients longer than most hospitals, but it's not an attempt to defraud insurance companies. It's because we don't believe in sending patients home early just to keep the costs down."

"They won't uncover anything fraudulent. But from what I understand, the investigator is going to interview anyone who might have information about the alleged fraud. That means doctors, nurses and the administrative staff."

"That will cast suspicion on everyone, which won't be good for morale. Besides, I'm not looking forward to having a stranger snooping around here. Not that I expect them to uncover anything." Simone chuffed. "You know, we have enough to worry about these days. Since the board rejected NHC's last offer, the takeover attempts could become hostile."

"I'm glad my father isn't alive to see what's going on. He loved this hospital."

Ella didn't mention it, but Simone wondered how James Wilder would have felt about his adopted daughter, Anna, working for the conglomerate that wanted to take over Walnut River General.

Not pleased, Simone decided.

"Are you going to attend the retirement party for Henry Weisfield on Sunday afternoon?" Ella asked.

Simone wasn't up for another party/dress-up affair.

But she'd have to at least make an appearance. "I may stop by for a few minutes."

"Long enough to have a glass of champagne?" Ella asked. "J.D. and I are having a private celebration." She grinned. "It's now official. He'll be taking over Henry's position."

"That's great news, but I'm afraid I've given up drinking champagne. It doesn't sit well with my resolve to remain unattached."

"Maybe you ought to drink more of it," Ella said with a smile. "You had a lovely glow that night we re-christened the hospital library."

Yep. Wrapped in Mike's arms, Simone had smoldered until dawn that night. And now she had a *pregnancy glow* to look forward to.

"By the way," Ella said, "I saw Mike walking Woofer and the puppy the other day. It looks like you two have figured out a shared-custody arrangement."

Simone's heart sank to the pit of her stomach, causing a wave of nausea to render her speechless.

"What's the matter?" Ella asked. "Is that a touchy subject?"

"It's just that…" Simone blew out a wobbly breath. Normally, she'd keep news like her pregnancy a secret. But it was going to be common knowledge as soon as she started showing.

Besides, she and Ella had become closer in the past few months.

Simone hadn't been sure how or when it had happened. She'd always respected Ella, but lately she'd come to enjoy her company, too.

So, she scanned the immediate area, checking to see

who might be listening in. When she was convinced their conversation was private, she cleared her throat. "Well, there's the dog thing, yes. But when you mentioned shared custody, I...well, it hit a little too close to home."

"What do you mean?"

"I'm pregnant."

Ella sat back in her chair, the springs creaking in protest. "Oh, Simone... Does Mike know?"

"Yes." Simone blew out a sigh. "And to make matters worse, Mike and I have opposing beliefs on what would be best for everyone involved."

"He wants to...?" Ella merely looked at Simone, prompting an answer she might have normally kept to herself.

"He wants to get married and live happily ever after."

"And you don't?"

"I can't, Ella."

Footsteps sounded, and both women grew silent. Simone was glad to refocus her thoughts on work.

If her mind would only cooperate.

Simone had just arrived home from the market and was unloading her car when Mike drove up in his Jeep. She watched as he got out of the vehicle and approached.

He was wearing a pair of faded jeans, a white polo shirt and an unreadable expression. Sheepish? Pensive? Intense?

"If I help you put away your groceries," he said, "will you take a ride with me?"

"Where?"

"It's a surprise."

A part of her was glad to know he hadn't shut her out

of his life completely, and since it was rare that anyone had a surprise for her, she was also curious.

"All right," she said.

Minutes later, after they'd placed the frozen food in the freezer and the eggs and dairy products in the fridge, they stacked the pasta, rice and canned goods in the pantry.

"Okay," Mike said. "Let's go."

Simone glanced down at the clothes she was wearing—a pair of black slacks, which had a little more room in the waistband and just seemed to feel better than her jeans these days. She also had on a lime-green, scoop-necked top with an empire waist. The shirt was stylish, yet she realized it looked a bit like a maternity blouse without all the extra material. Not that she needed a new wardrobe yet.

"Should I change my clothes?" she asked.

"No, you look great." The warmth in his grin convinced her of his sincerity.

So she grabbed her purse and, after locking the house, followed him to his Jeep. Before climbing into the passenger side, she again asked, "Where are we going?"

"Just for a drive. I want to show you something." He opened the door and waited for her to get in.

He always behaved like a gentleman around her, and she decided there was a lot about Mike to admire. A lot to love.

A wistful ache settled in her chest, and she wished she could let go of her fears and accept his optimism. He made it all sound so simple, when she was a realist and knew that having a relationship with him—at least, the kind he wanted and deserved—would be anything but easy for her.

After she slid into her seat, he closed the door, circled the vehicle and climbed into the driver's side.

Minutes later, they were driving through the tree-shaded streets of Riverdale.

She suspected he wanted to show her the Dennison place, or rather the home he'd just placed an offer on. And if truth be told, she'd like to see it, too.

After he turned onto Maple and passed the first curve in the road, she realized that's exactly what he had in mind.

He pulled along the curb in front of a three-story, pale yellow Victorian-style home with white gingerbread trim and shut off the ignition.

The house needed paint and some fix-it work done, but the place had enormous potential.

"The owners agreed to rent it to me before the close of escrow," he said. "So I moved in early this morning. Come on. I want to show you the inside, as well as the yard."

As he led her to the house, she realized that the lawn had been freshly mowed, trimmed and watered. She also saw that the sidewalk and porch had been swept clean and washed down. She suspected Mike had been eager to get to work on his new place.

Or had he wanted to make a good impression on her?

He unlocked the front door and waited for her to enter. Once they were inside the house, he pointed out the hardwood floors, a redbrick fireplace that bore smoke and soot stains from years of use and a curved banister that led upstairs.

The walls had been covered in a faded blue-and-yellow floral wallpaper that Simone suspected was part of the original decor. If not, it had been a part of the house for years.

There were five bedrooms upstairs and one down. It seemed like a lot of square footage for a single man. Still, she could understand why a guy like him might want to tackle a big renovation, as this was bound to be.

The kitchen, with its retro-style appliances and scarred gray linoleum, needed to be remodeled. The bathrooms—three of them—did, too. Yet there was a charm to the place, and she truly believed Mike had lucked out when it went on the market.

"The house is wonderful, Mike. You're really going to enjoy refurbishing it."

"I know. And I can't wait to get started." He placed a hand on her back and ushered her through the kitchen to the service porch, then out the door. The back lawn, like the one in front, had been newly mowed. A sprinkler had been turned on and was raining some much-needed water on the dried-out blades of grass.

She suspected, before long, it would soon be a lovely shade of green.

On the other hand, the shrubs, trees and bushes were in desperate need of a trim, and the flower beds could stand some attention from someone with a green thumb.

"The yard still looks like a jungle," Mike said, "but with some work, I ought to be able to whip it into shape before you know it."

"You're going to get lost inside of this old place alone. Are you planning to fix it up, then turn around and resell it?"

For a moment, his smile faltered, and his excitement

waned. But just for a beat. "I plan to get married and fill it up with kids."

She suspected he'd been thinking about her and knew she would have to disappoint him again.

Yet the thought of him finding a younger woman and creating a family with someone else twisted her heart in an unnatural direction.

Rather than deal with the emotional discomfort of either option, she clung to the silence.

Mike walked to the side of the house, where he turned off the sprinkler. "I'll take Wags with me when I drop you off."

She ought to be happy to have one less dog, but she'd gotten attached to the little scamp. Of course, she didn't dare mention anything like that.

"Would it be okay with you if I picked up Woofer sometimes and brought him over to visit Wags?" Mike asked.

"Sure." The dogs had become much closer these days, and she suspected they'd miss each other.

Shared custody, an inner voice whispered, bringing to mind that unsettling term again. But she quickly shrugged it off.

Mike grabbed some kind of electrical, long-handled tool that had been leaning near the back porch. "Do you mind if we make a stop before I take you home and pick up Wags? I have to return this edger."

She didn't mind. Nor was she in any hurry to get rid of that scruffy puppy with big, brown eyes. She was going to miss the little guy who met her at the door or the gate with a yappy bark and an I-need-you whine.

After locking up the house, they headed for his Jeep.

And moments later, they were on the road. Mike drove along Lexington to the other side of Walnut River and turned onto Cambridge Court.

When he parked in front of a white stucco house with redbrick trim, she asked, "Who lives here?"

"My folks. I borrowed the edger from my dad."

All the way across town? It would have been easier to drop her off at her house first. Of course, he also wanted to pick up Wags. Maybe he didn't want to take Wags to his parents' house.

Yet something told her he might have an ulterior motive for bringing her with him. Had he come up with a phony excuse to force her to meet his parents?

"Come in with me," he said, reaching for the door handle.

Simone stiffened. "Why?"

"Because I'd like to introduce you to my mom and dad."

Had he told them about the baby? About his plans to marry her?

A sense of panic settled over her, and she couldn't seem to move.

"You can wait in the car if you want," he said. "But you don't need to do that. Just come inside and say hello. We can leave whenever you want to."

Her stance didn't soften in the least. "Did you tell them about the baby?"

If he had, she wasn't sure what she'd do.

"No," he said, "I haven't said a word to anyone. Not even to Leif. But that's not because I didn't want to."

He seemed to have backed her into a corner, and while she didn't feel like going through the how-do-you-do and the nice-to-meet-you motions, she un-hooked her seat belt and got out of the Jeep.

As she strode up the walkway, she tugged at the hemline on her blouse, now really hoping it didn't look like a maternity top.

When Mike rang the bell, he didn't wait for anyone to answer. Instead, he swung open the door for Simone and called out, "Hey, it's me. Is anyone home?"

"Mikey!" a woman's voice said. "Come on in. I'm in the kitchen."

As Mike led Simone through the house, she couldn't help looking around the modest but cozy living room, with its display of family photos on the mantel of a brick fireplace.

The warm aroma of sugar and spice filled the air and suggested someone was baking. As Mike led her to a small but functional kitchen, the mouthwatering scent grew stronger.

Sure enough, she'd been right. A salt-and-pepper-haired woman wearing oven mitts was placing a cake onto an open breadboard to cool off. When she straightened, a loose curl flopped onto her forehead.

"Looks like we arrived just in time," Mike said to Simone. "My mom is the best cook in New England, if not the entire country."

Mrs. O'Rourke caught Simone's eye and grinned. "My kids are biased. But I do love to cook. And there's usually something on the stove or in the oven. I never know when one of them will come home. And when they do, they often have several friends with them." She removed the mitts and reached out a hand to Simone. "Hi. I'm Rhonda O'Rourke. And while you're welcome to have some carrot cake, it'll taste better after it cools and I can whip up the sour-cream frosting."

Simone took the older woman's hand in greeting as Mike introduced them.

"It's nice to meet you," Simone said.

"We won't be staying long," Mike added. "I just brought Dad's edger back."

"It's too bad that you can't stay," Rhonda said. "I've got some iced tea and leftover apple cobbler I can feed you. That is, if your father didn't get into it while I was at the market earlier this morning. He's got such a sweet tooth."

"I don't know about Simone," Mike said, "but I could probably be coaxed into staying long enough to have some coffee and cobbler. And speaking of Dad, where is he?"

"Outside." Rhonda brushed at the errant curl with the back of her hand. "He's working on the new gazebo. It's nearly done."

"My dad retired after forty years as a police officer," Mike told Simone. "And ever since he left the department, he's taken an interest in the yard."

"Actually," Rhonda said, "he's always liked working with plants and flowers, but when our children were young, it seemed as though every kid in the neighborhood used to hang out at our house."

Mike cupped his hand around his mouth as though he meant to whisper, yet he kept his voice loud enough for his mom to hear. "Our friends all wanted to play here because of all the cookies and brownies they used to get."

Rhonda laughed, a warm, hearty lilt that a person could get used to hearing. "Okay, so I used to like knowing where my kids were at all times. And I wasn't beyond bribing them and their friends."

"Aha!" Mike said. "And here I thought you spent so much time in the kitchen because you loved to cook and bake."

Rhonda crossed her arms and grinned. "A mom's gotta do what a mom's gotta do."

Even Simone found herself smiling.

"So," Mike added, "with five of us kids living here, the doors and gates were swinging open and closed repeatedly."

"That's true. And poor Sam couldn't seem to do much in the yard except mow. The kids trampled any flowers or shrubs he tried to plant."

"So now that we're finally adults, he's making up for lost time."

"You ought to see the new rose garden." Rhonda pointed to a vase on the kitchen table, where a bouquet of flowers in shades of red, yellow and pink was displayed.

"Come on," Mike said to Simone. "I'll introduce you to my dad."

"Will you excuse me?" Simone asked Rhonda.

"Of course. I'll put on a pot of coffee and dish up the cobbler while you're outside."

Simone followed Mike as he led her to the sliding glass door. Through the window, she could see a lovely backyard.

Mr. O'Rourke, a stocky silver-haired man wearing a pair of khaki shorts, a bright yellow shirt and a green baseball cap, had his back to the house and was stooped over, pulling weeds from around the base of a rosebush bearing red buds.

When Mike pushed open the sliding door and stepped onto the patio, the older man looked up and grinned.

"Hey, Pop." Mike placed a hand on Simone's back as he escorted her across the lawn. "I brought your edger back."

The man's grin stretched into a broad smile. "Looks like you brought more than a lawn tool."

Mike chuckled. "Yep. This is Simone Garner, one of the nurses at Walnut River General." He then went on to introduce her to his father.

"I'd shake hands," Sam O'Rourke said, "but I'm afraid that would get you all dirty."

"Your wife was right," Simone said. "That's a lovely rose garden."

"Thanks. It's coming along nicely, although I'm still learning how to take care of it properly." Sam reached into his hip pocket and pulled out a pair of clippers. Then he cut off a blood-red bud, leaving the stem long. He snipped off the thorns before handing it to her. "Here you go, Simone. If you put this in water, it'll bloom for days. And the fragrance will surprise you."

"Thank you." She took the rose and sniffed the blossom. Sam was right; it smelled wonderful.

"You might want to come inside and wash up," Mike said. "Mom's putting on some coffee and cutting into the cobbler."

"That little woman is a real prize, but I gotta tell you, I've put on twenty-five pounds since my retirement." Sam patted his stomach, which hung over his belt. "But I'm not going to worry about that until Monday, when I start my new diet."

They went inside, where the aroma of coffee mingled with the scent of cinnamon and nutmeg. Sam cleaned up at the kitchen sink, then joined everyone else at the table, where they made small talk while eating the best apple cobbler Simone had ever tasted.

Every once in a while, she caught one or the other of Mike's parents stealing a surreptitious glance her way.

Were they wondering if she and Mike were dating?

Did they know she was pregnant?

Before they'd come inside the house, Mike had insisted that he hadn't told them about the baby. Hopefully, he'd been truthful. It made her feel…uneasy to think Sam and Rhonda might be privy to the news, that they might sit in judgment over her decision to give up their grandchild.

But wouldn't it be worse to be a lousy mother?

Simone passed on the coffee, asking for water instead. And as they ate, Sam mentioned that Mike's sister Kathy had just been hired as a reporter for the *Walnut River Courier,* and that his younger brother Dave, was going to propose to the young woman he'd been dating since high school.

"Sammy has a Little League game on Saturday," Rhonda said. "He's going to play shortstop." She turned to Simone and explained, "Sammy is Aaron's son and our oldest grandchild."

"Are you going to the game?" Mike asked.

Sam beamed. "We wouldn't miss it."

"I'm even going to wear my lucky Baseball-Mama shirt." Rhonda turned to Simone. "I used to practically live down at the ball field when Mike and his brothers were young. And it's great to have a reason to go back and watch the kids play."

"I know it's only T-ball," Sam added, "but that boy is a natural-born athlete. And I'm not just saying that because he's my namesake."

"You ought to stop by on Saturday," Rhonda told Mike. "Sammy's game starts at noon."

"I've got to work," Mike said, "but I'll try to make the next one."

"And bring Simone with you," Sam said, a twinkle in his eye.

Simone didn't comment. She was both touched to have been included yet discomfited at the same time.

Before long, they'd finished their bowls of cobbler.

What was with all the conflicting emotions?

Simone found herself wanting to find an excuse to stay longer, but she wasn't any good at dealing with warm, fuzzy feelings. She always seemed to stiffen at the wrong time or say something that came across as awkward.

She did much better at the hospital, where she could just do the job she'd been trained to do. Where her efforts to provide comfort or understanding actually worked.

Fortunately, Mike stepped in and made it easy for her. "Simone and I have to go. I promised her we'd only stay a few minutes. Besides, I have a lot of work to do on that house."

"I can come over and help you rewire those electrical outlets," Sam said.

"Thanks, Dad." Mike gave his dad a hearty hug, then kissed his mom on the cheek.

It was nice to see the warmth the O'Rourkes showed each other.

Yet it also reminded Simone of all she'd missed growing up.

Chapter Eleven

Mike glanced across the vehicle to the passenger seat, where Simone sat, staring out the window at the passing scenery. "So, what did you think?"

She turned and caught his eye. "About what?"

"My parents."

"They're very nice. And you're lucky to have them."

The O'Rourkes could be her family, too, Mike thought. That is, if she was willing to accept them. But he decided it was best not to push her any more than he already had.

"What do you plan to do when you get back to your new house?" she asked.

Was she intentionally trying to change the subject?

Or did she just think it was time to move on to another topic?

Either way, he was okay with it—for now, anyway.

"Since I can't get the gas and electricity turned on until tomorrow afternoon, I figured it's a good idea to get those outlets changed. I also have a few light fixtures that need to be replaced. So I'm going to start with that."

"I guess that means you won't have lights or a television tonight."

He'd thought about that this morning, before he signed the lease and picked up the keys. But he had to work tomorrow and didn't want to put off moving in. He had a lot to do.

And a baby on the way.

"Most of my spare time will be spent on fix-it projects," he said, "so I won't be reading or watching much TV for a while."

"How long do you expect the project to take?"

Up until the baby was born, he suspected. "I'd like to have it done for the holidays, although I think the place will be an ongoing project."

"I'm glad it all worked out for you."

He probably would have bought that particular house anyway, even if Simone wasn't pregnant. Still, he was glad that things seemed to be coming together. "It's going to need new paint and window coverings, too, but I'd rather get the repair work done first. Of course, that's probably because I'm not that good at decorating. I never have had much of an eye for matching paint or fabric swatches."

"That's the fun part," Simone said.

That's what he'd been counting on. He slid another glance her way. "I don't suppose you'd mind helping me with that—would you?"

"*Me?*"

He didn't dare tell her the real reason he'd asked. That he hoped she'd live in the house with him someday. That he wanted her to leave her mark on their home, every wall, every room.

Instead, he told her, "You've done such a great job decorating your place, I thought you'd have some good suggestions for what I can do with mine."

"Thanks." She tucked a silky strand of hair behind her ear. "What did you want me to do?"

He didn't want it to seem like a big chore, so he shrugged. "Maybe you could come by later today or tomorrow and look around. I'm not all that fussy, but I would like the house to look nice inside. My folks always had off-white walls. But I've noticed some people get creative with colors these days. Not that I have time to look around when I'm called out on an emergency. But when it's a false alarm, I sometimes notice things like that."

"I guess it kind of depends upon what you like and the style of your furniture."

He laughed. "Other than a bedroom set, a state-of-the-art stereo system and a plasma television, I don't have furniture. In fact, I'll be eating out a lot because all the kitchen stuff belongs to Leif, and I had to leave it behind."

"That house is huge," she said. "So it's really going to look empty."

"I can always go to the thrift store and fill it up with things other people didn't want."

"Actually, because of the Victorian style, it might work to buy some antiques." She seemed to think on that for a while.

Before long, he pulled into Simone's driveway and parked. As they climbed from the Jeep, he spotted the dogs standing at the gate on the side of the house.

As Mike followed Simone up the walk, Woofer howled and Wags whined.

"Hey," Simone said to them. "Did you guys miss us?"

Miss *us?* He sure hoped she was starting to see them as a team.

He waited until she unlocked the door.

Once inside, she faced him, "Why don't you let the dogs in while I pack up a few things for Wags to take with him."

Moments later, while Mike stood in the living room, dividing his attention between the big and little dogs, Simone returned carrying a box.

"Thanks to Woofer, who seems to like the Puppy Bits much better than his own food, Wags is running low. He has enough to last him for a week or so, but you'll need to pick up some more the next time you go to the store."

"All right."

"And at night, I've been making him and Woofer stay in the kitchen, since he still tends to have an accident every now and then. But he's getting better." She scratched the puppy's ear. "Aren't you, little guy."

Mike couldn't help but notice that they'd been treating the two canines like children, that they'd both seemed to have taken on a parental role with the dogs.

Shouldn't Simone take that as a sign that she had a maternal streak after all and that she would love their baby?

That she wouldn't be a bad mother just because she'd been raised by one?

"You know, I was just thinking," he said. "Since I'll be working until it gets dark and I don't have anything in the kitchen to cook with, why don't I come back and take you out to dinner?"

"Won't you be tired?" she asked. "It sounds as though you have a lot to do."

He shrugged. "I still have to eat."

"Maybe it would be easier if I fixed dinner for you."

Mike shot her a crooked grin as he realized his game plan was moving along just fine. "I'd like that. Thanks for the invitation."

"What time will you be ready to eat?"

"You tell me."

"How about six?"

"Perfect. I'll see you then."

As Mike carried Wags out to the Jeep, he couldn't help but feel relieved.

Everything was coming together nicely.

After finishing the laundry and cleaning the bathrooms, Simone took a shower and shampooed her hair. She used a fluffy, white towel to dry off. As she bent to get her feet, a bout of dizziness struck.

Ooh. She carefully straightened and reached for the countertop to steady herself.

That didn't happen very often.

She'd gotten dizzy once before, though, and had fainted at the pet shop. Dr. Kipper had said it sometimes happened during pregnancy and had suggested she eat regularly and change positions slowly.

Should she mention it to the doctor again? Just to be sure?

She had more than herself to worry about these days.

Once she'd dressed, styled her hair and put on a dab of lipstick and mascara, she drove to the New England Ranch Market. Surprisingly, she got a spot right in front, which didn't happen often. The popular grocery store was pretty busy in the afternoons.

She snatched her purse from the passenger seat, slipping the strap over her shoulder, then locked the car and went inside.

A display of fresh flowers sat at the doorway, tempting her to buy an unadvertised special—tulips.

Why not?

She grabbed a yellow bouquet, placed them in her shopping cart and headed for the produce section, where she picked up potatoes, carrots, celery and several bags of fresh fruit. Next she went to the butcher shop, where she chose a small rump roast to make for dinner.

Should she make dessert or buy it?

While she was trying to decide, a male voice called out her name. "Simone! Fancy meeting you here."

She turned to see Fred Baxter, his cart filled to the brim. She greeted the man and asked about Millie. "I suppose she's holding down the fort at Tails a Waggin'."

"Actually, she picked up a flu bug and is home sick again today."

"That's too bad." Simone didn't like to see anyone feeling under the weather.

"Yes, it is. Poor thing. I worked part of the day, then closed the shop early." He scratched his head. "Do you know where I can find the chicken soup? Millie said they make a homemade variety in the back that doesn't have all the preservatives and stuff, and she thought that might help her feel better."

Besides its quality meat and produce, the New England Ranch Market also offered an assortment of home-style meals that could be purchased for those on the go.

Simone pointed to the east wall. "You'll find it in the refrigerator section."

"Thanks. The shopping is usually Millie's job, so I'm not familiar with the layout here."

For a guy who didn't know his way around a market, Fred had sure managed to find plenty of things to buy. She glanced into his cart, noting the sugary brand of cereal that kids liked, two gallon jugs of milk, individual packets of raisins, peanut butter, jelly, those little fruit juices that came in a ten-pack, Popsicles…

Somehow, she expected he'd be picking up more adult food, like steaks, potatoes, maybe even a six-pack of beer…

"What's the matter?" Fred asked.

"Oh, I…" She shrugged. "I don't know. I just noticed that you're buying a lot of things that children would like—which is fine. It surprised me a bit. That's all."

Fred chuckled. "Yes, I did my best to choose things that would appeal to kids. We got a call from the pastor of our church last night regarding some children that needed a temporary home."

"And you and Millie are going to take them?" Simone asked.

"It's only for a week, I guess. And even though Millie hasn't been able to keep much of anything down for the past few days, she insisted that they stay with us. Can you believe it?" Fred slowly shook his head. "I told her the timing was bad, and that maybe it would be better if someone else volunteered their home, but Millie…" Fred chuckled and gave a little shrug. "Well, you know Millie. She has a heart for kids."

That was so true. All Simone had to do was to offer her baby to the Baxters, and she knew Millie would be thrilled. But a sense of uneasiness settled over her, leaving her with second thoughts about giving up the baby.

Yet she was a realist.

She had to be.

It wasn't as if Simone didn't care about the baby. It was because she wanted to do the right thing. And it was obvious that Millie would make a much better mother.

"Well," Fred said, nodding toward the east wall. "I'd better go get that soup."

"I sure hope Millie kicks that virus soon," Simone said, "especially if she's going to have to babysit."

"Me, too."

"Be sure to tell her hello for me."

"I will." Fred began to push his cart down the aisle, then tossed her a grin. "Have a nice evening."

"Thanks. You, too." Simone glanced down at the pot roast and the yellow tulips.

Interesting enough, she *did* expect to have a nice evening.

Mike arrived at Simone's house about a minute or two before six o'clock.

He hoped she didn't mind him bringing Wags along, too. The poor little guy started whining up a storm when Mike tried to stick him behind the gate he'd stretched across the kitchen doorway. And he hadn't had the heart to leave him all by himself.

So with Wags cuddled in the crook of one arm, he used his free hand to ring the bell. He didn't have to wait very long for Simone to answer.

She wore a red apron over a pair of brown slacks and a cream-colored blouse. Her hair was down and curled at the shoulders—just the way he liked it.

He couldn't help thinking how great it would be to come home to her and the baby each night. According to his calculations, she was due around Thanksgiving.

As the middle child in a family of five kids, Mike's best memories were of holidays, campouts and outdoor games with his siblings. So he looked forward to seeing his son or daughter joining his or her cousins during the O'Rourke-family functions.

"Well, look who else came to dinner," Simone said.

"I…uh…" He glanced at the wiggly pup. "I hated to leave with him crying. I hope you don't mind that I brought him."

Her smile, which dimpled her cheeks and put a sparkle in her eyes, just about knocked the breath right out of him. "I would have been upset if you'd left him home alone in a dark house."

That was good to know. Wags had wormed his way into Simone's heart, just the way the baby would.

Simone gripped Woofer by his collar and held him at bay as Mike entered and caught the aroma of something warm and meaty—beef?—that permeated the air. He'd gone without lunch today and was starving, so he inhaled deeply and relished the hearty, mouth-watering smell.

Once the door shut behind him, he placed Wags on the floor so the two canine buddies could play.

"How was your day?" Simone asked as she led him to the small dining area that was an extension of the living room.

"It was great. My dad brought my brother Nick, and between the three of us, we changed out the plumbing and light fixtures before I had to be at work. So it was a good start." He watched the back of her as she walked, watched the gentle sway of her hips.

Yep. He could sure see himself coming home to Simone.

"I hope you had a good day, too," he said.

"Actually, I did. I ran some errands, cleaned out the fridge and fixed dinner—speaking of which, I hope you like pot roast."

"I sure do. And if it tastes as good as it smells, you probably won't have any leftovers to worry about."

She blessed him with a shy smile. "I don't usually cook for anyone, so it was…fun." She shrugged, a pair of pretty dimples forming.

Good. That was another indication that she might be warming up to the idea of home and hearth and family.

He noticed that she'd set the table, complete with linen napkins. The centerpiece was a white vase of yellow tulips. "That's a nice touch. The guys down at the department all take turns with the meal preparation, but none of them put flowers out."

She smiled. "I don't usually get fancy, but they were on sale at the market today, and I love tulips."

He made a mental note of that.

"If you'll take a seat," she said, "I'll bring out the food."

"Is there something I can do to help?"

"No, I've got it under control. But what can I bring you to drink?"

"Whatever you're having is fine."

"Milk?"

For the baby? Probably, which was another sign that she was slowly shifting into maternal mode.

Mike didn't drink much milk these days, but he would be supportive of her efforts to be healthy for the baby's sake. "Sure. Milk sounds good to me."

Minutes later, they sat across the table from each other. The pot roast, carrots, potatoes and gravy looked even better than they smelled, and it seemed as though he'd been invited to dine with the queen.

Of course, he suspected they could have been munching on bologna sandwiches and corn chips, and he would have felt the same way.

They talked about life in the E.R., as well as the fire department. Mike told her about some of the practical jokes he and Leif had pulled on their buddies, which she seemed to appreciate. So he went on to reveal a side of his friend and partner she hadn't been aware of.

"Mo Granger has this habit of sleeping with his arm under his pillow at night," Mike said, "so once, after having spaghetti for dinner, Leif, who had kitchen duty, snuck the table scraps into the bedroom, lifted the pillow from Mo's bed, and dumped a pile of noodles and sauce right on the mattress. Then he carefully replaced the pillow."

"Ooh." Simone scrunched her face, yet the hint of a smile remained. "That's gross."

"Yep. And you should have seen what happened when Mo climbed into bed that night and tried to get comfortable. His hand slipped under his pillow and right into a slimy mess. Mo was hopping mad, while the rest of us laughed our heads off."

"I can't imagine Leif doing something like that."

Mike laughed. "Apparently, he learned that trick on a Boy Scout campout, and now it's become sort of an initiation we do with each new rookie. We welcome them with a spaghetti dinner, making sure there's more than enough for everyone, then Leif hides the leftovers in their beds."

"That's terrible." A grin suggested she found it funny, too. "Those poor rookies."

"Hey, but what goes around comes around. Once, when some of us were off duty, we met at the Brown Jug, that bar located just off Lexington and Riverdale. After a while, Leif excused himself to go to the restroom. And when he came back, he'd forgotten to zip his fly."

Simone arched a brow, while a smile tugged at her lips.

"Wally Wainwright, one of the rookies who'd had the pleasure of Leif's leftover-pasta humor, spotted it first and offered him twenty bucks to stand on the table and tell a joke while facing a table of very attractive and obviously single ladies."

"Uh-oh." Simone leaned forward and placed her elbows on the table. "Then what happened?"

"Leif had a little liquid courage in his system, especially since I was the designated driver that night, so he took the bet and climbed on the table. Trouble was, he was flashing a pair of tightie-whities and didn't realize it.

"One of the ladies noticed, and they started nudging each other. The next thing you know, they all busted up laughing."

"That must have been a sight."

"'*Hey,*' Leif said to the women. 'Why are you laughing? I didn't even get to the punch line yet.'" Mike couldn't help chuckling himself.

"I had no idea Leif was a practical jokester," Simone said.

"Well, he is. But this time the joke was on him."

"I guess it was." Simone had fallen into an easy mood. It was great to hear her laugh. And sitting across from her, with the candlelight dancing upon the gold highlights in her hair and her eyes sparkling with humor, was a real treat.

He wished that she could see herself like this—the Simone he'd fallen in love with.

"By the way," Mike added, "Leif loves to sing, although he's not as talented as he'd like to think he is. So if you're into karaoke, we'll have to invite him to go with us."

"I'm afraid I'm not at all comfortable standing before a crowd, let alone entertaining one. But it would be fun to go out with Leif sometime."

"I'll see what I can arrange." A double date might be nice.

After dinner and a bowl of rocky road for dessert, Simone stood and began to clear the table.

Mike followed suit.

"You don't have to help," she said. "I can clean up after you leave."

"I can't let you do that. My mom would skin me alive if I left you with the mess. Besides, it's quick work when two people share the load."

And it was. Before long, they had the leftovers packed away and the dining room back in order.

Mike had just filled the dishwasher when Simone turned away from wiping down the stove, the dishcloth in her hand. She'd no more than started to walk back to the sink when Woofer came charging into the room with Wags at his heels.

The big dog's hind end, which had a tendency to sway to one side while his front end was going another, thumped into Simone and knocked her off balance.

Mike had always been quick on his feet, but the thought of her taking a tumble in her condition sent a jolt of adrenaline to jump-start his natural reaction.

"Are you all right?" he asked as he caught her in his arms.

"Yes, but darn that crazy dog…" She looked up at him, and their gazes met. Locked.

Something passed between them, something blood-stirring and heart-pounding. Something that set off the pheromones and hormones that always seemed to be buzzing and sparking between them like a swarm of fireflies.

Mike was doing his best to shrug it off, to keep his mind off what he'd been wanting to do again since the last time he'd kissed her.

But when Simone reached up and stroked his cheek, when her lips parted…

Well, damn. He was only human.

Chapter Twelve

As Mike took her in his arms and lowered his mouth to hers, Simone had only a moment to question whether she wanted to kiss him again.

But something had happened to her tonight. Something that hadn't been triggered or altered by a champagne buzz. And she wondered if maybe Mike could be right about her.

About *them*.

She certainly couldn't deny how badly she wanted to kiss him, how badly her body yearned for what only Mike could give her.

As his lips brushed across hers, as she allowed his tongue to sweep inside her mouth, she lost all conscious thought.

The only thing left for her to do was to hold on tight

and ride the wave of passion that swept through her, hoping that somehow she could get her fill of him.

As the kiss deepened, raw need took over. Hands explored, stroked, caressed, while breaths mingled and heat exploded in a sexual rush.

Simone hadn't wanted to get physically involved with Mike again, but she'd grown to care for him—more than she'd wanted to admit. And at this very moment, she knew she'd be a fool not to admit it or do something about it.

So she broke the kiss long enough to rest her cheek against his, to catch her breath and whisper, "There's no arguing that we have chemistry."

"That's for sure." His embrace loosened, yet he didn't let go.

She clung to him, too, savoring the musky male scent of his mountain-fresh aftershave for a moment longer. Then she slowly pulled away and raked a hand through the strands of her hair. "I still have reservations about us getting further involved, but I want you. And I want to make love again."

"I'm glad." Desire smoldered in his eyes as he moved slowly, deliberately, closing the gap between them.

He cupped her cheeks with his hands, and his thumbs caressed her skin, as the intensity of his gaze weakened her knees.

"You won't be sorry about this, Simone." The sincerity in his passion-laced tone reached deep into her heart, and she hoped he was right.

She might have reservations about making love with a man who wanted so much more than she was able to give him, but no one had ever made her feel so special, so desired. So…flawless.

What little apprehension she'd had left seemed to vanish within the sexually charged room, and she slipped her arms around his neck and pulled him back into another heated kiss.

Their tongues dipped and tasted, and she was lost in a mind-spinning swirl of heat and desire.

His hands slid possessively up and down her back, then he gripped her derriere and pulled her flush against his erection, staking his claim and letting her know that he wanted her as badly as she wanted him.

As his hands slipped under her blouse, his fingertips skimmed her skin, and her breath caught. She'd never been so fully aroused, and she had a sudden compulsion to shed her clothing, to remove all the physical barriers that kept her from enjoying him freely.

She tore her mouth away from his long enough to reach for the hem of her blouse and to say, "Wait a minute. Let me get this…"

He took the lead, helping her to slide the fabric over her head and to unhook her white, satiny bra. Before she knew it, she was tugging his shirt out of his pants and grappling for his belt at the same time.

Apparently, he was glad to assist, because he'd soon bared his torso, too.

Simone wanted Mike, wanted *this*. And nothing else seemed to matter. As she fell into his embrace, she relished the feel of her breasts as they pressed against his chest, the beat of her heart as it pounded against his.

But it wasn't nearly enough.

As he nuzzled the soft spot below her ear and trailed kisses along her neck, he whispered between ragged breaths, "I want to touch and kiss you all over."

He wouldn't get an argument from her. "Okay, but I don't think my knees are going to hold me up much longer."

"No problem." He scooped her into his arms, then carried her to the bed, where he gently laid her down and proceeded to peel her slacks over her hips. Next he took off her panties, leaving her completely naked.

"Now, you," she said, feeling like a seductress with her hair splayed upon the pillow sham. "I'm not the only one who's going to get kissed all over."

All over, huh?

Mike grinned. "Honey, I'm going to hold you to it." He peeled off his own pants and dropped them on the floor, then he joined her on the bed, where he loved her with his hands, with his mouth—slowly and methodically, as he savored each sensual touch, each breathy kiss, each flick of the tongue.

And he didn't let up the sensual assault until he'd made her writhe with need.

"I want you inside of me," she said, her voice ragged with desire. "All of you."

"You can have every last inch." Of course, he'd already given her more than that. She had him—heart and soul—but he didn't dare admit it. Nor did he mention that he'd been dreaming of doing this again since the end of February, when they'd made love the first time.

As he hovered over her, he inhaled the powdery, peach fragrance of her body lotion, as well as the musky scent of sex. And when she opened for him, he entered full hilt.

She arched to meet each thrust, in and out, until they peaked, until they pressed over the top and cried out in a mind-shattering, body-shuddering climax.

They continued to hold each other, as though neither wanted to be the first to move, the first to break the tenuous connection that stretched between them.

As the last wave of pleasure passed, Mike rolled to the side, taking her with him.

He expected her to pull away, to shut down like she had the last time. But she held on tight, her nails threatening to make crescent-shaped marks on his back.

It had been a sweet joining, one that he hoped meant she'd finally accepted his love and all he had to offer her and their baby.

It's what he'd been counting on—that she would finally be able to let go of the past and embrace the future.

A future with him.

As dawn cast its light in the bedroom, Simone lay cuddled in Mike's arms, her back to his front, her bare bottom nestled in the fold of his lap.

They'd made love several times last night, with each climax better than the last. So they'd found themselves in a sensual world of their own, oblivious to anything but each other.

The phone had rung around nine o'clock, but Simone had let the answering machine pick up. Nothing seemed to matter except pleasuring each other.

They hadn't even bothered to gate the kitchen, which meant the dogs had remained loose in the house last night, so she'd probably find a puddle or two on the floor.

Around midnight, since Mike had to go into the station in the morning, he got out of bed long enough to set the alarm.

Otherwise, they'd savored every moment together.

The very first time they'd made love, that night in February, Simone had awakened with a growing sense of regret.

She felt better about it today, though, and didn't have that same compulsion to retreat. Still, she was on edge.

Would she gradually get used to waking in Mike's arms? To having him in her life?

He seemed to think she would.

Woofer, who'd just trotted into the bedroom, placed his nose on the mattress and whimpered, letting her know he wanted to go into the backyard. So she carefully lifted Mike's arm and slid out of his embrace. Then she climbed from bed and pulled her bathrobe from the closet.

As her bare feet padded across the hardwood floor, the dogs eagerly followed her through the kitchen and to the service porch, where she opened the back door and let them outside.

Wags hardly made it to the lawn before squatting to relieve himself.

Hey. Maybe she wouldn't find any puddles on the floor after all.

"Good job, Wags! That's the idea." She pulled the lapel of her robe closer, shielding her naked body from the brisk morning air and wishing she'd taken time to put on her slippers.

She decided to leave the dogs outdoors to play for a while, then went inside and put on a small pot of coffee for Mike. In the meantime, the alarm sounded in the bedroom, then shut off. A moment later, the plumbing shuddered as the shower went on.

Mike would be leaving soon, so they'd have to discuss the future later, which was okay with her. She wasn't sure what she wanted out of a relationship with him anyway.

Whenever she thought about marriage, she still grew uneasy. And unfortunately, the white-picket-fence dream was still Mike's highest priority and Simone's biggest fear.

And why shouldn't it be?

No matter what Mike said, what he might think, Simone knew she would fall sadly short of the wife-and-mother image he had in mind. She'd never be like Rhonda O'Rourke, and Mike would end up disappointed down the road. And that wasn't fair to him.

Bottom line? Simone was a career woman, a medical professional who loved doing what she'd been trained to do.

Would Mike expect her to be a stay-at-home mother?

She certainly hoped not. That would be a huge conflict in and of itself. How could she give up the one thing that defined her?

She couldn't.

Would that make her a bad mother? Would Mike grow to resent her because of it? And worse—would the baby?

As the last bit of water trickled through the filter and filled the bottom half of the carafe with fresh coffee, she glanced at the answering machine that rested on the counter. A red light blinked to remind her of the call she hadn't wanted to take last night. So she pushed play, then listened for the message.

"Hi, Simone. It's Cynthia Pryor again. You know, your mom's friend and neighbor? I really hate to bother you, but I was wondering if—since you're a nurse—you could give me the name of a good counselor. I think your mother really needs to talk to someone, and…well, I'm out of my league when it comes to…some of her issues."

Had Simone's mom finally leveled with someone about the date rape?

If Simone hadn't found those journals, she might never have known why her mother couldn't stand looking at her.

"I hate to pry," Cynthia began, "but when I told Susan to call you, she admitted that your relationship wasn't very good, and that it was probably her fault."

Probably?

"Gosh," Cynthia said. "Here I am, rambling on your tape. You probably think I'm a mindless old busybody…"

Actually, the thought had crossed Simone's mind, although Simone suspected she meant well.

"But it breaks my heart to see the sadness in your mother's eyes, especially when I think there's relief out there—either with medication or by talking it out. So, anyway, would you please give me—or better yet, give *her* a call? Your mother really needs someone in her corner right now."

Cynthia went on to leave her number before hanging up.

Susan Garner *did* need help, and Simone couldn't help wondering where someone like Cynthia had been years ago. Back when Simone had needed someone in her corner. Back when Simone *also* needed a mommy.

So why should she get involved *now?*

The last time Cynthia had encouraged Simone to pick up the phone and offer some daughterly advice, it had taken her mother more than a week to return the call.

No, if her mom had wanted Simone to get involved, Cynthia wouldn't have had to interfere. Her mother would have picked up the phone and called herself.

Really? a small voice asked. *Considering how lousy your relationship has been?*

"That's *not* my fault," Simone muttered.

She opened the fridge, removed a carton of orange juice and poured herself a glass. Then she divided an English muffin and placed both sides in the toaster. She'd intended to fix Mike a hearty breakfast this morning, but the message from Cynthia seemed to have depleted her domestic energy.

"Good morning." Mike entered the kitchen wearing a towel wrapped around his waist and a carefree grin. His hair was wet and mussed, his body still damp from the shower.

She returned his smile, hoping it hadn't fallen short of sincere.

He bent to kiss her, and she offered her cheek.

Darn it. It was happening again. He was coming on strong, and she was pulling back.

She wished she could make an excuse for doing so. Or maybe find a way to regroup. But thoughts of her mother and old childhood pain had set her on autopilot.

Mike didn't seem to have let the proffered cheek bother him. "I'd like to take you to dinner as soon as we're both free. How does your schedule look?"

"I'm off tonight and work tomorrow." Actually, she was glad they would both be tied up for a few days. She was starting to gravitate toward him, yet old habits were hard to kick.

He closed the gap between them, and she forced her feet to stay still, her smile to remain in place.

See? She didn't have to retreat. She could make a conscious effort to remain emotionally connected.

He placed a hand along the side of her head, caressed the strands of her hair. Then he snagged her gaze with his. "Last night was wonderful for me. And it was great for you, too. You can't deny that."

"You're right."

"Why do I sense that you're having second thoughts?"

She couldn't see any point mentioning that her mother was still casting a dark shadow over her life. That there was still a little girl inside of Simone who hoped her mommy would get help, that she'd learn how to love the child she'd given birth to. "I guess it's just because I've gotten so used to living alone that I'm not sure what we're supposed to do now."

"Well, that's an easy decision this morning. I'm going to have a cup of coffee, get dressed and leave you to spend your day and evening any way you want." He placed a finger under her chin. "Then I'm going to work, where I'll probably think about you too damn much."

"The whole commitment thing scares me, Mike."

"I know it does, honey."

God, what did she do to deserve a guy like him loving her? He was so understanding. And she was so…

She blew out a ragged sigh. "I just need some time to get used to…this."

"Get used to what? *Me? Us?*"

She nodded. "I was raised differently than you. I'm not used to the home-and-hearth stuff. Heck, I don't even read romances or watch chick flicks. It's hard for me to relate to the characters."

"Fred and Millie are happily married. Are you uncomfortable around them?"

"No. Not at all."

"What about my folks? You seemed to enjoy yourself at their house."

"I did." Still, as nice as the O'Rourkes were, as accepting as they'd been, Simone had only been further convinced of the differences she and Mike had.

Rhonda O'Rourke might be the epitome of a loving mom and grandma, but being around her only made Simone realize how much she'd missed growing up.

"Then don't fight it, Simone. Just give it a chance, honey. You'll get used to me, to us. You'll see."

The English muffin popped up in the toaster, and she turned to get it, retreating from the intensity of his gaze, from the emotion of the topic.

"Maybe you ought to start reading more romances and watching more movies. It might help."

But before she could take a plate out of the cupboard to put the muffin halves on, she thought of something. Something she'd been wondering about.

She turned to face him again. "Why did you take me to your parents' house yesterday?"

"Because I wanted you to meet my mom and dad, to see what kind of grandparents they'll be."

"I have no doubt that they'll be wonderful," she admitted. "It's just that I still can't see myself making you happy in the long run."

"Let me be the judge of that."

"Making a marriage work is tough enough when people come from the same background," she said.

"Marriages are two parts love, one part compromise. That's something my parents always told me."

She supposed that was true. "It's hard to imagine them having to compromise about anything."

"Over the years, there were plenty of times. For one thing, my dad was raised Catholic, and my mom was Protestant. But they didn't let that stop them. They loved each other and were determined to make their marriage work."

Still, she couldn't help thinking that there'd be way too much compromising going on if Mike had his way. And she couldn't help thinking she'd be doing them all a favor by avoiding what would only be a star-crossed affair.

But truthfully, there was a part of her that really wanted to adopt Mike's optimism, his unshakable belief that everything would work out. That she would instantly fall in love with the baby the moment she laid eyes on it. That Susan Garner hadn't left any permanent scars on Simone's psyche, other than to make her grow up afraid to love, afraid to get involved with the nicest guy in the world.

A man any other woman would be thrilled to call her own.

A man who'd helped her touch the moon and stars last night.

"I guess I just need time to get used to this, Mike."

"No problem. You've got it." Then he brushed a kiss upon her cheek. "I'm going to get dressed, then get out of your hair for a few days."

That ought to be a big relief.

So why wasn't it?

* * *

Mike should have been walking on air after spending last night in Simone's bed and in her arms. In fact, up until six this morning, he'd thought he *had* been.

But Simone had done it to him again. She'd ditched the warm, loving woman she'd been at bedtime and morphed into someone he couldn't seem to get through to. A woman so reserved that she might shatter in his arms.

At the station, his shift had barely started when the crew was called out to rescue a child in a tree. It had been one of those so-called emergencies that was actually humorous.

Tommy the cat, a big orange tabby, had gotten stuck in a tree. And when little Jimmy Ralston took it upon himself to rescue the frightened feline, Tommy had scampered down, leaving the ten-year-old boy about twenty feet aboveground and afraid to move.

Twenty minutes later, they'd put the boy on the ground and placed him in the custody of his mother. They'd just started back to the station when another call came in. This time, it was a kitchen fire started by a woman who hadn't had a match to light her fireplace. Instead, she'd used a twisted-up paper towel that she lit at the stove. She'd started to carry it like a small torch into the living room, but the paper burned much faster than she'd intended.

The panicked woman rushed to the sink, only to watch the flame catch the curtains on fire.

Fortunately, no one had been hurt.

Now, as noon approached, Mike found himself sitting all by himself on the side of his bed, his mind on Simone and their problems. She was pushing him to the limit of his patience. He'd told her he would give her all the time she needed, but now he wasn't so sure he could do that.

Not if she refused to meet him at least part of the way.

"O'Rourke," Leif said as he approached. "What's wrong?"

"Nothing." What was he supposed to say? That he was bummed out because Simone was pulling away again?

Leif had already suggested he cut bait and run, so he knew what advice his buddy would give him this time.

Of course, things weren't quite as bad as they'd been at the end of February. And maybe she would realize that she'd still have plenty of space and alone time.

"What's eating you?" Leif asked.

Nothing Mike felt like sharing. "I'm just sorting through a few things. No big deal."

"Is Simone giving you fits again?"

Mike wanted to say yes, to lay his heart on the line. But somehow, it didn't feel right going into detail about the woman he loved, about their relationship—what there was of one, anyway.

"No. It's not that," he lied. "Don't worry about me. I'll be okay."

And he would be—one way or another.

Leif chuffed, then took a seat across the table. "I think you just need to get laid. That ought to put things into perspective for you."

Oh, yeah? He *had* gotten laid. And it seemed to have made things worse.

"Come on," Mike said, getting to his feet and trying his best to pull himself out of a bum mood. "Let's go watch ESPN. There's a game on."

Still, it was going to be tough keeping his mind on anything other than Simone.

Especially when she was frustrating the hell out of him, and he wasn't sure how much longer he could deal with her refusal to give their love—or their family—a chance.

What if she never would?

Chapter Thirteen

On Sunday afternoon, before starting her shift, Simone stopped by the solarium, where Henry Weisfield's party was being held. She really didn't feel like celebrating—or mixing—but she managed to put on a happy face, determined to make a showing and to wish the retiring hospital administrator her best.

Upon entering the festively decorated room, Simone surveyed her surroundings, as well as those who'd stopped to congratulate Henry.

She spotted Ella and J.D. mingling in the crowd, so she made her way to the happy couple to say hello and to congratulate J.D. on his new position, which he would assume Monday morning. By the time J.D. entered the hospital for his first day on the job, Henry and his wife would be flying over the Atlantic on their way to Europe, where they would set sail on a Mediterranean cruise they'd been planning for months.

After Simone chatted with J.D. and Ella for a few minutes, she excused herself to speak to Henry. Even though he'd recently been sympathetic toward an NHC takeover, she still appreciated his years of service.

"Enjoy your retirement," she told the older man. "And have a wonderful time on that cruise."

"Thank you, Simone. My wife and I are eager to do a lot of traveling." Henry shook her hand and grinned, then turned to the next person who'd approached to greet him and wish him well.

With the formalities out of the way, Simone stopped by the refreshment table and, using the ladle provided, filled a large glass of punch.

"I hope you're going to save some for me."

She turned to see Isobel standing behind her and smiled. "That shouldn't be a problem. Everyone else seems to be having wine or champagne."

While in front of the bowl, she prepared a glass for the hospital social worker.

Isobel didn't usually work on Sundays, so Simone was glad to see that she'd come. It would give her an opportunity to get the referral for a counselor.

"You're wearing scrubs," Isobel said, "so you're obviously working today."

"My shift starts in a few minutes, so I can't stay long, but I wanted to give Henry my best." Simone scanned the room, making sure she could speak in confidence, then lowered her voice. "I must admit, though, it's probably in the hospital's best interests that he's retiring."

Henry's empathy toward an NHC takeover had contributed to some of the dissension on the board.

"J.D. ought to be a good replacement," Isobel said, glancing around the room, as well, apparently satisfied that their conversation would be private. "By the way, I have a growing suspicion about the person who is leaking information about the hospital to NHC."

"What's that?"

"I think the mole is in one of the administrative departments."

That was unsettling, but certainly possible. "Do you think Henry is—or rather *was*—the mole?"

"I didn't mean to imply *that*. But it's obvious someone in that department has been talking out of turn."

They each took a sip of punch and watched the people who'd gathered in the solarium—those in street clothes who weren't working and those in lab jackets and scrubs who were.

"You know," Simone said, "I want to ask you something. My mom needs to see a counselor. She never sought any professional help after that date rape I told you about. Is there anyone you can recommend? She'd also do well in some kind of support group."

"If you'll walk with me to my office, I'll give you some names and contact numbers."

Simone agreed, and they left the solarium together.

"I've pretty much given up hope that I'll ever have a close relationship with my mother," Simone said, "but either way, she still needs to come to grips with what happened to her."

"Talking it out helps a lot of people."

Simone walked along in silence for a while, then

said, "Sometimes I think I might need to talk to someone, too."

"You'd be surprised at what an hour or two with a trained counselor can do."

"I'll give it some thought." Simone blew out a sigh. "You know, I've always had intimacy problems, so I tend to keep to myself. I was doing just fine until Mike came into the picture."

"That's understandable."

Was it? She hoped so. And she couldn't help adding, "I'm having trouble trusting him to love the real me."

"Sometimes, trust is a decision that's made."

"Like blind faith?"

"No. Not like that. Trust is earned, but there are times when you must cognitively decide to trust someone."

"And what if that person lets you down? Or, in this case, what if I disappoint Mike?"

"That's the risk we take in any relationship."

Simone offered her friend a wistful smile. "I'm not much of an emotional risk-taker."

"Then I suppose you have to ask yourself if you love each other enough to handle life's normal disappointments."

"That's the problem. I don't know what I feel for him. I think it's love. And if so, I'm not sure what my love—or *his*—can handle."

Isobel placed a hand on Simone's shoulder. "You can't change the past, but you can change your perception of it."

Maybe so. But as usual, she just couldn't seem to forget about the kind of mother she'd had. The kind of mother she was so afraid she would become.

"Families are created by love," Isobel said, "not necessarily by blood."

"I know. You're right." That's why Simone had hoped Millie and Fred could create that kind of special, loving family for her baby.

"I'd be happy to talk to you—as a friend," Isobel said. "Or I can refer you to a counselor, if you think that might be more helpful. A couple of sessions might be all it will take."

"You mean you don't see me needing extensive therapy?"

"In your case, I suspect the answer is already in your mind and in your heart. You probably just need someone to ask the right questions so you can sort through things and come up with your own conclusion, your own game plan."

Isobel opened her office door, then flipped through her Rolodex and jotted down a few names and numbers. "Give these to your mother. And if you decide you'd like a reference for yourself, let me know."

"All right. Thanks."

After Isobel locked up her office, the two women walked down the hall together. At the elevator, they went their separate ways—Isobel back to the party and Simone to work.

On the way to the E.R., she slipped her hand into her pocket, where she'd tucked the referrals, then made a detour to the hospital gardens, where she found some solitude.

She took a seat on one of the benches and pulled out her cell phone. She'd planned to call information to get Cynthia's number, but her movements froze.

Instead, she listened to her heart and dialed her mother's house. They'd been tiptoeing around an emotional quagmire for years, and Simone simply wasn't going to do it anymore.

When Susan Garner answered, Simone decided to be honest for the first time in her life. "Mom, it's me. I think you should get some counseling, and I have the names and contact info for some qualified therapists you might find helpful."

"I…well…actually, I've been thinking about it lately."

Good. They were on the right track, and she felt her heart swell with something she couldn't quite identify. Relief? Optimism?

"I'm glad to hear it." So she recited the names Isobel had given her, waiting as her mother made a note of them.

"Thanks," her mom said. "I may give someone a call. We'll see."

Simone decided to go one step further, again making the cognitive decision to trust herself and her instincts. "I never mentioned this to you before, but I know the circumstances surrounding my conception, Mom. And, well, I don't believe you've ever worked through your pain, which has crippled you in many ways. But I want you to know that I love you. And I'll be there for you…if you want me to."

For a long, drawn-out minute, the only response was silence.

Then came a gulp. "Oh, Simone…"

And the call ended in tears.

By the time Tuesday rolled around, Simone found herself restless and uneasy.

She also had a growing compulsion to talk to Mike. In fact, she couldn't get him out of her mind. He'd been on duty Saturday, and she'd had to work on Sunday, so she understood why they hadn't had any contact. In the past, she would have been happy to have the space, but for some reason she wasn't.

Then, late Monday morning, he'd called to say hello, but went on to tell her he had a full day scheduled at his new place.

That, too, was a reasonable excuse.

Still, she sensed a growing distance between them, which was unsettling.

She couldn't help wishing something would bring him to the E.R. Not that she wanted to wish bad health or injury on anyone. In the past, he'd managed to stop by a time or two, even without a patient. So it seemed like a reasonable wish on her part.

Throughout the day, she'd had a growing compulsion to pick up the phone and call his cell, yet she hadn't.

What would she have said? "I just wanted to hear your voice?"

It was true, though; she was definitely missing him.

But if she told him so, she wasn't sure if she was ready for what the truth might provoke.

So now Simone was in the midst of a day shift she was covering for Carol Harrington, an RN who'd sprained her ankle while playing with her granddaughter at the park.

As footsteps sounded and someone approached the nurses' desk, Simone glanced up from her work and saw Owen Randall, the new chief of staff.

Dr. Randall wore a pair of black slacks, a white shirt

and a lime-green-and-pink tie that would have been too bold for most men, but Owen was able to pull it off. "I thought I'd spread the word. Neil Kane, the insurance investigator from the state attorney general's office, arrived today and has begun a preliminary investigation of those allegations of insurance fraud."

Simone's stomach lurched. She knew the claims of fraud at Walnut River General made the possibility of a takeover more likely, so now that the investigation had begun, it all seemed real.

And threatening.

"Obviously, I'm not the least bit happy about Kane being here," Owen said, "but there's nothing I can do about it. Hopefully, he'll come to a quick conclusion about the integrity of the hospital, especially in regard to insurance billings."

"Have you met him yet?"

"Yes. Earlier this morning. I'm sure he'll eventually get around to interviewing you, so I wanted to give you a heads-up."

Great.

As Dr. Randall turned to go, Jennifer Dimon, one of the LVNs, approached the desk and called her name.

"Yes?" Simone answered.

"We've got a three-year-old little girl in bed five, and both parents are with her. She has an arm injury, and while I was getting her vitals, she claimed that 'Mommy did it.'"

Simone stiffened. She'd seen her share of child-abuse cases, and they never got easier. "I'd better talk to them."

Jennifer nodded. "Should I call Isobel?"

"Yes, we need to follow protocol." Simone stood. "I'll go back into the exam area with you."

Once behind the curtain, Simone introduced herself to the parents.

"It was an accident," the mother said, tears welling in her eyes. "I was trying to hold her hand, and she threw a fit. I didn't mean to jerk up as she was pulling away, and…"

The father slipped his arm around his wife's shoulder. "Lisa is a strong-willed little girl. And sometimes, she does that when walking with me. She'll just decide she doesn't want to go and lift up her legs."

"Those things happen," Simone said, still not sure if the mother had been abusive or whether it had been a routine accident.

They'd seen similar injuries before, when a child's shoulder or elbow was dislocated. But there were other situations in which the arm was twisted or jerked in an unnatural direction——the result of parental anger and abuse.

The pediatrician would have to make that call.

Still, her heart went out to the little girl, and she hoped this was merely the accident the parents claimed it was.

Simone couldn't help thinking back on the times when she'd been spanked or slapped for no apparent reason, times she'd cried herself to sleep, thinking she was a bad girl and trying to figure out what she'd done wrong.

Looking back now, though, she realized that her mother sometimes drank in the evenings, most likely as a way to cope with her own terrible demons. And that she probably hadn't been sober on those occasions that she'd lashed out at Simone.

But that hadn't made her actions less abusive.

Nor did it chase away the fear about her own mother- ing skills. Could her maternal instinct have been hampered or tainted by lack of bonding with her own mother?

One thing was certain, though. Simone would *never* strike a child—hers or anyone else's. So she wasn't the least bit afraid of that happening.

But would she have intimacy issues with her own son or daughter?

At this point, she hadn't heard a heartbeat or felt any movement. So it was hard to imagine a living, breath- ing child growing inside of her.

But there *was* a baby, a child who needed a loving mother.

Thirty minutes later, Dr. Wiley, the pediatrician on call, determined that the little girl's injury—nursemaid's elbow, he'd determined—was consistent with a normal parent/child incident and not a sign of abuse. And so there'd been nothing to report, which had filled Simone with a sense of relief. She was glad of the positive outcome for the family.

Isobel, who'd come to the E.R., was on her way back to her office, when she stopped to talk to Simone. "Did you have a chance to give those telephone numbers to your mother?"

"Yes. And she even admitted that she thought she needed some counseling, but when I told her that I knew about the date rape, she grew silent for a while. Then she started to cry, telling me she had to hang up. I have no idea what she'll do."

"Give her some time," Isobel said.

That's about all Simone could give her at this point. She'd taken the first step toward communicating with her mom on a different level, and now it was up to her mother to respond.

Was that what Mike was giving Simone? Some space and time to sort things out and decide what she needed to do?

Or was he making his own decision and trying to end their already rocky relationship?

That possibility sent a wave of nausea rolling through her tummy, and while the urge to call him grew stronger than ever, it was stilled by fear that it was too late.

Maybe she'd lost Mike already.

Mike arrived at the hospital at a little after four that afternoon, hoping Simone could take a break.

Over the past couple of days, he'd expected her to reach out to him. To miss him. To call.

But she hadn't.

He'd wanted to give her the time she needed and was willing to wait. But not if she didn't love him and didn't expect to ever have a future with him. If that was the case, he was spitting into the wind.

So the way he saw it, he'd been as patient as he could be. Now they needed to talk.

He entered the double doors that led to the waiting room, then stopped by the registration desk, while the woman in front of him signed in.

"I need to talk to Simone," he said when it was finally his turn. "Can you please tell her I'm here?"

The clerk, Carla Hawkins, nodded, then got up from her seat.

Mike stood to the side, arms crossed, and waited.

Several minutes later, Simone came to the window and motioned him to the security door, which she opened to let him inside.

"I need to talk to you," he said. "Can you take a break?"

Simone glanced at Jennifer, the LVN who was seated at the desk. "Can you cover for me a little while? I'll be in the garden. I have my pager, so let me know if you need me."

Jennifer nodded.

They walked side by side in silence to the door that led out to the hospital gardens, separated by more than the space between them.

Once outside, Mike crossed his arms and snared her gaze with his. "How do you feel about me?"

Her lips parted. "I…care about you. A lot."

"Do you love me?"

She seemed to ponder the question for a while, then slowly nodded. "I think so."

Damn. He'd told himself everything would be okay if she cared about him, if she thought she could grow to love him. But now he wasn't sure if what she might—or might not—be feeling would be enough.

"I want to create a family for our baby," he said. "And if marriage scares you, then I'm willing to try living together for a while. We can take things slow and easy, if you think that will help."

He studied her, watching for a sign that she was going to give in, that he'd somehow touched her heart. That he'd made her see that they were meant to be together. That they'd find a way to make things work.

Yet he feared that if she pulled back again…

Well, he wasn't sure what he'd do. There was always

plan B to fall back on, and as far as he was concerned, the ball was in her court.

Simone had her back to the open garden, yet she felt as though Mike had backed her into a corner. He was asking for a decision, a commitment.

And, apparently, he wanted it now.

"What exactly are you suggesting?" she asked. "That I give up my house and move into yours? That you let your new place fall out of escrow and move into mine?"

"I don't care either way. I'm willing to compromise. Are you?"

Was she? Quite frankly, she didn't know. She felt as though she were walking along a balance beam that stretched over a treacherous canyon.

The past was still etched too clearly in Simone's mind. Would she ever be able to forget her own childhood? Quiet all the doubts that tortured her? Put it all behind her and walk across that narrow beam that Mike swore led to a bright and happy future?

"I need an answer," he said.

She stiffened. Didn't he get it? Didn't he understand that she was in love with him? That she wanted to make that first step, but when he pressured her, she fell back into old habits and patterns?

"Don't push me," she said, unable to stop the words. "If it was just you and me, I'd consider it. But there's the baby to think about."

"What about the baby?"

"I'm afraid of failing it."

There it was. The horrible truth. The fear that loomed

over them both and prevented her from moving one way or the other on that precarious beam.

"Not *it*," he said, his tone a blend of anger and frustration. "You're pregnant with a little girl or boy just waiting to grow big enough to come out into the world."

"I realize that," she said, her voice growing softer, hesitant, and laden with what really concerned her. "But maybe he or she would be better off with another mother."

Mike bristled. "Are you still thinking about adoption?"

No, not as strongly as before. She now realized that while she feared she'd fail the baby somehow, she didn't want to give it up, either. Not to Millie, not to anyone.

"Damn it," Mike said, showing her a sign of righteous anger, of fierce determination he'd never fully revealed before. "You can get *that* thought out of your head right now."

What thought?

"My first plan was to marry you and create a home and family," he said. "But there are other options, and adoption isn't the only one. I'm not going to sign my son or daughter over to anyone. If you don't want it, I'll take the baby myself."

His words, his determination...his fierce loyalty, unbalanced her.

All along, she'd known Mike would be a fabulous father, but she hadn't thought he'd want to take the baby on his own. Or that he would be so determined, so adamant about it. And, if anything, she knew without a doubt that she would never give up her baby.

Not even to Mike.

"No, you—" Before she could finish telling him that he didn't understand, before she could explain that she wanted their child, too, a roaring buzz sounded in her ears, whizzing louder and louder.

And before she could utter a peep, the garden around them began to spin until her legs gave out and everything went dark.

Chapter Fourteen

Mike grabbed Simone just before she hit the ground, and he felt a rise of panic.

His training told him she'd had another fainting spell that was probably pregnancy related. But it wasn't easy being rational and detached from a patient when she was the woman he loved, a woman carrying the child they'd created.

Damn. Why had he pushed her?

Was he somehow to blame for this?

He dropped to his knees, taking her vitals, and watching her eyes flicker open. She moaned, and he felt both fear and relief.

"Mike?" she asked.

"Yes, honey. I'm here."

Her eyes searched his like a child awakening from a scary dream. "Please don't leave me."

"I won't," he said. And he meant it.

He could have called for help, but instead, he scooped her into his arms and carried her into the E.R., where he laid her on a gurney that had been parked in the hall. Then he wheeled her to the nurses' desk.

"Oh, God," Jennifer said. "What happened?"

"She fainted," Mike said. "Will you please call in an obstetrician?"

Jennifer's jaw dropped, and she paused for a beat before reaching for the phone.

"Call Dr. Kipper," Simone said softly.

Mike placed a hand on Simone's forehead, acknowledging that it was cool to the touch, then he caressed her hair, her cheek.

He'd pushed her too hard. But only because he loved her so much.

Moments later, an E.R. doctor hovered over Simone, checking vitals. The resident obstetrician, who explained he'd been sent by Dr. Kipper to make a preliminary exam, arrived and concurred with the diagnosis. The fainting spell had been a result of pregnancy, and Simone would be okay.

"Can we have an ultrasound?" Mike asked the obstetrician. "I want to make sure the baby's all right."

"Sure," the resident said. "I'll put in an order."

Mike stood beside the gurney and reached for Simone's hand. "I'm sorry for being so tough on you."

She gave his fingers a gentle squeeze. "You didn't cause me to faint, if that's what you mean."

"But I *did* upset you."

"Only because I'd begun to think you might be right about us. Then, before I could admit it to myself or to you, I felt you pulling away from me. And it was...more than a little unsettling. I can only imagine how you must have felt each time I did that to you."

Mike's heart took a tumble in his chest as he realized that they just might be able to work things out after all. "I wanted you and the baby to be a part of my life, and I tried to force your hand. I'm sorry."

"Apology accepted, but I'm afraid I owe you one, too. I love you, Mike. And that scares me. I've never had anyone love me back before."

Mike brushed a kiss across her lips. "It won't scare you for long. You're going to get used to it, to me. I promise. And as long as I know you love me, we can work it out."

"You've made a believer out of me."

She started to sit up, and he placed his hands on her shoulders and gently pushed her back down. "I'd feel better if you stayed still for a while. I don't want you passing out on me again."

Simone's gaze wrapped around his heart and held on tight. "I've never had anyone worry about me before."

Mike's grin brushed aside the concern on his face. "Then you'd better get used to it, honey. You've become a priority in my life. And I'm in this for the duration."

Simone studied the man who loved her, the man whose concern was so clearly written across his brow.

Isobel had said that trust was earned, and Mike had clearly earned hers. It was also a decision that was made. And today, at this very moment, she was going to consciously choose to trust Mike—now and forever.

You can't change the past, Isobel had said, *but you can change your perception of it.*

Simone realized her friend had been right. She'd thought that an emotionally distant mother and a bad childhood had been a millstone around her neck, an awkward set of baggage that would hold her down for the rest of her life.

But she'd come to realize that it had merely been one step in her life's journey, a journey that led her to Mike and the unconditional love she'd been craving for as long as she could remember.

"I can hardly believe it," she told him. "I'm going to create the family I never thought I could have—with you. It's going to be a new experience for me, so be patient."

"It's not so new. You've got a family of sorts in the hospital, people you respect and care about, people who respect and care about you, too."

He was right. She'd developed at least two close relationships with coworkers—Ella and Isobel.

But the most important relationship of all was the one she hadn't even expected, the one she had with Mike.

He loved her; he *really* loved her.

"What did I ever do to deserve you?" she asked.

He shot her a crooked grin. "You showed me the real Simone. And then I knew my bachelor days were over." He bent forward and brushed his lips across hers, gently but possessively. It was a kiss filled with promise.

"Excuse me," Jennifer said. "Simone, we're ready for that ultrasound."

Moments later, as Simone's belly was exposed and slathered with the cool gel, the resident obstetrician pointed to the black-and-white moving image on the screen.

"Everything looks good to me," he said.

Simone's breath caught, as her eyes focused on the form of a baby, its little heart pumping and beating strong, its arms and legs moving. A sense of awe filled her heart, her throat.

"Can you tell if it's a girl or boy yet?" Mike asked the doctor.

Simone turned her head to the doctor, listening intently. Suddenly, it mattered very much whether they would have a son or a daughter. She needed to start thinking about names and decorating a nursery.

"It's too soon to determine the baby's sex," the doctor said. "But what are you hoping for?"

"We don't care," Mike said, his eyes glistening with joy and wonder. "We just want the baby to be healthy."

He was right. Simone turned her head again, back to the screen. Back to their baby. And her own eyes filled with happy tears.

At that very moment, Simone knew that she would love their child no matter what sex it was, no matter who it looked like.

A bond had begun to form.

Or maybe it had begun to form the first time she'd looked into Mike's eyes and recognized the love that burned there.

"Well," said the doctor, "I think everything looks great and on schedule. Maybe you ought to just go home and take it easy for the rest of the day."

"Yes," Mike said. "Let's go home."

Simone had no idea if he was talking about his house or hers, but it no longer mattered.

Love was wherever Mike was.

* * *

On the way home, Mike mentioned that he needed to stop by his place and pick up Wags.

"Did you ever purchase more food for him?" Simone asked.

"Uh-oh. I meant to do that, but I haven't gotten around to it yet. Do you mind if I get some now? The pet shop is just ahead on Lexington."

"No, that's fine. It'll give me a chance to check on Millie. Fred said she had a flu bug that was giving her fits."

Moments later, Mike pulled in front of Tails a Waggin' and parked the Jeep. Once they'd both exited the vehicle, they walked hand in hand into the pet store.

Something felt very good and right about being with Mike, and Simone suspected that it wouldn't take any time at all for her to get used to being part of a couple.

When they entered the store, they'd agreed to separate, though. Mike went after the puppy food, and Simone wanted to say hello to Millie.

For the first time during one of her visits, she wasn't greeted by Popeye Baxter.

She spotted Millie, though.

Her friend was seated on a stool behind the cash register. She'd bent forward on the counter, where she was resting her head on her folded arms.

"Millie?" Simone asked. "Are you okay?"

The brunette looked up and managed a smile. "Oh, hi. I was just resting my eyes. I've been so tired lately that I find myself wanting to nap constantly."

"Are you still fighting that virus?"

"I'm afraid so." Millie blew out a weary sigh. "I just can't seem to kick it. Fortunately, it seems to come and go. But that's probably because of the excitement at our house these days."

"Fred mentioned you were going to have a few kids for a while. Are they still staying with you?"

"Yes, they are."

"How long are you going to have them?" Simone asked, wondering if Millie ought to be more concerned about her health.

"It's kind of a long story. Joe and Connie Prescott, a couple in our church, were foster parents for three small children. The girls are three and five. And the boy is nine. But when Joe had to transfer out of the country for business, they weren't going to be able to take the kids. Those poor little ones had been through a lot already, and the Prescotts hated to see them split up, which could have easily happened. It's so hard to find foster parents willing to take more than one child."

"Where are the kids now?" Simone asked.

"Greg, the boy, and Fred are at Little League practice. And Kimmy and Julie are with Gladys, Fred's mother. They're making cookies." Millie yawned. "Boy, I hope Fred gets back soon. I'd love to close up early and go home."

"Have the children found a permanent home yet?" Simone asked.

A broad smile stretched across Millie's face, dimpling her rosy cheeks. "As a matter of fact, they *have*. Fred and I have applied to be foster parents with the agreement that we eventually be allowed to adopt them."

"That's wonderful. How's it working out? I would imagine your lives are going to change dramatically."

Millie chuckled. "That's for sure. But Fred and I

don't mind a bit. And we couldn't be happier. The same goes for Popeye, who refuses to leave the children's side. The cats and the bird are still getting used to the hullabaloo, though. But I'm sure it won't take them very long."

"That's probably true."

"You know," Millie said, "I have to admit I was a bit worried about Fred's health. I hoped having the children wouldn't add too much stress to his life."

Simone nodded, sharing her friend's concern.

"But it's the weirdest thing. Since those kids came to live with us, Fred's coloring is much better, which leads me to believe that his heart condition is showing signs of improvement. I don't know if it's a divine miracle or just the result of sheer happiness. But we're not going to worry about it."

Simone wasn't sure what was going on, but she was glad to hear that Fred was feeling better.

"Now," Millie said, "if I could just kick this lingering virus that I've got, we'd all be happy. Thank goodness neither Fred nor the kids have caught it from me."

"What are your symptoms?" Simone asked.

"I seem to feel just fine when I wake up in the morning, but as the day wears on, I start feeling more and more nauseous. And I just seem to be tired all the time." She blew out a sigh. "But maybe juggling parenting duties with Fred and trying to work in the store has taken a bit of a toll on me. I'm sure I'll be feeling better soon."

"You're probably right." Still, Simone couldn't help wondering if the intermittent bouts of nausea and being tired might be pregnancy symptoms. She'd heard of cases where couples who'd been trying unsuccessfully to conceive for years finally gave up, only to find themselves pregnant when they least expected it.

But she didn't want to offer Millie false hope.

Either way, it seemed as though the Baxters had been granted the family they'd always dreamed of having.

Just as Simone had.

As Mike approached carrying a sack of puppy food, he tossed a smile Millie's way, greeting her. Then he waited as she rang up the charges.

After paying for their purchase, they were back in the Jeep and on their way to pick up Wags and take him home.

Home. Never had the word held so much love, so much hope.

Could Simone be any happier?

Ten minutes later, they arrived at Simone's house, and Mike carried Wags inside.

They still hadn't made any plans about where they would choose to live, but it seemed as though they had all the time in the world to decide.

Simone suspected they would live at her house while working together to fix up the old Dennison place. In the meantime, as the dogs played happily in the backyard, apparently glad to finally be together, she and Mike closed the back door and walked through the kitchen on their way to the bedroom.

He'd insisted that she lie down for a while and agreed to rest with her.

As was her habit, she glanced at the counter, where her answering machine sat, the red light indicating that she had a message.

So she stopped long enough to punch the play button and wait for the recording to sound.

"Simone? It's Mom. Please give me a call when you get in."

She glanced at Mike, who gave a little shrug. "If you decide to call now, maybe you should do it from the bedroom so you can at least put your feet up."

His concern for her well-being strummed something deep in her heart. "I feel fine, but if it makes you feel better, I'll lie down while I talk to her."

"It *does*," he said with a smile.

She returned her mother's call, and interestingly enough, they didn't have to play phone tag.

"Hey, Mom. It's me. What's up?"

"Oh hi, Simone. I just called to let you know that I spoke to one of the counselors you suggested."

"How did it go? Did you find it helpful?"

"As a matter of fact, I liked her. A *lot*. We had our first session last night, and I think it went...very well. I probably have a long way to go, but I wanted to thank you for encouraging me to contact her."

"I'm so glad you think she'll be helpful, Mom. And if you ever want or need to talk to me about it, you know you can, right?"

"Thanks, Simone. I know that I wasn't always there for you when you grew up, and I'm sorry. With Cynthia's friendship and Dr. Daniels's help, I'm hoping that things will...get better."

"I'd like that." Simone glanced at Mike, saw him watching her closely. Still, she wasn't sure if he knew how much this meant to her.

For as long as she could remember, she'd hoped

and prayed her mom would be normal, that they'd have what other mothers and daughters had. And she'd all but given up.

"I know I've never said it," her mother added, "but I do love you. And I want you to know that I blame myself for the bulk of the problems we've had. But I'm going to try and work on becoming a…better person, if not a better mother."

All she had any right to ask of her mother was that she at least try to get help. And, apparently, she was.

"I'm glad to hear it, Mom. And I have a few things that I probably ought to work on, too. I've pulled away a lot in the past, so it didn't help us find any common ground."

Silence stretched across the line, which Simone realized was par for the course for the two of them. But she hoped that, with time, the awkwardness would eventually lessen.

"While I have you on the line," Simone said, hoping her news would be helpful and not hinder her mother's progress, "there's something I want to tell you. I've fallen in love with a wonderful man. His name is Mike O'Rourke, and we plan to be married."

"That's…a nice surprise. I'm…happy for you. When is the wedding?"

"It's all in the planning stages now." Simone glanced at Mike and held on to the love glowing in his eyes. "I'll let you know when we decide on a date."

"Is he good to you?" her mother asked.

"Unbelievably so." Simone placed a hand on Mike's cheek and basked in all she'd found in his arms. "I'm the luckiest woman in the world."

"You deserve the best, Simone."

"Thanks, Mom." Simone chose to believe her mother was being sincere. "And, by the way, there's even more good news. We're also going to have a baby."

"A baby?"

"Yes, Mom. You're going to be a grandmother by the time next Christmas comes around."

"Imagine that. Time has a way of changing things."

Yes, it did.

They told each other goodbye and promised to chat again later, a promise that rang true.

Simone wasn't sure what the future would bring, but she was hopeful that, with counseling, her mom would work through the issues she should have taken care of right after the rape happened.

She knew she could never really change what had happened between them in the early years, but maybe her mother would be a better grandmother.

Mike kicked off his shoes, then stretched out upon the bed. He rolled to his side and patted the place beside him.

Words weren't needed. Simone was eager to curl up next to him. As much as she looked forward to making love again, the doctor had said to take it easy. And she didn't want to take any chances by overdoing it today.

So instead, she relished the feel of Mike's arms around her, the hint of his musky, male scent, the comfort that the gentle rise and fall of his chest provided.

"Do you know what?" Mike asked.

"What's that?"

"I recognize how hard you've worked to become the nurse that you are. So I don't expect you to be a stay-at-home mom unless you want to. I'm willing to either take care of the baby myself or juggle my schedule any way that will allow you to continue working."

She ran her fingertips along his cheek, felt the faint bristle of his beard. "You're a sweetheart, Mike O'Rourke. We'll just have to wait and see what the future brings." Then she cupped his jaw and pressed a kiss on his lips, allowing her hand to linger on his face. "Right now, I can't imagine wanting to give up my job completely, so I appreciate your willingness to work out a day-care solution."

"I'm sure my mom wouldn't mind helping out some, too. She loves babies."

That thought held a lot of appeal.

"You know," Simone said, "I like your mom. And your dad is great, too. I hope, when they get to know me better, that they'll feel the same way about me."

"They'll love you." He took her hand from his cheek and kissed her palm. "And so will the rest of my family. As big and boisterous as the O'Rourkes can sometimes be, they've always welcomed each new in-law and baby with open arms. So you'll be one of them, too."

A family of her own. Imagine that.

"I love you," Simone said, enjoying the sound of her words and realizing they came easier each time she said them.

"I love you, too."

They lay like that for a while, caught up in the intimacy they shared. An intimacy Simone no longer found the least bit scary. Not with Mike.

"Thanks for seeing something inside my cool exterior," she said. "And for being persistent about making me see it, too."

"I didn't have to look that deep. I've got an eye for inner warmth and beauty."

Simone smiled, her heart swelling to the bursting point.

Mike had set his sights on her, just as he had that old Victorian on Maple Drive that he'd purchased. He'd sensed what a little tender loving care could do and was determined to renovate the run-down house into a happy home.

There was no doubt that he would succeed.

After all, that's exactly what he'd done with Simone's heart.

* * * * *

HER MR RIGHT?

BY
KAREN ROSE SMITH

Award-winning author **Karen Rose Smith** has seen more than fifty romances published. Each book broadens her world and challenges her in a unique way.

Readers can e-mail Karen through her website at www.karenrosesmith.com or write to her at PO Box 1545, Hanover, PA 17331, USA.

To the "gathering" group
from York Catholic High School's class of '67.
It's been wonderful reconnecting again.
Thanks for the friendship and good times.

Chapter One

"You work with elderly patients. Is that correct, Miss Suarez?"

Isobel felt as if she had been viewed under a high-powered microscope for the past five minutes. Neil Kane had the power to make her pulse race simply by passing her in the hall. It wasn't his status as an investigator for the Massachusetts Attorney General's Office that rattled her most. Rather it was her response to him as a man, with his sandy-brown hair graying at the temples, his strong jaw with its cleft at the center, his tall, trim and fit physique under a charcoal suit. He was attractive enough to turn the heads of most women.

She didn't want her head turned—especially not by a man who was trying to pin wrongdoing on hospital personnel. Who was attempting to discover fraud that could be the downfall of Walnut River General, or more insidiously, make a takeover by Northeastern HealthCare a probability instead of a possibility.

"Miss Suarez?" the investigator repeated, those gold-flecked brown eyes sending a tingle up her spine.

Isobel intended to select every word carefully. "I'm a social worker at this hospital, Mr. Kane. I tend to any patient whose case history finds its way to my desk."

They sat alone in his temporary office, a small conference room, with the door closed. A laptop was positioned in front of Kane and a legal pad sat beside it. From her seat around the corner of the table, she couldn't see what was on the screen of the laptop.

When the investigator leaned back in his chair and rubbed the back of his neck, his knee was very close to hers. She didn't move an inch.

"I think everyone who works at this hospital has taken a course on how to be evasive," he muttered.

She didn't comment. By age thirty-five, she'd learned when silence had more effect than a retort.

He blew out a breath and she suspected his day had been as long as hers. From what she'd heard, he'd been interviewing personnel in this room since seven-thirty this morning; he'd been here eleven hours straight.

"Miss Suarez. You told me you've worked here ten years." He leaned forward. "In that amount of time, what age group has occupied most of your attention?"

She could only pick up a hint of his cologne, something woodsy and very masculine. "I haven't kept track."

"Well, then, isn't it a good thing we have records and computer programs that *do* keep track." His voice had an edge to it that was part frustration, part anger.

Her own temper was precariously perched. "Why are you

asking me the question if you already have the answer? You know, Mr. Kane, if you try hard enough to catch a fish, you might catch the wrong fish."

His brows arched. "Meaning?"

Impatiently, she shoved her very curly, chin-length auburn hair behind her ear. "Meaning…everyone I work with at this hospital is dedicated to his or her profession. We're here to take care of patients, not in any way to take advantage of them. I don't know what you're specifically investigating—there are so many rumors floating around, I can't count them all—but whatever it is, maybe someone made a mistake. Maybe there was a computer error. Maybe there's no culprit or fraud or theft at all."

He studied her for a few very long moments. "What would you have our office do, Miss Suarez? Ignore the possibility of wrongdoing? Wouldn't the guilty love that!"

The buzz around the hospital was that Neil Kane was the enemy. Everyone from the chief of staff to the night security guard had banded together to treat him as if he were. They believed in each other and the work they did here. This hospital was about patient care. That could change drastically if Northeastern HealthCare took over. If a conglomerate ran Walnut River General, the hospital would consider financial well-being more important than helping the residents of Walnut River.

Frustrated herself by a long day made longer by Neil Kane's hard-edged questioning, she made a suggestion. "If you want to know what I do and who I help, shadow me. Shadow the doctors and nurses. See what we do in a day. Do that, and then ask your questions. At least then you'll be asking the *right* ones."

They sat in silence for a moment, both stunned by her outburst. Eager to avoid his gaze, Isobel looked down and dusted some imaginary lint from her skirt. She had worn a

lime-green suit today to celebrate spring and the beginning
of May. This was the time of year she liked best, and she
wanted to bring the idea of new beginnings inside. The
longish jacket hid the extra pounds she'd put on since she'd
moved back in with her dad. The chunky jasper beads she
wore around her neck carried shades of green and brown that
coordinated well with her tan silk shell. Neil Kane was
studying her necklace, studying her face, studying *her.*
Because she was being confrontational? Or because…

A man hadn't looked at her as an attractive woman in over
two years. She wasn't feeling attractive these days—not with
the extra fifteen pounds, not with her mass of curls needing
a trim, not with the circles under her eyes showing her fatigue.

Kane's voice lost its sharpness as he asked, "What *are* the
right questions?"

Was he serious? Did he really want to know? "The right
questions are the ones that matter. Do the professionals who
work here *care* about the patients? Do they punch in and punch
out, or do they work when they're needed? If they aren't
making salaries commensurate with pay at a larger hospital,
why do they stay? *Those* are the questions that would be a start."

"Tell me what *you* do in a day."

In spite of herself, Isobel noticed the stubble shadowing
Kane's jaw. She saw the tiny scar over his right brow. She
wondered if there was someone in his life who could ease the
creases around his eyes into laugh lines. Amongst all the
other rumors about him, she'd heard he'd once been a
homicide detective with the Boston P.D. Was that why he
seemed so… so…unyielding?

Leaning back a few inches, she took a calming breath. "I
check on patients I'm following to see how they fared over
night. My supervisor hands me the files on new admission

that I can help. I'm always writing progress notes. I meet with families, confer with therapists and find placements in rehab facilities and nursing homes."

"Do you find yourself giving more time to some patients than others?"

He'd asked the question mildly as if it were just another in a long list. But for some reason, it put her on alert. "Some cases are more complicated."

"What do you do when there isn't family to consult?"

"I try to do what's best for the patient, of course."

"Of course."

The way he said it made her hackles rise, and her temper flipped to the ruffled side. "Are you accusing me of something?"

"Did it sound as if I was?"

"Talk about evasive," she murmured.

"*I'm* asking the questions, Miss Suarez. This isn't give and take. It's an investigation."

"A *preliminary* investigation. Doesn't that mean your office isn't even sure if there's anything to investigate?"

"You know the saying, where there's smoke…" He trailed off, letting her fill in the rest.

"There's another old saying—when a man looks for dirt, he'll miss the gold."

"Where did *that* come from?" He seemed mildly amused.

Isobel frowned. She felt as if he were laughing at her. The quote came from her dad. At sixty-eight, he spouted as much wisdom as he did complaints these days. "Do you have any more questions for me?" she asked curtly.

"Yes, I do. Tell me about Doctor Ella Wilder and J. D. Sumner."

Isobel considered how best to answer him then finally decided on "They're engaged to be married."

"How did they meet?"

"Is that another question you already know the answer to?"

"Humor me."

Everyone knew how Ella and J.D. had met. "Mr. Sumner had an accident. He slipped on the ice."

"Here at the hospital?"

"Yes, in the parking lot."

"And Dr. Wilder treated him."

"Yes."

"Do you know any more about it than that?"

Now Isobel was really puzzled. "I'm not sure what you mean."

"Did you know the nature of Mr. Sumner's injury?"

"I believe he had torn cartilage in his knee."

"Isn't arthroscopic surgery for torn cartilage usually done on an outpatient basis?"

Now she saw where this was going. "Mr. Sumner's case was a little different."

"Why is that?"

"In February he was a representative from Northeastern HealthCare."

"So he received extra special treatment?"

"All of our patients receive the same treatment, but J.D. was a stranger in town. He didn't know anyone, and he didn't have anybody to help him."

Kane leaned forward, his gaze piercing. "You were called in on the case?"

"No. There was no need for that."

"Because Dr. Wilder took a personal interest in him?" Kane asked mildly.

His tone didn't fool her for a minute. "What do you want to know?"

After a thoughtful pause, the investigator was blunt. "I want to know if he was charged for special treatment. He was kept longer than necessary."

Her defensive guard slipped into place once more. "I understand since you're from the Massachusetts Attorney General's Office that you have access to medical records as well as financial records. If that's true, you can verify why Mr. Sumner was kept."

"The medical records say he had a fever."

She shrugged. "And what does Mr. Sumner say?"

"He said he had a fever."

"Then why wouldn't you believe that?"

When Neil Kane wouldn't answer her question, she suspected why. Someone was feeding his office information—*false* information. There was a leak in the hospital and she guessed that someone in the administrative ranks was doing the damage. Someone had their own agenda to make the hospital look bad so Northeastern HealthCare could take over more easily.

Neil Kane seemed very close, though he hadn't moved and neither had she. "Patient records aside, can you tell me if Dr. Wilder transported Mr. Sumner at any time?"

"Why is *that* important?" she fenced, leaning back, putting more distance between them.

"I'm trying to understand what's fact and what's fiction, what are legitimate charges and what aren't."

The long day caught up to her. There was nothing of substance she could tell this man even if she wanted to. "My area is social work, Mr. Kane. Unless I'm following a case, I don't have contact or interaction with the other patients in the hospital."

"Oh, but I'm sure you hear plenty in your position. Besides

the fact that I understand that you and Dr. Wilder and Simone Garner are friends."

At that leap into personal territory, Isobel stood. "I understand you have an investigation to conduct. I don't like talking to you about my cases, but I will if I have to. But I *won't* discuss my personal relationships."

When he stood, too, she noticed he was a good six inches taller than she was and seemed to take up most of the breathable space in the room. That was her very overactive imagination telling her that, but nevertheless, oxygen seemed a little harder to come by. He wasn't menacing, but he *was* imposing.

"Are you going to stonewall me?" he asked in a low, determined tone.

"No. I'm just setting boundaries."

He frowned. "And what happens if I have to cross them?"

"I'll clam up and not talk to you at all."

As he studied her, he seemed to gauge her level of conviction. "There are consequences to obstructing an investigation."

"Do I need a lawyer?" she returned.

He blew out a long breath. "All right. You want to leave for now? Fine. Leave. But we're not done. I need answers and I intend to get them."

She could tell him he'd get those answers when hell froze over, but he *was* the one who held the power here. She was usually law-abiding and cooperative, but so much was at stake—the survival and reputation of Walnut River General.

Swallowing another retort, she picked up her purse, went to the door and opened it. Neil Kane didn't say another word, but she could feel his gaze on her back as she left the conference room. She suspected he wasn't the type of man who would give up easily. Still, round one went to her.

She wouldn't think about round two until it was staring her in the face…until Neil Kane was staring her in the face.

Then?

Then she'd deal with him again after a weekend of chores, sleep and gardening. Next week she was sure she wouldn't react to him so strongly. Next week she'd figure out how to be diplomatic. Diplomacy was usually her middle name. She'd just have to figure out why Neil Kane got under her skin…and make sure he didn't do it again.

Most of the houses in Isobel's childhood neighborhood had been built in the 1950s. She'd been five when her family had moved into the house on Sycamore Street, her sister Debbie seven, their brother Jacob three. She remembered the day they'd moved in to the modest brick two-story with its flowerpots on either side of the steps and the glassed-in back porch where she and her brother and sister played whenever the weather permitted. The neighbor on the left, Mrs. Bass, had brought them chocolate-chip cookies. The neighbor in the small ranch house on the right, Mr. Hannicut, had given her dad a hand unloading box after box from the truck someone had loaned him.

Isobel had never expected she'd be living back here again after being on her own since college.

The detached garage, which sat at the end of their lot in the backyard, only housed one car—her father's. Because of the shoulder surgery he'd had two weeks ago, he couldn't drive now. He hated that fact and so did Isobel because it was making him grumpy. Lots of things about his recuperation were making him grumpy.

She parked in front of the house knowing that he'd had his physical therapy appointment today. One of his senior center buddies had taken him.

Although May in Massachusetts brought warmer days, the nights could still be cold. Without a coat to protect her, she quickly opened the front door and called over the chatter of the television, "I'm home." She'd phoned him late this afternoon to see how his session had gone and to tell him she'd be late. He'd been monosyllabic, not a good indication that he'd be in a better mood tonight.

After a glance at Isobel, her father flipped off the TV. "It's about time."

He rubbed his hand over his shoulder as if it ached.

Isobel tried to put her fatigue aside and remind herself what her dad must be going through. "I'm sorry I'm so late. As I told you on the phone, I had a meeting."

"You need a job that doesn't run you ragged fifteen hours a day." John Suarez lowered the leg lift on his recliner, pushed himself to the edge of the seat, then used his right arm to lever himself up.

He was a stocky man who stood about five-eight. At sixty-eight, his black curly hair had receded but was still thick. His eyes were the same dark brown as Isobel's. She'd gotten her red-brown hair from her Irish mother.

The stab of memory urged Isobel's gaze to the photos of her family on the mantel above the fireplace.

Her father must have noticed. "She'd want you to slow down, go out and meet a nice young man and have some kids."

"As if wishing could make it so," Isobel murmured, then smiled at her father. "I like my work. You know that. And if Mom wants me to get married, she's just going to have to toss the right guy down here in front of my nose."

"I still don't understand why you broke up with Tim. He treated you nice. He owned his own business. Bicycle shops are really taking off these days. Sometimes I think you're just too picky."

Picky? She supposed that was one way of putting it. After her mother died, she'd moved back in with her father to ease his grief, to help with the chores, never intending to stay permanently in her childhood home. But her dad had begun having shoulder problems and was limited in what he could do for himself. Isobel had always liked cycling and she'd bought a new bike. The owner of a cycle shop, Tim, had asked her out and over the next year they'd gotten serious.

But Tim had never liked the fact that she lived with her dad. He'd insisted that if her father needed help, he should move into an assisted-living facility. Isobel had already lost one parent and she'd known how much the family home meant to her father. How could she suggest he leave when he still felt her mother's presence here? In the end, her father had been the reason she and Tim had broken up. Family was important to her. She'd never ignore or abandon them and that's what Tim had wanted her to do.

"Tim just wasn't right for me, Dad." She headed for the kitchen. "Give me ten minutes and I'll have that roast beef and mashed potatoes from last night warmed up."

"Cyrus and I finished the pie Mrs. Bass made, so there won't be any dessert," he called after her. "You really need to go to the store. We're out of ice cream and orange juice, too."

"I'll shop first thing in the morning, then I want to get out into the garden."

"If you plant flowers, they could still freeze overnight."

"I'll cover them." She just needed to work her hands into the earth, feel the sun on her head, and forget about everything going on at the hospital…especially Neil Kane.

For the next fifteen minutes, Isobel tried to put a meal

together. Unfortunately, she left the roast beef in the micro-wave too long and the edges turned into leather. The mashed potatoes weren't quite hot enough. The frozen broccoli was perfect—except her dad didn't like broccoli. It had been the only vegetable left in the freezer.

After he tried to cut a piece of meat with one hand, he grumbled, "Spaghetti would be easier for me than this. Now if I could saw it with both hands—"

Isobel felt tears burn in her eyes. "It was the best I could do for tonight. Sorry." She really wanted to yell, "This isn't the life I'd planned, either."

So many thoughts clicked through her head, memories of the meals her mother had made that had always been perfect in her dad's eyes, the family get-togethers around the table every Sunday. But with her mom's death and her sister's divorce, Sunday dinner had dwindled into now and then. Life had changed whether they'd wanted it to or not. But her dad, especially, didn't like the changes.

"Maybe we should keep some frozen dinners in the freezer," he suggested helpfully.

Frozen dinners. Her mom would turn over in her grave.

"No frozen dinners. At least not the ones bought in the store." She turned to face her dad. "What I should do is spend all day Sunday cooking, make some casseroles that we could freeze and you could just take one out and put in the oven when I'm late."

"Did you have plans for Sunday?"

She didn't have *specific* plans for Sunday. She'd just been looking forward to a day off, a day of rest, a day to catch up with her sister and her niece and nephews, maybe go for a walk along the river now that the weather was turning nicer. Maybe go cycling again.

Instead of telling her dad about her hopes, she gave him a smile and answered, "No plans. I'll fill the freezer so we don't have to worry about meals for a couple of weeks."

He gave her a sly smile. "When you go to the store tomorrow, don't buy any more broccoli, okay?"

"No more broccoli," she agreed and started loading the dishwasher, exhausted, eager to go to bed so that she could get up early tomorrow morning to get grocery shopping out of the way and spend a couple of hours in the garden before she did laundry and the other household chores.

Isobel basked in the sun's warmth, digging her hands into the ground, making another hole for a Gerber daisy. It was the last of the six, a beautiful peachy-pink color she'd never seen before. She'd have to cover the flowers at night for a little while, but it would be worth the extra bother.

A shadow suddenly fell over her.

"Miss Suarez?"

She knew the voice without turning around to see who it belonged to, the voice she was so familiar with after just one meeting. She knew its timbre and depth and edge. It was Neil Kane's voice.

In some ways she wished she could just disappear into a hole in the ground. She was wearing a crop-sleeved T-shirt that came to her waist and old jeans that were grubby at the knees and too tight across her rear. She had no doubt she'd brushed peat moss across her cheek and her hands were covered with dirt.

Sitting back on her haunches, she closed her eyes, took a deep breath, then looked over her shoulder.

"Mr. Kane. To what do I owe this pleasure on my weekend off? It's supposed to be wild and fun and free." She couldn't help being a little bit sarcastic. He was making everyone's lives at the hospital miserable. Did he have to chase them down at their homes, too?

"If you don't want me here, I'll leave."

His sandy hair blew in the breeze. He was dressed in a tan-and-black striped Henley shirt and wore khakis. She spotted the sandy chest hair at the top button of his shirt. His three-quarter-length sleeves were snug enough that she noticed muscles underneath. His eyes were taking her in, not as if she were a grubby Little Orphan Annie, but as if she were Miss USA! Was there interest there? Couldn't be. She felt mesmerized for a moment, hot and cold and just sort of mushy inside.

Feeling defenseless on the ground with him looking down on her, she put one hand on the grass to lever herself to her feet.

He offered her his hand. "Let me help."

She would have snatched her hand away, but she probably would have tumbled back down to the ground in a very unladylike position.

His hand was large, his fingers enveloping and she felt like a tongue-tied naive teenager with a crush on a football player.

As soon as she was balanced on her feet, she pulled out of his grasp and saw his hand was now covered with dirt. "I'm so sorry." She caught a towel from her gardening basket and handed it to him.

He just wiped his hands together. "I'm fine. But I can see I'm interrupting you. Can you take a break?"

Actually she was finished but she didn't know if she wanted to tell him that. "You didn't answer my question. Why are you here?"

"I didn't like the way our meeting ended. You were upset and I didn't mean to upset you."

"I wasn't upset," she protested.

"Okay, not upset, angry. Everyone seems to be angry—if not downright hostile. We're not going to get anywhere like that. I know I'm asking pointed questions, but I have to get to the bottom of the rumors and complaints. If there is insurance fraud, don't you want to know? If you cooperate, wouldn't that be better for both of us?"

"I *am* cooperating."

The corners of his mouth definitely twitched up in a semblance of a smile. "If that was cooperation, I'd like to see resistance."

She felt her face getting hot, and not from the midday sun. "I feel as if you're trying to entrap me or the staff. As if you want to catch us in some little discrepancy—"

"I want the truth."

There was something about Neil Kane besides his sex appeal that got to her. Maybe it was the resolve in his eyes that told her he was sincere.

"I stopped by today to see if we could discuss everything more calmly over lunch."

"You're asking everyone you question to lunch?"

This time, a dark ruddiness crept into his cheeks. "No, but I don't get the feeling you're hiding anything. You seem to want to be careful so no one gets hurt. I understand that."

"In other words, you think I'm a pushover."

He laughed and it was such a masculine sound, her tummy seemed to tip over.

"That's exactly what I mean," he explained. "Although you try, you really don't watch every word you say. I get the feeling you're a straight shooter. So am I. I thought we could make some progress together."

Having lunch with the enemy wasn't a terrific idea. On the

other hand, Neil Kane wasn't going to go away until he was
satisfied with the answers he got. No one would have to know
she was talking to him and maybe, just maybe, she could do
some convincing of her own.

"I found a place I like," he coaxed. "You can probably go
like that if you want."

At first she thought he was laughing at her, but then she
realized he wasn't. He was serious. Where was he going to
take her—to a hot-dog stand?

"I'd like to change and wash the dirt off my face." She
crouched down, gathered her gloves with the small gardening tools and plopped them into her basket.

Neil picked up a hoe and a rake lying beside the garden.

"You don't have to—" she began.

"Someone could trip over them." Now he was smiling at
her.

She couldn't help but smile back. "You can just leave
them on the porch."

"I can wait there."

"That's silly. No, come on in. My dad's watching TV. He
might ignore you, but at least you can find a comfortable
chair." She started up the stairs and he kept pace with her. As
he propped the tools against the wall, she said, "Mr. Kane,
about my dad—"

"Do you mind if we drop the formality? My name's Neil.
We might feel less confrontational if we can at least call each
other by our first names."

"Isobel's fine."

Their gazes caught…met…held. Until finally he asked,
"What about your dad?"

Whenever she looked into Neil's eyes, she lost every
coherent thought in her head. She made the effort to concen-

trate. "If he seems to ignore you or is grumpy, it's just him, not you. Please don't feel offended. He had surgery on his shoulder two weeks ago and he's not happy about it. He's limited as to what he can and can't do, and that frustrates him."

"It would frustrate anyone."

Neil seemed to understand and that was a relief.

As they crossed the foyer and went to the living room, her father didn't say a word, just kept his eyes glued to the TV where a biography of Dwight D. Eisenhower played.

"Dad, I want you to meet—"

"Not now. Shhhh."

She felt her cheeks flush and was about to apologize to Neil when he said, "My father told me he visited the Eisenhower farm when he was a boy."

Isobel's father swung his gaze to Neil. "No kidding. How'd that happen?"

"My grandparents apparently knew a friend of the family."

"You're from Pennsylvania?"

"No. I was born and raised in Massachusetts, but we took a couple of vacations there when I was a kid. I was interested in history so the Gettysburg Battlefield fascinated me. I enjoyed it almost as much as Hershey Park."

To Isobel's surprise, her father laughed, and then his gaze went to her, expecting introductions.

"Dad, this is Neil Kane. He's…he's…"

"An investigator for the state Attorney General's Office," Neil filled in.

"So *you're* the one who's been snooping around the hospital."

Instead of taking offense, Neil smiled. "Investigators always get a bad rap when they try to find the answers, don't they?"

Her father just grinned and pointed to the sofa, which sat at a right angle to his recliner. "Sit down and tell me about those trips to Pennsylvania. My parents moved up and down the East Coast. My dad had trouble finding work until they settled here."

Isobel was absolutely amazed her father had started talking to Neil like this. But then maybe he sensed another history buff.

Who would have thought?

As she ran up the stairs, she mentally pictured everything in her closet, trying to decide what to wear. Then she chastised herself. What she wore simply didn't matter. She wasn't going to try to impress a man who would be here today and gone tomorrow. She wasn't going to try to impress a man who thought she or other personnel at the hospital had committed some kind of crime.

No matter how easygoing Neil seemed today, or how gentlemanly, she had to be on her guard. Her future as well as the hospital's depended on it.

Chapter Two

"I never expected you to bring me here. Only the locals know about this place." Isobel's eyes were the deep, dark brown of rich espresso. Her smile was even a bit friendly.

As Neil sat with Isobel in his car parked on the gravel lot of The Crab Shack, his gut tightened. How long had it been since a woman gave him an adrenaline rush? How long had it been since he'd actually felt happy to be somewhere *with* someone?

Happiness had been a commodity he couldn't quite get a grip on ever since he'd lost his brother. Guilt had been a factor in that, a guilt he'd never been without.

But today, just looking at Isobel in her bright yellow T-shirt, her pin-striped yellow-and-blue slacks, he felt...good, damn good. And he shouldn't. He'd only stopped by her house and brought her here to get information. He normally didn't fraternize with witnesses in an investigation. He always proceeded by the book.

But stonewalled by most of the staff...

"Not everyone in Walnut River considers me an enemy," he joked, returning her smile. "I'm staying at the Walnut River Inn. Greta Sanford told me about this place. She said to ignore how it looked on the outside and ignore some of the customers *inside* and just concentrate on the food."

"You haven't tried it yet?"

"I haven't had the chance to explore."

He'd arrived a few days ago and since then he'd spent most of his time in that hospital conference room.

"I heard you stayed at the hospital most nights until after nine."

"Does someone post my whereabouts on a Web site so everyone can check what I'm doing?" He was half kidding, half serious.

She didn't get defensive but rather looked sympathetic. "Scuttlebutt in small towns travels at the speed of light. Especially if it can impact jobs and careers."

Neither of them was going to forget for a minute why he was here. If he thought he could make Isobel forget...

Why did he *want* to make her forget?

So she'd let her guard down.

Isobel unfastened her seat belt, opened her door and climbed out of the car.

The Crab Shack was just that—a shack located along the river about a mile out of town. There were about fifteen cars parked in the lot and a line of patrons extended out the door. The weathered gray wooden building looked as if it might collapse in a good storm.

"There's always a crowd on the weekends and evenings

are even worse," Isobel explained as they walked toward the restaurant. "There are a couple of tables by the river, though, that are empty. We could just order the food and sit there."

Neil had dated women who would never sit in the open air, let alone go near one of the weathered benches. Isobel didn't seem to mind the breeze riffling through her hair. Her curls always seemed to be dancing around her face. His fingers itched to see if they were as soft as they looked. He couldn't help but notice the way her knit top fit her breasts—not too tight, not too loose. A stab of desire reminded him again that he hadn't slept with a woman in months. But that was because not just any woman would do. Isobel, however…

"A picnic table's fine with me," he agreed, his hand going to the small of her back to guide her.

She glanced up at him. Their gazes held. She didn't shift away…just broke eye contact and walked to the end of the line.

Fifteen minutes later, they were seated across from each other on the gray-brown benches. Half their table was shaded by a tall maple. Neil had bought a basket of steamed crabs for them to share. Isobel had insisted that was plenty, and that was all she wanted. But he couldn't resist the cheese fries.

He set those on the table between them.

Isobel laid a stack of napkins next to the crabs. "This always gets messy."

He also didn't know many women who would agree to picking steamed crabs for lunch. "Have you lived here all your life?" His information-gathering on Isobel Suarez had to start somewhere.

"Yep. Except for college."

"You have a master's degree, right?"

Reaching for a crab, she expertly cracked it. "I went

straight through, summers too. I was lucky enough to earn a few scholarships to take some of burden off of Dad. The rest were loans, but I finished paying them off last year."

She sounded glad about that and he realized she was the responsible type. Unable to take his eyes from her, he watched as she picked apart a crab, slipped some of the meat from one of the claws, and popped it into her mouth. She licked her lips and he felt as if his pulse was going to run away. She seemed oblivious to the effect she was having on him.

"Did you go to college?" She colored a bit. "I mean I heard you were a detective with the Boston P.D. before you took a job with the state." She used her fingers to separate another succulent piece of crab.

"I went to college and earned a degree in criminal justice before I joined the police force."

"Why did you leave the Boston P.D.?"

He went silent for a moment, realizing just how uncomfortable it could be to answer questions that went too deep or zeroed in on what he wanted to talk about least. "I left because I was getting too cynical." He nodded to the dish of cheese fries. "Sure you don't want one? Mrs. Sanford said they're as good as everything else here."

Isobel took a good long look at them, then at the crab she was picking. Finally, she smiled. "Maybe just one." She picked up a fry with a layer of cheese, took a bite from the end…and savored it.

Neil shifted on the bench. Damn it, she was turning him on with no effort at all. He felt as if he'd been in a deep freeze and Isobel had suddenly pushed the warm current button.

She took another bite of the large fry and set it down on a napkin. "Why is it that everything that's pleasurable comes with a price tag?"

"Don't most things come with a price tag?"

Their table was cockeyed on the grass and they could both see the river. She looked toward it now. "You know that old line, *the best things in life are free?*"

He nodded as he studied her profile, her patrician nose, her high cheekbones, the few wisps of stray curls that brushed her cheek in front of her ear.

She went on. "I used to believe that was true. And maybe it *is* true when you're young. But as you get older, everything seems to have a price."

He wondered what she was thinking about that made her sad, but he knew exactly what she meant. His gaze followed hers to the water and he almost recoiled from it. The sight of the river brought memories that were painful. He never should have brought her here. He'd thought his mind would be on the investigation and he would dive into the usual background questions. He never imagined they'd get into a conversation like this.

"Are you involved with anyone?" he asked her, surprising himself.

Her big brown eyes found his and for a moment, he thought she wasn't going to answer him, or that maybe she would say it was none of his business, which it wasn't.

"No, I'm not involved with anyone. How about you?"

"Nope. No strings. No ties that bind. With my job, any kind of a relationship would be difficult. I travel. I have a home base but I'm rarely there."

"Boston?"

"Yeah. It's home, but not really. Do you have family?" he asked her. "I mean besides your dad."

"I have a sister, Debbie, who lives here in Walnut River. We were always close but since her divorce, I think we've gotten even closer. We have a younger brother, Jacob, who's an adventurer. I don't think he'll ever settle down. One month he's in Australia surfing, the next he's in South America helping to save the rain forest."

"Lives in the moment?" Neil asked.

"Totally."

"How long ago did you lose your mom?"

"Four years ago. I moved back in with Dad after she died because he just seemed so…lost. He was having more problems with his arthritis and had fallen down the basement steps one day when he'd done some laundry and hurt his shoulder. So it just seemed the right thing to do."

"You were on your own before that?"

"Oh, sure. Since college. I had my own apartment over on Concord."

"It must have been hard for you, moving back home." He absolutely couldn't imagine it, but then he didn't have the relationship with his parents that Isobel obviously had with her dad.

"It was really odd moving back home. I mean, I had been in and out of the house ever since college, dinners on Sundays, stopping in to see how my parents were. But when I moved back into my old room, it was like I recognized it but I'd outgrown it. I didn't want to change anything because Mom had decorated it for me and that was part of her. Yet it was a young girl's room and I wasn't young anymore."

"What did you do?" he asked, curious.

"I packed away my cabinet of dolls, put the cupboard in the basement and moved in my computer hutch and printer. I couldn't bear to part with the latch-hook rug my mom had made, but I hung a watercolor I had at my apartment and bought new curtains. A mixture of yesterday and today."

"So living with your dad isn't temporary?"

"I don't see how it can be. He needs me and I can't turn away from that."

Neil admired what Isobel was doing. How many thirty-somethings would give up their life to help out a parent? "You're fortunate to be close to your family."

"You're not?"

He'd left himself wide open for that one. "There's a lot of distance between us, especially between me and my father."

She broke apart another crab. "Is that your doing or his?"

If anyone else had asked him that question, he would have clammed up. But Isobel's lack of guile urged him to be forth-right, too. "I'm not sure anymore. At one time *he* put it there. Now we both keep it there."

"That's a shame. Because anything can happen at any time."

That was a truth he'd experienced as a teenager.

They ate in silence for the next little while, listening to the birds that had found their way to the maples, to the sound of the breeze rustling the laurels and the foliage along the river, to the crunch of gravel as cars came and went. Whenever their gazes met, he felt heat rise up to his skin. It was the kind of heat that told him taking Isobel to bed would be a plea-surable experience. But as Isobel had said, most things had a price. He had the feeling she wasn't the type of woman who lived in the moment. She was the type of woman who wanted a marriage like her parents had had and wouldn't even consider a one-night stand as an option. He wasn't consid-ering it, either. This was an investigation, not a vacation.

After she wiped her hands with a napkin, she smiled at him. "I'm full."

His pile of crab shells was much larger than hers, and he'd finished all but two of the fries.

"I really should get back," she said. "I have laundry to do and cleaning. I play catch-up on weekends."

His weekends were usually his own. The cleaning lady took care of his apartment and he sent out his laundry. Suddenly his life seemed much too easy compared to Isobel's.

They finished their iced tea and cleaned up the remnants of lunch. His hand brushed Isobel's as they reached for the same napkin. The electric charge he felt could light up the restaurant for a week.

She seemed as startled as he was. She blushed, shoved more crab shells onto a paper plate, then took it to a nearby trash can to dump it. Five minutes later, they were in his car headed for her father's house. He'd felt comfortable talking to her while they had lunch, but now, there was an awkwardness intertwined with their silence.

Before he'd even stopped the car, her hand was already on the door. She unfastened her seat belt. "Thanks so much for lunch."

He clasped her arm. "We didn't talk about the hospital."

"No, we didn't," she responded softly.

"I need to ask you more questions. Can you stop by my office after you're finished work on Monday?"

"I never know exactly when I'll be done."

"I know. It doesn't matter. When I'm not doing interviews, I'll be going through records."

She looked as if she wanted to protest again, to tell him no one at the hospital had done anything wrong, but then she gave a little sigh as if she knew any protest wouldn't do any good. "All right."

He felt as if he had to tell her this lunch hadn't been all about his investigation because he finally had to admit to himself it hadn't. "I enjoyed lunch with you, Isobel."

She didn't say anything, just stared at him.

He leaned in a little closer. The scent of her lotion or her perfume reminded him of honeysuckle. If he kissed her, would she taste as sweet as she smelled?

If he kissed her—

Mentally he swore and shifted away.

She opened the door and quickly climbed out.

Neil watched her walk up the path to the door. She didn't look back.

And neither did he. Something told him his attraction to Isobel Suarez could bring him nothing but trouble.

On Monday afternoon, Isobel stopped to say hello to the nurses at the desk on the surgical floor, then continued down the hall and rapped lightly on the door to Florence MacGregor's room. Her son, West, worked in the accounting department at the hospital.

As a high thready voice called for her to come in, Isobel pushed open the door. "How are you doing, Florence?"

The thin, petite lady almost looked swamped by white in the hospital bed. Her surgery had been recent—on Friday—and she was still pale with dark circles under her eyes. This was her second hip replacement. Her first had been about six months ago. She'd done well with that operation. But Isobel and the staff had noticed disorientation and memory problems even back then. Isobel had spoken to West about it, believing Florence should be evaluated for Alzheimer's. But as far as Isobel knew, West hadn't done that yet.

Isobel drew up a chair beside the bed and sat down. "How are you feeling today?"

"My hip hurts. West said you might be stopping in because I can't go home when I leave here." She sounded upset by that.

"No, I'm afraid you can't. Remember when you went to Southside Rehab after your last operation?"

Florence's eyes were troubled. "I remember exercising. I should be feeling better, don't you think? My surgery was so long ago."

Isobel realized reality for Florence slipped from now to the past, even to the future. "You just had your second surgery on Friday. That's only three days ago."

"Three days?" She looked down at her hip and leg and frowned. "Maybe I can't think straight because of the pain medicine they give me."

With Florence's first surgery, the staff had thought that might be the case. But a nurse had made notes on the intake sheet that Florence's memory seemed to fade in and out. Ella Wilder, her orthopaedic surgeon, had noted the same was true during her visits and checkups.

Isobel and West had spoken more than once about the responsibility of elderly parents and how they felt about it. They were of like minds. West lived with his mother to watch over her. However, Isobel was afraid Florence couldn't stay by herself even during the day for much longer even if she recovered completely from surgery. The staff at the rehabilitation hospital would talk about that with West, she was sure.

Isobel noticed the beautiful bouquet of flowers on the windowsill in a glass vase. "What pretty flowers."

"West sent them," Florence said proudly. "He knows I like pink and purple." There were pink carnations and purple mums, tall lilies, too.

"West came in just a little while ago to eat lunch with me. Have you had your lunch, dear?"

Isobel smiled at Florence's concern for her well-being. Her

lunch had been yogurt and salad in between patient visits. "Yes, I did have my lunch. Was yours good?"

"Oh, yes, very good. I had…I had…I know I had meat loaf yesterday. What did I have today?" Her blue eyes were confused and she looked frustrated. "I hate when I can't remember. I know West worries about that. He worries about other things too and I—" She stopped abruptly.

"What other things, Florence?"

Florence thought about Isobel's question, looked a little guilty, and then said, "Oh, I don't know. I can't remember that, either."

But this time, Isobel wasn't so sure that Florence didn't remember. What was she hesitating to say?

"Have you had any visitors besides West?"

"Lily. We've been friends for a long time."

"I'm glad she came. Maybe she can visit you while you're working on getting stronger, too."

"You mean at that place where I'm going to have physical therapy?"

"Yes. West and I will sit down with you tomorrow and show you the pictures from two different facilities. He's going to show you the one he thinks is best for you."

"He has pictures at home, too…in his desk."

After Florence's first surgery, she'd been transferred to Southside Rehab Facility. But her son hadn't been entirely satisfied with her care. So this time, he'd also gathered brochures on Pine Ridge Rehab.

Isobel checked her watch and saw that if she didn't leave now, she'd be late for a meeting in a conference room in the tower. Walnut River General had four floors but it also boasted a tower that had been a later addition, with conference rooms, boardrooms and guest suites for consulting physicians. The new chief of staff himself, Owen Randall, had asked her to attend this meeting so she didn't want to be late. The way this day was going, she might be here until nine o'clock tonight answering Neil's questions after she finished with her last case.

When she thought about Neil, her tummy fluttered and she remembered the way he'd leaned close to her in the car… when she'd thought he might even kiss her. But of course he wouldn't do that. Her own reaction to him had just colored her perception.

She had so many questions where he was concerned. Why had he changed careers? Why was there distance between him and his parents? Had he taken her to lunch to further his investigation…or because he liked her?

She might never know the answers.

"Why are you frowning, Isobel? Are you troubled by something?"

Florence's mind might be fading into the past, but she was still caring and helpful and kind. Isobel could see why West was determined to take care of his mother the best way he knew how.

"I'm sorry I can't spend more time with you, but I've been called to a meeting that starts in a few minutes and I don't want to be late." Standing, she pushed her chair back and then laid her hand on top of Florence's. "I'll stop in again tomorrow with West and we'll talk about rehab."

"Thank you for coming by. I wish West would meet a nice girl like you. Then he wouldn't worry about me so much."

Isobel just smiled and waved goodbye as she left Florence's room. From what Isobel knew of West MacGregor, he went for the intelligent, geeky types. He'd been dating someone in the records department but Isobel hadn't seen him with anyone lately. His hours were long ones, too, and with taking care of his mother…

Isobel knew all about those commitments.

Neil strode into the conference room knowing full well no one wanted him there. Owen Randall—with his silver hair and stocky build, his red tie perfectly knotted—came over as soon as he spotted him.

"I still don't understand why you'd want to sit in on a meeting to discuss the hospital's possible investment in a fitness center with a warm-water pool. No insurance would even be involved. This would be a center for recuperating patients who could follow a regimen of their own because they no longer need direct patient care."

Neil wasn't only at Walnut River General to investigate insurance fraud. Someone from the hospital was feeding his office information, and they didn't know who their informant was. Neil wanted to find that out as well as get to the bottom of the allegations. If he could put his finger on the informant, he might be able to figure out if this was a move by someone who wanted the takeover to take place quickly, or if it was someone who was genuinely worried about the way Walnut River General did its business. His interviews so far had turned up nothing.

Except a mighty potent interest in Isobel Suarez.

Trying to brush Isobel from his mind, and not entirely succeeding, he gave the chief of staff an answer. "I'm going to investigate every aspect of this hospital, right side up and inside out, any way I have to. You might as well get used to that." He was investigating in his get-it-done-by-the-book manner.

Randall didn't like his answer one bit and Neil could see that. "I want this investigation over and done with so we can fight this takeover with our armor intact."

"Then tell everyone to cooperate with me," Neil suggested.

"I have," Randall returned indignantly. "And so has J. D. Sumner."

"Where *is* the hospital administrator today?"

"He had a meeting in Pittsfield. There's a trauma center there and if he likes what he sees, we'll model ours after theirs."

Neil had to admit the people he'd talked to here seemed like good people, but he knew from experience the real story was often hidden beneath the surface.

Although Peter Wilder and his fiancée, Bethany Halloway, gave him a nod, none of the other board members acknowledged his presence. He was used to being treated as an outsider and an enemy. But sometimes he wondered what it would be like to be an *insider.*

Owen had just introduced the board member who was going to run the meeting when Isobel opened the door and came hurrying in.

"Sorry I'm late," she murmured, slipping into the empty seat across from Neil. When she saw him, she looked surprised, but then she gave him a little smile.

He didn't know why that smile was so welcome. Why it warmed some place cold inside of him. Or why Isobel suddenly seemed to be the only other person in the room.

Paul Monroe, a board member who owned his own contracting firm, stood at the head of the table holding a sheaf of papers in his hand. He passed a handout to each person at the table. "This is the result of our feasibility study. There's no question that a fitness center subsidized by clients as well as the hospital would be a success in Walnut River. With the number of residents in the general community who we believe would use this facility, we could easily break even or turn over a small profit."

One of the female board members asked, "And how would this be different from a health club?"

"Isobel, would you like to answer that?" Monroe asked, then went on to explain to the board, "Isobel has contacts with medical personnel, rehab facilities and doctors' offices that she deals with. She left questionnaires in all those offices and doctors had their patients fill them out."

Isobel looked a bit flustered, but stood and smiled at the group. "Anyone who would use this fitness center would need a prescription from his or her primary physician, which would indicate a medical condition. On the questionnaires many patients commented that they hate the regimen, the cost and the insurance hassles with physical therapy. With this center, they would pay a monthly fee, like a commercial gym."

"Would needing to lose weight apply?" asked a male board member who was about twenty pounds overweight.

"It would," Isobel answered, then continued, "As long as the patient is being monitored by his doctor."

"Why a warm-water pool?" the man next to Neil asked. "Who would want to swim laps in warm water?"

Isobel didn't seem ruffled at all as she answered calmly, "If a patient can swim laps, he probably wouldn't need the use of *this* pool. But anyone with arthritis, fibromyalgia, sports injuries, even continued rehabilitation after a stroke would benefit from a warm-water pool." She gestured to a pretty young woman. "Melanie, do you want to explain the benefits?"

Melanie Miller introduced herself as a physical therapist and Neil listened with half an ear. His attention was still on Isobel—her sparkling brown eyes, the professional way she fielded questions, the energy she brought to a room. She was wearing a conservative royal-blue suit, yet the silky top under her jacket was feminine. She wore a silver chain around her neck with one dangling pearl. He was too far away to catch the scent of perfume but he remembered the honeysuckle sweetness he'd inhaled on Saturday.

While Melanie answered questions, Isobel took her seat again, and her gaze met his, once, twice, three times. After a moment or two, maybe feeling the same connection he did, she looked down at her notes, at another board member, anywhere but at him.

Was this attraction one-sided?

Damn it, there shouldn't be any attraction. Isobel was under investigation just like everyone else.

The discussion continued for about a half hour and then, as at most meetings like this, nothing was decided except that the hospital would have to consult with a fund-raising expert.

Randall took the floor once more. "I'll send a memo to all of you as to the time and place of our next meeting. We'll be sure J.D. is present so he can give us his thoughts, as well as any other staff member who is interested. Thank you all for your time. Your attendance is appreciated."

Neil took note of which board members spoke to other board members, and of how Melanie conversed animatedly with Isobel. Most important, he noticed who seemed to be the most hostile, who ignored him, and who didn't seem to care that he was there. Nonchalantly he stood and walked out into the hall, catching bits and pieces of conversations.

When Isobel emerged, she saw him propped near a window, merely observing. The hallway was empty for the moment as she approached him. "I was surprised to see you at the meeting."

"I'm poking my nose into everybody's business. That should ruffle feathers and shake loose some information."

Another board member exited the conference room, spied Neil, and headed in the opposite direction.

"I'm sorry everyone's being so cool to you."

He shrugged. "It goes with the territory. I have a thick hide. I can take it."

"I imagine you can, but it's not a pleasant way to work."

Much of his work wasn't pleasant, but it *was* challenging. The only thing he didn't like particularly was all the traveling. That traveling had broken up his marriage. At least that's what he and Sonya had blamed it on. Now he wasn't so sure. He'd done a lot of soul-searching since his divorce and a contributing factor was definitely his penchant for keeping his own counsel, for not letting anyone get too close, including his ex-wife. During the marriage he hadn't realized he was closing Sonya out. But afterward…afterward he'd understood he'd closed people out since his brother had died when Neil was in high school. He had good reasons for wanting to protect himself, for not confiding in anyone, for dodging his feelings. Preventing self-disclosure had become a habit, a habit he'd taken with him into his marriage.

Skipping over Isobel's comment, he said, "You seem to be the go-to person for Randall on this project."

"Peter Wilder suggested Mr. Randall include me in the discussion."

"The Dr. Wilder who was chief of staff after his father died?"

"That was only temporary. Peter's not a paper-pusher. He likes treating patients. But yes, he's the one."

"And Peter Wilder is Ella Wilder's brother, correct?"

"Yes."

"And also Dr. David Wilder's brother—the physician who was called in to help with the little girl who needed plastic surgery."

"Yes. Their father was well-loved as chief of staff. He was an extraordinary man. His children are as dedicated as he was. Except…"

"Except?" Neil prompted.

"Anna Wilder. She's Peter, Ella and David's adopted sister. Ironically, she happens to work for Northeastern Health-Care."

Neil looked shocked. "Now *that* I hadn't heard."

Isobel looked troubled. "I probably shouldn't have said anything."

"I'm glad you did. Isobel, I need to know the ins and outs of what's going on here right now. That's the only way I'll get to the truth."

Two more board members and Owen Randall emerged from the conference room. All three exchanged looks when they saw Neil and Isobel together talking.

Isobel's cheeks reddened and she murmured, "I have to get back to work."

"You'll stop at my office before you go home?"

"Yes." Without a "goodbye," "see you later" or "it was nice talking to you," she hurried to the elevator.

Randall was staring after Isobel thoughtfully.

Neil would give her a couple of minutes to get away from him and then he'd take the elevator to his office. Better yet, maybe he'd just take the stairs.

He knew why Isobel had hurried away. She was a member of this hospital community. She had respect here and lots of friends. She didn't want to be seen consorting with the enemy.

Neil hated the idea of being Isobel's enemy. His job had never interfered with a personal relationship with a woman before.

But there was *no* personal relationship here. He was just going to do his job and return to Boston.

So why had Isobel's rushing away gotten to him?

Chapter Three

Neil definitely had a height advantage.

When Isobel entered his office and he stood, she felt small. His size could be intimidating if he wanted it to be.

He'd been working at the table again, printouts spread all over it. He motioned to the extra chair. "Did you get a breather or did you come straight from working?"

"No breather. I had a consultation with one of the doctors about a patient."

She lowered her briefcase and purse to the floor and sank into the chair. She knew she had to be alert and on guard in this setting with Neil. Maybe in all settings with Neil. She didn't know if he separated the personal from the professional and couldn't take the chance that he didn't. She'd been a little too open during their lunch, not that she'd revealed anything she shouldn't have. She wasn't a guarded person by nature.

But she didn't know what Neil might use against her, against other personnel, against the hospital.

He looked at her as if sensing her apprehension. "Isobel, I'm not going to attack you," Neil said quietly.

"Of course, you aren't. I mean, I didn't think you would."

"As soon as you sat in that chair, your shoulders squared, your chin came up and you looked at me as if I were the enemy. I'm not."

But his saying it didn't make it so.

He sighed. "Let's start with something easy."

She didn't comment.

"You mentioned Anna Wilder works for Northeastern HealthCare. Has that caused a rift in the Wilder family?"

"You'd have to ask the Wilders." Peter had come to her last month in confidence to talk over the situation. She was afraid she hadn't been much help. Peter, David and Ella were on one side and Anna on the other. Every conversation they had seemed to push them further apart.

"I *will* talk to the Wilders," Neil assured her. "But I just wondered if Peter, David and Ella are really all on the same side. They might portray a united front, but could one of them want to help their sister? Could one of them be feeding information to my office?"

This wasn't the kind of questioning Isobel had expected. She'd thought he'd be asking about dollars and cents and patient charges.

Considering his question, she answered honestly, "I think it's highly unlikely. Peter, Ella and David are very straightforward in what they believe and they've all been vocal in how they feel about the takeover."

"But it's possible one of them could be sympathetic to Anna?"

She thought about her strong relationship with her sister, Debbie, and her brother, Jacob, and remembered what Ella had told her about the bonds between her and her adopted sister, Anna, when they were small. "I suppose it's possible."

Neil looked thoughtful and glanced down at the legal pad where Isobel could see a list of scratchings. She couldn't make out most of the writing, but her name was clearly printed at the top.

"I understand no one objected when Peter Wilder temporarily took over the position of chief of staff." Neil was fishing again. "Was anyone surprised when Peter didn't keep the position? Were *you* surprised?"

"Actually, I wasn't sure what Peter would do. I mean, I knew patient care was important to him. He's the epitome of a caring doctor. Yet maintaining his father's legacy was important, too. So I imagine the decision he made wasn't easy. In the end, I guess he did what he knew would make himself happy, and that was taking care of patients. Why are you so interested in the Wilders?"

"Because they're involved in everything—the running of the hospital, interaction with patients, the board, as well as their connection to the takeover. I imagine a family like that is not only respected but can make enemies just by being who they are. If, as you believe, the allegations my office is investigating have no merit, I have to look for other reasons why anyone would want me to give them credence."

Could someone be feeding false information to the state Attorney General's Office because he or she had a grudge against the Wilders? That was possible, Isobel surmised.

"Tell me about David Wilder. Why did he return to Walnut River?"

Isobel leaned forward and accused, "That's another one of those questions you already know the answer to."

A small smile played across Neil's lips and she couldn't seem to move her gaze from them.

"Indulge me," Neil suggested once again.

"David's a renowned plastic surgeon. He came back to Walnut River to help a little girl who needed reconstructive work done."

"Not because of the takeover attempt?"

"I don't think so. But I don't know for sure. He probably knew about it but he was here to help Courtney's little girl."

"Courtney Albright who works in the gift shop?"

"Yes."

"But she and David Wilder are now engaged."

"Yes."

"Do you know if his airfare was charged to a hospital account?"

"I don't know. But if it was, there wouldn't be anything wrong with that, would there? After all, if he was asked to come as a consultant—"

The beeping of Isobel's cell phone in her purse interrupted them. "I need to check that," she said. "It might be my father. With him at home alone—"

"Go ahead." Neil didn't look impatient or even annoyed, and that surprised her. Didn't he want to get this questioning over and done with as much as she did?

She opened her phone, saw her sister's number on the screen and became alarmed. What if something *had* happened to their dad?

"Debbie, what's wrong? Is Dad okay?"

"Sorry to scare you, Iz. Dad's okay as far as I know, but I need your help."

"What's wrong?"

"Chad had an away game and his bus broke down on the way home."

Isobel's nephew Chad was sixteen and hoping to get a baseball scholarship to college. Since his mom and dad had divorced two years ago, he'd become more quiet, more withdrawn. He obviously missed his father who had moved to the Midwest to take a better job and start a new life. Chad was a big help with his younger brother and sister but sometimes Isobel thought Debbie's older son felt he had to take his dad's place, and that could be a burden for a sixteen-year-old.

"What do you need?"

"Can you come over and watch Meg and Johnny while I go get Chad? I wouldn't lay this on you but I can't find anybody else."

Isobel's niece was six and her nephew was four. "I can come over but I'm in a meeting right now and I'll have to stop and pick up Dad first. He's been alone so much lately, I hate to have him spend the evening at the house by himself."

"Isobel." Neil's voice cut into her conversation with her sister.

"Hold on a minute, Debbie."

"What's going on?" Neil asked.

Succinctly she told him.

"I have a few more questions for you but they aren't as important as helping your sister. Why don't I go pick up your father and bring him to wherever you need him to be?"

Isobel was stunned. "Are you serious? Why would you want to help?"

"Maybe because I'm a stranger in town and I have nothing else to do."

Sure, Neil might just want to fill his time, but she saw a

kindness in him she hadn't seen in a man for a long while. Should she accept his offer? What would he expect in return?

"Isobel?" her sister called to her from the phone.

"What?"

"The boys are standing by the side of the road and I really want to get there as soon as I can. Can you cut your meeting short?"

Isobel's gaze met Neil's. She wasn't sure what she saw there. Curiosity? Interest? Desire? Was her imagination tricking her into thinking this man might be interested in her? She didn't even want his interest, did she?

Yet being closed in this office with him, inhaling the musky scent of his cologne, appreciating the baritone of his voice as well as his desire to get to the truth, she had to admit she did want to get to know him better, in spite of the consequences or the risk.

"You're sure you want to do this?" she asked him.

He nodded. "I'm sure. I can have all this packed up in three minutes. Tell your sister you'll be there as soon as you can."

As Isobel did just that, she wondered if she was making a terrible mistake.

Neil gave Isobel's sister's kitchen a quick study as he pushed open the screen door for John Suarez and juggled two pizza boxes.

A little girl came running to meet the older man, her dark-brown pigtails flying. She looked to be about the age of a first-grader.

"Grandpa, Grandpa. Will you play dominoes with us? Aunt Iz said I should ask."

Aunt Iz? Neil had to smile as he followed her father

inside the cheery kitchen with its purple-pansy and yellow-gingham theme.

A little boy in jeans and a Spider-Man T-shirt added, "Will you play with us? Will you play with us?" to his sister's question.

Neil leaned close to Isobel. "Aunt Iz?"

"Only my family uses that nickname, so don't get any ideas."

He inhaled the honeysuckle scent surrounding her and right away noticed her change of clothes to jeans and a powder-blue T-shirt with a sleeping cat on the front. Printed under the white feline, the print said Don't wake me unless there's an emergency.

When she spied him reading her T-shirt, she explained, "I always keep a duffel bag in my car with a change. It comes in handy." Monitoring what her niece and nephew were doing, she warned gently, "Don't pull on Grandpa's arm."

"I smell pizza," the little boy said and came over to stand in front of Neil. "Who are you?"

Neil hadn't been around children much, but he appreciated forthrightness in anyone. He crouched down to the little boy's level, pizza boxes and all. "I'm Neil Kane. I'm working at the hospital right now with your aunt, and I brought supper."

The supper part of the explanation intrigued Isobel's nephew most. "Mom only lets us order pizza one time a week." He held up his index finger and stared at the boxes with longing. "I like pepperoni. Did you bring pepperoni?"

Neil laughed and stood. "Yes, I did. Your grandfather said that was your favorite."

"Can we eat now?" the boy pushed.

Isobel ruffled her nephew's hair. "Why don't you tell Mr. Kane your name first."

"My name is Johnny, after Grandpa." He pointed to his sister. "And her name is Meg. *Now* can we eat?"

"You get the napkins. I'll get the silverware. Neil, can you set those on the table?"

Isobel was a manager, no doubt about that.

After they were all seated at the table and Isobel's father had rolled his pizza so he could eat it one-handed, she asked him, "How did physical therapy go today?"

"They're trying to turn me into a muscle man. I just want to be able to use my arm again."

"You're doing exercises with repetitions now?" she asked.

"Yeah." Isobel's dad studied his grandchildren happily munching their pizza and then turned to Isobel and Neil. "This was a good idea, Iz."

"It was Neil's," she admitted, looking up at him, a slight flush on her cheeks.

Was she feeling the heat, too? Had she been fantasizing about a kiss between them? Maybe more?

As if maybe, just maybe, the same thoughts were running through her mind, she broke eye contact and concentrated on cutting her pizza into little pieces.

"Do you always eat it like that?" Neil asked her.

"I'm only having one piece and it will stretch it out."

"My daughter believes she needs to lose weight," John explained. "What do *you* think, Neil?"

"Dad!" Isobel protested, sounding horrified he'd bring up the subject at the table.

"I think Isobel's perfect the way she is," Neil said, meaning it.

John Suarez cocked his head and with a twinkle in his eye, asked, "How long are you going to be in Walnut River?"

"As long as it takes to finish my investigation. Probably about three weeks."

"That's a shame. Do you think you'll ever consider settling down some day?"

"Dad!" Isobel protested again.

"I don't know, Mr. Suarez. I've been doing this job for a long time. Traveling is a big part of it."

"Life changes. Needs change," Isobel's dad advised sagely. "Have you ever been serious about someone? Just wanted to be where they were?"

This time when Neil glanced at Isobel, she didn't protest, she just looked mortified. She murmured, "Dad doesn't respect boundaries."

"Boundaries, schmoundaries," her dad muttered. "Maybe it's a question you've wanted to ask him and didn't have the guts."

Isobel looked as if she wanted to throw her napkin at her father. But instead, she put it in her lap, her lips tight together. She was probably biting her tongue.

Meg and Johnny seemed oblivious to the conversation as they stole pieces of pepperoni from each other's slices of pizza.

Neil knew he could joke off the question. However, if Isobel had wanted to ask it and was too shy to, he might as well give her the answer. "I was married once, but traveling was hard on the relationship."

"That's why you split?" John pressed.

"Not entirely. But it *was* a major stumbling block. My ex-wife and I were naive to think we would stay close when we were miles apart most of the week."

Isobel's father finished another roll of pizza and wiped his mouth with his napkin. "Naive... Or maybe the two of you didn't want to *be* close."

"All right, Dad." Isobel stood. "Meg, Johnny, if you're

finished playing with each other's pizza, why don't you wash up? We could set out the dominoes on the coffee table and we'll all play a game." She looked at Neil. "Unless you need to leave."

He was still trying to digest the fact that Isobel's father had gotten to the bottom of the problem with his marriage with such clarity. "No, I don't have to leave yet." Then he turned to John. "How long were you married?"

"When Brenna died, we'd been married forty-one years. We weren't apart even one night, not even when she had our babies. I remember they tried to keep me out of the labor room with Isobel, but I wouldn't let them. I told them Brenna was my wife and I was staying. When she got sick—" He shook his head as if the memories hurt him deeply to remember. "I stayed in that hospital room every night. My doctor got me special permission because he understood. When you love someone, you walk through hell for them. Getting a crick in my neck sleeping on one of those hospital chairs was nothing compared to the comfort of holding her hand." He sighed. "But I don't think young people understand that kind of love anymore."

"You and Mom had something special. Jacob, Deb and I knew that," Isobel remarked in a quiet voice.

"Then why can't the three of you find it?" her father demanded. "Jacob runs off here and there as if he's searching for something and he doesn't even know what it is. Debbie…Debbie divorced her husband after his affair. They didn't even try to work it out."

"Dad, you don't know—"

"What else Ron did to her," he finished as if he'd heard it all before. "Maybe I don't. She won't talk about it with me. And then there's *you*. You work, work, work. I think that's the reason you and Tim broke up, though you'll never tell me the truth about *that,* either."

The tension and strain of having dirty laundry shaken out in front of Neil made Isobel's body taut. Beside her, Neil could feel it. Then she took a very big breath, seemed to somehow relax her muscles, and said to her father without any anger at all, "I know you must have a good reason for wanting to talk about all this in front of Neil, but it's making me uncomfortable and it's probably making him uncomfortable, too. Can we just relax the rest of the night? Play a little dominoes and talk about anything that isn't serious?"

John waved at his daughter. "That's her assertive, social-worker's side coming out. I hate feeling like I'm being handled," he grumbled. Then he smiled at his middle child. "All right, I'll keep my mouth shut."

"I don't want you to keep your mouth shut, Dad, but I would imagine that you and Neil can find a hundred topics more fascinating, especially since you both watch the History Channel."

Neil couldn't help but chuckle. When he looked over at John, the older man gave him a wink. "My daughter does have a point."

Isobel wasn't simply a caring daughter. She was an intelligent and beautiful woman who could turn him on with just the hint of a smile.

But this attraction could go nowhere. When he left, he'd go back to his life and she'd stay in hers.

End of story.

An hour later, when Isobel's sister and her older son came home, Neil was making a quarter disappear for Johnny. The little boy had gotten tired of dominoes.

After Chad and Neil were introduced, Neil asked him, "So do the Sox have a chance at the pennant this year?"

Chad had reddish-brown hair like Isobel and the same brown eyes. He gave Neil a crooked smile. "As good a chance as last year. You follow baseball?"

"Since I was eight."

"You play sports in school?" Chad asked.

"Basketball."

"What did you play?"

"Center," Neil answered. "How about you?"

"Point guard."

"So you're busy all year."

"Mom wants to see me busy so I stay out of trouble."

His mother didn't deny it. Debbie was taller and thinner than Isobel, but had the same dark-brown eyes. Her hair wasn't as curly and it was more brown than red but the resemblance was there.

Chad spotted the pizza box. "Was there any left over?"

Neil nodded. "It's in the refrigerator."

Johnny came running over and tugged on his brother's arm. "He can make a quarter disappear."

Chad gave his brother's shoulder a little bump. "You can make quarters disappear when you go to the candy machine in the mall."

"Not like that," Johnny protested. "Show him," he demanded.

Neil suddenly realized how much he was enjoying the evening, how long it had been since he'd spent time with a real family. During investigations he usually felt isolated. Each meeting was a confrontation and he spent every night by himself. Looking around at this close family, he realized how tired he was of the whole routine. His gaze fell on Isobel. She was sitting on the sofa with Meg and tying her niece's shoe. She held the little foot in her hand so gently, smiled so tenderly at Meg, that Neil actually felt his heart lurch.

What was happening to him?

Whatever it was, it unsettled him. Didn't he have the life he wanted? Hadn't he decided an intimate relationship only brought pain and disappointment?

Yet whenever he looked at Isobel, he had a yearning inside that told him that maybe the life he'd been leading wasn't fulfilling enough.

Disconcerted by his thoughts, his life, an investigation that seemed to be going nowhere fast, he checked his watch. "I'd better be going. I still have some work I want to do tonight."

"Thanks for bringing me over here," John said, "and for the pizza. Don't be a stranger. I could use a little company now and then."

"I'll keep that in mind," Neil told the older man.

Isobel crossed to him and walked him to the door. He'd discarded his suit coat long ago, tugged down his tie, rolled up his shirtsleeves. She was taking him in, just as he was taking her in. The chatter of her family behind them in the kitchen reminded him they weren't alone.

"You have a nice family."

"They liked you. I could tell."

"That's because I know how to make quarters disappear."

Isobel laughed. "I think they like you for more than magic tricks."

"You're fortunate to be able to be around people who care about you."

"Sometimes they annoy me," she admitted with a sly grin. "But most of the time I know they love me. I'm sorry you don't have that kind of support."

Neil shrugged. "I've gotten used to it. I'm basically a loner so I don't miss it."

Isobel tilted her head and studied him. "I think you've convinced yourself of that, but I don't know if it's true."

He wasn't going to delve into his personal history or give her a glimpse into his family's dynamics. They hardly knew each other. Yet in some ways he felt Isobel knew him better than most people did.

He reached out and brushed a few curls away from her cheek, his fingers burning from the contact. Touching Isobel was such a temptation!

He caught the spark of desire in her eyes and fell back on the investigation that was always between them. "I still have some questions for you, but my next few days are booked solid. I'll call your office at the end of the week and we can set up another appointment."

He found himself not wanting to leave Isobel and that was absolutely crazy. Also, out of the question. He always left. That's how he lived his life.

Alone.

As soon as Neil drove away, Isobel touched her cheek where his fingers had grazed her skin. She could still feel the tingling heat of his touch.

Debbie opened the screen door and stepped outside. "Your taste in men has improved. This one is not only good-looking, but he seems to like family."

"My taste in men had nothing to do with Neil being here. We were having a meeting and he offered to help out."

"He wouldn't have offered if he wasn't interested."

"In me?" Isobel laughed. "I doubt that. We're on opposite sides of an investigation."

"He looked at you as if he's interested. I was watching."

She and Debbie didn't have many secrets. "The truth is—

I don't know if I can trust him. He might just want to get more information out of me."

"You have good radar, Izzy. What's it telling you?"

"My radar usually isn't compromised by an—"

"Attraction?" Debbie smiled. "You like him."

"Even if I did, that doesn't matter. He'll be leaving in a few weeks. You know I'm not the type to live in the moment."

"Maybe living in the moment wouldn't be such a bad idea. It might even be fun. Think about it, Iz…having fun. If you're given the chance, maybe you should try it."

Isobel didn't want to have fun now and exchange that for heartache later.

But when she thought of Neil's touch and the exciting golden light in his eyes, she was afraid he could convince her otherwise.

Chapter Four

As West MacGregor hurried down the hall to his mother's room on Tuesday afternoon, one of the nurses waved to him. Tami had a nice smile and was always friendly. With her divorce final now, maybe he should ask her out. He straightened the knot on his tie. Unlike many men, he felt comfortable in a suit and tie. His professional attire defined him, gave him purpose and his place in the world. As an accountant at Walnut River General, his services were necessary to the running of the hospital. Tami was one of the people here who respected his position.

His position.

He'd led his life on the straight and narrow—his mother had taught him well. His father had split before he'd entered first grade. His mom's secretarial skills and her promotion to executive secretary to the vice president of an engineering firm had supported them well enough for her to buy a small house and even give West money toward college. He owed her. He owed her for raising him right. He owed her for making sure he had a place to go after school when she had to work. He owed her for just being there whether it was for his school concert or parents' day at college. She'd been a wonderful mother, giving him everything she possibly could, and he wasn't going to let her down now when she needed him most.

That's why being a corporate spy didn't bother him as much as it should.

West glanced down at the brochures for rehab facilities in his hand, then thought about the "other" pamphlet in his desk at home, along with the information packet about Fair Meadows. Fair Meadows had everything his mother would need when she could no longer stay alone. They could be at that point in four to six months, maybe a year if they were lucky.

After she'd recuperated from her first hip operation, he'd taken her to Boston for an evaluation. He'd wanted the best doctors in the Alzheimer's field looking after her. He also hadn't wanted hospital scuttlebutt talking about it, her or them. Driving her to Boston had enabled him to do what he was doing now without throwing any suspicion on himself.

He wasn't doing anything illegal, exactly. He was just feeding information that was a bit skewed to the Massachusetts Attorney General's Office, as a favor for Northeastern HealthCare. The conglomerate was funding his mother's care until she needed to be admitted to Fair Meadows. Not only was he receiving a lump sum for whatever his mother might need, but the head honcho at Northeastern HealthCare had promised to find a room for her at Fair Meadows when she needed it. The facility's waiting list was a mile long.

West really had no choice but to help NHC. His salary wasn't enough to cover long-term care, and he would not let his mother become a ward of the state in some second-rate nursing home where she'd be miserable and he'd worry daily about her care. She deserved more than that, and he was going to see that she got it.

As West approached his mother's room, he heard voices coming from inside and recognized Isobel Suarez's. He liked Isobel—he really did. They had the same consideration for family. But he'd caught her talking to Neil Kane more than once and that worried him. Not because they were talking, but because they'd looked *friendly* while they were talking. If everyone treated Kane like the enemy, it would take him longer to get to the bottom of the information West had fed his office. He'd find most of the allegations groundless, though a few could be considered in the gray area. But the longer Kane's investigation took, the more headway North-eastern HealthCare could make in staging their takeover.

West strode into his mother's room determinedly cheerful as he always tried to be when he was with her.

She spotted him and her blue eyes danced a little, the way they used to. "Here's West now. Maybe he remembers that trip I took to Puerto Rico with Lily and Mary."

The trip to Puerto Rico. West had heard about that often but it had taken place before he was born.

Instead of walking down that road of conversation, he nodded to Isobel, smiled and suggested, "How about considering taking a trip when you're finished with rehab? You always wanted to visit Las Vegas. We can play the slots and go to shows."

"Could we really do that?"

"I have vacation time and it would be a great incentive for you to get better fast."

Isobel was taking in their conversation. "So you like to play the slot machines?" she teased his mother.

"West took me to Atlantic City a few times. I won a two-hundred-dollar jackpot once."

That had been about five years ago. Sometimes his mother's memory was more detailed than his. He'd once heard that if there was a lot of feeling attached to memories, they lasted longer. Holding up the brochures, he went to the bed and pulled a second chair over beside his mother. "Okay, Mom. I know Isobel's time is limited. Let me tell you why I think you should go to Pine Ridge this time around. Then you can tell me how you feel about it."

Isobel gave him an approving nod. They'd talked more than once about letting their parents make as many decisions as they could themselves to give them control over their lives.

He handed his mother the two brochures and while she examined them, he asked Isobel in a low voice, "How did your meeting with Kane go?"

Isobel looked disconcerted for a minute, maybe even a little guilty, but then she replied, "It went all right. But we were interrupted again. My sister needed me and I had to leave."

"I'm sorry. Anything serious?"

"No. Chad's bus broke down on the way home from the game and she needed me to babysit while she went to get him."

"So when do you talk to Kane again?"

"I'm not sure. Maybe at the end of the week. He said he has interviews lined up back-to-back for the next few days."

West frowned. "Yeah, I know. I'm one of them. Is he tough?"

"I don't know if *tough*'s the word. But his questions *are* pointed. And he doesn't like it when his interviewee hedges."

"That's what you tried to do?"

"*Tried* is the operative word," Isobel said with a small smile. "I'm sure we all feel a little defensive, but he cuts right through that."

From the bed, Florence pointed to the one brochure. "I like the one with the blue rooms and the dining room where everyone eats together."

West smiled. "That's Pine Ridge and that's my choice, too."

Somehow this was all going to work out. Then he could stop worrying about his mother and the rest of her golden years.

"Wait up," a now-familiar male voice called from the fourth-floor landing as Isobel hurried down the stairs. For the past few days she'd used the staircase at the back of the hospital, having decided the exercise would be much better for her.

Apparently Neil used the stairs, too. She waited halfway down the flight as he joined her. "Are the elevators too slow for you?" he asked with a smile.

"And sometimes too crowded. I was thinking about everything else I had to do this afternoon and didn't want to get caught up in a conversation."

When he frowned, she said quickly, "I didn't mean I don't want to talk to *you*."

"If you need to think, we can take the rest of the steps in companionable silence," he joked.

If he was walking beside her, she wouldn't be *able* to think.

"Thanks again for bringing my dad over to my sister's and buying the pizza."

"Your father's an interesting man. I enjoy talking with him."

She cocked her head. "What does *your* dad do?"

After a moment's hesitation, he answered her. "My father's a judge."

A judge who didn't get along with his son? "How long has he been a judge?" she asked, curious to know more about Neil's background.

"Since I was a teenager."

"Was that tough?"

Neil's expression, open and friendly before, was now closed and guarded. "I'd rather not talk about my father."

"I'm sorry. I just thought since we were talking about mine—" She didn't know where to go from there and now she felt awkward. "Never mind." She turned away from Neil and started down the stairs again.

But he caught her arm and was beside her before she could take another breath. "I told you, I'm not close to my family like you are to yours. Talking about the reasons why doesn't change anything."

She could tell him that talking might give him another perspective. She could tell him that talking *with* his family might even be better.

"I can hear the wheels turning," he said seriously. "I know in your professional position, you're good at mediation and counseling. But I don't want any counsel. And mediation isn't something my father would ever consider. So let's drop it."

"Sure," she murmured feeling unreasonably hurt.

She had no right to feel hurt. Neil Kane was nothing to her. They'd shared a few conversations. They'd enjoyed an evening with her family. But they weren't involved and probably never would be. If Neil was guarded in this area, he was probably guarded in others. He was probably wounded from his divorce. He probably didn't feel attracted to her at all, not the way she felt attracted to him.

She was trying hard not to show any emotion, but something must have shown. He took a step closer and cupped her chin in his palm. "Isobel," he said softly, with such tenderness Isobel's throat felt tight.

He ran his thumb along her cheekbone and she trembled. She knew he could feel it.

"Damn," he growled. "I never get involved or even friendly with someone in my investigation."

His finger was still on her cheek and she could feel it touching someplace deep inside. "Because you lose perspective?" she wanted to know.

"Because the guilty can seem innocent and the innocent can seem guilty. I never take the chance that I'm wrong. I always go by the book. It was the way I was raised, the way I was taught and the way I've lived my life."

So his father had an influence even though Neil hadn't wanted him to? She didn't ask that question out loud because she was too lost in the heat in Neil's eyes, too lost in the way he was looking at her.

There was complete silence in the stairwell. The steel fire doors kept the busy noise in the halls from entering the staircase. Her heart was pounding in her ears, racing with anticipation and expectation.

Neil's hand slid to her neck under her curly hair. The warmth of his skin felt so good...the touch of his fingers against her scalp so sensually right. When he tilted her head up and lowered his, she knew exactly what was going to happen. He paused just an instant in case she wanted to back away. She knew she *should* back away, but she definitely didn't want to. Curiosity and need were much stronger than any sense of propriety, or any admonition from her good sense that she was consorting with the enemy. Right now, Neil didn't feel like the enemy and she refused even to consider the fact that he might be.

It had been almost three years since she'd been kissed by a man…three years since she'd had any intimate contact at all. When Neil's lips touched hers, she savored the sensation, recognizing the chemistry that was stronger than any she'd ever experienced. She could shyly wait to see what he'd do next but she didn't. Her arms went around his neck and when they did, his tongue slid into her mouth. The material of his suit coat was smooth against her arms. His hair was thick and coarse under her fingers. The scent of his cologne and something more basic intoxicated her until she forgot she was a social worker who worked for Walnut River General and she became totally a woman in Neil Kane's arms.

When his tongue probed her mouth, she stroked against it and heard him groan. Pressed together on the narrow step, they hardly moved for fear they'd teeter off. But Neil's tongue moved, his hand on her back moved, and she pressed into him seeking his arousal, proving she was as hungry as he was. After his hands crept up and down her back, they settled in her hair. His fingers tangled in her curls as if they couldn't get enough of the feel of them.

Abruptly—all too soon—his hands stilled and he broke away. "I feel like a teenager in high school between classes."

She almost lost her balance and his arms went around her again. "Are you okay?"

"Just fine," she lied, still in a daze from the erotic sensations running through her.

"We wouldn't want anyone to see us together like this," he said somberly.

"No, we wouldn't," she agreed thinking about her career, her friendships, Neil's investigation.

"That's been an event waiting to happen since the moment we met."

Apparently he'd felt the sparks, too. Now that it had happened, she didn't know quite how to put her feelings into words. Taking a deep breath, she ran a hand through her hair, straightened her jacket, and pasted on a smile. "I have to get to Admissions. I have a meeting there in…" She checked her watch. "Ten minutes."

"I was on my way to X-ray. There are some reports there I need to look over."

She knew better than to ask questions because Neil wouldn't answer them.

They began descending the steps together but this time they didn't converse, and this time the silence wasn't companionable. There was too much electricity still crackling between them, too much uncertainty about what had happened and what should happen next.

When they stood silently on the first-floor landing, Neil pulled open the heavy fire door and Isobel preceded him through it. She heard voices right away—raised voices—just around the corner. She recognized them.

"I can't make Anna see reason any more than *you* can," Peter Wilder said to his brother David.

"Can't you talk sense into her?" David asked Ella. "You two used to be so close."

"*Used to be* is the operative phrase," Ella responded sadly. "Ever since she quit med school, too much distance has grown between us. It's partially my fault, partially the family's fault. I think Anna feels like an outsider with us because she's different in so many ways."

"Maybe so," David agreed. "But that doesn't excuse her now, working for a company that's trying to destroy Dad's legacy."

Peter added, "She doesn't see it that way. In fact, she

insists if Northeastern HealthCare takes over, we'll have access to the latest research and technology. She doesn't realize how the company's deluding her."

"They're in it for the money," David insisted. "And as long as she's working *for* them, she's working *against* us. Dad's lifelong pursuits and our careers don't seem to mean anything to her anymore."

Neil clasped Isobel's elbow and whispered in her ear, "We've got to let them know we're here." Taking a step back, he opened and closed the stairway door once more, letting it bang loudly.

The conversation around the corner stopped. Neil guided Isobel toward the Wilders. Ella smiled at Isobel. David eyed Neil suspiciously. Peter just looked resigned.

They would have walked by the Wilder clan, but Peter called out, "Isobel, may I speak with you?"

When Neil released her arm, she felt the absence of his touch. Neil nodded at Peter then his gaze met Isobel's. His expression was neutral but there was still heat in his eyes, heat that she felt, too. "I'll call your office soon," he said, "and we'll finish up with those questions." He didn't look back as he strode down the hall, leaving her with Peter Wilder.

"Everything okay?" Peter asked her, his gaze still on Neil's back.

"Everything's fine." If you could count being kissed senseless as being fine, she thought.

"Do you think you could clear a few minutes in your schedule for me? There's something I need to discuss with you. I'm tied up tomorrow. Thursday I have more wiggle room."

Isobel mentally went over her schedule for the week. There was never enough time in a day but she could give Peter a few minutes of her lunch hour. "I can see you at twelve-thirty on Thursday unless there's an emergency."

"That sounds good, thanks. Can you come to my office?"

Isobel knew that something had been troubling Peter lately. She'd assumed it was the takeover attempt and now the investigation. But maybe there was something else, something more personal. Whatever it was, she hoped she could help him with it. "Sure. I'll call you if something comes up."

After Peter turned away, Isobel hurried toward Admissions, all the while not thinking about Peter or the discussion she'd overheard with his family. Only one thing filled her mind—Neil's kiss and how she'd felt when she'd kissed him back.

"You're better than I thought you'd be," Chad muttered as Neil prevented another of the sixteen-year-old's shots from flying into the basket.

They were playing basketball in Chad's driveway and Neil was enjoying it. He'd been surprised when Isobel's nephew had phoned him earlier and asked if he'd like to shoot some hoops. Neil had agreed, knowing he could use the exercise, suspecting Chad wanted some older male company. He obviously missed his dad.

"We're even. I can't let you drop another one in," Neil insisted as a car drew up at the curb. It was Isobel's car.

He and Chad were hard at it again when Isobel walked up the driveway and stopped to watch them. "This is a surprise." Just that moment of inattention, of listening to her voice, was all Chad needed to score on Neil.

"I won," Chad crowed, then did something unexpected. He tossed the ball to Isobel.

She easily caught it.

"Want to play, Aunt Iz? I've got homework to do."

Isobel must have stopped at home before coming over.

She was dressed in jeans, a sweatshirt and running shoes. "Maybe Neil's not up for another game. You might have tired him out."

He could hear the mischief in Isobel's tone. She was daring him to play basketball with her. He never turned away from a dare. "We have a half hour of daylight left. I've got enough energy left to make eleven before you see five."

"You're on." She threw the ball to Neil and, taking her shoulder bag from her arm, she tossed it to Chad. "Take that inside, would you?"

Her nephew saluted, grinned and loped off. Isobel's fingers went to the waistband of her sweatshirt.

Neil found himself holding his breath as she pulled it up and over her head, revealing a red T-shirt that fitted snugly against her breasts and defined her waist. The next thing he knew, she'd pulled a headband out of her pocket and slipped it on. She looked too sexy for words. His mouth went dry and he didn't know how he was going to guard her when he'd much rather pull her into the garage and kiss her blind. He hadn't been able to forget their encounter in the stairwell—not one little detail of it.

"Ready when you are," she said sweetly.

He tossed the ball back to her. "Try to make a basket."

As they did a side dance, first to the left and then to the right, she asked, "So what are you doing here?"

When she tried to throw, he easily blocked her, snatched the ball, pivoted on one foot and shot. The ball swooped through the basket.

Catching it on a bounce, he handed it to her. "Try again." When she didn't move, he replied, "Chad called me and asked if I wanted to play basketball. I'd given him my card last night. Since I needed the exercise, I said yes."

Isobel dribbled thoughtfully. "He needs a male role model."

"How often does he see his dad?"

"Not often enough. A week in the summer, every other holiday." Craftily she slipped under Neil's arm and made a basket.

"So you're going to be sneaky," he teased.

"I aim to win."

"Not if I can help it."

They went at their game seriously then.

After Neil had scored two and Isobel one, he spotted the determination in her eyes. She was going to try to mow him down. He could have moved out of the way. He could have simply blocked her with one long arm. But the devil inside him made him stand perfectly still as he took her shoulder into his chest. She pushed and he didn't push back. Her curls were damp around her face, her breath was coming quick and hard, her breasts pushed into him and his arm came around her, holding her still. The ball fell from her hand, bounced and rolled away. When she looked up at him, the sizzle that had begun the moment they'd met snapped and sparked.

"I've got to…" she stopped. "I've got to get the ball."

"We could try another kiss instead of playing basketball," he suggested, his voice huskier than he'd like.

Instead of considering that option seriously, Isobel pushed a curl from her cheek, stepped back and responded, "My sister would ask too many questions if we did that."

"Maybe the questions would be worth it," he remarked.

"Maybe another kiss would take us somewhere we don't want to go." She looked as serious as he'd ever seen her and he knew she'd meant what she said.

"I'll get the ball." He needed to move before he took her

into his arms and kissed her into oblivion, making her wish they'd never stop.

The ball had rolled off the tarmacadam to the side of the garage where Chad's bike stood tilted against the forsythia bush.

Isobel came over and laid her hand over the seat on the racing bike.

"It's a nice bike." His comment was lame, but he needed something to get them back on easy footing.

"Chad's father gave it to him for his birthday. He told him to go down to the bike shop and pick out the one he wanted."

Neil stood by her shoulder, watching the shadows from falling dusk play over her face. "You sound as if you don't approve."

"Chad likes the bike and he knows his mom never could have afforded one like it. But the truth is, he would have appreciated his dad flying in here and spending a weekend with him a lot more."

Playing devil's advocate, Neil offered, "Airfare's expensive."

"If you have kids, they should come first, foremost and always," she said vehemently.

"You mean when *you* have kids that's what will happen."

"I think that's what should happen for every child. And yes, when I have children, I'll put them first."

He knew he was stepping into private territory but had to ask, "You want children?"

She looked down at the bike then up at him. "Very much. How about you?"

"I'd like to have kids someday. I've often thought about joining a Big Brother program."

"Why haven't you?"

"Because when I make a promise or a commitment, I believe in keeping it. My job sometimes takes me away unexpectedly and I wouldn't want to have to break a planned trip to a ball game or a movie or a day at the park. That wouldn't be fair."

"You said you believe in keeping promises and commitments. How did you look at getting a divorce?" As soon as she asked the question, her cheeks turned red and she shook her head. "Never mind. I'm sorry, I shouldn't have asked that."

If anyone else had asked, he probably would have gotten angry. But Isobel… He knew she wasn't making a judgment, she just wanted to know.

He slid his hands into his jeans pockets, gazed down the treelined street then answered her. "My marriage to Sonya never should have happened. I don't know how much in love we were. We met after I quit the Boston P.D. We liked each other. I think we saw marriage as a convenient way to get on with our lives."

He brought his gaze back to Isobel now. "But she didn't anticipate how much I'd be away. I didn't know how much I didn't want to share myself with anyone. Your father was right last night. Although neither of us understood what we were doing, we set boundaries we didn't want to cross. Since then, I've realized a couple can't have boundaries like that. They have to be willing to go deep into each other's territory, even if it's uncomfortable, and even if it hurts. Sonya and I weren't willing to do that, so we were never as close as we should have been. Eventually closeness became something we avoided."

The furrow between his brows deepened when he added, "In spite of that, I was committed to her and to our marriage.

But she was lonely, and she found someone who would make her feel less lonely. So to answer your question, I rationalized. I told myself she broke our vows first by being unfaithful. But in reality, maybe I broke our vows first by isolating myself from her."

"You've thought a lot about this," Isobel remarked quietly.

"I don't like to fail at anything. That's not the way I'm made. I grew up believing success was the bar every man should use to determine whether he's had a good life."

"We learn more when we fail than when we succeed," she suggested.

"You're a deep thinker, aren't you?" he asked.

She smiled wryly. "I'm not sure that's a compliment."

"Sure it is. You don't just consider the surface, but what's *below* the surface."

The screen door slammed. Chad jogged to where they were standing by his bike.

"We were just admiring it," Neil told him.

"I remembered I didn't put it away. I have to be careful and chain it up wherever I take it."

"Unlike *my* bike," Isobel teased him. "Nobody would want it."

"Do you ride much?" Neil asked.

Before she could answer, Chad did. "She used to ride at least ten miles every day. But she doesn't have time since she moved in with Grandpa. Do you ride?" Chad asked Neil.

"I used to. Now I spend more time on the life cycle at the gym than on a real bike."

"If you want to use mine to go riding with Aunt Iz, you can."

"I'll think about that," Neil assured him.

As Chad wheeled his bike around to the side door of the

garage, he called over his shoulder, "Mom said she baked a chocolate cake today. It's on the table whenever you're ready." Once Chad had taken the bike inside the garage, Neil realized the sun was setting and in a few minutes, the shadows would turn to darkness.

"We could go riding sometime," he said casually. It wasn't so much an invitation as a gambit to see what Isobel would say.

She shook her head. "That's probably not a good idea."

"Because we're on opposite sides?"

"Because your job is still the main priority in your life and when this investigation is over, you'll be headed for the next one."

She was right. If it weren't for his job—

Would he still be married?

Would he have kids?

Would he be living in the suburbs with a picket fence and a minivan?

"You're a planner, aren't you, Isobel? When you take a first step, you want to know what the next one will be."

"Is there anything wrong with that?" She sounded a bit defensive.

"I just wonder if you're not missing out on joy and excitement along the way."

"I'm not a risk taker."

"I'm sorry you're not." He'd like to get to know her better. He'd like to take more than a bike ride with her, but he could see she wasn't even going to give them the chance to enjoy a few hours together. He represented danger to her—danger because the risk of getting involved with him would only hurt her. He couldn't blame her for wanting to keep her heart safe, but he was filled with regret that they wouldn't be taking a step past the first kiss.

"I guess we'll have to call our game a draw," he decided.

"You were ahead," she reminded him.

"Being ahead doesn't mean I won."

"Neil, I wish—"

Before she could move away, he hung his arm around her shoulders, ignoring the stirring in his body that told him he wanted a hell of a lot more than the casual contact. "Don't wish. You have to be true to what's right for you. In the meantime, we'll eat chocolate cake and have a damn good time doing it."

He thought her eyes looked unnaturally moist but with darkness falling, it was hard to tell. As he guided her inside, he felt as if he'd lost something important to him.

Because of his past?

Because of his job?

Or because he still wasn't ready to open his heart?

Chapter Five

Isobel was out of breath as she braked to a stop on her bike in front of the Walnut River Inn. When she'd started out, she'd really had no intention of coming here.

Neil might not even be here.

She could just tell him she'd been out for an evening ride and…what? She just *happened* to pass the Inn?

She was almost ready to turn around and head down the street when she heard, "Isobel."

That was Neil's voice. He was standing on the porch wearing black jeans and a red polo shirt that seemed to emphasize his broad shoulders. His sandy-brown hair blew in the breeze. She couldn't see the color of his eyes from here but she knew their golden depths were trained on her.

He was coming down the steps now and she couldn't

pretend she didn't hear him call her. Wheeling her bike up the curved path, she parked it beside the porch.

"Hey," he said with a smile. "Did you just happen to be passing by, or did you come for a reason?"

Leave it to Neil to be blunt. When he wanted to know something, he just asked.

"I don't think that was a difficult question," he remarked, grinning now.

She felt foolish. Her hair was damp from her exertion but she had chosen a crisp yellow cotton blouse and her best pair of jeans to ride in. "Both, I guess. I didn't particularly have this destination in mind when I started out."

"If you want to talk, we can go up to my room. Or if you'd rather, we could go for a walk. But then, of course, some of the fine citizens of Walnut River might see you with me."

Pulling her helmet from her head, she hung it on her handlebars. Should she go to his room? This conversation would be short, and at least they'd be able to discuss things in private. "Do you have any water in your room?"

"In fact, I have a small refrigerator stocked with juice, soda and water."

She wasn't afraid of Neil. He was the kind of man a woman could trust. No, she hadn't been around him that much, but she did have sensitive radar in her line of work. "Juice would be terrific."

Opening the door, he led the way through the foyer and to the staircase. She admired the hardwood banister, the fine-quality blue-and-white wallpaper.

Neil had let her go first and at the head of the stairs, he directed her, "Second room on the left."

Neil was staying in the Lighthouse Room. It overlooked the backyard with its profusion of bushes and trees, which were all green with spring life. But she hadn't come here to admire the inn or the nautical décor in the room. She could see Neil had made himself at home. His laptop was open on the small blue desk and there was a stack of papers beside it. He was wearing deck shoes but sneakers were tumbled haphazardly under a straight-back chair next to the double bed. On the nightstand, a psychological thriller lay open next to the phone.

She'd come here tonight for a reason and one reason only. "I think we should talk about what happened in the stairwell."

Neil closed the door and the little click made her realize how alone they were, and more aware of how attracted she was to him—his height, the sandy hair on his forearms, his strong chin. He motioned to the red upholstered chair by the window, but she shook her head.

"So I guess this is going to be a short conversation," he remarked glibly.

"How can you joke—"

"I'm not joking, Isobel. Apparently you came to get something out of the way. You just want to do it and go on home again. No muss, no fuss."

He sounded almost angry and she had no idea why. "I don't want to take up any more of your time than I have to. And for your information I'm working on a fund-raising auction for the senior center. We have two more weeks to get donations and there's still a lot to do."

"Then why do we need to talk about the kiss at all?"

"Because…because it affects our interaction together—professionally," she added quickly.

"Oh, you mean whenever you see me at the hospital, you're going to think about the kiss?"

"Why are you making this so difficult?" She really was puzzled.

"Tell me something. Are you and Peter Wilder involved?"

"No." Isobel was so shocked she couldn't think of anything else to say.

"When I left the two of you, you looked pretty chummy."

"Peter is engaged to Bethany. They're getting married next month."

Neil's expression didn't change.

Now *she* was getting mad, too. "Do you honestly think I'd even be tempted to get involved with someone who is already promised to someone else?"

When he didn't answer, she had had enough. "If you do think that," she headed for the door, "I shouldn't be here at all."

He caught her arm. "Isobel, wait. No, I don't think that. But you seemed very friendly with Wilder."

"Are you digging now? For professional reasons, or personal ones?"

He frowned and admitted, "Personal ones."

She could see that Neil was serious, that maybe after their kiss he'd even been a little bit jealous. That idea made her heart flutter faster. "Peter and I..." She stopped and shook her head. "We're colleagues."

"And you can't say more than that because he's perhaps consulting you about something?"

She kept silent.

Releasing her arm, he placed a hand on both her shoulders and nudged her a little closer. "So..." he drawled. "What did *you* want to talk about?"

After a shaky breath, she laid it out. "I can't get involved with you. There's no point. Not when you'll be leaving after a few weeks."

"Isobel," he said in a soft, gentle voice that made her name sound romantic. "Have you ever taken a roller-coaster ride?"

Her eyes widened because she absolutely didn't know where he was going with this question. "Actually no, I never have."

His brows arched and he rubbed his thumb back and forth over her collar bone, distracting her immensely. "You don't know what you're missing. As an amusement-park ride, it's meant for fun and excitement and thrills. You start out slowly and you think, *Oh, this isn't so scary,* but then you start mounting the first hill. The excitement builds. You're still going very slowly but although the earth is far below, you don't seem to be in any danger. But then you come to the top of the hill. It seems like you're suspended there for a moment, just a moment, and then, so fast that you don't know what hit you, you're over the top, down the dip, on a straight stretch into another dip, up another hill, down with a whoosh. There's absolutely nothing like it, except maybe a kiss like we shared. Except maybe *thinking* about another kiss."

"Neil," she protested softly.

He nudged her a little closer and at the same time, he moved in, too. "Tell me you don't want to experience another dip and whoosh."

"Fun and excitement and thrills have never been driving forces in my life." She practically squeaked because she was so deprived of air.

"Maybe it's time to change that."

Getting hold of herself, she managed to ask, "How many affairs have you had since your divorce?"

Now it was his turn to look startled. "I thought *I* asked tough questions," he commented wryly.

She waited.

"I'm not a thrill-seeker either, Isobel. I've only dated two other women since my divorce."

If he was telling her the truth, that information truly astonished her. "Two women in two years?"

"I've gone out with a few others, but nothing developed from it. I don't take every woman I date to bed. I'm careful, I'm selective, and to be honest, I work too much to have a social life."

"So you see me as a diversion from your job?"

"No, Isobel. I see you as someone special. The moment you walked into my office, I felt it. Didn't you?"

If she admitted that—

"I thought it was a fluke," he went on. "I thought I'd been cooped up for too long, asked too many questions, interviewed too many personnel. So when an attractive woman walked in, sure, she got my attention, but then minute by minute, that current between us never subsided. By the time you left, I was having a hell of a time keeping my mind on what I was supposed to be asking you."

"You could have fooled me."

"Yeah, well, usually I'm great at compartmentalizing. I can separate the work from my personal life. That's why I've never dated anyone involved in a case."

"Never?"

"Never."

"So...are you considering dating me?"

He laughed. "Dating? Let's put it this way. I'd like to spend more time with you."

"And what about the investigation?"

"I've been doing this a long time, Isobel. You're not involved in anything going on at the hospital. *If* something is going on. In fact, I think you could be a help to me."

"What kind of help?"

"I'd like you to go through some of the files and computer data with me and answer questions I might have. No one else is willing to do that, either because they don't want to get the hospital in trouble, or because they do. I can't trust either side because of the takeover issue. But I think you would be honest with me. You're an insider. You know the goings-on. I think you could be an asset. No one has to know you're helping me if we do it in our off-hours."

"You really trust me that much?"

"I do."

Could he be playing her? Could he be using her? Could he be telling her he trusted her to get her to trust him?

"So many suspicions," he said with a rueful shake of his head. "Maybe this will help prove I'm telling the truth."

She'd thought about Neil's kiss since it had happened. She hadn't been able to think about much else. But now she had the opportunity to kiss him again. Did she want to take that roller-coaster ride? Did she want to change her life and put a few thrills in it?

Staring into Neil's forthright brown eyes, she simply couldn't resist the romantic notion that he was attracted to her, or the excitement of being desired.

She lifted her lips and he didn't hesitate. His kiss took her back to the stairwell and then sent her head spinning. His tongue was so erotically sensual, all she could do was hold on, breathe in his scent, feel his strength and ask for more. Not in words, but by stroking his tongue, by pressing her breasts against his chest, by letting her leg settle between his.

He groaned, pressed her even closer, then broke the kiss and lifted his head. "Damn it, Isobel. If you don't want to end up in that bed, we've got to stop now."

She almost smiled—almost—though her heart was still racing, her body still tingling. Neil was looking at her as if she *were* "special." That was almost hard to take, hard to accept, hard to feel because she'd never felt that kind of special with a man before. Finally the haze of sensual hunger diminished as each second ticked by.

She backed away from him another step. "I'd better go."

"You didn't have your juice."

"I'd better go," she said again.

His face was stoic now as he nodded and let her precede him out the door. They didn't speak as he walked her down the steps, as they made their way through the foyer and out over the front threshold.

He looked as if he might want to kiss her again. She knew if she let him do that, they'd end up back in his room, on his bed, *in* his bed.

She descended the porch steps.

"Isobel."

She turned to look at him.

"Will you help me?"

There was only one rule of thumb she used to guide her actions. Not what other people thought, not what her friends might say, not even what her coworkers might do. It was something her mother and dad had taught her well. She always tried to do what was right. And helping Neil get to the bottom of the hospital's problems seemed *right*.

"Yes," she said softly.

Without looking at him again, without witnessing a desire in his eyes he couldn't quite bank, without feeling the yearning for yet another kiss, she flipped up her kickstand, wheeled her bike to the sidewalk, hopped on and rode away.

* * *

The following afternoon, Isobel stopped by Peter's office, curious as to why he wanted to see her.

"I suppose you didn't eat lunch," he began.

"I blocked off this time for you today. I'll grab something later."

"I know the hours you put in. Everyone here appreciates that."

"You're not chief of staff anymore," she reminded him with a smile.

"No, I guess I'm not. Some habits are hard to break. I still care too much about this hospital and everyone in it."

"Can you care *too* much?"

Peter ran his hand through his dark-brown hair. "I try to put the investigation and the takeover bid out of my head when I'm seeing patients. But those are always there, like swords hanging over my head."

"Is that why you wanted to talk to me?"

He leaned back and took a deep breath. Then he pulled a letter out of the inside of his suit jacket. "No. I want to talk to you about something my father left."

She could see the legal-size envelope had the name *Anna* written on it. As was Isobel's usual habit, she didn't poke or prod. She let Peter set the pace.

"I've had this since my father's estate was settled. His lawyer gave it to me."

"Something for Anna?"

"It's a letter within a letter. My dad wrote to me explaining what this letter was, that he wanted me to make the decision of whether to give it to her. It's one hell of a responsibility."

"Do you know what it says?"

"Not explicitly. But it does explain to her that she's our *half* sister, not our *adopted* sister."

"That must have been difficult for you to learn."

"It was. But even more shocking…" He paused for a moment, then went on. "My father had an affair and my mother never knew about it. Anna was the result of that affair."

"That *is* a bombshell. It was a huge secret for your father to keep. And now you're considering keeping it, too?"

"It's really Anna's secret. Still, I don't like keeping something so important from David and Ella, either."

"So if you give this letter to Anna, would you be giving it to her for *her* sake or for your sake?"

He smiled wryly. "This is exactly why I wanted to talk to you. To try and figure that out."

"I'm sure it isn't anything you haven't thought of already."

"No, I guess it isn't. I just don't know what to do, Isobel, because of the tension with Anna right now. She works for the company that wants to destroy everything my father spent his life building! At least that's the way Ella, David and I see it."

"That's business, not personal," Isobel reminded him.

"You think the two can be separated?"

"Maybe not in *your* mind, but maybe in Anna's mind they can."

"I can understand if she wants to be loyal to the company that pays her, but that's clashing with *family* loyalty."

"If you give her this letter, what do you think it will do?"

"It will either put her on the family's side, or make her stand even firmer against us because of what my father did and never acknowledged. I have to ask myself how I would feel having lived in a house all those years with a man who claimed to be my adopted father, yet who was my *real* father and he never told me."

"Do you believe it's better if she never knows?"

"I don't know what I believe, except that a secret carries weight and that weight is a burden. On the other hand, I can't believe a person wouldn't want to know the truth about their life, their parents, their real family. How can I possibly keep that information from her?"

Isobel let the question hang in the air.

"I guess I knew the answer all along, didn't I? But I just can't spring this on Anna, either. I'm going to have to find the right time to give it to her."

"You'll know the right time," Isobel assured him.

Peter stood and so did Isobel. "Thank you for stopping in. I just needed to…lay it all out in front of someone objective."

"Have you told Bethany?"

"Yes. We don't have secrets. But she can't be objective because she loves me." He grinned. "I wouldn't trade that for anything."

"I wouldn't, either," Isobel agreed.

As she moved toward the door, Peter asked, "You *are* coming to our wedding, aren't you? The invitations go out next week."

"I wouldn't miss it."

After a goodbye and Peter's thanks, Isobel left his office and passed his exam rooms, going through the door to the reception area. Five minutes later, she was back at her office. To her surprise, she found Neil waiting for her.

"You just happened to be passing by?" she teased as she unlocked the knob, her fingers fumbling with the key.

He took the key from her hand. "Want me to try?" He was so very close to her, his arm brushing hers, his fit body a reminder of how she'd felt pressed against him.

He easily slid the key into the lock and opened the door. Then he followed her inside.

"I thought we could work on the files tonight," he explained. "Your place or mine? I'll spring for dinner."

"I put stew in the slow cooker this morning. It will be ready when I get home. Do you want to come over to my dad's place?"

"Are you sure he won't mind someone barging in?"

"I'm positive. So much of what I do is confidential and I can only talk about it in broad terms. Dad gets tired of that. He likes specifics. Unless I've gotten an e-mail from Jacob or something new happens with Debbie, our dinner conversation is pretty dull."

"What would we do without the weather?" Neil asked, sounding serious.

"That's what you talk about with your parents, too?"

"Yeah, that's the main topic of conversation. Why don't I stop at that bakery on Lexington and pick up something for your dad's sweet tooth. What's his favorite?"

"Anything with chocolate."

"Is chocolate your favorite, too?"

The timbre of his voice created pictures in her mind of satin sheets, naked bodies, strawberries dipped in chocolate and whipped cream. "Like father, like daughter," she answered flippantly.

Neil dragged his finger from her cheek to the corner of her lip. He looked as if he wanted to kiss her, but he knew where they were and so did she. "I'll meet you at home."

When she nodded, Isobel knew deep down that she was just asking for trouble and she didn't care.

It was so obvious to Isobel that her father liked Neil. Throughout dinner they talked and Isobel enjoyed just sitting there and listening, seeing her father totally engaged. After she had cleared the table, her father watched Neil set up his laptop computer.

"So you're both going to work now?" he grumbled.

"Isobel's going to help me go through some files," Neil explained.

"And you don't want anyone at the hospital to know you're helping him, do you?" her dad asked her.

Isobel and Neil exchanged a look. Both of them wondered how much her father knew. To distract her dad, Neil asked him, "Have you ever worked on a computer?"

John frowned, apparently knowing full well what Neil was doing. "I sold out my hardware business before I had to computerize. Ledgers were always good enough for me. I didn't need a machine that could make everything disappear with the tap of one wrong key."

"I think you might like where the Internet could take you, especially with your love of history."

"What does history have to do with it?"

"You could find sites devoted to any subject you wanted to read about. Some senior centers are setting up computer banks and teaching seniors how to use them." Neil glanced at Isobel. "You said you're helping with an auction to raise funds for the senior center. It would be a project to suggest."

"Would you be interested in something like that, Dad?" Isobel asked, curious.

"You mean I could look up Eisenhower or Truman or Thomas Jefferson?"

"You certainly could. Do you go to the senior center? You could ask your friends if they'd be interested."

"I haven't gone since I had this shoulder operated on."

"You know Mr. Bruckenwalt told you he'd pick you up and take you whenever you wanted to go," Isobel reminded him.

"It's bad enough Cyrus has to take me to and from PT. I'm not going to ask him to chauffeur me to the senior center. Besides, I can't even lift my own lunch tray yet. A man's got his pride."

"Your pride is keeping you cooped up in here. That's why you're bored," Isobel offered gently.

"Do you miss your friends?" Neil asked.

Her dad shrugged, not wanting to admit it. "I keep myself occupied. I do crossword puzzles. Now that the weather is nicer, I can take walks."

"And soon you're going to be using that arm again," Isobel said encouragingly.

"You and your positive thinking. Sometimes it makes a man tired." He sank down heavily into his recliner.

"When you went to the senior center, what did you do there?" Neil asked.

"Ate lunch, played cards, yakked about the old days."

"Is there any reason why you can't invite some of your friends here? You could order a pizza. You wouldn't have to worry about carrying a tray."

Isobel's dad was silent for a few moments.

"I never thought about doing that. I know Benny doesn't like to go to the senior center anymore, either, because he can't hear very well. He might like to come over, too."

"We've got at least three decks of cards in the desk drawer," Isobel commented nonchalantly, thinking Neil's idea was a good one.

"Yeah, we do, don't we?" Her dad rubbed his chin and pushed himself out of the recliner. "Maybe I'll call Benny now and see what he thinks. Then I'll turn in for the night. You two aren't going to be any fun if you're going to work."

Her dad smiled at them to take the sting out of his words, then headed for the stairs.

After she could hear her dad's footsteps in the upstairs hall, Isobel sat down next to Neil on the sofa. "I wish I had thought of your suggestion. I don't know why I didn't."

"You've had a lot on your plate. One person can't think of everything."

Their gazes met and held for one very long minute. Neil had tossed his suit coat over the back of the sofa and tugged off his tie. His white oxford shirt was rumpled from a day of wear, but with the cuffs rolled back, he looked incredibly relaxed—and sexy. The temperature in the room seemed to climb another ten degrees. With the warmer weather, the house was a little stuffy.

"Do you need to be hooked up to the phone line?" she asked him.

"No, I have everything on the flash drive. I just need an outlet. Why?"

"Because we could go out on the sunporch and work. I can open the window."

"That sounds like a great idea. Grab my briefcase. I'll get the computer."

Five minutes later, they were set up on the glassed-in porch. The light beside the wicker sofa burned brightly. Darkness had fallen and the scent of just-blooming lilacs wafted in from the open window that looked out onto the backyard.

Side by side they sat there, breathing in the spring flowers and dampness, night settling in and each other. Oh, they worked. Neil brought up page after page that Isobel examined with him, searching for charges that didn't fit, checking anything that seemed over the top, showing him her own billing sheets. She explained basic charges, time allotments, services rendered.

Still, their arms brushed often, his shirtsleeve against her bare skin. When she pointed to something on the screen, he leaned close, his mouth almost touching her cheek. By the time they had spent an hour and a half examining and checking, silence and shadows and the perfumes of spring wrapped them in an intimate cocoon.

"This is tedious work," Isobel murmured as they finished another page.

"It's not so bad doing it with you." Neil's voice had a husky quality that brought her eyes to his. The desire she saw there made her breath catch and her mouth go dry.

After a moment she asked, "Would you like me to get us something to drink?"

"I'd like something else a lot more."

She didn't have to ask what Neil wanted because she wanted it, too. Leaning into him, she raised her lips to his.

Chapter Six

Time, place and consequences had no hold on Isobel as she gave herself up to the delight of Neil's kiss. That delight, however, soon morphed into desire and thrills and novelty that made her gasp in pleasure and moan in surrender.

The wicker couch's floral cushions gave with their weight as Neil's arms wrapped around her and they leaned against its back. His lips were on her cheek, on her eyelids, then they returned to her mouth. His hands smoothed over the back of her silky blouse then roamed into new territory. They were at her waist, on her stomach, almost touching her breasts.

Isobel's slim skirt rode up her thighs as she restlessly reached for handfuls of Neil's shirt and pulled it from his trousers. She didn't think twice about what they were doing. She didn't think at all. She'd never experienced such mindless pleasure or basked in a man's hungry desire. She and Tim—

well, they'd been attracted to each other, but she'd never wanted to put her hands all over him the way she wanted to put her hands all over Neil. She'd never wanted to get into Tim's skin the way she wanted to get into Neil's. She'd never before felt the heat and the urgency to make love because she knew when she did, she'd rocket straight away from earth. Neil had that effect on her, whether he was just looking at her, kissing her or touching her. There was an innate virility that poured from him—an alpha determination he couldn't keep in check. Yet he could be kind and gentle, too. That mixture in a man was totally irresistible.

He stroked her hair back from her face. "Do you want this, Isobel? Are you sure?"

Beyond rationality, her body cried out for more—more of touching, kissing, holding and most of all, completion. "I do," she murmured, reaching for his belt buckle.

She didn't stop to admit that the illicit nature of making love on the back porch with her father upstairs had an element of danger she found enticing. She'd never realized the extent of the excitement that danced around danger—the danger of being heard or found or seen.

Still, she knew the glassed-in porch was so separate from the rest of the house, so far away from her father's room, he couldn't possibly hear them. Once he went upstairs for the night, he didn't come down again. Those steps were hard on his knees. As far as neighbors…their yard was bordered by maples, spruce and oaks. There might be a stray cat lurking out there, but not much else. A spirea hedge surrounded the yard and gravel from the alley beyond would alert them to a neighbor taking a walk, or a car backing in for the night.

All of those thoughts were extraneous as she trembled while Neil undressed her…as he shrugged out of his shirt and she unzipped his fly. Naked on the sofa, Neil pulled her onto his lap, caressed her breasts and kissed her lips. She could feel his arousal beneath her thigh. He was hot and hard and big. The excitement he created had her reaching between them, stroking his stomach, moving lower. He slid forward with her on the cushion, turned her on his lap so she was facing and straddling him. She'd never made love like this…this was over-the-top exhilarating, tempting, brand-new.

They didn't speak. They were too busy nibbling, kissing, tasting.

Neil turned from her, grabbed his trousers, fished in a pocket for his wallet. Moments later he was pushing into her, she was melting around him and desire was a newly awakened hunger that made a need so far deep inside of her, she didn't know how she'd satisfy it.

But Neil did. His hands slipped under her buttocks and he pushed in deeper, farther, groaning as his own hunger was partially satisfied. His lips clung to hers, his tongue never stopped moving, his body rocked closer, his hands guided her movement and they created an irresistible friction. She pushed, he thrust, they rocked until her muscles tightened, her nerve endings lit up with excitement and her world shattered into a thousand pieces around her. In the throes of her orgasm, she felt Neil's final thrust, held him as he shuddered, and sighed when his lips broke from hers. He caught her tight against his chest.

But after a few moments, he leaned against the back of the sofa, taking her with him. Her heart was beating hard against his chest and she could feel the racing of his heart, too. The primitive pounding in her ears slowed as they began to breathe normally again. Their bodies were glazed with their exertion and she loved the scent of Neil…the scent of the two of them together. He held her for a very long time.

She was almost lulled by a happiness she'd never experienced until she started thinking again. Neil had been prepared with a condom. That wasn't so unusual, she guessed, lots of men were. Still…

"Do you always carry a condom in your wallet?"

He was silent and she didn't look up. Finally he inquired, "Why are you asking?"

Now she sat up and awkwardly disengaged herself from him. She should get dressed, but she had to know something first. "I'm trying to put two and two together and I'm getting five. You said you haven't slept with many women, only a few since your divorce. Was the condom old or new?"

"Because you're concerned you might get pregnant if it's old?" His voice was gruff.

"Because if it's new, I have to wonder if you planned this. If you want to keep me close so I'll help you. If you want to get me on your side so you can get the information you need."

"Isobel." Her name was a protest tinged with anger.

She went on anyway. "You said you never get involved with someone in an investigation. Why now? Why me?"

His thumb nudged her chin up so she was gazing into his eyes. "Are you so lacking in self-confidence you don't know how beautiful you are?"

Although she wanted to cover herself, she couldn't look away. Did he mean that?

"I haven't had men rushing to take me out."

"Then you haven't met the right men."

He *was* angry, but at least his anger was honest. She could tell that. Had tonight been as important to him as it was to her? Or could he separate emotion from pure physical desire? Perhaps tonight had just been about slaking that desire.

"I told you I don't do one-night stands," she murmured.

"So why did this happen tonight?" he asked reasonably. "You know I'm not staying in Walnut River. You know I'll be gone when the investigation's over."

"I got caught up in—"

"In desire? In passion? There's nothing wrong with that, Isobel."

"Yes, there is. When there's no commitment, it shouldn't happen. That's the way I was raised. I want what my parents had."

"Life's too short to wait forever for perfection."

The bitterness in his voice surprised her. "Perfection?"

His hands slashed through the air. "The right place, the right time, the right decade. For a few moments, Isobel, you and I had something special. Wasn't that good enough?"

"A few moments isn't enough for me."

Now Neil levered himself off the couch, turned aside, then grabbed his clothes. "You should take your special moments where you can get them."

There was pain under his proclamation and she wanted to know where it was coming from. His divorce? "I don't understand."

After a prolonged silence he finally responded. "My brother died when he was twelve. He never had the chance to wait for special moments. He never had the chance to live."

"Neil, I'm sorry."

Neil pulled on his trousers and buckled his belt. His fingers flew over the buttons of his shirt. "This is my fault. I knew you were a woman with traditional values. I just…I just let my libido wallop my good sense. It won't happen again." He looked at her. "But just for the record, Isobel. I had no ulterior motive. I wanted you because I'm attracted to you. And that has nothing to do with the investigation."

Isobel picked up her clothes, too, and shrugged into her blouse without her bra. But before she could even button it, Neil was completely dressed and had gathered his laptop and files. "I'll see you around the hospital."

She was confused, not sure of his motives and not sure of hers. She simply didn't know what to say.

She didn't have to say anything because he left without another word. She knew she wouldn't be seeing him at the hospital, not unless she searched him out. But what was the point? To help him? He didn't really need her help and she… she couldn't let him make love to her again without losing her heart.

She realized she wouldn't mind losing it. She just didn't want Neil to crush it.

On Monday morning at 7:00 a.m., Isobel stopped by Pine Ridge Rehab to peek in on Florence and see how she was adjusting since her move there last week.

West's mother was having breakfast. Florence's face lit up when she saw Isobel. "Did you come to have breakfast with me?"

"I already had breakfast." If she could count the glass of orange juice as breakfast. "So I'll just keep you company and find out how you like it here."

"The food's pretty good," Florence told her, taking another bite of her pancakes. "But you know what? They make me walk." She pointed to her walker. "I'm beginning to hate that thing."

Isobel smiled. "Soon you'll graduate to a cane and then to nothing at all."

"I'll have to be very careful when I go home."

Isobel went on alert. "Very careful of what?" she asked softly, not wanting to jar Florence out of her confiding mood.

The little woman took a piece of bacon, crunched on it a while, and answered, "A while back, I left a pot on the stove. It scared West. When he came home, he said he smelled something awful."

"What were you making?"

"I was cooking noodles and all the water burned away. He said if he hadn't come in when he did, we would have had a fire."

This was exactly the kind of thing Isobel was worried about. If Florence was becoming that forgetful that she would cause herself harm, she had to be watched. "Can you tell me something, Florence?"

"What would you like to know, dear?" Florence picked up her coffee cup and took a sip, then settled the cup back down again. She pushed her tray toward Isobel. "Are you sure you don't want a slice of bacon?"

"I'm sure, but thank you for asking." Isobel thought about how she should phrase her question. She didn't want it to be in any way threatening or even nosy, because then Florence would clam up. "When I was driving in this morning, I noticed the daffodils blooming. You have those in your garden, don't you?"

"Well, yes, I do. I love the smell. I have a favorite vase I use to put them in the middle of the kitchen table."

"Do you walk up and down your street very often? To see the flowers? It's good exercise, too."

"West doesn't like me going out alone for walks."

"He doesn't? Is he afraid you'll fall?"

Florence stared down at her pancakes for a long time. Finally in a small voice, she admitted, "One time when I took a walk outside, I ended up over on Maple and couldn't get back home. Mrs. Johnson was out for her walk and she saw me, so she showed me the way home."

"Did West know you'd gotten…lost?"

"Oh, yes. She told him and that's why he doesn't like me to leave the house when he's not there. But I do sometimes. I just don't tell him. The thing is, that'll be harder now. He's already found someone to stay with me when I go home. I guess she'll take walks with me."

So West *was* aware of the care his mother needed. Thank goodness.

Isobel checked her watch and stood. "I really have to be going."

"So soon?"

"I'm sure after breakfast you'll be starting your therapy and you'll be busy, too."

"I just want to get well."

As Isobel gave Florence a hug and said goodbye, she realized how coherent and lucid Florence had been today. Isobel hoped her good days kept outnumbering her bad ones.

Yesterday Isobel had taken a ride to the cemetery before going to dinner at Debbie's for Mother's Day. She had felt the loss of her mom all day. She was glad West was doing everything he could for Florence while he still had her to love.

Though Isobel had been busier than busy all day, her work load didn't prevent thoughts of Neil from sneaking in, from capturing her at the first unguarded moment, from lingering in her mind underneath everything else. When she least expected them, pictures of her and Neil popped into her head: as they sat side by side in her dad's sunporch, as they'd kissed, as Neil had undressed her, as she'd made love to him.

She also remembered every word she'd said to him...her accusation...his reply. Most of all, his comment about his brother. *He never had the chance to wait for special moments.*

Was it any wonder she was hesitant to see Neil again? His office was on the same floor as hers but on the other side of the building. It was well after six and personnel from the fourth floor had mostly gone home. Maybe Neil had left, too. Avoiding him, though, would only postpone the inevitable.

She stopped in the restroom to make sure her hair was in some semblance of order, to add a dash of lipstick, to make certain her flowered spring dress still looked presentable. Telling herself to stop stalling, she headed for Neil's office. As she glimpsed the closed door, she thought maybe he had left. Then she saw his shadow through the frosted-glass window, and she knocked.

His "Come in" could have been for anyone. After she turned the knob and stepped inside, Neil's head came up from his computer and his gaze locked to hers.

"Are you busy?" she asked, and as soon as she did, she understood what a totally silly question that was. Of course, he was busy. Papers were spread all over the table and he'd been typing something on his laptop.

He pressed a key, typed a few letters, and pressed another. "I have a few minutes. What can I do for you?"

He could kiss her again. He could tell her he understood her fears about getting involved with him. He could say he forgave her for making the wrong assumption.

She didn't know where to start, but she could see he wasn't going to help her. She walked over to the chair on the other side of the table from him, pulled it around the corner so she was facing him. She sat in it because her knees were wobbly.

He looked away, adjusted a few papers into a pile, and didn't bring his gaze back to hers.

To save them both any more uncomfortable moments, she said, "I'm sorry."

If she thought that would soften the set of his jaw, the guarded look in his eyes, she was wrong. "About what? You didn't do anything wrong. *I* was the one who should have known better. I should have stayed away from you."

If he *had* stayed away from her, she would never have known how beautiful making love could be. At least, that's what *she'd* been doing. "I'm sorry for what I thought and said."

He shifted in his chair, ran one hand agitatedly through his hair. "Did you honestly think I'd have sex with you to get information? And don't just tell me what you think I want to hear. I want the truth."

What *was* the truth? "On a deep level, I didn't think that. I never would have let anything happen if I had any real suspicions. But afterward, on another level, I was scared and unsure and regretful. Believing you just wanted to use me helped...it helped me push you away."

Maybe Neil wasn't used to that kind of honesty because he looked very surprised. "I can't believe you're admitting that."

"It's the truth."

His serious eyes searched her face and then he seemed to relax a bit. "I wanted you, Isobel. That's why I was carrying a new condom. But I was also afraid I'd taken advantage of you. I'm the one in a position of power and—"

"Says you," she cut in.

Surprised again, he smiled. "You think you have some power?"

"Of course, I do. I'm the one who decides what I do and who I do it with. Your position has nothing to do with that."

He grinned slyly and she felt her whole face heat up. "You know what I mean."

Leaning forward, he took her hand and looked down at it. "I don't want to hurt you. I don't want to push you into something that isn't right for you."

Now, with Neil simply holding her hand, she wasn't sure what was right for her and what wasn't. "Last night, you mentioned you had a brother who died. How long ago did that happen?"

Releasing her hand, he stood and went to look out the window at the grounds below. She had the feeling he wasn't seeing anything out there. "Is that something else you don't want to talk about...like your father?"

He glanced over his shoulder at her. "You listen too well and see too much."

She could tell him she'd been practicing for years, that listening well and seeing a lot was part of her job. Not only part of her job, but who she was. But she knew he didn't want to hear that.

After the silence had stretched a little longer, he answered her. "It was the summer before my senior year in high school. Garrett had just turned twelve. He'd gone fishing with a friend at the river. No one was sure exactly what happened, whether he lost his footing, or whether he and his friend were simply fooling around as boys do. But he got towed by a strong current and drowned."

Unable to stay across the room from him, Isobel rose to her feet and crossed to Neil. "I'm so sorry," she said again. "Was it just the two of you, no other brothers or sisters?"

Neil nodded and finally looked at her. "Just the two of us.

I was an only child, groomed to be the perfect son my father wanted, until Garrett was born when I was six. He and I were very different. No one could resist Garrett from the moment he was born."

Isobel filled in what Neil wasn't saying. "At six, your parents didn't feel you needed much attention, so the baby got it all?"

Neil shrugged. "I've got to admit, I was happy as an only child. I loved Garrett and would have done anything for him because I fell under his charm, too. He was a great kid, always happy, everybody's friend. But more than once, I wished he wasn't around."

"Oh, Neil, don't tell me you felt guilty when he died."

"Wouldn't *you* have felt guilty? I know it was irrational. I didn't have anything to do with what had happened, but I still felt responsible. If I had been with him that day instead of with *my* friends... He'd asked me to go along. But I wanted to hang with guys who were making college plans and telling the most popular girls about them. I grew up the day Garrett died. I started to learn what was important and what wasn't."

Her heart went out to the teenager Neil had been. She also realized he carried that sense of responsibility with him today.

"How did your parents react to losing Garrett?"

"They were never the same. Their marriage was never the same. My dad was never overly demonstrative or even generous with compliments. But after we lost Garrett, he became even more remote, closed off from Mom and me. God knows I tried to make up for their loss. I had concentrated on basketball and the debate team. Garrett ran track. So I added that to my schedule too. Even won a few trophies. But nothing seemed to impress my father. At first I intended to be a lawyer and follow in dad's footsteps, but then when I saw it didn't matter what I did, I decided to do what made me feel successful. That's why I joined the Boston P.D."

"Have you and your father ever talked about all this?"

Neil just shook his head. "He didn't seem to want to hear what I had to say."

"What did he say when you told him you weren't going to be a lawyer?"

"He said that he'd give the money he'd put aside for my law-school degree to a local scholarship fund."

"Did he know why you weren't becoming a lawyer? Or did he just see it as rebellion against what he wanted?"

"I don't know what he thought or how he felt. My mother knew I was tired of school and I wanted a real life. I got it. Being a detective showed me more than I ever wanted to see. When I hit thirty-eight, I wanted something different, maybe a life *with* someone. So I took the job with the state."

"And you like what you're doing?"

"I still like it, at least the gathering-evidence part of it. When I'm questioning someone, I'm pitting my mind against theirs. It's a challenge."

Neil was definitely a complicated man. No one went through life without baggage and he had his share. But she knew he was an honorable man. Her accusations had been defensive rationalization on her part.

The longer they stood there, the more heat she could feel surrounding them. Making love hadn't diminished it. In fact, it had hiked up the vibrations to a new level.

The look in Neil's eyes told her he was thinking about kissing her again, but he was restraining himself because she'd told him that wasn't what she'd wanted. She'd told him she didn't want an involvement.

What good can come of it if he'll be leaving? she asked herself again.

His voice was gruff as he said, "You'd better go."

She mumbled, "I just wanted to apologize."

He nodded, standing perfectly still, his arms straight at his sides.

Her throat tightening, Isobel hurriedly left Neil's office.

If he had called her name, she would have turned back. She would have surrendered to the feelings that seemed right and wrong and everything in-between.

But he didn't, and tears of disappointment and regret filled her eyes.

Chapter Seven

Breathless from exertion, Isobel opened the back door and stepped into the kitchen. Even though it was only 6:45 a.m., her father was sitting at the table reading the morning paper.

"You're up early," he remarked as his gaze swept over her windblown hair, light jacket and workout pants.

She knew he expected an explanation. "I'm going to start cycling regularly again. This morning was the first."

"How many miles did you do?"

"Five. I'll add one each day."

"Pretty soon you'll be getting up at three in the morning to cycle."

"I do have some common sense, Dad. I know I need sleep before I can work."

"What's brought back this sudden interest in bicycling?"

She went to the refrigerator and took out a quart of orange

juice. "No sudden interest. I'd wanted to get back to it. I need the exercise."

"Or maybe you just want to get into better shape for a certain gentleman investigator?"

Was *that* what she was doing? She shook her head. "No, that's not the reason. I've been slacking off."

"You could have fooled me. You usually run around here so fast going from one thing to the other, it makes my head spin."

"I've been slacking off in taking care of myself."

Her father went silent for a few moments, and then said, "Because you've been taking care of me."

"No, Dad, of course not. Life has just gotten busy and I let exercise get lost in the shuffle, that's all."

His brows arched. "And Neil is showing you what you need in your life?"

"Let's just leave Neil out of this, okay?" She poured a glass of juice and quickly downed it.

Her father was still studying her. "You can fool yourself, but you can't fool *me*…about anything. I know you'd rather be living on your own, not having anyone to answer to or do for. Maybe we should consider—"

"Stop telling me what I want, Dad. I'm perfectly happy living here with you, helping you when you need it. Pretty soon that shoulder's going to be better and you'll be driving again."

"Yeah, but I'll still be sixty-eight with creaky bones and arthritis and you'll worry about me. Seriously, Isobel, you should think about getting your own place again."

She could see her dad wasn't going to let this go until she agreed with him. "I'll think about it."

After a few moments her father informed her, "You don't have to worry about supper tonight. A few friends are coming over. We'll order pizza."

"You're going to have fun for a change?" she joked.

"About time, don't you think? You should have some fun, too. Get out more."

A half hour later, Isobel was still considering her conversation with her father when she stepped off the elevator onto the fourth floor of the hospital. She heard a woman's strident voice as she walked down the hall and realized the commotion was at Neil's office door. Mrs. Donaldson, a board member who always held a strong opinion on everything, apparently had her temper up and was pointing her finger at Neil.

Mrs. Donaldson's overstyled ash-blond hair wobbled with her words. "Everyone in this hospital is walking on eggshells around you. They're all afraid to tell you what they think. Well, I'm not. These good people don't deserve the treatment you're giving them. You're even asking *personal* questions. It's none of your business who Peter Wilder is going to marry, or Ella or David. The Wilders practically built this hospital brick by brick. James was a man of integrity and his children are good doctors."

Neil's shoulders were squared and his body tense, his face set on neutral. Isobel knew he was too much of a gentleman to tell the woman what he was thinking. He was too much of a professional to spill his investigation into the hall. But Isobel couldn't let Neil take venom he didn't deserve.

Mrs. Donaldson was pointing her finger again. "Your investigation and your methods are unjust."

Isobel stepped up beside Neil to face Mrs. Donaldson with him. "Mrs. Donaldson, maybe you should think about this more rationally. If something unethical is going on, it should come to light to save Walnut River General…to save James Wilder's legacy. If there *is* wrongdoing, we can't let it destroy the good we do."

Mrs. Donaldson's eyes narrowed and now she targeted Isobel. "You, my dear, are a traitor. The rumors are all over this hospital about your after-hours tête-à-têtes with Mr. Kane."

With that, the woman spun on her heels and headed for the elevator. Several people had come out from their offices and were standing in their doorways listening.

Isobel's eyes suddenly filled with tears. *Were* there rumors about her all over the hospital? *Was* she considered a traitor?

Apparently Neil saw how Mrs. Donaldson's words had affected her because he took her by the elbow and tugged her into his office. After he shut the door, he took her by the shoulders. "You need to forget what that woman said. Someone who searches for the truth is *not* a traitor."

A tear ran down Isobel's cheek and she just let it.

Neil pulled her into his arms, held her for a moment, his chin resting in her curls. "Isobel," he murmured.

As she looked up at him, the few inches of space between them seemed to be too much. His eyes told her he'd missed her and he wanted her. She couldn't deny the missing or the wanting and she lifted her face. He kissed her tears away first and took her lips with a possessiveness that excited her. His tongue didn't wait for an invitation but plunged into her mouth, seducing her into the same rich passion they'd shared before. She blanked out everything but the feel of his hair under her fingertips, his taste, his strength and his desire. Lost in whatever happened whenever they were together, she jumped when there was a sudden knock on the door.

Neil swore. "I'm scheduled for a session with West Mac-Gregor and Richard Green, the lawyer who's filling in for the hospital attorney."

Away from Neil now, letting common sense reign once more, Isobel took a deep breath and pulled herself together fast. She ran a hand through her hair, took a small mirror from her purse and saw the mess her lipstick had become. With a tissue, she eased away the smears as best she could, but she knew she still looked just-kissed.

"Isobel, you're fine. Everything's going to be fine."

How she wished she could believe Neil—but now she felt more like a traitor than she had before…even if there was no basis, even if she was just trying to do what was right.

There was another knock. Neil went to the door and glanced at her. "Ready?"

"As ready as I'm going to be," she assured him.

As he opened the door, she plastered on a bright smile, murmured, "I'm running late. It's good to see you again, West," and then she was practically running down the hall to her office and away from the two men who could probably see she'd been doing more than talking with Neil Kane.

A few hours later, Neil had to admit he was looking for Isobel, not taking a stroll around the hospital to pick up any unusual undercurrents. When he spotted her in a lounge on the second floor talking with a couple, he stopped and observed. He didn't know who the couple were or what they might be discussing. The woman looked distraught, with tears on her cheeks. The man appeared to be upset, too, but was trying to conceal whatever he was feeling to listen to Isobel. Neil could easily see the compassion on Isobel's face. She was leaning into the couple, not backing away. There was no partition that she hid behind. He'd witnessed detachment on social workers' faces, on doctors' faces, so they didn't become too involved with whoever they were helping. Not Isobel. She was right there. That was the thing. She was always right there. Whenever he looked at Isobel, he knew he was missing something important in his life, something he'd done without for far too long. She made him dream again, and he didn't know if that was good or bad.

After a few more minutes she stood, picked up the file folder on the table beside her and left the lounge. She looked startled when she spotted Neil, and glanced at her watch as if she didn't have much time to talk.

"On your way somewhere?" Neil asked.

"Back to my office for a conference call."

Two women brushed by them into the lounge.

"We can talk in the elevator."

"Neil—"

"What? You don't want to be seen walking to the elevator with me?"

"That's not it at all. It's just everything between us is becoming too...too explosive."

Gazing into her dark-brown eyes, wanting to feel her in his arms again, more than ready to take her to his room at the Inn, he knew exactly what she meant. "Come on. The elevator will contain the fireworks."

She shook her head as if she couldn't believe her own stupidity in walking with him and kept pace beside him as he headed for the elevator. Fortunately, he snagged a car that was empty.

As soon as they stepped inside and the doors closed, he assured her, "MacGregor and Green couldn't see us this morning. That frosted window in the door prevents anyone from looking in."

"They didn't have to see us to know what we were doing. One look at my face and hair probably told them everything."

He turned to her and clasped her arm. "What do you want to do?"

She looked troubled and confused and way too vulnerable. "Maybe we need some breathing space."

"Together or apart?"

She just rolled her eyes as the bell in the elevator dinged, announcing their floor.

He pressed the button to keep the door closed. "You want me to stay in my office and keep away from yours. All right, I'll do that. But answer me one question first."

"What?"

She was obviously expecting something personal and that wasn't where he was going. "Who do you think the informant is?"

Her eyes went wide. "The informant? I don't know. I..."

"You said you don't think it's one of the Wilders. What's your gut instinct telling you?"

After she thought about his question, she replied, "The questions you've asked me lead me to think the allegations are about overcharges, or in J. D. Sumner's case, being kept longer than you thought he should be."

Neil didn't confirm or deny that.

"If that's the case, then I think someone in the administrative department is feeding your office the information. I really can't see other personnel knowing as much about it."

"You mean someone in the billing department?"

"Yes, or accounts receivable or even one of the data-entry employees."

"Thanks for narrowing the field," he said wryly.

"I have no clue as to who the person is, Neil. But I think only someone who has access to computer files could be giving you the information."

He nodded, though he didn't say anything. That was the conclusion he'd come to also. He couldn't completely rule out a doctor with a gripe, or one who wanted this takeover to happen. But the kind of information his office had received suggested someone other than a doctor. Maybe more than one person. A doctor being helped by someone in an administrative role?

Isobel hit the open door button on the elevator panel.

"Thanks for your help," Neil told her. "Why don't you head down the hall ahead of me? I'll take my time."

When her gaze met his, he knew what she was thinking. They'd had sex. They'd been as intimate as two people could be. But now they were going to act like strangers because that was easier for her.

And him?

He didn't want to be a stranger to Isobel Suarez, but he couldn't offer her what she obviously deserved—romance, whole-hearted commitment and happily ever after.

He couldn't take his eyes off her as she walked down the hall. He wished he could find the answers he was searching for. He wished he and Isobel could forget the investigation and just live in the moment.

However, he didn't know if living in the moment was enough for him anymore. Maybe he needed to think about the future, too, and whether or not he wanted to live it alone.

An exhausted Isobel walked into her house that night at seven-thirty and was appalled. Cigar smoke stung her nostrils and her lungs as she stepped into the living room. Windbreakers and sweaters were tossed onto the sofa. The remains of a pizza, leftover hot wings and several soda bottles sat on the coffee table and end table. Paper plates were strewn here and there. Men's voices sailed to her from the kitchen. When she headed that way, the smoke was even thicker and she coughed.

Her father had told her he was having friends over, but she'd never expected the place would be totaled.

"A couple more hands, Iz, and we'll be finished."

"If I'm not home by eight-thirty, my wife will be calling every five minutes," Mort Thompson grumbled.

"She worries about you since you had your heart attack," John Suarez insisted.

"She worries too much," Mort murmured.

The men were playing cards around the kitchen table and snacks were tossed here and there and sat beside cups of soda. The smell of burned popcorn hung in the air.

It was going to take hours to clean the place up.

Finding a smile somewhere, she managed to say, "Enjoy your game." To her dad, she said in a low voice, "I'll be down after everyone leaves."

It was her father's turn to play a card but he studied her for a moment and asked, "Are you okay?"

"Tired, Dad. Just tired. I'll take a shower then be back down in a while."

He gave her another careful once-over and then nodded.

Isobel tried not to think or feel as she undressed, took a terrifically long hot shower and towel-dried her hair. She tried to obliterate from her mind the mess downstairs, the work she'd brought home, the moment she'd walked away from Neil, telling herself staying away from him was the best thing to do.

Was it? Didn't she need something else in her life, other than working and taking care of her dad? Didn't she need to be touched and kissed and cared about?

An hour later, dressed in sweats, still wishing she could simply crawl into bed and pull the covers up over her head, she went downstairs and found all the men had left. Her father was transferring snack plates to the kitchen counter, then he attempted to pick up a carrier of soda with his left hand.

When he winced, she hurried over to him. "Dad, you know you have to be careful."

"I never intended for you to have this much of a mess to come home to."

The apology almost made Isobel want to cry. "I know you didn't."

Turning away so he didn't see her emotion, she opened the window over the sink, letting the cool night air push the smoke away.

"I know you hate smoke," he mumbled.

"We'll get it aired out. I can leave the window open overnight."

Wearily he sat down at the table, looked around the room again, and then said determinedly, "This is no life for you—taking care of me, cleaning up after me, doing all the chores you should be doing for your own family."

"*You're* my family."

"Yeah, well, that's probably another reason why you don't have your own family. Besides working so much, I mean."

"Let's not get into this tonight."

"We have to get into it sometime, Iz. Why do you think Jacob stays away? He doesn't want to be saddled with all this." He waved his good arm over the table—the crumbs, napkins and cigar butts.

"You are *not* the reason Jacob stays away. As you said before, he's searching for something."

"Jacob's a good boy at heart, but if he were back here, he'd feel responsible for me, too. Miles away, he doesn't have to worry so much."

In part, Isobel knew that was probably true.

"I should sell the house and look for a small apartment. That way you could get your own place and get on with your life."

"You'd hate a small apartment."

"I'd get used to it. They're building apartments for seniors on the north side of town. I should go look at them."

Her dad took joy in walking around his own yard and remembering the rosebushes he'd planted for their mother, smelling the lilacs and remembering when the girls had cut them to take to teachers at school. There was the sandbox Jacob had turned into a home for a turtle and the fence they'd all helped paint when they were teenagers. There were years of memories in every room in the house, too.

"Tell me something, Dad, if you hadn't hurt your shoulder, would you even be thinking of selling?"

"Probably not."

"In six weeks, two months, you'll be better. You can't make a rash decision you're going to regret."

"It might get better, it might not. If it's not the shoulder, soon it will be something else. I'm getting older, Iz. What I want won't count for much when I can't do for myself."

She went over to him and crouched down beside his chair. "That's why I want to help you. I'm not here because I have to be. I'm here because I want to be."

"For my sake, not yours."

"Have I complained?" she asked.

"No, but then you wouldn't. That's who you are."

"And I know who *you* are. You want to control your own destiny. I can help you do that."

He patted her shoulder. "You're a good daughter, Isobel." He called her Isobel on important occasions; when she'd learned to ride her first bike, he'd told her, *Now, Isobel, you can go where you want to go.* When she'd earned her driver' license, he'd said, *Driving is a big responsibility, Isobel don't take advantage of it.* When she graduated from high school and college, he'd insisted, *You're on your way now Isobel. The whole world's in front of you.*

She wanted the whole world still to be in front of her dad too. As he'd aged, it had grown smaller. She wanted to keep it as big as she could for him, as long as she could.

"You should never make an important decision when you're tired," she warned him.

"You think something will be different in the morning?"

"I think everything could look different in the morning. She stood and began stacking the dishes in the sink again.

"What can I do to help?"

She knew her father wanted to feel worthwhile, wanted t take some of the burden away from her. "Can you empty th ashtrays? It will get the smell out of here."

"That I can do."

As Isobel watched her dad move around the kitchen an living room, she knew she'd meant everything she'd said t him—but she had to wonder if her life would ever be her ow again.

The next morning, when Neil parked in the staff parkin lot at the hospital, he noticed Isobel's car rumbling in as h locked his car doors. They hadn't spoken since he'd held th door in the elevator. That seemed like years ago instead c less than twenty-four hours.

The parking space next to his was vacant and although sh hesitated a few moments as she drove down the line of slot she finally turned in beside him. She was wearing a conse vative, black two-piece dress today, trimmed in white at the sleeves, lapels and hem. She looked like a million bucks. And she had that unselfconscious style about her that said she didn't know it.

After she pulled her briefcase from her car, she locked her doors.

He went over to her, not knowing if he should. But there'd be no harm in walking her into the hospital. "Good morning."

As he approached her, he could see there were circles under her eyes and she looked pale. But she gave him a forced smile and returned, "Good morning."

He couldn't keep from asking, "Is everything okay?"

She looked so vulnerable for a moment he wanted to gather her into his arms.

"Nothing you'd want to hear about." She started walking toward the building, but he clasped her shoulder and tugged her around.

"Don't make decisions for me, Isobel."

She sighed. "It's just...I didn't sleep well last night. Dad and I had a conversation that bothered me."

"About?"

When she still hesitated, he squeezed her shoulder. "I like your dad and I think he liked me. Is there anything I can do to help?"

"Stop the hands of time," she answered with a sad smile.

"Is your dad not feeling well?"

"It's his emotional state I'm worried about. Last night he told me he should sell the house—"

Her words caught and Neil could see how upset she was. He hugged her. He couldn't help it. At first she was stiff in his arms, but then she seemed to need the contact, too. Finally she looked up at him and, oh, how he wanted to kiss her. But they were standing in the public parking lot and he knew how she'd feel about that after it was over, especially if there were witnesses.

He glanced up at the row of hospital rooms that over-looked the lot.

She realized what he was thinking and quickly pulled away from him.

"Do you know what I think?" he asked.

"I'm afraid to ask," she murmured.

"I think we both need to get away."

She sighed heavily. "That's the whole point, Neil. I can't. I'm taking care of my dad."

"Don't tell me you can't get away for a weekend."

"Away where?"

"You said you were working on an auction for the senior center and you needed donations. How would you like some-thing really great?"

"What kind of great?" she asked warily.

"Maybe an antique?"

"And you know someone who will be willing to donate an antique?"

"I might. Come away with me this weekend and we'll find out."

He could see the thoughts flipping through her mind.

"Look, I know what you're thinking. But this weekend can be whatever you want it to be. My parents live about two hours north. I haven't seen them for a few months and when I called Mom on Sunday to wish her a happy Mother's Day, she dropped a big hint that, though she liked the flowers I sent her, she'd like a visit from me even more. Antique shops are pretty common in their area. I happen to know the owner of one fairly well. You can pick out what you want, and I'll donate the antique. We can stay at an inn…in separate rooms, of course."

Isobel didn't say no right away and that was a great sign. But she did study him carefully. He could feel her gaze as if it were a touch on his eyes, on his mouth and back to his eyes again.

"Why are you doing this?" she wanted to know.

"I'm doing it because we both need a respite. I'm tired of feeling as if I'm in a fishbowl every time I talk to you. Besides that, I need perspective on the investigation and maybe you need perspective on what's going on with your dad."

"No *maybe* about it," she murmured.

He knew he couldn't push Isobel into this. It had to be a free decision on her part.

"I could ask Debbie if she'd mind if Dad stayed over with her this weekend."

"There's another solution," Neil offered. "Maybe Chad could just stay with your dad. He could keep a watchful eye on him, but your father wouldn't feel as if he's being coddled."

Isobel looked uncertain.

"I know, you probably need time to think about all this. Have dinner with me tonight. If you decide you want to do it, we can stop at your sister's and you can ask."

"Dad might not be all bent out of shape about it if Chad stayed with him," she agreed. "But I won't have time for a long dinner—"

"We can stop for fast food if you want. I don't care."

"The Chinese Kitchen is fast," she offered, finally accepting his invitation.

"The Chinese Kitchen it is." He suddenly realized that no matter what happened today, he'd have Isobel to look forward to this evening.

That thought could keep him smiling through anything.

Chapter Eight

Isobel had just finished with a patient one of the E.R. docs had referred to her when Simone Gardner snagged her arm. "Got a minute?" the pretty brunette E.R. nurse asked.

Isobel and Simone had become good friends over the past six months—good enough friends to confide in each other about their lives and pasts. "I always have a minute for you. I've been meaning to call you. How are you feeling?"

Simone was three months pregnant and glowing with the promise of motherhood. Some of that glow might also be due to her upcoming wedding to medic Mike O'Rourke. A one-night stand had led to what they'd hoped would be a lifetime of happiness.

Isobel thought of Neil, felt a pang of envy, and then quickly brushed it away. She was happy for her friend. That one-night stand had turned out well for her. Isobel considered the upcoming weekend, what might or might not happen. *Her* circumstances were very different. Neil didn't even live in Walnut River.

"I'm feeling good," Simone responded, answering her question. "I've had some morning sickness but it seems to be getting better now."

"How are the plans for the wedding?"

"They're going fine. I invited my mother."

Simone and her mother had long had a difficult relationship. "How do you feel about that?"

"I'm okay with it. She's attending the date-rape support group you recommended. I've noticed an improvement in her outlook since she's going to the group. She actually seems pleased to know that my future looks bright and happy. She's even a little bit excited about the wedding. It's going to be small," Simone went on. "But I'd like you to be my maid of honor. Will you? You don't need a special dress. I'm wearing a white suit."

"You've set the date?"

"The last Saturday in May in Mike's parents' backyard. Are you free?"

Would Neil still be around at the end of May? Probably not. "I'll be there. Just let me know what time."

Simone nodded and then leaned a bit closer. "I hear you're on a first-name basis with that investigator. What goes with that?"

Isobel didn't know what to say. She didn't want to lie to her friend, and she knew Simone would keep whatever she said in confidence. But what was there to say?

"Uh-oh, don't tell me the rumors are true," Simone surmised, probably correctly.

"What rumors?"

Simone hesitated.

Isobel knew her friend was not one to gossip. "I need to know, Simone."

Her friend finally revealed, "You've been seen outside the hospital with Neil Kane, at The Crab Shack, at the Walnut River Inn. Are you involved with him?"

Again, Isobel wasn't sure how to respond. So she simply said, "I like him."

Simone studied her more closely. "Oh, Isobel."

"What?"

"I can see it in your eyes. You've fallen for him."

In a quiet voice, she answered, "Maybe I have."

"Is there a future in this?"

"How *can* there be when he'll be going back to Boston when he's finished here?"

"Are you going to be with him while he's here?"

Simone knew all about falling in love against her will. Sometimes the heart made the most important decisions. Isobel knew she could trust her friend. "I'm going away with him this weekend. We're going to pick up an antique for the senior citizen auction."

There was a knowing look in Simone's eyes.

"We're going to have separate rooms," Isobel insisted.

"That doesn't mean you'll *stay* in separate rooms."

Just thinking about that possibility, Isobel's heart raced. "I'm not sure what I'm going to do. I do know that for once in my life, I'm not going to plan the future. I might even live in the moment. That will be a first."

"And damn the consequences?" Simone asked.

"And damn the consequences. Being with Neil for more than a snatched hour here and there might show me I don't care about him the way I think I do. This could be an eye-opening experience."

Simone clasped Isobel's arm. "I don't have any advice to give. Look what happened to me." She patted her tummy, which wasn't yet round. "But I can tell you I'm happier than I've ever been and that's all because of Mike."

Isobel gave her friend a hug. "I'm looking forward to your wedding."

"You can bring a guest," Simone suggested slyly.

"I'm not planning the future, remember?"

"Right."

A voice on the loudspeaker paged Simone.

"Break's over. I've got to scoot. I know you do, too." Before she hurried away, Simone suggested, "If you need someone to talk to when you get back, call me."

Isobel nodded, grateful Simone was her friend. Maybe when she returned to Walnut River, she wouldn't feel as confused as she did right now.

"So Cyrus is visiting with Dad?" Debbie asked Neil and Isobel as she brought the two of them sodas.

Neil was sitting on the sofa next to Isobel, his arm and leg lodged next to hers. He hadn't even kissed her yet tonight. In some ways, he felt like a teenager again, trying to read his date's cues.

"Cyrus was there when I got home," Isobel explained. "He said he was taking Dad to Burger King for supper. By the time I'd changed, they'd gone."

"Good for Cyrus. I'm grateful he's getting Dad out of the house."

"Actually your dad is why I'm here," Neil explained. "I want Isobel to go with me this weekend to my hometown.

I think I can finagle a couple of antiques for the senior center's auction."

"That would be great," Debbie said enthusiastically. "Do you want Dad to come over here?"

Isobel jumped in now. "I don't know how he'll feel about that, if he'll think we're taking care of him again. But Neil had a good idea. How do you think Chad would feel about staying with Dad Saturday and Sunday, instead of Dad coming over here?"

Debbie thought about it. "That might work. Chad's responsible enough. But he has to feel comfortable with doing it." She yelled, "Hey, Chad! Come here a minute, will you?"

The teenager emerged from his room in an oversize T-shirt and torn jeans. When he saw Neil, he grinned. "Did you come over for another game?"

"Not this time. Your aunt has a favor to ask."

Chad looked at Isobel. "What's up?"

She told him.

"So you want me to make sure Gramps eats and doesn't fall or anything?"

"Only if you're comfortable with staying," Isobel assured him.

"It will be cool. He can get out all those old photograph albums and tell me stories, and we can play cards. I know I might have to watch the History Channel with him, but I've got my iPod."

"You really don't mind?" Isobel asked.

"Nope. Stephanie's out of town this weekend so I'm high and dry."

"Except for that paper that's due," his mother reminded him.

"I'm going to finish that up tonight."

Apparently Stephanie was Chad's girlfriend. Neil could see the teenager really wouldn't mind looking after his grandfather.

Isobel assured Chad, "I have casseroles in the freezer I can take out before we leave for Saturday night and Sunday. There should be enough of everything else in the refrigerator—eggs, deli meat for the rest of the meals."

"We can always order pizza," Chad joked. "While you and Mom talk about what we're going to eat and all…" He cast a look at Neil. "Can I talk to you for a minute?"

Neil was surprised at the request. "Sure." Chad motioned to him. "Come back to my room. I want to show you something."

Still puzzled, Neil followed Chad to his bedroom. It was decorated like any teenage boy's bedroom with a poster of Carrie Underwood on one wall, an enlarged photo of David Ortiz at bat on the other. A computer sat on a small hutch.

"What did you want to show me?" Neil asked.

"Nothing really. I wanted to ask you something."

"About?"

"Well, Mom said you were married once."

"Yes, I was." He wondered if this was about Chad's dad and the divorce.

"But you're single now, right?"

"Sure am."

"And you like Aunt Iz?" Chad raised his brows.

There was no use denying it. "Yes, I do."

"Do you date a lot?"

"Not so much. I'm working most of the time."

"But you *do* date?"

"I do."

"See, I'm dating this girl," Chad explained.

"Stephanie."

"Yeah, and she's really hot. She's nice, too, and I like her a lot."

"So what's the problem?"

"I want to buy a car. Mom says she won't get me one and she won't let Dad get me one. But if I save up on my own and find one, she won't say I can't buy it. So I want to work all summer and save the money."

"That sounds like a plan."

"It *was* a plan until Steph asked me to go to the beach with her and her family for the month of July. They rent a house and her relatives come and go."

"So if you go with her for the month of July, you won't save nearly as much money."

"Right. But if I stay here and work, she might break up with me."

"How much does she mean to you?"

Chad looked down at his sneakers and rubbed his toe against the carpet. "A whole lot. She's the kind of girl I could see marrying some day. You know what I mean?"

"Can you live without the car?"

"I really want wheels."

"It's not an easy decision, Chad, but you're going to have to decide what's more important to you and live with whatever you decide."

"I want to work it so I can do both."

Neil chuckled. "Don't we all! But life rarely gives us everything we want. If Stephanie likes you as much as you like her, maybe she'll live without you for the month, and then get back together with you when she returns."

"Or, she could meet some surfer dude down there and I'd be toast."

"That's the chance you'd have to take."

Chad frowned. "I thought you'd have some answers."

Neil almost laughed out loud but he didn't because he was afraid Chad would misunderstand. "If you think you're going to find the answers as you get older, I can tell you you'll find some of them, but mostly you'll just find out what means the most to you."

"And that's what I have to figure out? Whether Stephanie's more important than the car?"

"Or whether trusting her is as important as the car."

"That's a different take on it," Chad mumbled. After a few seconds of silence, he shook his head and grinned ruefully. "And here I thought guys your age knew what to do about women."

"Not a chance. Even the ones who pretend to know what they're doing don't."

Chad gave him a sideways glance. "So what about you and Aunt Iz? Is something really happening?"

Neil was tempted to say, "After this weekend I'll let you know," but he knew better. He also knew after this weekend things could even be more complicated than they were now, especially if he took Isobel to his parents' home. "I don't discuss the women in my life. That's something I *have* learned in forty-two years."

Ten minutes later, after Chad showed him the iPod his father had gotten for him—another toy to make up for not being with him—Neil went back to the living room. All he wanted to do was take Isobel back to the Inn and spend the night with her. But he knew that likely wouldn't happen tonight. So instead, he waited until she'd ironed out every detail of Chad staying with her dad and then they left.

At the car, he opened the door for her. She slid inside and then looked up at him. He was broadsided by that look, by the beauty in Isobel that she couldn't herself see. Tonight she was dressed in a red-checkered blouse and navy slacks. Large red hoops swung from her ears. They both seemed lost in the moment because neither of them moved and neither of them spoke.

Suddenly he realized Isobel's sister was probably watching from a window, maybe even Chad, too. "Do you know how much I've wanted to kiss you all night?"

"No," she said with a shy smile.

"Will you come back to the Inn with me?"

"I don't think that's a good idea."

His heart sank. Maybe this weekend was going to be merely about antiques.

But Isobel hurried on. "I really don't want to be the butt of gossip."

He understood that the rumors really bothered her. But Isobel was always used to being in the right place at the right time and doing the right thing. Being with him wasn't wrong, but clearly it didn't seem right, either.

He closed her door none too gently, rounded the front of the car, and climbed into the driver's seat. After he did, she surprised him and leaned over, kissing him softly on the lips. She was there and then she was gone and he wanted a hell of a lot more.

"What was that for?" he asked, his voice husky as he backed out of her sister's driveway.

"For being so patient and letting me and Debbie iron out everything. What did Chad want to show you?"

"He showed me his iPod, but what he really wanted was to ask my advice on a girl problem. For some reason he thought I'd have the answer."

"And did you?"

"No, I just gave him food for thought. He's only trying to figure out what will make him happy."

"Good luck to him. At thirty-five, I'm still not sure," Isobel remarked.

Neil knew exactly what she meant.

They'd almost reached her dad's house when she said, "Cyrus's car is still parked in front. Don't stop. Go down to the next block and make a left turn."

"Where are we going?"

"You'll see." She directed him to make another left and he turned onto the gravel alley that stretched in back of the houses.

"There's a parking space next to Dad's garage. Pull in there and cut the lights."

After he did as she directed, he had to laugh. "I feel like a teenager again doing something illicit," he said with a smile.

"Doesn't that make it all the more fun?"

He couldn't see her in the pitch-blackness but he could hear the excited amusement in her voice. After he unfastened his seat belt, he took her into his arms, then he kissed her as he'd been wanting to kiss her all night. His hands were in her soft curls but his tongue was teasing her lips apart. His body was thrumming with all the restrained desire he'd been keeping in check.

She reached for him in the same hungry way, her fingers digging into his shoulders, her body straining toward his, her soft sounds of pleasure giving him all the permission he needed to take the kiss deeper, make it hotter and wetter. The steering wheel was in his way and the last thing he wanted to do was dig his elbow into the horn.

He broke away from her and leaned his forehead against hers. "Let's move into the backseat. We'll have more room."

She stilled. "Neil, I don't know if I want to—"

"I just want to hold you without wrecking the GPS or alerting the whole neighborhood we're here by hitting the horn."

After a long moment, she whispered, "Okay."

After they'd moved to the backseat, he gathered her into his arms for a long hug. He kissed her temple and ran his hand through her hair. "This isn't about me wanting sex again. It's about me wanting *you.*"

She turned her head into his neck and her breath was warm against his skin when she said, "I'm scared, Neil. We could be over in a blink of an eye."

"Do you want to go in?" He wasn't going to coax her into something she wasn't sure about, no matter how much his body tried to persuade him otherwise.

"Can we just stay here like this for a little while?"

Holding her and breathing her in was better than leaving her at her door. It was better than going back to that lonely bed at the Inn…better than erotic dreams that left him sweating and needing, with his arms empty.

"I'll hold you for as long as you want me to." Tonight, Isobel needed him in just this way. His needs would just have to be put on hold until she decided whether or not an affair with him would be worth the heartache.

Seizing the moment didn't seem so simple anymore.

As Neil drove two hours northeast to the town of Cranshaw on Saturday, Isobel couldn't believe how patient he'd been with her this week. She remembered how he'd held her without pushing for more on Wednesday night, how he'd kissed her, restraining himself from letting desire get out of control. Thursday night she'd been on call and had to handle a readmission. Last night…

They'd parked by her dad's garage again and Neil had sensed how much she'd needed to cuddle with him again in the silence.

It was scary sometimes how much he understood her. How was that possible in such a short time?

They didn't talk as they drove, just listened to music and held hands now and then across the middle of the car.

When they reached the outskirts of Cranshaw, she saw Neil stiffen, his hands becoming tighter on the wheel. How hard was this trip to his parents going to be?

"Your mom knows we're coming?"

"Yes, she does. Believe me, I'd never surprise them with an unexpected visit."

"Why not?"

"My parents aren't like your dad, Isobel. They're not all-embracing. Mom wants to be, but Dad is too…unrelenting. She'll pull out all the stops tonight, though, so be prepared."

"Pull out all the stops?"

"White linen tablecloth, candles, good silver, her mother's china."

"Does she do that for you?"

"Sometimes. She feels she's making my homecoming special that way. But tonight, she's doing it because I'm bringing a guest." As they drove through the center of town, they passed a huge brick-and-stone building with marble steps.

"The courthouse?" she asked.

"Yep. Dad worked there most of his life. I was really surprised when he retired two years ago. But he's writing a book on sentencing and the prison system. That's been keeping him busy."

The square in Cranshaw was the busiest intersection. Two streets later, Neil took a left turn, then a right. There was a row of shops, each painted a different color—yellow, royal blue, red and one white one. Antiques and More was the red structure which stood on the end. The other businesses housed a women's boutique, a flower shop and an optician.

All had similar window boxes filled with flowers and dark wood doors that stood open on the warm afternoon.

"The proprietors of all four shops decided they wanted to stand out. Even with the strip mall at the south side of town and a major mall on the north, these specialty shops do a good business. Come on, I'll introduce you to Mrs. Springer. She was my high-school math teacher."

Neil didn't give Isobel time to comment. He just hopped out of the car and came around to her door.

When she took his hand to climb out of the car, she asked, "Is Mrs. Springer going to tell me some good stories about you?"

"Not if I can help it."

A bell over the door jingled as Neil and Isobel went inside the shop. There were old photographs on the walls, furniture here and there, china and collectibles in cases. The woman at the cashier's desk was tall and thin, with gray hair piled into curls on the top of her head. She wore bright pink lipstick and a smock over her knit shirt and jeans.

When she saw Neil, she hurried toward him and gave him a big hug. "How are you doing, Neil? It's so good to see you. What's it been? Two, three years?"

"About that. It's good to see you, too, Mrs. Springer. I'd like to introduce you to Isobel Suarez. She's the woman I told you about who's collecting items for the senior citizens' auction in Walnut River."

"How many times do I have to tell you it's Helen. You're out of school now, Neil…been out a long time." She vigorously shook Isobel's hand. "It's good to meet you."

"Neil just told me you were his math teacher."

"That I was. He was one of my most promising students. He could have been a mathematician—clearheaded, fast thinking, calculated quicker in his head than anyone could on the calculator."

Isobel quirked her eyebrows at Neil. "A hidden talent you haven't told me about?"

"One of many," he joked. "Actually what I do isn't that different from mathematics. I add up the information, subtract whatever is irrelevant and figure out the solution."

"Your dad was right, you know. You would have made a good lawyer," Mrs. Springer commented.

Neil went silent.

Mrs. Springer, sensing she'd said the wrong thing, clasped Neil's arm. "But I understand you had to take your own road. It's just hard for a lot of parents who have their minds made up about what their children should be to accept something different."

Avoiding the topic altogether, Neil motioned to the merchandise in the shop. "So do you think you can help us? I'm searching for a couple of pieces I can buy and donate to the auction."

"Price range?" Helen asked.

"About five hundred total."

"Neil!" Isobel was shocked. "You don't have to donate that much. I never dreamed—"

When Neil hung his arm around Isobel's shoulders, she felt as if she belonged there, next to him, by his side. "Let me do this, Isobel. It's a worthy cause and I'll be able to see directly where it's going."

Her heart tripped. "You think you'll be coming back to visit after the investigation?"

Gazing down at her, he nodded. "I'd say that's a likely possibility."

Helen was watching them, taking it all in. She motioned to

them. "Come into the back room with me. I have a couple of pieces I just touched up. You'll want something useful that even someone who doesn't know antiques might buy. I have a Chippendale chair that's just been reupholstered and a nice claw-foot side table. If you have enough time, I can show you some pieces I've been saving for the summer tourist rush—Roseville pottery."

"Now *that* I could fit in my car. We have plenty of time, Helen." In Isobel's ear, he whispered, "We don't want to arrive at my parents' house any sooner than we have to."

Isobel hadn't been particularly nervous before, but now...

Neil's parents certainly wouldn't be ogres, but the way he was describing his dad, she suspected tonight could be uncomfortable at the least, confrontational at the worst, and maybe not even friendly.

What had she gotten herself into?

Chapter Nine

"My father inherited the house from his father," Neil explained as he drove up a treelined drive.

If a house could impress Isobel, the Kanes' house would. Stone and brick, it sat atop a hill with a long drive leading up to it. Surrounded by oaks, maples, spruce and pine, the three-story dwelling was stately and elegant, just like the property.

He added, "The Kanes helped settle Cranshaw and they've always been instrumental in running the town. My grandfather, who was also once a criminal defense attorney, became mayor after he retired."

"So he was around when you were growing up?"

"He was. We lived on the other side of town, and I used to ride my bike over. I could spend hours in his library. He died when I was in college. When my parents moved in, I chose a room on the third floor. It's like being at the top of the world up there."

She peered at the third-floor gables. "I can see why. It's a beautiful house."

"My parents finally seemed happier after they moved here. Maybe because there weren't any reminders of Garrett."

This was the first Neil had mentioned his brother since that one reference to him dying. "Were *you* happier?"

His answer was quick in coming. "I had moved on. But happier? No."

She could see now that his brother's death had affected him deeply.

They parked in front of a three-car garage that was attached to the house by a breezeway. Instead of going to the front door, Neil led Isobel to the breezeway door and they stepped inside.

She could see the area was sort of like her dad's glassed-in porch. The furniture was verdigris with huge soft cushions. The tables were metal and glass, and the ceramic-tile floor was the same rust shade as the cushions. A small gas-burning stove filled one corner.

"This is lovely," Isobel remarked, trying to take it all in. The backyard was immense.

"I spent a lot of time out here when I came home from college."

Because he'd still felt separated from his parents? Choosing a room on the third floor set him apart from them. Had he stayed removed because of guilt? He'd told her that when Garrett had been born, he'd felt displaced. After his brother had died, he'd felt responsible. At a time when a boy needed his parents most, she had the feeling a wall of pain had blocked Neil from his. She suddenly realized that she not only recognized Neil's pain, but actually *felt* it. She hurt for him; she hurt with him. And now she knew why.

She loved him.

She didn't know when or how it had happened. But she was head over heels. He'd become integral to her life, and in such a short time. The reality of love was so huge, the rush of emotion so great, it frightened her.

Without thinking twice, she slipped her hand into his.

The doors of the house flew open and Neil's mother—at least Isobel assumed she was Neil's mother—stood there grinning at them. In her mid-sixties, Alice Kane was still a beautiful woman. Her frosted-blond wavy hair was styled attractively around her face. She was wearing a pale-peach sweater, shirt and knit slacks. Her eyes were the same golden brown as Neil's. Although she appeared glad to see him, she didn't run forward and embrace him, nor did he embrace her.

Isobel keenly felt the absence of that hug.

When Neil released Isobel's hand and hung his arm around her shoulders, he said, "Mom, I'd like you to meet Isobel Suarez. Isobel, this is my mother, Alice Kane."

Isobel extended her hand. "It's nice to meet you, Mrs. Kane."

"Call me Alice," the older woman insisted. She stepped back and motioned them into the kitchen. "Come on in." She said to Neil, "I baked your favorite oatmeal cookies." As he passed her, she laid her hand on his shoulder.

Isobel could feel that these two wanted to be close, yet something was standing in their way. The judge, maybe?

"I have trays set up in the parlor," Alice hurried on. "We have coffee, tea, hot chocolate, whatever you want."

Isobel glanced around the bright kitchen with its birch cupboards, stainless-steel appliances and an island in the center. A bright-red table and chairs sat under a flowered chandelier, and Isobel could peek into the large dining room beyond. The teakettle simmered on the stove and the aroma of fresh coffee floated through the air. Cookies were laid out on a beautiful glass tray covered with plastic wrap.

"You don't have to carry everything into the parlor. We can just sit at the table," Neil suggested.

"Oh, but your father said he'd prefer—"

An older man who Isobel guessed was in his late sixties entered the kitchen then. He was tall, with glasses and completely gray hair. He was wearing an oxford-cloth shirt and casual slacks and loafers. His cheekbones were higher than Neil's, his jaw a little less defined, but she could see the resemblance.

"What do I prefer?" he asked with a tight smile and a nod toward Neil and Isobel.

Awkwardness filled the kitchen but Neil replied easily. "I told Mom she didn't have to go to all the trouble of setting up the parlor. We're fine at the table."

Already Isobel felt the tight wire of tension pull between the two men. "That's fine," Neil's father agreed, not making it an issue. "Introduce me to your…friend."

Neil made the introductions while his mother bustled about, putting the cookies on the table, gathering cups and saucers and goblets.

"My wife tells me you're a social worker, Isobel," the judge remarked. "You must see as much dirty family laundry as I did when I was on the bench."

"I get involved in family dynamics," she admitted. "Fortunately, I feel I can make a difference. I imagine it was frustrating for you to see the results of family situations gone wrong."

"That's perceptive of you," he said, studying her more closely, waiting for his wife to pour his coffee.

Neil remained silent. Still, his father targeted him next. "We've heard all about the Northeastern HealthCare takeover attempt in Walnut River. We're afraid they might try here next. Are you investigating what they're trying to do?" he asked his son.

"No, I'm not."

"And of course you can't say more about it."

"No, I can't."

The judge crossed his arms over his chest. "How soon will you be returning to Boston?"

"I'm not sure, a week or two."

The judge assessed Neil's neutral expression, then gave his son a slight smile that didn't carry much warmth. "Have you thought about what I advised the last time you were home—running for office? Even though you're not a lawyer, with the experience you've gotten, you could make a place for yourself in the State House, maybe even run for governor someday."

"I told you before, Dad, getting involved in politics is the last thing I'd ever consider," Neil said calmly as if the calmness was hard to come by.

"You're really satisfied with what you're doing?"

"Let's not get into this now, Dad, okay? Isobel and I just dropped by for a friendly visit."

As if his mother heard the restrained impatience in Neil's tone, she rushed in. "Did you find any antiques at Mrs. Springer's?"

"We did. Isobel thinks they'll go over well at the auction."

"Auction?" his father asked.

"It's a charity auction at the senior citizens' center in

Walnut River. Neil kindly bought a few items at Mrs. Springer's and is donating them." Isobel flashed a smile at Neil's father.

"Oh, he did?" Neil's father gave his son a long look and then appraised *her* carefully. His perusal was making her uncomfortable so she filled in the silence.

"Mrs. Springer even donated a small table we could fit in the back of the car. I might end up being auctioneer unless we can find someone more experienced. I'll be familiar with each item, but I've never done an auction."

"I helped with a silent auction last year," Alice said cheerily. She began telling Isobel about the charity benefit.

As Isobel listened, she wondered if this family had experienced any truly happy moments since Garrett had died. There was a chasm between Neil and his father that his mother obviously tried to fill, yet she couldn't, because she felt torn between the two of them.

Isobel felt Judge Kane's constant regard as Neil's mom gave her a tour of her gardens and they talked about flowers and landscaping. She felt his gaze on her often throughout dinner.

Afterward as dusk began to fall, Neil pulled her outside onto the patio. She supposed he wanted to give both of them a break.

The night air was cool and Neil stood close enough that she could feel his body heat. "Do you want to go to the inn now? We don't have to stay."

"You haven't seen your parents in a while, Neil. Don't you want to spend some time with them?"

"You've gotten a taste of what it's like being with my parents. I don't want you to feel uncomfortable. This was a bad idea. I don't know what I thought I'd accomplish."

"Did you want *them* to meet *me,* or *me* to meet *them?*"

He didn't pretend not to know what she meant. Had he brought her here so his parents might approve of her? Or had he brought her here so she could get a peek into his life, what it had been and what it was now.

"I'm not sure. Every time I come home I think things might be different. They never are."

"Your mom is sweet. She tries to make up for the tension between you and your dad."

"If it weren't for Mom, I wouldn't come home."

Suddenly the patio lights went on. They lit the perimeter of the flagstone and dispelled the approaching shadows. The French door that separated the dining room from the patio opened and Judge Kane stepped outside. It was obvious he noticed how close Neil and Isobel were standing.

He wore a light jacket and he brought Isobel's sweater to her. She'd left it in the kitchen. "I thought you might need this."

Neil silently took it from his father and held it while Isobel inserted first one arm and then the other. "Thank you," she told the older man, looking for signs of softening in his face. There weren't any.

He addressed Neil. "I'd like to talk to Isobel for a few minutes. Alone."

"Why is that necessary?" Neil countered, on the defensive, ready to protect her.

Isobel wanted to know what the judge was thinking and to get a glimpse behind the stoic facade he wore. "It's all right, Neil."

"You're sure?" It was his investigator's voice that wanted the truth.

"I'm sure. I'd like to get to know your dad better."

"I'll be in the living room," he told her as he went inside. She knew if she needed him, all she had to do was call.

A slight breeze ruffled the leaves on the decades-old trees and blew Isobel's hair across her cheek. She swept it away and just waited.

"Let's get to the bottom line," the judge decided. "Are you and my son serious?"

"Maybe you should be asking *him* that," she responded softly.

He frowned. "I didn't come out here to spar with you."

"Why *did* you come out here?"

He looked a little surprised that she was questioning him. "I want to know what Neil's getting himself into. It's been a long time since he brought a woman here."

"Exactly how long has it been?" she asked.

As if debating whether he wanted to answer her or not, he took a few moments, then he replied, "He hasn't brought anyone here since his divorce."

Could Neil really be serious about her? Did they have a chance to be together beyond his investigation?

Before she could even answer those questions in her mind, the judge warned, "Don't think you're going to get your hands on his money. After one failed marriage, I'm sure he'd ask for a prenuptial agreement."

"I didn't know Neil had any money," she blurted out honestly.

The judge motioned to the house and the surroundings. "When you saw this, you knew. I'm sure Neil indicated the lifestyle he grew up with."

"Your property and standard of living has nothing to do with Neil now."

"He'll inherit someday. A smart woman—and you strike me as a smart woman—will consider that."

Up until now, Isobel had tried to remain polite. After all, these were Neil's parents and, truth be told, she wanted them to like her. But the judge already had a preconceived notion of who she was. So maybe she needed to do some plain speaking to get her point across.

She looked him straight in the eye. "Money can't buy happiness. If I wanted proof of that, I can look at you and your wife and know it."

He blustered. "Who do you think—?"

She held up her hand to stop him. "I know about loss. My mother died four years ago. Not a day goes by that I don't miss her. No amount of money will bring her back. I suspect that's what you feel about the son you lost. Neil told me there's distance between you two, and that's what I can't understand. You lost one son, but you still have Neil. You should be proud you raised such a wonderful man and you should be doing everything in your power not to lose him, too!"

Silence stretched long between them until the judge decided, "This isn't any of your business."

"You made it my business when you came out here to question me."

After he studied her for a few tense moments, he looked into the darkness and the trees in the backyard. "Neil and I haven't been close since before Garrett died."

"Is that because Garrett was your favorite?"

When the judge's gaze found hers, she knew she was right.

"Maybe he was after he was born, but I was always proud of Neil. I had great expectations for him. He could have been anything he'd chosen to be. If he didn't want to go into law, he could have become a doctor, a physicist, absolutely anything. But he has no ambition. You heard what he said about going into politics."

She leaned forward, interested in how Neil's father

thought. "Why do you believe ambition has to be lofty? Neil became a police officer so he could catch the bad guys. Now he holds a trusted position in the Attorney General's Office. Why isn't it enough for you that he cares about what he does, that he thinks he can right wrongs his way?"

Neil's dad fell into silence again. Finally, he asked, "That's the way he sees it?"

"Yes, that's the way he sees it. As a judge, you see the results of a situation. Neil takes an active part in finding out the truth, making sure the right person gets blamed, which doesn't always happen in the legal system."

When Neil's father didn't respond, Isobel wondered if maybe she should leave him and go inside.

His voice was somewhat less arrogant when he concluded, "You and my son have more than a…surface relationship."

She knew what those code words meant. The judge thought they were sleeping together and that's what had brought them together. Maybe their attraction had brought them together, but she and Neil communicated on lots of other levels, too. "Yes, we do."

"I don't meet many young women who say what's on their mind in such a thoughtful manner," he admitted a bit awkwardly.

"I handle sticky situations a lot, so I've had practice."

The judge gave a light chuckle. "You're a match for Neil. I can see that. He needs a strong woman. He has a stubborn streak that I'm sure he didn't inherit from me." There was some slight amusement in Neil's dad's words and she wondered what would happen if he and his son had an honest and heartfelt conversation.

The subtle relaxation of tension between them led Isobel to say, "I think you and Neil are more alike than you realize."

"But we don't want to admit it?"

With her cards on the table as well as his, she could afford to be diplomatic, "Something like that."

"I think I just saw Neil's shadow pass by the French doors. We'd better assure him I haven't upset you to the point of tears."

"You haven't upset me, Judge," she assured him.

He opened the door. "Good, because I think I'd like to have more conversations with you in the future."

Neil was standing inside, and he studied her closely. "Everything okay?"

To Neil's surprise, the judge patted his shoulder. "If she can hold her own with me, she can hold her own with anyone." He shrugged out of his jacket. "I'm going to find your mother and see if I can rustle up another piece of that apple pie. If you're interested," he pointed his thumb at the kitchen, "I'll be in there."

After his dad left the room, Neil took Isobel by the shoulders. "I hope he didn't insult you. He has a way—"

"He didn't. Actually I think your dad and I understand each other."

Neil finally broke into a smile. "The same way *your* dad and I understand each other?"

"Precisely."

He shook his head. "You'll have to tell me about it. Do you want a piece of pie?"

She didn't, but she could nibble while Neil and his father took a few tenuous steps toward each other. "I'll have a cup of tea. You have a piece of pie and we'll see if we can't have some conversation that doesn't put everyone on edge."

"That'll be the day." Neil brought her into his chest for a tight hug and a quick but deep kiss. When they broke apart, he said, "We have separate rooms at the inn and that's the way it will stay if you want it that way. But I—"

Neil's cell phone rang. After he fished it out of his pocket, he checked the caller ID. "It's my office. I need to take this."

Apparently Neil's office never shut down and he was always on call. She wished their kiss had been longer, deeper, more intimate. Tonight...

She still hadn't made up her mind about tonight. She reached up and stroked his jaw. "I'll save you a piece of pie," she assured him, and went to the kitchen, considering the consequences of joining Neil in his room tonight...considering her regrets if she didn't.

Neil's phone call had troubled him, Isobel could tell. He'd acted as if it hadn't. He'd eaten his piece of pie, complimented his mother on it again, and asked his dad how his book was going. But underneath it all, she could see in his eyes when he looked at her that the call had bothered him.

He'd been so careful with her as they'd checked in at the Victorian inn where he'd reserved their rooms. He'd kissed her good-night at her door—the other room on their floor was unoccupied—with more restraint than she'd ever felt him use. It hadn't been what she'd expected at all. She'd expected to be swept away. She'd expected him to kiss her senseless until there was no decision to make. But he hadn't. He'd told her he'd see her in the morning and went into his room, next to hers.

Isobel changed into her nightgown. She attempted to read and didn't absorb any of the words on the page. She tried to sleep but thoughts of Neil and what they could be doing together kept her awake. Then there were the sounds from his room, the creak of the floorboards, first on one side of the room and then the other, the hum of the small printer he carried with his computer that told her he might be working, the sound of his door opening as he went into the bathroom, ran the shower, and then returned once more to his bedroom.

Maybe if she took a shower she'd be able to sleep, maybe it would relax her. Twenty minutes later, Isobel had showered, too, and dried her hair. It was a soft mass of wild curls all over her head. After she slipped on her nightgown once more, she studied her face in the mirror.

What do you really want? she asked herself.

That answer was easy—another night with Neil, a whole night with Neil, maybe every night with Neil until he left Walnut River. Sure, she could try to keep her heart safe. She could pretend the love she felt for him would go away after he was gone. She could deny the desire that right now made her feel more alive than she'd ever felt before.

Or…

She could take the risk of finding out if he wanted her as much as she wanted him.

Sliding into the satin mules that matched her gown—the slippers, gown and robe had been a set Debbie had given her last Christmas—she left the robe hanging on the bathroom door. She hesitated in the hall outside Neil's room. Was she being altogether foolish?

There was only one way to find out. She knocked.

When Neil answered his door, his face was more stoic than she'd ever seen it. He looked down over the pale-green, satin nightgown, his gaze lingering on her breasts, on the curve of her hips, before returning to her face. "Do you need something?"

His voice was gravelly and she hoped that was because she was affecting him the way he was affecting her. He wore navy flannel jogging shorts and a drawstring dangled tantalizingly at his navel. She was going to hyperventilate if she didn't get this over with and find out if she was going to sleep in her room or his.

"Can we talk?" she asked, her voice hardly more than a whisper.

The nerve in Neil's jaw worked. "If you come in and go anywhere near the bed, I might not let you leave until morning."

"Maybe I won't want to leave until morning."

"Are you saying—"

She blurted out, "I'm saying that I've never stood at a man's door like this before…that if you don't let me inside, you'll have to carry me somewhere."

Instead of stepping back so she could enter, he folded his arms around her and held her tight. "Knees still wobbly?"

She wrapped her arms around his neck. "Yes, but it doesn't matter. I know you'll catch me if I fall."

Then his smile faded. "I didn't want to force you into anything you didn't want…or that you'd regret."

"I'm here of my own free will. My only regret would be *not* coming to you tonight."

This time when Neil kissed her, he did sweep her away. He didn't hold back. He took as much as she could give and then he took some more. She couldn't distinguish his taste from hers and she didn't want to. She couldn't remember what it was like to take a breath and she didn't care.

Neil was hard against her. She could feel his heat through his shorts, through the thin layer of her gown. With him six inches taller than she was, neither of them could get the satisfaction they wanted. His hand slid down her back to her buttocks and lifted her. She wrapped her legs around him and her slippers fell off. He walked backward until they reached the bed and then he sat with her, kissing her, until they tumbled onto the mattress, each reaching for the other. They were as hungry for each other as they had been the first time. Even hungrier.

In spite of their eagerness, Neil didn't rush. He pushed the spaghetti strap of her nightgown off one shoulder and tasted her skin along her collarbone down to her breast. Her nightgown kept getting in the way so he helped her out of it, then dropped his shorts.

After a long, teasingly seductive kiss, he whispered against her lips, "Don't go away. I'll be right back."

She kept her eyes closed, still lost in desire. But she heard him rifle through his duffel bag. In no time at all he was back. Now she did open her eyes and what she saw in his took her breath away.

"I want you so much my fingers are shaking," he admitted wryly as he tore open the condom packet.

"And I want you so badly I'm shaking all over," she confessed. Taking the packet from him, slipping out the condom, she waited for him to lie back so she could prepare him.

"Are you going to torture me?" he asked with a crooked smile.

"I wouldn't call it torture." Her voice was as sensually enticing as her fingers as they teased and tempted and then finally rolled down the condom to cover him.

As soon as she finished, he pulled her to him for a kiss and then rolled her over so he was on top. "This time I'm not going to hurry."

"You hurried before?" she teased.

"I lost control before."

Then his mouth was on hers again and Neil filled her

senses and her mind and her heart. As he promised, he didn't rush. He kissed every inch of her until she was mindless with need, calling his name, begging for fulfillment. Finally he entered her slowly, oh so slowly. When she lifted her hips to take more of him, he chuckled, then continued his tempting possession. By the time he filled her completely, she was halfway there, rising fast, reaching for the farthest star. He began thrusting, taking her farther and farther until she caught the starburst and let it break all around her. His release sounded just as satisfying, just as wrenching, just as heart-enveloping. He said her name so tenderly tears burned in her eyes. Moments later, he was cuddling her, holding her so close she still felt one with him. She fell asleep that way, dreaming of tomorrow.

Isobel had fallen asleep by the time Neil slipped away from her and went into the bathroom. His mind was a turbulent maze, his thoughts scattered and unfocused because of what had just happened between them. She'd given herself to him completely.

So now what was he going to do? The phone call from his supervisor, Derek Grayson, was a complication he'd never expected. The mole, whoever it was, had digitally altered his voice every time he called. Today he'd left a message on Neil's supervisor's answering machine. Derek had repeated it verbatim.

As Neil climbed into bed beside Isobel once more, he studied her, knowing that this newest information certainly wasn't true. The gist of it was that Isobel Suarez was taking kickbacks from Pine Ridge Rehab.

How he wanted to tell her about it and trust her with the information. But he couldn't. He had to go by the book. He couldn't prejudice this investigation in any way.

Doesn't sleeping with her prejudice it? the devil's advocate inside his head asked.

No. Because he knew she wasn't guilty. He was absolutely certain.

He needed time to figure out what to do. But how much time could he give it? Could he get to the truth in the questioning he had left to do?

Or would he have to formulate a plan that could tear them apart?

Chapter Ten

The past week had been...

Neil couldn't even describe it as he lay beside Isobel in his room at the Inn after the senior center auction.

He ran his hand tenderly through Isobel's curly hair. She was cuddled naked by his side, nestled into his shoulder, and he wished he could keep her there forever. But after tomorrow, she'd look at him differently. He had hoped he wouldn't have to take the allegations against her to her supervisor. He'd hoped he'd have figured out over the past week who the mole was, that the information his office had received was groundless. But that hadn't happened and he had to get to the truth. His investigation had to take precedence over anything personal, didn't it?

Would Isobel ever forgive him for following regulations and keeping the charges against her to himself until they

could be handled as *his* supervisor suggested? He hadn't
needed Derek to remind him that if he gave the information
to Isobel, she could clean up anything she'd been involved
in. They had to go through the proper channels. As soon as
he reported the claims against Isobel to her supervisor, he'd
be on the phone to Pine Ridge, warning the administrators
there not to talk to Isobel until the investigation was over.

"I can't believe we raised almost nine thousand dollars,"
Isobel mumbled against his chest.

"That's what you're thinking about at a time like this?" he
teased, partitioning off his work from his personal life as he
had all week. Each day they'd managed to steal time for
themselves. This afternoon, they'd come back to the Inn,
eager to undress and please each other in bed.

"What better time?" she returned. "I want to know why a
bachelor needs a handmade quilt." There was a twinkle in her
eyes as she sifted her fingers through his chest hair.

"My mother likes anything hand-crafted. It will make a
wonderful birthday gift."

"You don't need it to keep you warm on long, cold nights
in Boston?"

She was fishing and he knew why. What would happen to
them once he was gone? Would he return to Walnut River?
Would she come to see him in Boston? Would he date other
women? He couldn't imagine ever dating anyone else. In
fact, Isobel was the be-all and end-all of women for him. He
found himself thinking about that house and picket fence
and dreams he'd never imagined he could make come true.

Would she date other men? The thought of Isobel dating
anyone else made his blood run cold.

"My condo has a great heating system." He had to keep
this light. He couldn't get into anything deep, not tonight. All

week he'd searched for ways to settle this investigation without using Isobel. But through his conference call with Derek yesterday, he'd realized there weren't any.

"Is something wrong? You're awfully quiet today."

"No, nothing's wrong. I'm just enjoying holding you like this. Besides, you wore me out yesterday, helping you get ready for the auction."

"I didn't wear you out. You were even running circles around Chad."

"He's a good kid. Did you know he's thinking about becoming a pharmacist?"

"Really? He told you that?"

"When we were carrying all those boxes to the storeroom in the senior center," he teased.

She lightly jabbed her elbow into his ribs.

Over the past week he'd learned her ticklish spots and he tickled her side. She squealed and wiggled away but he caught her and kissed her—longingly, sensually, almost desperately. When this was all over, how could he make her understand? How could he make her see that he was doing this for her, too? That if everything worked out, he'd clear her name and the hospital's, as well as find out who the informant was.

When he finished kissing her, he needed her all over again.

"I have to go soon," she murmured.

"Soon, but not now," he protested gruffly, caressing her face, running his thumb over her lips.

"I wish I could spend all night with you."

"You can."

"No, I can't. Dad would…he just wouldn't think it was right. And if anyone saw that I stayed over with you—" She shook her head. "I can't stay, Neil. I have to go home."

He knew she was right, yet he wanted another whole night, too. He wanted endless nights. That thought unsettled him, almost as much as the depth of his feelings for her. His emotions had been frozen for so long, he wasn't used to the happiness and the novelty of thinking about another person besides himself.

"Stay until dark," he coaxed, drawing her body on top of his, feeling her breasts against his chest, her softness against his hardness, her legs stretched out on his.

"So nobody sees me leave?" she asked.

"No, so we have at least another hour."

Isobel smiled at him. With her hands on his shoulders, she pushed herself up and straddled him. "Just what do you think can happen in another hour?"

"We can take each other to paradise."

Moving down lower on him, she let her hair brush his navel, then below his navel. He groaned.

"How about if you start the journey first," she suggested.

Then Neil couldn't speak as her lips surrounded him. He vowed when it was Isobel's turn, he had to make love to her as she'd never been made love to before.

If he did that, maybe when this was all over, she'd forgive him.

On Monday morning, at Northeastern HealthCare's main office in Boston, Anna Wilder adjusted her charcoal suit jacket and stepped up to the receptionist's desk in her boss's office suite.

Anna plastered on her professional smile. "Mr. Daly buzzed me this morning when I got in. He said he wanted to see me immediately." She shouldn't be nervous about this meeting but she was. She'd had only two other face-to-face meetings with Alfred Daly. One when he hired her, the other for a six-month evaluation. So why today?

His receptionist nodded. "Go on back. He's waiting for you."

The NHC building was plush. The company's logo was maroon and gray and the offices all kept that same theme, along with off-white leather furniture, contemporary artwork on the walls, and solid wood doors no one could hear through. That made her a little uneasy at times.

The door to Mr. Daly's office was open. When he saw her, he motioned her inside.

Daly was in his fifties, with brown hair combed over his bald spot. He wore suits that cost more than a month of her salary. And his ties? Some of his ties should hang in an art museum— many were one of a kind. When she saw him around the building, he never stopped to chat with anyone. He was always on the move, not unfriendly, just focused. Right now he focused on her.

"Anna, have a seat."

He stayed behind his monstrous mahogany desk, laid his reading glasses on the blotter and looked her straight in the eye. "I'll keep this short and to the point. I want you to go to Walnut River."

"Why?"

"There are many reasons, but mainly because you are a Wilder. Your sister and brothers are doctors at a hospital we want to bring into our family. Influential doctors. I know full well they're against the merger, and you've got to change their minds."

"I've talked to them many times. Their minds are set. I'm sorry, but there's nothing I can do about it."

"That kind of attitude won't get you far here, Anna. I want

you to make the merger between Northeastern HealthCare and Walnut River General happen."

"Even if I could convince my brothers and sister, there are many other doctors who are against it, as well as administrative personnel. How do you think I'm going to influence all those people?"

"That's my point, Anna. You have a job here for a reason. You're a smart woman. It's up to you to figure out how to accomplish the takeover. If you don't complete the merger, you will no longer have a job here."

Anna couldn't believe what she was hearing. Her whole professional career depended on this one assignment?

The truth was, for years she'd felt inferior to Ella and David and Peter. Now she had the chance to prove she wasn't. Now she had the chance to prove she could do what was asked of her and be successful in the hardest endeavor.

But what if she couldn't be? What if nothing she said or did made a difference?

Old insecurities die hard. She couldn't listen to them. "How soon do you want me to leave?"

"You and Holmes are working on the Carson Memorial Hospital merger. He tells me that's going well and you should have loose ends tied up in about a week. Is that right?"

"Yes, that's right."

"I don't want you to drop the ball there. I know you were instrumental in making it happen. So take this week to close that deal. But then I want you in Walnut River. I know you can do this, Anna. Don't let me down."

Anna stood. "I won't, sir."

As she left the office, she knew all she had to do was make the impossible happen.

If she thought about it too much, panic would overtake her.

For the next week, she'd concentrate on Carson Memorial. And then? She'd formulate a plan and go home to execute it.

Home. Where she didn't belong any more...where she'd never quite fit in.

And completing the NHC takeover would ensure she never did.

When Isobel returned to Walnut River General from an outside appointment early Monday afternoon, there was an e-mail from her supervisor, Mrs. Palmer, asking Isobel to come to her office as soon as she got back.

Margaret Palmer had hired Isobel and she'd always gotten along well with the woman. Margaret was in her late forties, knew that her social workers were overworked, and tried to be fair about assignments and their caseloads.

Isobel tucked her purse into the drawer of her desk and went down a short hall to Margaret's office. When she stepped inside, she was met by the most serious expression she'd ever seen on her supervisor's face. Margaret's ash-blond hair was styled in a pageboy, her bangs brushed to the side. Her glasses gave her a professorial look. Right now, Isobel saw confusion in her eyes and a frown on her face.

"You wanted to see me?"

Margaret motioned to the chair in front of her desk. Once Isobel was seated, her supervisor leaned forward and crossed her arms on her blotter. "I had a troubling report given to me this morning by Neil Kane."

A report from Neil? He hadn't said anything to Isobel about it. She remembered how quiet he'd been yesterday. Her heart began hammering. "What was in the report?"

"Mr. Kane has been made aware of a complaint against you."

"What?" Nothing could have surprised her more.

"A serious charge has been made against you, Isobel. Mr. Kane has received a complaint that you're taking kickbacks from Pine Ridge Rehab."

Isobel was so astonished, she couldn't form a coherent thought, let alone a coherent sentence.

"I have to take this seriously," Margaret went on, "especially since it's coming from an investigator from the Attorney General's Office. You're going to have to face the hospital review board and defend yourself." She hesitated. "Your review is set in two weeks. I'll have to suspend you until this is all cleared up."

"Suspend me? I haven't done anything wrong! All I've done is place patients the way I'm supposed to…in the best circumstances for *them*."

As Margaret studied Isobel carefully, her expression became empathetic. "I know you're a hard worker, Isobel. I know you'll be able to clear this up."

Could someone be setting her up? Doing more than delivering rumors? "Is there any proof of this charge?"

"Mr. Kane didn't say if he has hard evidence or not. He'll be turning over whatever he has to the board."

"Don't I have a right to know what it is?"

"I suppose you can discuss that with Mr. Kane. You'll be receiving an official letter tomorrow. It will list the areas the review board will go over with you."

"I suppose my pay will be suspended, too."

"I'm sorry, Isobel, but yes it will be, until the review board makes a decision."

Isobel was still in a state of shock when she walked out of her supervisor's office fifteen minutes later after discussing who would work the cases under her supervision now. For the next half hour, she sorted her files and gave them to the case workers who would be attending to them. They shot her odd looks, and she wondered if they'd already heard about her review and suspension.

As she returned to her desk for her purse, she couldn't understand why Neil hadn't told her. Over the weeks he'd conducted his investigation, he'd come to believe the informant was giving him unfounded information. So why had he gone to her supervisor? Why was he pushing for a formal review? When she thought about the hours they'd spent together, the weekend they'd spent together, the emotional intimacy she'd never shared with anyone else, she felt betrayed and absolutely devastated. She was going to confront him to find out why he'd kept this from her, but she had to calm down. First, she'd visit her patients and tell them someone else would be handling their cases. She would assure them they were in good hands.

And then she'd go to Neil's office and confront him.

The fourth floor was quiet when Isobel approached Neil's office door. She was still shaken by what her supervisor had told her. The idea of confronting Neil hurt her heart. *Why* hadn't he told her?

Determined to learn the answer, determined to find out if she'd meant anything to him at all except a diversion while he was in Walnut River, she sharply knocked on the door.

With a cordless phone at his ear, he opened it.

She thought she glimpsed a flicker of…something in his eyes, but then it was gone. His expression showed not one iota of what he was thinking or feeling.

He motioned her inside while he crossed to the far end of the office to finish his call.

But she didn't sit. She unabashedly listened to his conversation as he said, "I have a few different options. I'll call you when it's over."

After he clicked off the phone, he laid it on the table beside his computer and focused his attention on her. "Did you speak to your supervisor?"

All of the hurt and sense of betrayal was pushing against Isobel. It wanted to come rushing out, but she held it off. She thrust it behind a dam of resolve. When she did, anger stole hurt's place. It fortified her and gave her the strength to meet Neil's gaze head-on. Her voice clipped and even, she demanded, "Why didn't you tell me there was a complaint against me?"

Still with no expression she could read, Neil suggested, "Calm down, Isobel. *Sit* down and we'll go through this."

"Don't patronize me, Neil. If you had to go before a review board, *you* wouldn't be calm, either. This could go to the state licensing board. Why didn't you tell me about the complaint?" she repeated. "And how long have you known about it?"

Neil turned the chair toward her. "Please," he said quietly.

She sat, not because he told her to, but because she was feeling shaky and didn't want to fall apart in front of him.

He lodged himself on the corner of the table, much too close to her. In spite of everything, she wanted to touch him, to feel his arms around her, to feel his skin pressed against hers.

Never again. Once trust was broken...

"I had to tell your supervisor first because this is my job. It's what I do. I have regulations to follow and I can't let anything interfere with those."

"How long?" She had to know if he'd been keeping this to himself while he'd made love to her. Had sex with her, she reminded herself. He couldn't love her and do this to her.

This was the first time since she'd entered Neil's office that he looked uncomfortable. "I learned about it last weekend. The call I received at my parents."

Her hurt won the battle to be released. "I thought we were...close."

"We were." His jaw set.

"No. If we were close, you never could have kept it from me while we...while we were in bed."

"I had to decide what to *do* about the information. I was hoping I'd find the mole and not even have to bring it to light. But by this weekend after talking with my supervisor— You've got to understand, I have to go by the book."

Hurt beyond words, she kept silent.

"Isobel, I'm doing this for a reason. I hoped you'd trust me."

"Trust you? I'd trust you if you'd told me about the complaint without going to Mrs. Palmer first."

"If I had told you, you could have tampered with possible evidence—spoken to contacts at Pine Ridge, wiped your hard drive of correspondence. With this review, our investigation of you is official."

Their eyes locked for a few seconds.

Neil's voice gentled. "I don't believe you're guilty."

That was something, she supposed, but not much. She understood about jobs and rules. To her, though, people came first. The people she loved came first.

Neil went on. "I want to use your stint in front of the review board to lure out the mole."

"How is ruining my professional reputation going to do that?"

"Obviously, you'll be able to answer every question and refute every charge. After you do, I'll announce that the allegations against you are groundless, just like every other charge I've investigated. I'm hoping the mole will get desperate and up the ante, give us more, let something slip."

"You're going to go public with my review?"

"I'd like your permission to do that."

She could see the merit in his idea. If the mole had a grudge…or if he was getting paid to aid NHC in the takeover, he wouldn't stop. He'd want to stay in the fight and damage the hospital even more thoroughly. But Neil was using her career and her reputation as the means to his end.

"In other words, you want to use me as a pawn."

He contradicted her. "You need to look at this differently. You'll be my partner, not a pawn."

"You're *using* me, Neil. Don't delude yourself that you aren't. I understand why. You're stumped. You don't know where else to go. Walnut River General can't fight this takeover attempt until you're gone. Because of that, for the sake of the hospital, I'll help you with this. I'll do what you want. But on a personal level, I don't want any more to do with you."

She heard him call her name as she ran out of his office, as she kept running down the hall to the back stairway and took each step faster than she should have. Neil didn't come after her and she wasn't surprised. He didn't care about her after all—he cared about his investigation. He saw her as an easy way to make the days in Walnut River go faster. She'd been the foolish one to fall head over heels in love with a man who saw her as a means to an end.

She could lose her job. Oh, maybe that wasn't what he had in mind. Maybe that wasn't what he'd intended. But anything could happen with something like this, especially if someone was trying to set her up to prove wrongdoing at Walnut River General. Why couldn't Neil see that? Why couldn't he see that if he'd come to her with the complaint, they could have figured out together what to do with it?

Now, she was suspended. Her dreams were yesterday's news and Neil's so-called ethics had betrayed her.

A small voice inside her challenged her. *He's just doing his job.*

If doing her job meant hurting someone she cared about, she wouldn't be able to do it. It was as simple as that. Black and white.

Neil looked at life in black and white, too. Obviously, rules and regulations came first with him.

At the bottom of the stairwell, she pushed open the outside door and stepped into the warmth of the May day. But she didn't feel the warmth. She was cold inside. She needed to clear her head so she could start functioning again.

Her life would go on without Neil Kane in it. End of discussion.

When she reached Sycamore Street, she parked two houses down from her dad's. She didn't want him to know she was home. Some nights she was much later than this so he wouldn't worry. Thank goodness she kept a duffel bag in the car with a change of clothes.

After changing into workout clothes in the garage, she tied her running shoes and tried not to think. More importantly she tried not to feel. She knew there were tears on her cheeks and hoped the wind would dry them.

Wheeling her bike out of the side door, she bumped it over the grass until she had it on the gravel alley. Then she hopped on and took off as if she were in the most important race of her life. She didn't even think about where she was headed. She just rode, down neighborhood treelined streets, pedaling hard up the hills, letting the wind and speed take her as far as it would. She barely noticed when she veered off the side streets onto the secondary road.

When she came to an intersection, she turned right, aware cars were passing her and that her bike lane was very narrow. But the cars zooming by didn't distract her because she was so intent on not feeling, not thinking, not caring. Through all the "nots," however, she couldn't blank out the image of Neil's face. She couldn't forget how the gold flecks in his eyes were more prominent after he kissed her or how his hair dipped over his brow when they tussled in bed. Most of all, she couldn't eliminate from the tapes playing in her head the sound of his gentle voice saying, *I don't believe you're guilty.* He'd been sure of her honesty. Yet he still wanted to use her? And if he'd use her in this...

Had she ever really been his lover? Or had she been just a plaything? Tim hadn't cared enough about family. She'd thought Neil was different. He'd interacted with her dad and her nephew so well. Had that all been an act, too?

"What is real?" she shouted to the trees and the sky and anyone who cared to hear.

As she looked up to heaven, praying for an answer, she missed seeing the pothole until it was right in front of her. Maybe on a normal day, she could have navigated it. But today—

She hit the edge of the pothole, skidded on the loose chunks of asphalt, banged into the weather-worn crater and tumbled onto the lower shoulder of the road, hitting her head hard on the edge of the concrete.

Chapter Eleven

Isobel regained consciousness in the ambulance and panicked when she saw the IV, felt the oxygen at her nose, and realized she couldn't move. Her neck was held into place by a brace and she was lying on a body board.

Paramedic Mike O'Rourke, Simone's fiancé, patted her arm. "It's okay, Isobel. We're going to take care of you. We have you strapped down pretty tight just to make sure nothing moves until we can get some tests at the hospital."

Her face felt raw and burned like crazy. Her head hurt, too. A lot. And her ankle ached more than she wanted to think about. "I...I hit a pothole, didn't I?"

"That's what a witness at the scene said. He pulled over and called 911 on his cell phone." Mike pumped up the blood-pressure cuff on her arm. "What were you trying to do? Win the Tour de France?"

The memory of her disastrous meeting with Neil came rushing back. Tears swam in her eyes.

"Hey now," Mike said as he grabbed a tissue and dabbed at a tear on her cheek. "I told you, you're going to be fine."

The other attendant adjusted the IV line. "ETA two minutes."

Isobel had to admit she didn't like being on the receiving end of care at Walnut River General. She had no control and she hated that.

A few minutes later, Simone was by her side when the gurney was wheeled into the emergency room. She looked worried. "What did you *do?*"

"I rode my bike too fast," Isobel said, trying to joke.

"Do you want me to call your family?"

"Can you call Debbie? But tell her not to call Dad until I have whatever tests the doc is planning. I don't want Dad to worry. I don't even have my insurance card. It's in my purse in the garage. Debbie might have to tell him what happened if she picks that up."

"All right, Isobel," Simone soothed, looking worried. "Stop trying to plan everything. Let's just get you taken care of."

Mike wheeled her gurney into an E.R. cubicle and there the examination and questions began.

Three hours later, Isobel felt as if she'd been poked and prodded and examined and tested to the limit. Her father, Debbie and Chad stood around the gurney in the emergency-room cubicle looking at her with concern and worry. "I'm fine," she told them again. "I just have to wait for the doctor's final orders, then I can go home."

"You have a concussion," Chad reminded her.

"Only a slight one."

"Thank goodness you were wearing your helmet," her father mumbled, "or you could have cracked your skull wide open. I don't know how you're going to climb the stairs with that ankle all wrapped up like that."

"That's why it's wrapped, Dad, so I can put some weight on it."

Debbie muttered, "You should have let me call Neil."

"No!" Isobel said with a firmness that told her sister not to bring it up again.

Chad turned away from the bed, stepped toward the door to look out into the hall and check his watch. Isobel knew he was probably concerned about his brother and sister. A neighbor had come over to stay with them.

To her relief, the doctor hurried into the small room, studying her chart. He was tall and thin, probably in his late forties. Dr. Ruskin was fairly new on the staff, so Isobel hadn't had many dealings with him. But she knew Simone liked him.

"You're going to hurt tomorrow," he said, shaking his head. "Put ice on your ankle as needed for the next twenty-four hours. After that, warm baths will help. I have a prescription here for anti-inflammatory medication. I'd rather you not take anything for pain for twenty-four hours. You've had a concussion and I don't want medication masking that. You'll need someone with you for the next day or so. Through the night, I want someone to awaken you every three to four hours to make sure you're alert, conscious and have all your faculties."

"Is that really necessary?" Isobel wanted to know. "I just have a headache."

"It's necessary, Miss Suarez, and I can't let you go until I know someone's going to do that for you."

"I'll stay with her tonight and check on her every few hours," a deep male voice said from the doorway.

To Isobel's surprise and dismay, Neil stood there in jeans and a black T-shirt. His hair was wet as if he'd just taken a shower.

"What are *you* doing here?" Isobel asked with as much heat as she could muster. He was the last person she wanted to see. She didn't know when she'd felt quite this bad and she was sure she looked worse than she felt. She had scrapes on her cheek and probably a bruise was beginning to show. The doctor had put a dressing on it and she was supposed to change it in the morning. Her hair still had gravel in it from her brush with the side of the road and the scrapes down one arm had also been bandaged. Her ankle, which had twisted on the pedal when she'd fallen, was throbbing almost as much as her head. On top of all of that, she was wearing a very flimsy hospital gown that had seen way too many washings.

Isobel turned accusing eyes on Debbie.

"Don't look at me," her sister said, holding up her hands in surrender.

"I called him," Chad admitted, stepping up to the side of the bed. "I thought he'd want to know."

She could have groaned. She hadn't told anyone what had happened between her and Neil. She'd just insisted that she didn't want Debbie or her dad to call him. But Chad, who thought he knew best—

Neil came over to stand beside Chad and clapped the boy on the shoulder. "He was right to call me, Isobel. Your dad can't drive and you know he has trouble with the stairs. He also needs his sleep. I can run up and down and stay awake all night. I'll only stay as long as necessary, tonight and tomorrow, then you can kick me out."

Both her father and Debbie were looking from Neil to her and back again as if trying to figure out what was going on. She couldn't explain it now. She wasn't about to explain it now. Maybe not ever. Just why Neil was doing this, she didn't know.

But then he murmured in a low voice near her ear, "I feel responsible for what's happened. And you know your dad's not up to par yet. You don't need to burden him with your care right now."

"What happened is my *own* fault," she whispered back. "I ran into a pothole."

"Right. Would you have done that if you weren't so upset?"

Taking a glance over Neil's shoulder, she saw her sister and dad were trying to overhear. All of a sudden she felt such fatigue she couldn't fight them all anymore.

"All right," she said loud enough for the doctor to hear.

Neil straightened. "Is there anything else I should know before I take her home?"

"The nurse will give you a list of instructions when she brings the wheelchair."

"Wheelchair?" Isobel and Neil exclaimed at the same time.

The doctor gave Isobel a sly smile. "You work here, Miss Suarez. You know it's standard procedure, even for you."

Debbie slipped over to Isobel's side. "I brought you a clean pair of sweats. I'll help you get dressed."

"We'll be in the waiting room," Neil said as he and her dad stepped into the hall.

Though the doctor followed them out, Chad lingered behind. "Did you and Neil have a fight or something?"

"Or something," Isobel mumbled. Then seeing Chad's glum expression, Isobel gave him a small smile. "It's okay.

I know you did what you thought was best. Dad won't worry about me so much if Neil's there."

She could handle this, she told herself. She could. She'd just pretend Neil was a stranger checking on her now and then. In many respects, he was.

"Maybe you and Neil can work out whatever's wrong while he's there," Chad suggested.

Chad was too young to realize what a rare commodity trust was. She felt so betrayed by Neil she could never trust him again—not trust him to put her first, not trust him to feel what she did for him, not trust him to stay rather than go. She and Neil wouldn't be working on any differences. Not tonight.

Not ever.

Awkward didn't begin to cover the way Isobel felt as Neil hovered over her after her dad opened the door.

Taking Isobel's elbow, he helped her up the step into the house. Although his touch wasn't meant to be personal, even almost clinical, it *was* personal. She could remember every way and every time he'd touched her.

"They should have given you a cane," he remarked gruffly.

As she hobbled to the foot of the stairs, just wanting to make it to her own room and shut the door, she said over her shoulder, "I'm fine. Really."

Her father announced loudly, "I'm going to watch the History Channel for a while. If you need me, you holler."

She turned toward her dad, trying to ignore Neil's tall presence beside her. "Thanks for coming to the hospital."

"You know I'd do anything for you, Iz," her father returned.

Her eyes misted over and she grabbed onto the banister to lever herself up to the first step.

"If you think I'm going to stand here and watch you try to hobble up each one of those stairs, you're mistaken."

The next thing she knew, Neil had swept her into his arms and was carrying her up the staircase. She was too surprised to protest. Even if she had protested, by the look on Neil's face, she knew it wouldn't have done any good.

At the top of the stairs he asked curtly, "Which way?"

She pointed toward the door to her room.

Carrying her inside, he gently set her down on the bed. Only the glow of the hall lamp shone into the room and she couldn't see his expression. Before he slipped his arms away from her, she thought she felt him hesitate. But then he was standing beside the bed, turning on the lamp, looking down at her as if he were mad at the world.

"This wasn't your fault, Neil, and I'm not your responsibility. So why don't you just go back to the Inn?"

"Your dad's worried sick about you. He'd be climbing up and down these stairs, not getting any sleep, checking on you every hour. Is that what you want?"

"Of course that's not what I want!"

"Then stop fighting me. At least on this. You didn't have any supper tonight. What can I get you?"

"I really just want to wash up and go to bed."

"You need to take your anti-inflammatory pill first and it has to be taken with food. So what's it going to be?"

If she weren't hurting so much, if she weren't so exhausted, she might laugh. Somebody taking care of her was indeed a novelty. *She* was the caretaker and she didn't like this reversed role.

Surrendering, she suggested, "A piece of toast and a glass of apple juice."

"Coming right up." Soberly he left her room.

As soon as Neil closed the door behind him, Isobel moved. When she did, her head pounded, but she ignored it. After she grabbed her nightgown and robe from her closet, she hurried out into the hall to the bathroom. She did as best as she could in the amount of time she had, washing away any remaining grime with her washcloth, using her honeysuckle soap to do it. A few minutes later, she was crossing the hall to her room again, holding on to the door frame for support when Neil came up behind her.

"Are you feeling light-headed?"

He carried her toast on a dish with a vial of pills, the juice in his other hand.

"A little. I have an awful headache. I'll be fine once I can close my eyes and turn out the lights."

Once she'd settled in bed again without his help, this time under the sheet, he watched her eat and take her pills.

He ran his hand gently over the gauze on the side of her face. "Does this hurt?"

If she told him it didn't, he'd know she was lying. "I think it's going to look worse than it feels," she joked. Then she added, "I hope I have some gauze patches in the linen closet. I need to change this in the morning."

"I'll check before I go downstairs. I'm only going down to keep your dad company for a few minutes, though. I'll be sleeping in the spare bedroom. I'll set my alarm and check on you every few hours. If you need anything— *anything,* Isobel—you call me. In fact, do you have your cell phone?"

"It's in my purse." She pointed to the other side of the bed.

Neil didn't ask her permission but rather went around the bed, fished in her hobo bag, and found it. Opening it, he said, "I'm going to put my cell number on your speed dial. I'm

sure I'll hear you if you call me, but if I don't, use this."
Coming around the bed again, he set it on the edge of her
nightstand.

He was looking at her as if he wanted…wanted to…kiss
her? No, couldn't be, and she certainly didn't want to kiss
him. So she concentrated on the pounding in her head, the
soreness on her cheek, the thump of her ankle.

Pulling the sheet up to her chin, she said, "Good night,
Neil."

She didn't thank him because she couldn't. She didn't
want him here. Just looking at him made her hurt even more.
Her heart felt as if it had a hole in it and that was worse than
any bicycle fall, any concussion, any physical injury.

As if he understood that, he nodded. "I'll check on you in
a little while."

When Neil left the room, she let the dressing on her cheek
catch her tears. Then she turned onto the side of her face that
didn't hurt, eager to escape her life for sleep.

Neil lay on the spare-room bed in John Suarez's house,
staring at the ceiling. There was an almost-full moon
tonight and the shadows played around the room. He concentrated on their lines and edges, trying to stop his mind
from clicking through recriminations that were too many
to count.

Isobel's accident was *his* fault. Everything about this
messed-up situation was his fault. The best thing he could do
for Isobel was stay away from her. She'd never forgive him
for putting rules and regulations before her. For the first time
in his life, he was questioning the way he lived it.

The alarm on his watch beeped. Immediately he swung his
legs over the side of the bed, willed his thoughts and reac-

tions into neutral and headed for Isobel's room. There he stood at her bed, watching her sleep in the moonlight. She was curled up on her side, facing away from him, her hand tucked under her uninjured cheek. As John had said repeatedly, thank goodness she'd been wearing a helmet.

Isobel's curly hair was a mussed tangle. It lay on her pillow and he longed to stroke his fingers through it, catch them in the curls and feel their silkiness once more. She'd only used the sheet to cover herself. He could see the outline of her beautiful body underneath it and his gut tightened. How could he even be thinking—

As if she sensed him watching her, she uncurled her legs and turned over onto her back. "Neil?" Her voice was soft and feathery, filled with drowsiness. The fact that she recognized him was a good sign.

He hunkered down by the side of the bed. He could ask the usual questions—what's your name, where do you live, who's the President of the United States—but he opted for, "How do you feel?"

"Like a truck ran over me. A very big truck."

"Do you know where you are?"

"In my old room in my dad's house."

He hated to bring it up, but a reality check was a reality check. "Do you know what happened to you?"

She hesitated a moment, gazing straight into his eyes. He could almost hear her thinking, *Neil Kane happened to me.* However, she answered, "I was riding my bike on the highway and hit a pothole in the bike lane."

She'd given him details so he'd know she remembered all of it. She was alert, even while sleepy, and he was relieved.

"Are you dizzy?"

She shook her head and winced. "No, but I feel a whole

lot better if I don't move my head. Was Dad all right when he went to bed?"

Even in her condition, hurting all over, she worried about the people she cared about. He was no longer in that circle. And the idea that he wasn't gave him a feeling of loss he'd never experienced before. "I reassured him that you just need a few days and you'll be feeling a lot better."

As they stared at each other in the shadowy room, Neil couldn't look away. So many emotions bombarded him, his chest tightened.

Before he could stop himself, he reached out and cupped Isobel's uninjured cheek in his palm, his thumb tracing her nose and the curve of her upper lip. "I wish I could take all the hurt away." He wasn't just talking about her bike accident.

She lay perfectly still, then she moved away from his hand and whispered, "You'd better go."

Moving away from her was so difficult…but necessary.

Standing, he jammed his hands into his pockets. "I'll be back in a couple of hours. I'll leave after I make you and your dad breakfast."

She closed her eyes and he knew why—so she didn't have to look at him and remember how he'd reported her to her supervisor…so she could block him out of her life.

Feeling numb inside, he turned and left her room. Numb was better than feeling too much.

In the morning, Isobel knew she looked worse than she had the night before. The bruising had set in and the adrenaline that had rushed through her after the accident had ceased. She absolutely didn't want to get out of bed. More because she didn't want to face Neil than anything else.

Even her suspension.

What was going to happen to her professional reputation? Would she always have a questionable cloud hanging over her head from the review?

Frustrated, she hiked herself up, took a deep breath, and swiveled until her feet were on the floor. If she couldn't keep her job in the social work field, she'd find *something* else. Even if she had to wait tables until she figured out what to do.

Fifteen minutes later, she'd dressed and was stepping into a pair of deck shoes when there was a knock on the door. "Isobel, are you up?"

If she didn't answer, would Neil go away? Didn't she *want* him to go away?

"I'm up," she called.

He came in and saw immediately she was dressed in a pale-green T-shirt and matching knit shorts. "I thought you might need help going downstairs."

She wished he'd waited to come up, or not felt as if he had to help her at all. "I have to change my dressings and retape my ankle."

"I'll help you. It's hard doing that for yourself."

She could protest from here to next year and he wouldn't listen. She already knew that about Neil. When he found a direction, he took it.

After Neil took the gauze pads from the linen closet, she sat on the bed. He used antiseptic on her face, fumbling once. Did he just feel awkward or…?

Was his heart racing, too? Did he feel as unsteady as she did?

She wasn't even sure if she meant anything to him… anything more than a responsibility.

She hardly took a breath. He must have showered this

morning because he smelled like the bathroom soap. He hadn't shaved, though. The beard stubble gave him a rough, sexy look.

As if he could *look* any sexier…

They avoided each other's gazes until the gauze pad slipped again and she caught it. His hand covered hers and for an interminable second, neither of them moved or breathed.

When he took the gauze from her hand, he assured her, "I'll be finished in a minute."

And he was.

Why couldn't she stop wanting him? Why couldn't she stop feeling as if she needed him? He certainly didn't need her. She was expendable, a blip in his investigation that he could use to find out what he wanted.

In spite of all that, she couldn't forget the dream that she'd found her Mr. Right. Yet he wasn't right. He was all wrong for her. Wasn't he? Hadn't he betrayed her? In spite of that deep sense of betrayal, his body seemed to pull hers toward him. She could hardly keep from leaning in… couldn't stop wishing he was touching her in a much different way.

When he finished gently taping her ankle—his long fingers on her leg and foot much too tempting, much too personal, much too intimate—she felt wrung out.

After her murmured thanks, Neil set her foot on the floor. "If you're worried about being reported to the state licensing board, you shouldn't be. I know the complaint against you has no legs. There weren't any witnesses to back up the charges."

"Unless someone is setting me up. What if somebody really wants to harm me?"

Neil adamantly shook his head. "This is about NHC, not about you."

"I hope so," she said in a low voice, turning away. She couldn't look at him and not remember what she thought they'd been to each other. Apparently he couldn't look at *her*, either.

Closing the box with the gauze pads, he suggested, "It would be a lot easier if I carried you downstairs."

"No!" There was no way she was going to let him hold her in his arms again. No way at all. "I have to do it on my own so I know I can. I'll use the banister. I'll be fine."

"Just because you keep saying that doesn't make it so. Come on. I'll go down the steps ahead of you so you don't fall."

She'd already fallen. That was the problem. She'd tumbled head over heels in love with Neil. But she'd get over it. She'd get over him.

She had no choice.

A few minutes later, after Neil watched her hobble to the stairs, he went down sideways, watching her as she held on to the banister and maneuvered down each step.

"You *are* going to stay downstairs for the day, aren't you?" he asked with a frown.

"What I do isn't any of your concern anymore."

At her words, his frown deepened to a scowl, but he didn't argue with her, just studied her like the proverbial hawk until she was on the first floor.

Her father, in the kitchen reading the morning newspaper, smiled at her. "How are you doing this morning?"

"Much better."

"Liar," Neil whispered into her ear so close she could feel his breath on her neck. Her chin went up.

"I'm not dizzy anymore and the headache's better. I'll be

able to go back to work—" She stopped. She couldn't go back to work even if she did feel better.

The expression on her face must have given something away because her dad asked, "Isobel?"

"We'll talk about work later, Dad." She glanced over at the man who had unsettled her life. "After Neil leaves."

As Neil ignored the dig and took a frying pan from the cupboard, her father's gaze swung from one of them to the other. "All right, tell me what's going on."

"Not now," Isobel insisted as she made her way to the table and sat in one of the chairs.

"Yes, now," her father demanded. "I want to know why Neil feels he has to take care of the two of us, and why you're treating him like a stranger."

The silence stretched, becoming a heavy weight in the kitchen until Neil broke it. "My office received a complaint about Isobel. I reported it to her supervisor."

Isobel's dad studied her expression. "It sounds as if Neil was caught between his job and you. Is that why you're so upset?"

"I'm upset because he didn't tell me about it. Because he didn't give me a chance to explain or figure out what was wrong before he blew my career to bits."

"There are channels and regulations," Neil protested, cracking an egg savagely.

"And there was *us*," Isobel maintained, her voice shaking.

"I think you two have a lot of talking to do." Her dad pushed himself up from his chair.

"There's nothing to talk about. I'll be lucky if I still have a job when this is done," she blurted out, close to tears. "I'm suspended, Dad, until everything is cleared up. When I feel better, I'll look for something to hold us over."

"You're acting like a martyr," Neil grumbled. "The hospital review is less than two weeks away."

"If this were *your* job on the line, you wouldn't be so glib," she tossed back as her father slipped out of the kitchen to give them privacy. But she didn't want privacy, didn't even want to be in the same room as Neil. Everything would be different if he had just told her. If he'd told her, they could be getting to the bottom of it together. If he'd told her, she wouldn't feel so alone. If he'd told her, she would have known they really were lovers, not only in bed, but in life.

Close to tears again, she managed to say, "I'd like you to leave now. Dad and I can handle breakfast on our own."

"Isobel—"

"Please go."

He must have heard the finality in her voice, because he didn't glance back at her as he left the kitchen.

A few minutes later she heard the front door close. She dropped her head into her hands and cried.

Chapter Twelve

Ever since her meeting with her supervisor—and her confrontation with Neil—Isobel had vacillated between anger and hurt.

She hadn't spoken to him since he'd left her dad's house last Monday. Did he know if the hospital had turned up any concrete evidence against her? Even if he did, he wouldn't tell her. He went by the book, she thought bitterly.

Unable to do her job, she was going to visit Florence MacGregor—unofficially. After all, they'd become friends and she wanted to know how the older lady was doing. There was no chance of running into West on a Monday afternoon. He'd be working. Maybe her visit would make Florence's day a little brighter, and would, in turn, brighten hers. It was worth a try.

Pine Ridge Rehab was located on the west side of town, surrounded by lawns and, of course, pine trees. The one-floor facility was sprawling and accommodated about fifty residents at any one time.

Since Isobel didn't know if the staff had heard about the accusations against her, she decided to avoid the main lobby and reception area. She entered through a side door and stepped into a hall south of the dining room. Since it was almost three, Florence should be back in her room resting.

Isobel heard applause from the game show channel as she stopped at the door to Florence's room and peered inside. The older woman was seated in an armchair, her walker beside her. She pointed to one of the contestants on *The Match Game*. "I told you the answer was pink. It's *pink* elephant."

Isobel smiled, rapped softly on the door and stepped inside.

"Isobel!" Florence exclaimed. "I haven't seen you for—" She stopped as if she couldn't remember. "For a very long time."

Isobel's ankle was healed now and she just had a few remnants of the scrape on her cheek that she'd managed to cover with makeup. "I've been a little under the weather. I had an accident on my bike."

Florence examined Isobel's face. "West told me that you weren't at work. That you had a concussion. Do you still have headaches?"

Isobel could see this was one of Florence's more alert days. "Not anymore." She pointed to Florence's walker. "How are you doing? You should be able to go home soon."

"Tomorrow or the next day," Florence assured her. "That's what West said. But I don't know how long I'm going to be at home. West tells me I'm going to take a trip."

"To Las Vegas?" Isobel wouldn't be surprised if West took his mother there to have some fun after she'd recovered.

"No, not Las Vegas. Let me see. Where did he say we were going?"

Maybe Florence just imagined she was going on a trip. "It doesn't matter. Wherever you go, I'm sure you'll enjoy yourself."

"He told me the leaves would be magnificent in October. That's when we're going. October."

All of New England was beautiful in October. Then again, maybe Florence was confusing this October with last October. Isobel recalled West had taken some vacation time last fall, too. "Has West mentioned where you'll be staying when you go away? What hotel?"

Florence looked absolutely blank for a moment. "He told me but I can't remember. Why can't I remember, Isobel?"

She leaned closer to pat Florence's hand. "It's not important. I'm sure he picked out a very nice hotel." Since his mother liked to gamble, maybe he was taking her to Foxwoods Resort in Connecticut. But Isobel didn't want Florence to get more upset or frustrated when she couldn't find what she was looking for in her memory.

"Lily came to see me again," Florence told Isobel.

"She did? That's terrific. It's good to have visitors. It makes the time go faster."

"She came when I didn't have therapy. She stayed a long time."

Isobel guessed Florence's friend had come on Sunday afternoon. "She brought me candy," Florence announced like a little kid who had received a Christmas present she liked. "Chocolate-covered creams. They're in that box over there if you want one."

Isobel spotted the box on the bedside table. "Would you like one?" she asked Florence, guessing that might be why she brought it up.

"Sure."

Isobel rose and went to the nightstand. Bringing the box back to Florence, she lifted the lid and the wonderful smells of chocolate and mint floated up.

Florence pointed to the square ones. "Those are mint. They're my favorite."

"What are the round ones?"

"They're coconut or vanilla."

Isobel reached for one of those, though she wasn't hungry. She hadn't had any appetite since last week. But maybe the sugar would give her some of the energy she was lacking. And sharing the treat with Florence formed a bond.

Florence took a mint one and poked it into her mouth. She smiled as she enjoyed the candy. "Do you like to cook, Isobel?"

"I do when I have the time."

"A young lady here was talking to West about when I go home. She told him I should have someone stay with me and cook for me."

Isobel had wondered what Florence's caseworker here at the rehab facility would recommend to West.

"He said he found someone—a college girl who's living at home for the summer. She's going to spend her days with me."

"She'll be nice company for you."

"I guess. Do you think she'll like to watch the game show channel?"

"I don't know. You'll have to ask her when you meet her."

"She'll have to go back to college, though. That's why West is taking me to Fair Meadows when we go on our trip." Florence snapped her fingers. "That's the name of the place I'll be staying. Fair Meadows."

Isobel went still. Everyone in health care in Massachusetts knew about Fair Meadows, outside of Boston. It was one of the elite nursing-care facilities for patients with Alzheimer's. Politicians sent relatives there, and so did movie stars. How could West afford the place?

Not exactly sure where to go with this, but knowing she had to go somewhere, Isobel commented, "I think you'll like Fair Meadows very much. I've heard the grounds are beautiful with lots of gardens. There's a sunroom. They even have someone on staff who'll give massages."

"They have a hair salon, too," Florence interjected.

How would West's mother know that? Unless she'd seen a brochure, or maybe a promotional DVD. "I guess West told you all about it."

"I saw it. I went to that hospital in Boston and then he took me to Fair Meadows. He wanted to see if I would like it."

Isobel's suspicions grew. "Do you remember when you went?"

"Not so long ago. It was…let me think…it was before Christmas." She thought some more. "Before Thanksgiving."

Apparently West had taken his mom to Boston last fall for a medical evaluation. Why wouldn't he have told the staff here? Why wouldn't he have mentioned it to Dr. Wilder?

Isobel was getting a very bad feeling about this. "Tell me something, Florence. I know West works very hard to take care of you. He puts in a lot of hours at the hospital. But I was just wondering, does he have another job, too?"

"How did you know?"

Maybe this wasn't what Isobel thought. Maybe West actually was working two jobs in order to pay for Fair Meadows. But even with two jobs…

"Does he do work at home at night for someone else?" She felt terrible pumping Florence, but if her suspicions were true, she had to know what else West was doing.

"He gets papers at home sometimes. You know, that machine he has beeps. And he's on his computer a lot."

"It could be work from the hospital that he's taking home."

"No, I don't think so. Because I found an envelope with money in his desk from somebody else. Not Walnut River General."

"Were there any papers with the money? A pay stub?"

"Let me think. The money was new. I could tell. There wasn't a paper with it. But on the envelope up at the top in the corner there was a little picture of one of those things a doctor wears."

Isobel's heart thumped harder. "A stethoscope?"

"Yes, that's it. A stethoscope."

"And beside the stethoscope were there letters? NHC maybe?"

"Oh, I don't remember the letters, but I do remember the stethoscope."

That was good enough for Isobel. NHC's gray-and-maroon logo with initials and a stethoscope was well-known by now. West MacGregor was the mole who was siphoning information to Neil's office.

Chad's basketball ran around the rim and then dropped into the basket. "I'm three up on you," he crowed. "You said you wanted to play but I think your mind is somewhere else."

Neil caught the ball as it bounced on the asphalt. Yeah, his mind was somewhere else all right. When Chad had called him after school, asking if he wanted to play after he got off work, Neil had agreed. He needed the exercise. He needed to expend some energy. He needed to stop thinking about Isobel.

When Neil dribbled the ball, Chad dashed in front of him

to guard him. "Aunt Iz was over here yesterday. She wasn't limping. She said her head didn't hurt anymore. But..."

Neil stopped dribbling. "But?"

Snatching the ball from him, Chad made another shot. "See what I mean? Distracted. Because of her, I'll bet. She didn't seem very happy, either."

"I guess not," Neil muttered.

"I heard her telling my mom you got her suspended and she might even lose her license."

"That's *not* going to happen." He'd been tempted to go to Pine Ridge and question the staff himself. But the hospital's lawyer was doing that. And Neil couldn't interfere. The phrase *by the book* rang in his ears again.

"Neil?" Chad asked him.

"What?"

"Aren't you and Aunt Iz even talking?"

"No."

"How are you going to get back together if you're not even talking?"

Back together. Had they *been* together? He thought about the weekend in Cranshaw. He thought of the week afterward. Of how many times they'd made love. The ways they'd made love. The conversations after they'd made love. He'd talked about his childhood and so had she. They'd talked about their college years. They'd kissed and connected and—he'd known all that time he'd have to report Isobel to her supervisor.

By the book. His job didn't give him the satisfaction it used to and he'd hated keeping something from Isobel.

"What's the problem, Neil?" Chad asked, standing still now.

"My job's the problem." Then he thought about *that* statement. "Nix that. *I'm* the problem. For so many years I've lived by rules and regulations that they've become second nature to me. I put my job and what I'm doing here ahead of Isobel's feelings."

After a thoughtful silence, Chad asked, "Remember when you asked me if my wanting a car was more important than Stephanie?"

"I remember."

"Is your job more important than Aunt Iz? If it is, then what she thinks and feels doesn't matter. But if it isn't, if *she's* more important—"

Chad had decidedly turned the tables on him. Neil thought about not caring about Isobel, what she thought and felt. He considered not seeing her again. Not kissing her again. Not holding her again. A video played in his mind of the last couple of years, of his work, of his life, of his practically empty apartment, of the days on the road and the nights in motels. The work had been important. But now, being here in Walnut River, this job, this investigation, seemed to be all smoke and mirrors. He'd let it come first out of habit, not out of a great deal of thought. Whenever he pictured himself going back to Boston without Isobel, not seeing her for weeks on end, now maybe not seeing her ever, he knew that wasn't right for his life. He knew—

That he loved her.

How could he have thought that this affair with her was just about sex? How had he ever thought that betraying her wouldn't push them apart?

Deep down, had he wanted to push them apart? Did he feel that unworthy of being loved?

The question was immense and couldn't be answered easily. Couldn't be answered here and now.

Chasing the ball that had rolled down the driveway, he

scooped it up and dribbled it back to the net. "Game on," he said to Chad. "I bet I can recover those points."

The beep-beep-beep from his cell phone, which was lying with his keys and his wallet and duffel bag near the porch, stalled the game once more. As he jogged to retrieve it he called to Chad, "We'll get this going again in a minute." He opened the phone and saw Isobel's number. His heart began racing. Did she want to talk to him? Was it possible she could forgive him?

"Isobel?"

"Neil, I need to talk to you. I've been driving around and around, trying to decide what to do."

"What happened?"

She hesitated.

"Isobel, you can trust me."

"No. No, I can't."

His heart ached when she said those words, but he knew they were true. She didn't think she *could* trust him. Coaxing wouldn't make her open up to him. But *she* had called *him,* so he waited, hoping.

"I have to see you. I might have information that could end your investigation."

The constriction in his chest loosened a little because she wanted to see him. "I'm at your sister's, playing basketball with Chad. Do you want to come over here?"

Silence echoed back and forth for a few moments.

"I don't want to get Debbie involved in this. The Crab Shack is closed today. How about if I meet you there?"

"You want to make sure you're not seen with me."

"You don't want to be seen with me, Neil. Remember? Your investigation comes first. I'm putting it first. I'll see you there in ten minutes."

He took the phone from his ear, stared at her number and then closed it. She'd told *him*. And there hadn't been a hint of forgiveness in her tone. Maybe betrayal didn't deserve forgiveness. But he was glad she had called him. And whatever she had found out, he'd use it to clear her, to get this job over and done with and then to get on with his life.

Right now, he just wasn't sure whether Isobel would be in it or not.

Fifteen minutes later, Neil waited for Isobel at the same table where they'd shared a basket of crabs after he'd first arrived in Walnut River. As he watched her park and climb out of her car, he knew she was remembering, too. Her eyes were bright with unshed tears and her expression was sad.

Wearing jeans and a red knit top, she approached him slowly. He could tell she'd lost weight. From the bike riding regimen she had started? Or because, like him, she had no appetite anymore?

It was the last week in May. Birds twittered in the trees and the long, green grass swayed in the wind. Yellow and blue irises bloomed in clumps along the path to The Crab Shack, while tiny yellow flowers blossomed in the field. He wished, oh, how he wished, he was meeting Isobel here for a romantic rendezvous.

Stopping a few feet from him, she glanced over her shoulder as if she were afraid someone was following her. "I know who your mole is. It's West MacGregor."

The accountant. Neil remembered the man who had been cooperative, but not too cooperative—who had defended Walnut River, but who had asked questions of his own. "How do you know?"

"I went to visit his mother at Pine Ridge." If Isobel

expected a comment from him, she didn't get it. If she wanted to visit her former patients, that was her business—at Pine Ridge or anywhere else.

"I heard from one of the aides I interviewed that she has dementia?"

Without commenting on that, Isobel explained, "Today Florence was alert and quite talkative. I thought West took her on a vacation last fall. That was the story they both told. But today I learned he took her to Boston, probably to be evaluated for Alzheimer's. He also showed her around an upscale nursing facility for Alzheimer's patients. And I do mean upscale. It's nothing he could afford on *his* salary. When Florence told me about it and I questioned her more, it seems West is being paid by Northeastern HealthCare. Their logo is a stethoscope with their initials. Florence described it as being on an envelope with cash she found in West's desk."

Neil considered everything Isobel had told him. "He could deny all of this. It's his word against his mother's."

"You mean this information isn't useful?" Isobel looked crestfallen. She'd thought she had discovered the answer to the problems at Walnut River and he'd just told her she hadn't.

He reached out and grabbed her arm. "We can use this, Isobel."

When she pulled away from him, their gazes met, and he saw the distrust in hers. "I'll make something work. I want your name cleared as much as you do."

His words obviously surprised her. "I doubt that."

"I will do *anything* to clear your name. I got you into this mess. If I hadn't pushed so hard, if I had stayed away from you, no one would have seen you as a threat."

She seemed to consider that. "What are you going to do?"

"I'll have to convince someone to feed information to West MacGregor—information he can use against the hospital. If he calls it into my supervisor's office again, then we'll know he's the mole."

She stood very still and studied him carefully. "I'll do it."

"No. I don't want you any more involved in this than you are."

"We don't want him to get suspicious."

"You're suspended. You don't have the opportunity to tell him anything."

"I'll make the opportunity to drop off some papers to Margaret that I filled out for the review. I know when West takes his break. He does it like clockwork. I'll pretend I'm looking for Simone in the lounge."

"And what if someone else walks in?"

"I'll make it work, Neil. I don't know why you're having a problem with this. You were ready to use me as a pawn before the review board."

He couldn't deny her accusation and her blow struck hard. If he told her now he'd made a mistake—

Anything personal between them had to wait until this was all over. He didn't want her to feel used again. He didn't want to make her promises he couldn't keep. He had to make a few decisions on his own before he could tell her what she meant to him. He had to be ready for action…because words wouldn't mean anything now. Not to Isobel.

"Are you sure you want to do this? A few of the personnel I interviewed this week want to get to the bottom of this as much as I do. I think they'd be cooperative and could feed information to West."

"I know West. He'll believe me. And he has to believe what we tell him."

"Do you know what you'll say?"

"I'll keep it simple. I can be righteously indignant about the whole proceeding, proclaim my innocence, then tell him I know specific instances where patients were charged for medicine they never received."

"Were they?"

"No. But West doesn't have to know that."

"He might want specifics."

"I'll give him specifics. I'll give him fake names."

"He could check." Neil knew he was playing devil's advocate, but he wanted this to work.

"Yes, he could. But I doubt if he will. Sure, everything's computerized. But you saw what it was like trying to go through the files. Sometimes you can find what you're looking for and sometimes you can't. Do you know how many patients go through our hospital in a year? He'd never expect *me* to lie to him."

"What if Florence tells him you were there asking questions?"

"I didn't really ask questions. I just guided her. He won't think it's unusual that I stopped in if she even remembers to mention it. If we do this right away, we should have our best shot."

"I admire your courage in doing this." He wanted to kiss her, give her a hug, show her how much he *did* care.

"It's not courage. It's fear and desperation."

"You'll tell him tomorrow?"

"Tomorrow." She checked her watch. "Dad will be worried about me. I need to go home." She turned to walk away.

"Isobel?"

Although she stopped, she didn't turn around. Maybe because she guessed he had something personal to say.

"When this is all over, you and I need to talk."

If she heard him, she didn't acknowledge that she did. She went to her car, climbed in and drove away.

Neil was so tempted to go after her. Even if he did, she still wouldn't trust him. Even if he did, she still might not forgive him.

He had to prove to her he cared about her. And he would, when this was all over.

When this was all over.

Chapter Thirteen

"I don't like this," Neil said for at least the fifth time, as his fingers accidently brushed the undercup of Isobel's bra.

In the garage to the rear of her dad's property, he finished fastening a piece of tape on the wire that Isobel would be wearing during her conversation with West MacGregor. The warrant that he'd picked up from the district attorney was stuffed into his inside jacket pocket. The Walnut River chief of police, Rod Duffy, would be meeting him at the hospital in plain clothes.

Isobel didn't flinch at his almost intimate touch. But she didn't look at him, either. This was probably more difficult for her than for him. After all, he wanted to be touching her. She didn't want *him* anywhere near *her.*

"West is the mole," Isobel protested. "If I can get him to admit it and you have it on tape, you can close your investigation."

The information Isobel had fed West yesterday had been called into Neil's supervisor. West was obviously desperate, using anything he could get hold of. But they needed the proof that he was the man behind the digitally altered voice.

"I don't want you to push him." Neil finished with the adhesive tape and adjusted the wire. Afterward he took Isobel by the shoulders. "If you can't get anything out of him, you leave. Owen Randall, the chief of police and I will be two offices away. That one was empty and we won't arouse anyone's suspicions by being there."

Isobel buttoned the blouse that complemented her skirt and reached for her jacket. "You'll be able to hear everything?"

"Everything."

Neil stooped to the ground to toss the tape into the duffel bag he'd used to carry the equipment. He glanced over at Isobel.

Staring at the bag, her voice was soft and shaky when she asked, "I don't really know you at all, do I?"

They had to be at the hospital in fifteen minutes and couldn't talk about this now. "You *do* know me, Isobel. This is just another part of my job. White-collar crime is still crime."

She finished buttoning her jacket, felt for the small microphone and asked, "Can you see anything?"

Her face reddened when he took an extra few seconds to assess her appearance. "You look normal. I can't tell a thing. Give me a five minute head start. After I park at the back entrance, I'll come up the stairs. And don't worry. I'll be in place before you get to West's office."

"How will I know for sure?"

"You're going to have to trust me, Isobel."

Neil could feel her eyes on his back as he left, hoping their plan worked…hoping even more fervently Isobel would place her trust in him again.

* * *

Isobel shook as she stood outside West's office, praying Neil was ensconced in the empty one down the hall. Sure, she was nervous about confronting West. But she couldn't forget the feel of Neil's fingers on her skin as he'd arranged the wire and then taped it. She'd tried to pretend he was a stranger, just doing his job, but the look in his eyes said he wasn't. The look in his eyes said that he had regrets, too.

Attempting to shake off her feelings about Neil, she focused on what she had to do. West's door was partially open. She poked her head inside. "Can I talk to you?"

The accountant looked surprised to see her but then he pasted on a genial smile. "Isobel. Did you have another meeting with Margaret?"

Why else would she be here? After all, she was suspended. And that was *his* fault. "No. I came to see you." Inside his office now, she closed the door. "You've been outed, West."

Was that fear she saw in his hazel eyes? "I don't know what you mean. Explain yourself, Isobel." Her colleague wasn't smiling now.

"I told you about overcharges in drugs to Mrs. Johnson and Mr. Talbot."

West was wary. "So you did."

"That information was called into the State Attorney General's office. Neil Kane knows about it."

West tried to play the conversation with nonchalance. "Are you and Mr. Kane speaking again? Rumor has it there was a rift between you two."

"It's over, West. I told Neil there *were* no charges. I just gave you that information to see if you were the mole. And you are." She wanted to make this sound as if it were *her* idea…that she intended to trap him to save herself.

Shaking his head in denial, anxiously balling one hand into a fist, he said, "They can't prove anything, Isobel. It's my word against yours. I can claim *you* called in the information. After all, with a device to disguise your voice—"

Isobel cut in. "How do you know the mole disguised his voice? There's only one way. You made those calls, West."

Sweat broke out on his brow and he appeared almost desperate. Then he sat up straighter. "As I said, you can't prove it. No one can. It's not as if I even did anything illegal. I called in rumors—rumors that deserved to be investigated. They were based on facts."

"Why? Why did you do this? You put the reputation of the doctors here in jeopardy, the reputation of the hospital itself."

Now some of the panic left his face and he appeared almost defiant. "Why? Oh, Isobel, grow up. There's only one why. NHC is paying me. I need the money for Mom's care. She deserves the best and I'm going to give it to her. She's not going to end up a ward of the state. I know what those nursing facilities are like. No one cares there. I need to have her someplace where I don't have to worry about her twenty-four hours a day. You know what that's like. We've talked about it. What would you have done if this was your father?"

What *would* she have done? Sold his house and everything he owned so she could pay a year or two of good care?

"I don't know what I would have done, West. But not this. I wouldn't have affected other lives."

"Don't be so righteous. You're on the outside looking in. When you're on the inside, you get a different picture. Black doesn't stay black and white doesn't stay white. They merge into gray."

She could see how that had happened for West.

He was frowning now. "I never intended things to go this

far. NHC approached me. They knew I had taken Mom to Boston for an evaluation. They knew her prognosis wasn't good. They said if I helped them with the takeover they would make sure she had a place at Fair Meadows, and I wouldn't have to worry about her care."

"That's what you're getting out of this?" Isobel asked, feeling sorry for him in spite of herself.

"They gave me money to cover her needs for home care until I'm ready to put her in Fair Meadows. How could I refuse that, Isobel? How?"

He had asked her what she would have done. And the answer had seemed so simple, so easy. But now looking at it from his perspective, wanting the best for his mother, life definitely *wasn't* black and white.

The door to West's office opened and Neil burst in. Behind him she caught a glimpse of Owen Randall and the chief of police.

West stood and stuttered. "What's this? Why are you here?"

Isobel said sadly, "I'm wearing a wire, West. They've recorded everything you said." Then she added, "I'm sorry." Because she was. She and West had been friends of sorts. She hated deception of any kind. And she'd just deceived him. For the greater good.

For the greater good. Is that what Neil had done to her? She glanced up at him. "Do you need me here?"

His voice was gentle. "Just leave the equipment in the office down the hall. I have to tie up loose ends here."

He motioned West back into his chair. "Have a seat, Mr. MacGregor. I have a ton of questions and we'll be here all night if we have to be."

"I want to sit in," Owen interjected forcefully.

"You can if you wish, but I don't think there's any need,"

Neil concluded. "My findings aren't official yet, of course, but as far as *I'm* concerned this investigation is over."

Rod Duffy extended his hand to Isobel. As she shook it, he said, "You did good work here today."

Owen nodded in agreement and added, "As soon as we verify that MacGregor's information was false, I'll notify Margaret. We'll be canceling your review. Why don't you take the rest of the week off and start back on Monday?"

Start back on Monday. As if everything was going to go back to normal. As if none of this had even happened. She suspected Northeastern HealthCare would deny they'd requested West MacGregor's help. They still wanted to take over Walnut River General and that endeavor wouldn't stop just because Neil had uncovered West's role in it.

When she moved to pass Neil, he clasped her arm. "I admire your courage."

Admiration? Did he feel anything else?

Today had been enlightening in so many ways. One point that had been driven home was that the situation hadn't been black or white for Neil, either. Would he call her later? Did she want him to?

She was so confused she just didn't know.

Although West had been silent since Neil's entrance, he said now, "I'm not going to answer any of your questions. I want a lawyer."

"You can call a lawyer. But if you tell me what you know, I can put in a good word for you with my boss." Neil reminded him, "We have you on tape and Isobel is a witness."

West rubbed his forehead wearily. Finally he nodded. "All right."

Neil gave Isobel one last look before she left West's office, and she couldn't decipher its meaning.

She needed time to think, time to put everything into perspective.

And if Neil didn't call?

She'd go on as she had before, working and taking care
of her dad.

Isobel couldn't have been happier for Simone and Mike.
The blue sky, puffy white clouds and golden sun had been
a perfect backdrop for their ceremony in the rose garden of
Mike's parents' backyard. Now Isobel, along with Mike's
huge family, Simone's mom, Ella Wilder and her fiancé
J. D. Sumner tossed birdseed along with good wishes at the
bride and groom as they ran around the side of the house
to Mike's SUV, climbed inside and drove away, waving
back through the words *Just Married* written in soap on the
rear window.

Isobel and the other guests smiled at each other as the
couple drove away.

Mike's brother motioned to all of them. "Come on. There's
a lot of party left in that backyard. My mother doesn't want
leftovers for the next week."

As everyone laughed, Isobel trailed behind Ella Wilder as
she and J.D. settled at one of the linen-covered tables under
the canopy. Mike's mother cut second pieces of cake for all.
Isobel sat staring at hers, not in the least bit hungry. It had
been a beautiful late-afternoon ceremony, but her heart had
felt like a rock in her chest as she'd witnessed the happy
couple share their vows, exchange rings and dance their
wedding dance.

The past two days she'd had time to think about Neil and
everything that had happened. Had he been torn by what he'd
had to do? Had turning the information over to her supervisor

been difficult for him? *Had* she been more than a diversion while he was in Walnut River?

He hadn't called her before he'd left. From what she'd heard, he'd left the same day West had confessed. That hurt, too. Granted, she hadn't given him reason to think—

Ella, who was planning a wedding with J.D. for the fall, turned toward Isobel. "I just love your dress."

Isobel had found a calf-length, multicolored, flowered dress with a sweetheart neckline and a pencil-slim skirt at one of Walnut River's boutiques. "Simone insisted I buy something I could wear again."

"It's perfect for a wedding or anything dressy in the summer. I love the style. Maybe my bridesmaids could find something like it in fall colors."

There were weddings all around Isobel. Peter and Bethany's next month, Ella and J.D.'s, Courtney Albright and David Wilder's the weekend before Thanksgiving.

"Are you getting excited?" Isobel asked Ella, knowing the answer already from the sparkle in her eyes.

"I started writing my vows," Ella admitted. "J.D. said it's the perfectionist in me. I want them to be perfect."

J.D. draped his arm around Ella's shoulders and gave her a hug. "I told her I'm just going to stand up there and say what I feel. But she thinks I should write down the words so I don't forget."

Suddenly, Ella and J.D. were staring over Isobel's shoulder.

Isobel glanced behind her—and was astonished to see Neil Kane. He was wearing a suit and tie and was too handsome for words. Her heart skipped a beat, then ran so fast she could hardly catch her breath. Why was he here?

Finding her voice, she managed to say, "I—I thought you'd left."

His gaze focused on her as if she were the only guest at the reception. "I did. I had a lot to accomplish in two days, but I managed it, and that's why I'm here." He held out his hand to her. "Will you come talk with me?" He nodded to the patio and the glider there.

Isobel didn't know what to say or what to do or how to act. But she knew if she didn't take Neil's hand, she'd forever have regrets. When she put her hand in his, his fingers enveloped hers. She stood, her mouth bone-dry, and followed him to the patio, away from the crowd of guests. She knew everyone was watching them. But Neil didn't seem to be bothered by that.

When he motioned to the glider, she sank down onto it and he lowered himself beside her, still holding her hand. It was as if he didn't want to break the connection, however tenuous it might be.

"I was wrong." His deep voice was strong, sure and apologetic.

Now she definitely couldn't breathe.

"I was wrong to put my job before *you*. Doing that made you think I didn't care about you, that I just wanted to use you to get to the bottom of the investigation. That wasn't true, Isobel. I've done a lot of soul-searching since the day I turned the information over to your supervisor. Ever since I met you, you rocked my world. The night we spent together in Cranshaw— I'd never had a night that intense with a woman before. The following week I told myself we could continue the affair long-distance. I thought I could control my emotions about you, that I could set them apart from the investigation. But I couldn't. Remember what your father said? That I worked the way I did because I didn't want to be close to my ex-wife?"

Isobel nodded.

"I realized that, yes, I was doing my job the 'right' way by going to your supervisor. But by doing that I was also pushing you away, even though what I wanted most was to be close to you. I told you I felt responsible when Garrett died, whether my feelings were rational or not. I think all these years I've believed I didn't deserve love because I didn't love him enough. I was pushing you away because I didn't deserve you...didn't deserve to be loved by you."

"Oh, Neil."

He squeezed her hand. "Let me finish. I guess I've come to realize the best way to serve Garrett's memory is to love *more*, not less. To accept love whether I deserve it or not. I love you, Isobel. I don't want an affair with you, I want to spend my life with you. I know I've hurt you, and I have to do more than say the right words. So...the past two days, I've been rearranging my life. I've resigned my position at the Attorney General's Office, effective in two weeks."

"You're not serious!"

"Yes, I am. I'm going to get my private investigator's license and do investigative work for the D.A.'s office in Pittsfield."

"Pittsfield?" It was actually dawning on her that Neil had arranged his life around hers.

"Yes, Pittsfield. It's only a half-hour commute. I'll probably still have odd hours. This isn't nine-to-five work. But we can live in Walnut River. We can buy a house or build a house with an apartment for your dad."

"You want my dad to live with us?"

Neil smiled at her words. "Yes. Remember? He and I get along really well." His smile faded away as he asked, "Can you forgive me? Can you believe that from this day on I'll put you first?"

Gazing into his eyes, seeing truth and love there, her reply came from her heart. "Yes, I can forgive you. I've been doing a lot of thinking, too. I've realized that just because you followed the rules didn't mean you didn't care about me. You were caught in the middle. I guess I…was still insecure… afraid my feelings were one-sided. I should have tried to understand."

Instead of kissing her, which is what Isobel wanted Neil to do, he stood. Before she could grasp what was happening, he went down on one knee before her, holding a beautiful marquise-shaped diamond ring between his fingers. "Up until now I've handled everything all wrong. Now I intend to handle it right. I want to start my life with you today. Will you marry me, Isobel? Will you accept this ring as a promise that I will join my life with yours and make you as happy as I possibly can?"

She was overcome by the love and the hope in Neil's eyes. Tears welled up in hers as she easily found the answer to all of her confusion and all of her questions. "I love you, too, Neil. Yes! Yes, I'll marry you."

After he slipped the ring on her finger he stood, pulled her to her feet and wrapped his arms around her. His kiss told her everything that was in his heart. It was a promise that their future lay before them and that they would walk into it together.

Their hunger for each other was intense and demanding. Isobel received Neil's passion and gave her own until—

The sound of applause finally penetrated the haze of desire, love and need surrounding them. Neil broke away, and still holding her, murmured close to her ear, "I think we have an audience."

They both turned their attention toward the guests gathered

under the canopy. The clapping grew louder until, with one arm still around her, Neil held up a hand.

Grinning, he declared, "She said yes."

There were cheers and calls of congratulation. And then Neil was kissing her again, lifting her into his arms and carrying her away from the rest of the guests.

"I didn't give up my room at the Inn. How about if we go there for a while and then tell your dad the good news?" he proposed.

"A while?" she teased.

"Why don't you call your dad on the way? Tell him I'll bring you home after we've made wedding plans."

"Is that what we'll be doing?" she asked innocently.

"Yes. In between showing each other the perfect married couple we're going to be."

"Perfect," she agreed, knowing she *had* found her Mr. Right.

She held on to him as he carried her to his car and he held on to her, ready to start the journey of promises, commitment and love that would last a lifetime.

* * * * *

hands...' he thought. 'Hey I'm happy now louder enough with one arm still shaking, he could hold the jump.'

'Emma's here, he didn't care?' she said she's...

'Then when others and tells its importanthah...' And then Neil was say us, he came, his...' the after life his anniversary' the emotion away from the idea of the abuse.

'I didn't realise how much' he said she 'but, if we get there for a while and then tell whatever the good news...' he passes to...

'A smile' she reached 'hm.'

'Why don't you call with once on the town? I'll find it bring you home after he or may breathing again...'

'Ps that what we'll be doing,' she gazed impatiently.

'Yes,' he nod and how much each like the silent morning coup...we'll get close to see.

'Perhaps,' she sighed enjoying she had found her. Me Right...'

She held as to time to be carried out to his consent be held to this sneaky part in the journey of prove a permanence and love complicated as a lifetime.

A MERGER
...OR MARRIAGE?

BY
RAEANNE THAYNE

Raeanne Thayne finds inspiration in the beautiful northern Utah mountains, where she lives with her husband and three children. Her books have won numerous honors, including a RITA® nomination from Romance Writers of America and a Career Achievement Award from *RT Book Reviews* magazine. RaeAnne loves to hear from readers and can be reached through her website at www.raeannethayne.com.

Chapter One

So this was what it felt like to be a pariah.

Anna Wilder tilted her chin slightly higher, tightened her grasp on her briefcase and walked firmly past the two gray-haired biddies at the information desk in the lobby of Walnut River General Hospital.

She didn't need to keep them in view to feel the heat of their glares following her to the gleaming elevator doors. She also didn't need to fully hear their whispers to catch enough to make her ulcer go into overdrive.

It's her, Anna Wilder.

The traitor.

James and Alice must be rolling in their graves.

She did her best to ignore them—and the hurt that settled like greasy black bile in her stomach. Still, to her great shame, she wasn't quite able to control the slight tremble of her hand as she pushed the elevator button to go up.

One of the two cars appeared to be permanently stuck on the second floor but the other one at last began creeping downward in what felt like excruciatingly painful slow motion.

She prayed the blasted thing would hurry up and arrive—not only to allow her to slip inside and escape the stares and whispers but, more importantly, because she was late.

She really hated being late.

The elevator stopped on the second floor and paused there for a few moments before continuing its descent. Suddenly a new apprehension fluttered her ulcer.

Why hadn't she been smart enough to take the stairs? The only thing worse than being late for her meeting would be the social discomfort of encountering one of her siblings in the elevator during her first few minutes at the hospital.

She didn't know which one would be harder to face right now. Ella? Peter? David? It probably didn't matter. They were all furious with her and would no doubt love a chance to let her know.

Just before the elevator arrived, one of the two volunteers at the information desk raised her voice in what had to be deliberate malice so Anna couldn't miss her words.

"She might have the Wilder name," she said in a carrying voice, "but she's not a true Wilder. How can she be, since she's in bed with those who are trying to sell out this hospital and this town?"

Anna inhaled sharply. Apparently the doctors weren't the only ones at Walnut River General who could wield a scalpel. The words effectively sliced straight to where she was most vulnerable.

Her hand tightened on the briefcase as she ruthlessly tried to ignore the hot tears burning behind her eyelids.

It didn't matter what a couple of dried-up old prunes had to say about her. Why should it? They had nothing better to do with their time than sit around gossiping and watching all the human suffering march through their lobby.

She knew she was doing the right thing—the *best* thing—for Walnut River and its citizens. She just had to convince everybody else in town.

No problem.

At long, long last, the elevator car arrived and the doors whooshed open. She considered it nothing short of a miracle that it was blessedly empty. Not a Wilder in sight.

Only after the doors slid shut did she close her eyes and slump against the wall of the elevator, pressing a hand to her stomach before she dug in the pocket of her suit jacket for an antacid.

She did not want to be here. In Walnut River, at the hospital her family had all but founded, in this blasted elevator.

It helped nothing that she had expected the reaction she had received from those two volunteers and she expected much more vitriol in the days ahead.

She had read the reports and knew the merger she had been sent here to expedite wasn't popular among the staff at WRG. Not that she had needed reports. Her family's unreasonable opposition was all the evidence she needed. They had all made no secret that they were furious at her.

Traitor.

Not a Wilder.

She screwed her eyes shut. Focus on the job, she chanted to herself. That was all that mattered. Move in fast and hard and wrap things up so she could return to New York.

She had no choice, not if she wanted to keep her job. And she certainly did.

She loved working for Northeastern HealthCare, one of the fastest growing health care conglomerates in the region. She was on the fast track there and had great hopes of making vice president within the next five years. That goal would be even closer if she could pull this deal off.

Mercifully, though the elevator stopped on the second floor to pick up a couple of nurses, she didn't recognize them and they didn't seem to know her. One of them even gave her a friendly smile.

So maybe David hadn't yet gotten around to plastering up wanted posters throughout the hospital of her wearing devil horns.

Beware of the evil HMO-mongerer.

She wouldn't put anything past her second-oldest brother, a gifted plastic surgeon who had recently returned to Walnut River as well. Unlike her, he had come back to a warm welcome, embraced by one and all—the prodigal son giving up a lucrative career in L.A. as plastic surgeon to the stars to share his brilliance with patients in his own hometown.

On the fourth floor, the nurses exited with her. Anna stood for a moment, trying to catch her bearings.

This part of the hospital had been renovated in the past few years and she was slightly disoriented at the changes.

She remembered it as slightly old-fashioned, with wood-grained paneling and dark carpeting. Now everything was light and airy, with new windows and a far more modern feel.

"Do you need help finding something?" one of the nurses asked, noticing her confusion.

"Yes. Thanks. I'm looking for the administrator's office."

"Down the hall. Second door on the right," she said.

"Thank you." Anna gave a polite smile, grateful for any help she could find here in this hostile environment, then headed in the direction the woman indicated.

The receptionist's nameplate read Tina Tremaine. She greeted Anna with a friendly smile, her features warm and open.

"Hello. I'm Anna Wilder. I'm here for a three-o'clock meeting with the hospital attorney and the administrator."

The instant she heard Anna's name, the woman's smile slid away as if a cold breeze had just blown through the room.

"I'm here for a three o'clock meeting with the hospital attorney and the administrator."

"Phil Crandall, the hospital attorney, is not here yet, Ms. Wilder. But Mr. Sumner and your attorney are in the boardroom. They're waiting for you."

Though she spoke politely enough, Anna thought she saw a tiny sliver of disdain in the woman's eyes.

She fished around in her mind for something she might say to alter the woman's negative impression, then checked the impulse.

She was working hard to break the habits of a lifetime, that hunger for approval she couldn't quite shake. Did it really matter what J.D.'s receptionist thought of her? It certainly wouldn't change anything about her mission here in Walnut River.

"Thank you," she answered, mustering a smile she hoped was at least polite if not completely genuine. She headed for the door the receptionist indicated, tilting her chin up and hoping she projected confidence and competence.

This was it. Her chance to cinch the promotion at NHC and cement her growing reputation as a rainmaker there.

Or she could blow the merger, lose her job, and end up begging on the street somewhere.

Think positive, she ordered herself. *You can do this. You've done it before.* As she pushed open the door, she visualized herself handing over the signed deal to her bosses, both her direct supervisor, Wallace Jeffers—vice president for mergers and acquisitions—and the NHC chief executive officer who had given her this assignment, Alfred Daly.

It was a heady, enticing image, one she clung to as she faced the two men at the boardroom table, papers spread out in front of them.

Two men sat at a boardroom table talking, papers spread out in front of them. She knew both of them and smiled at J. D. Sumner and Walter Posey, the NHC attorney.

"I'm sorry if I've kept you waiting. I didn't realize there would be so much construction surrounding the hospital."

J.D. nodded. "Walnut River is growing. You just have to walk outside to see it."

"Which is one factor that makes this hospital an attractive opportunity for NHC, as you well know."

J.D. had first come to Walnut River as an employee of NHC. He had ended up falling—literally—for her sister, Ella, resigning from NHC and taking the job as hospital administrator.

She didn't know all the details but she knew Ella had treated J.D. after he was injured in a bad tumble on some icy steps when leaving the hospital. Something significant must have happened between them to compel a man like

J.D. to fall for his orthopedic surgeon and leave a promising career at Northeastern HealthCare to take the reins of Walnut River General Hospital.

She couldn't imagine giving up everything she had worked so hard to attain for something as ephemeral as love, but she had to admit part of her envied her sister. J.D. must love Ella very much.

She could only hope his relationship with Ella had turned him soft. Judging by his track record at NHC, Anna feared he would be a formidable foe in her efforts to make the merger happen.

"Our attorney was caught up in the traffic snarl, as well," J.D. answered. "He just called and was still parking his car but he should be here any moment."

Though he spoke cordially enough, there was a reserve in his voice she couldn't miss.

She had only known him casually when he worked for NHC, but their interactions as coworkers had always been marked by friendly respect. Now, though, they were on opposite sides of what was shaping up to be an ugly fight over the future of the hospital.

He didn't seem antagonistic, as she had feared, only distant. She had to admit she was relieved. He and Ella were engaged, from what she understood. This was bound to be awkward enough between them without outright antipathy.

"I'm going for some coffee before we get started," the NHC attorney announced. "Can I get either of you anything?"

Anna shook her head at Walter, whom she had worked with before on these due diligence reviews. "None for me, thanks."

"Sumner?"

J.D. shook his head. "I'm good."

As soon as Walter left the room, J.D. leaned back in his chair and studied her carefully, until Anna squirmed under the weight of his green-eyed gaze.

"So how are you? I mean, how are you *really?*"

She blinked at the unexpected personal question and was slow to answer, choosing her words carefully. "I'm managing. I suppose you heard I tried to stay out of this one, obviously without success."

He nodded, his brow furrowed. "I heard. Does Daly really think your family connection will make anyone happier about NHC's efforts to take over the hospital?"

"Hope springs eternal, I suppose," she muttered.

J.D. laughed. "Alfred Daly obviously doesn't know your stubborn siblings, does he?"

If her boss had any idea what he was up against, Anna had a feeling he never would have initiated the merger proceedings at Walnut River General.

"How's Ella?" The question slipped out before she could yank it back.

J.D.'s eyes widened with surprise for just an instant that she would ask before they softened into a dreamy kind of look that filled her with no small amount of envy.

"She's great. Wonderful. Except the wedding next month is making her a little crazy. I told her to just leave the details to someone else, but she won't hear of it." He paused. "She misses you."

I miss her, too. The words tangled on her tongue and dried there. She couldn't say them, of course. She could never tell J.D. how she hated this distance between her and her sister.

They used to be so close—best friends as well as sisters, only a year apart. They had shared everything—clothes, secrets, friends.

She remembered lying on her stomach in their backyard, daydreaming and giggling over boys.

"You're going to be my maid of honor," Ella declared more than once. "And I'll be yours."

"One of us will have to get married first," she remembered answering. "So one of us will have to be a matron of honor."

"That sounds so old! Like one of the gray-haired ladies at the hospital! How about we'll both still be maids of honor, even if one of us is already married?"

Anna remembered shaking her head at Ella's twisted logic but in the end, she had agreed, just like she usually did.

That had always been their plan. But now Ella and J.D. were getting married in a month and Anna wasn't even sure she would receive an invitation.

Especially not if she successfully carried out her objective of making this merger a reality.

Her career or her family.

A miserable choice.

"You should talk to her," J.D. said into the silence, with a sudden gentleness that made her want to cry again.

"I wish this were something that a little conversation could fix," she murmured. "I'm afraid it's not that easy."

"You never know until you try," he answered.

She didn't know how to answer him, and to her relief she was spared from having to try when the door opened.

She looked up, expecting Walter with his coffee, then she felt her jaw sag as recognition filtered through.

"Sorry I'm late, J.D. That traffic is a nightmare," the

newcomer said. He was tall and lean, with hair like sun-light shooting through gold flakes. His features were classically handsome—long lashes, a strong blade of a nose, a mouth that was firm and decisive.

The eight years since she had seen Richard Green had definitely been kind to him. He had always been sexy, the sort of male women always looked twice at. When they were teenagers, he couldn't seem to go anywhere without a horde of giggling girls around him, though he had barely seemed to notice them.

Now there was an edge of danger about him, a lean, lithe strength she found compelling and seductive.

J.D. rose and shook his hand. "I appreciate you filling in for Phil at the last minute."

"No problem."

The attorney looked over J.D.'s shoulder and she saw shock and disbelief flicker across the stunning blue eyes that had lost none of their punch even after eight years.

"Anna!"

In a different situation, she might have rushed to hug him but he was sending out a definite "back off" vibe.

"You two know each other, obviously," J.D. said.

She managed to wrench her gaze away from Richard, wondering how she could possibly have forgotten his sheer masculine beauty—and how she ever could have walked away from it in the first place.

The reminder of how things had ended between them sent a flicker of apprehension through her body. He looked less than thrilled to see her. Could this merger become any more complicated? Her family was fighting against her tooth and nail, the hospital administrator was marrying her sister in a month's time, and she and the hospital attorney had a long and tangled history between them.

How was she supposed to be focused and businesslike around Richard when she couldn't help remembering exactly how that mouth had tasted?

"Richard lived only a few blocks away from the house where we were raised," she finally answered J.D., and was appalled to hear the husky note in her voice. She cleared her throat before continuing. "We went to school together and were…good friends."

Friends? Is that what she called it?

Richard listened to her with a mixture of anger and disbelief.

He supposed it wasn't strictly a lie. They had been friends through school. Both had been on similar academic tracks and had belonged to many of the same clubs and after-school organizations. Honor Club, Debate, Key Club. Even later when they went off to different universities, they had stayed in touch and had gotten together as often as possible with their other friends.

Yeah, they had been friends. But there had been much more to it, as she damn well knew, unless she'd somehow managed to conveniently wipe from her memory something that had certainly seemed significant—earthshaking, even—at the time.

What the hell was she doing here? Why hadn't somebody—J.D. or Peter Wilder or Phil Crandall, his absent partner—warned him?

He had heard from Peter and Ella that Anna was working for Northeastern HealthCare, their dreaded enemy. He just had never dreamed she would be a part of the conglomerate's efforts to take over Walnut River General.

She had changed. She used to wear her hair down, a long, luscious waterfall. Now it was tightly contained, pinned back in a sleek style that made her look cool and businesslike. Her features were just as beautiful, though some of the bright, hopeful innocence he remembered in the clear blue of her eyes had faded.

How could she sit across the board-room table, all cool and gorgeous like some kind of damn Viking princess, acting as if her very presence here wasn't a betrayal of everything her family had done for this hospital and for this community?

The depth of his bitterness both shocked and disconcerted him. What did it matter if the NHC executive was Anna Wilder or some other mindless drone they sent?

Either way, the outcome would be the same.

NHC was determined to purchase the hospital from a city council eager to unload it and a solid core of doctors and administrators was just as determined to prevent the deal.

Richard numbered himself among them, even though he was here only in a fill-in capacity for his partner.

Yeah, he had been crazy about Anna once, but it had been a long, long time ago.

That fledgling relationship wasn't significant in the slightest. It hadn't been important enough to her to keep her in Walnut River and whatever might have been between them certainly had no bearing on the current takeover situation.

"Shall we get started with the hearing?" he said icily.

She blinked at his tone—and so did J.D., he noted with some discomfort.

Richard had built a reputation as a cool-headed attorney who never let his personal feelings interfere with his legal responsibilities. He supposed there was a first time for everything.

After a long awkward moment, Anna nodded.

"By all means," she replied, her voice matching his temperature for temperature.

Chapter Two

Two hours later, Richard understood exactly why Anna Wilder had been brought into this takeover.

She was as cold as a blasted icicle and just as hard.

While the NHC attorney had been present to vet the information offered by the hospital side, all of them recognized that Anna was truly the one in charge.

She had been the one leading the discussion, asking the probing questions, never giving an inch as she dissected their answers.

Richard had certainly held his own. Anna might be a tough and worthy opponent but he had one distinct advantage—he was absolutely determined to keep NHC from succeeding in its takeover efforts while he was still alive and kicking.

"Thank you, everyone." Anna stood and surveyed the men around the boardroom table with the sheer aplomb of a boxer standing over the battered and bloody body of an opponent.

"We've covered a great deal of ground. I appreciate your forthrightness and the hospital's compliance with the municipal council's disclosure order. You've been very helpful. I'll take this information back to my superiors and we can go from there."

Richard gritted his teeth. Until they could find a way out of it, the hospital administration had no choice but to comply with the municipal council's strictures.

For now, city council members controlled the purse strings and they appeared eager to escape the costly hospital business that had been a drain on taxpayers for years.

Even the NHC contretemps a few weeks ago involving charges of corporate espionage hadn't dissuaded them.

The only bright spot in the entire takeover attempt was that the municipal council seemed genuinely committed to listening to the opinion of the hospital board of directors before making a final decision to move forward with the sale of the hospital to NHC.

Right now, the board members were leaning only slightly against the sale, though he knew the slightest factor could tip that ultimate decision in either direction.

Who knows? Maybe the NHC bigwigs would take a look at the hospital's tangled financial and personnel disclosures and decide another facility might be more lucrative.

Though he was committed to doing all he could to block the sale, Richard was nothing if not realistic. He wasn't even the hospital's lead attorney, he was only filling in for his partner, who had called begging the favor only an hour before the meeting.

Before he knew Anna Wilder was on board as the NHC

deal-closer, he would have jumped at the chance to step up and handle the merger discussions. Seeing her at the board table with her sleek blond hair yanked ruthlessly into a bun and her brisk business suit and her painfully familiar blue eyes changed everything.

He sighed as he gathered his laptop and papers and slipped them into his briefcase. He was zipping it closed when Anna managed to surprise him yet again, as she had been doing with depressing regularity since he walked into the boardroom.

"Richard, may I speak with you for a moment?"

He checked his watch, his mind on the very important person waiting for him. "I'm afraid I'm in a hurry," he answered.

"Please. This won't take long."

After a moment, he nodded tersely, doing his best to ignore the curious glances from J.D. and the NHC attorney as they both left the room.

Anna closed the door behind the two men and he was suddenly aware of the elegant shape of her fingers against the wood grain and the soft tendrils of hair escaping her pins to curl at the base of her neck.

She had changed perfumes, he noted. In college she had worn something light and flowery that had always reminded him of a sunwarmed garden. Now her scent was slightly more bold—and a hell of a lot more sexy, he had to admit. It curled through the room, tugging at his insides with subtle insistency.

She turned to face him and for an instant, he was blinded by the sheer vibrancy of her smile. "Richard, I know I didn't say this before, but it's really wonderful to see you again! I've wondered so many times how you were."

He found that hard to believe. She had to know where he was. If she had wondered so much, she could have found out as easily as sending a simple e-mail or making a phone call.

"I've been fine. Busy."

Too busy to spend time mooning over the only woman who had ever rejected him, he wanted to add, but managed to refrain.

He was an adult, after all, something he would do well to remember right about now.

"Rumor has it you got married," she said after a moment. "Any kids? I always thought you would make a wonderful father."

"Did you?"

She either missed the bite in his tone or she chose to ignore it.

"I did," she answered. "You were always so great with the neighborhood children. I can remember more than a few impromptu baseball games with you right in the middle of the action. You didn't care how old the players were or anything about their ability level. You just tried to make sure everyone had fun."

He was trying really hard to ignore the softness in her eyes and the warmth in her voice.

She had walked away from everything he wanted to offer her, without looking back. He had a right to be a little bitter, eight years later.

"So do you have any children?" she asked. She seemed genuinely interested, much to his surprise.

"One," he finally answered, not at all pleased with her line of questioning. He didn't like being reminded of old, tired dreams and newer failures.

"Boy or girl?"

"Boy. He's just turned five."

And he would be waiting impatiently for his father to pick him up if Richard didn't wrap things up quickly and escape.

"I do the best I can with him, especially since his mother and I aren't together anymore. The marriage ended right after he was born. I have full custody."

He wasn't sure why he added that. It wasn't something he just blurted out to people. If they hadn't been friends so long ago, he probably would have kept the information to himself.

Shock flickered in the depth of her blue eyes. "Oh. I hadn't heard that part. I'm so sorry, Richard."

He shrugged. "I'm sorry she's chosen to not be part of Ethan's life, but I'm not sorry about the divorce. It was one of those mistakes that make themselves painfully clear minutes after it's too late to be easily fixed."

"That doesn't make it hurt less, I would imagine," she murmured softly.

"No, it doesn't," he answered, his voice short. He regretted saying anything at all about Ethan and especially mentioning his failed marriage that still stung.

He gripped his briefcase, desperate to escape this awkwardness, but her words stopped him before he could do anything but put his hand on the doorknob.

"Can I ask you something?"

He eased his hand away, flashing her a wry look. "You haven't seemed to have any problem asking questions for the last two hours. You're amazingly good at it."

"That was different. Business. This is...not."

For the first time since the meeting she seemed to reveal her nerves weren't completely steel-coated. Wariness flickered in her eyes and she appeared to be gripping a file folder with inordinate force.

He ought to just push past her and get the hell out of there but he couldn't quite bring himself to move.

Instead, he shrugged. "Go ahead."

"I just wondered about this...hostility I'm sensing from you."

Apparently he wasn't as good at concealing his inner turmoil as he'd thought. "I'm sure you're imagining things."

"I don't think so," she answered, her voice pitched low. "I'm not an idiot, Richard."

Abruptly, suddenly, he was furious with her, as angry as he'd ever been with anyone. She had no right to come back, dredging up all these feelings he had buried long ago. The rejection, the hurt, the loss.

He had thrown his heart at her feet eight years ago. The hell of it was, he couldn't even say she had stomped on it. That might have been easier to handle, if she had shown any kind of malice.

But he supposed that would have been too much bother for her and would have required her to care a little. Instead, she had politely walked around it on her way out the door.

And then she dared to stand here now and ask him why he wasn't thrilled to see her!

This wasn't personal, he reminded himself. Or if some part of him couldn't help making it so, he shouldn't let everything between them become about their shared past. He couldn't afford it, not in his temporary role as hospital counsel.

"Why would I be hostile?" he said instead. "You're

only the point man—or woman, I guess—for a company trying to destroy this hospital and this community."

She blinked a little at his frontal assault, but it only took her seconds to recover. "Not true. I would have thought as an attorney you could look at this with a little more objectivity than..." Her voice trailed off.

"Than who? Your family?"

She sighed. "Yes. They won't listen to reason. Peter and David think I've betrayed the family name and Ella...well, Ella's not speaking to me at all."

He didn't expect the sympathy that suddenly tugged at him, fast on the heels of his own anger. Her family had always been important to her. Sometimes he thought she placed *too* much importance on their opinions. She had always seemed painfully aware that she was adopted and struggled hard to find a place for herself among the medicine-mad Wilders.

As a single child himself, he could only imagine what she must be feeling now—alienated by her siblings and bearing the brunt of their anger over her role in the NHC takeover attempt.

On the other hand, he instinctively sided with her siblings in this situation, not Anna.

He pushed away the wholly inappropriate urge to offer her comfort. "How did you expect them to react, Anna? This hospital is in their blood. Your family is basically the heart of Walnut River General. Everyone here knows that. And the soul, the essence, of this place is the sense of community—neighbors reaching out to help neighbors. That's what has made this hospital such an integral component to the quality of life in Walnut River. No one likes to go to the hospital, but the ordeal is made a little easier here when you know you'll be treated with respect and dignity, often by someone who has known you all your life."

She blinked with surprise. "Times change," she answered. "The health-care industry is changing. Independent community hospitals just don't have the competitive edge anymore."

"Nor should they. It's not about making money. It's about helping people heal."

"Exactly! And if Northeastern HealthCare can help them heal in a more efficient, cost-effective way and provide better access to cutting-edge procedures not currently available in this market, don't you think that will be better for everyone in the long run?"

"Will it?"

"Yes!" she exclaimed. "Walnut River would be part of a powerful consortium of health-care providers. With that backing, the hospital can afford to bring in state-of-the-art equipment and the newest procedures. NHC is already talking about building a cancer treatment center so patients don't have to drive twenty miles away for radiation treatment! And they're talking about an entire renovation of the labor and delivery unit and an after-hours Instacare facility for parents who work during the day to bring their children to see a doctor...."

Her voice trailed off and color brushed her cheeks like the first hint of autumn on the maple trees along the river. "I didn't mean to ramble on. I'm afraid I get a little... passionate sometimes."

She obviously believed the NHC takeover would truly be best for the hospital. Richard had to admire her passion, even if he disagreed with it.

"You certainly are free to believe what you want," he said. "And I'll do the same."

After a moment, she nodded. "Fair enough. But that doesn't really answer my question."

"What question would that be?"

She opened her mouth to answer but before she could, the boardroom door opened and Tina Tremaine, J.D.'s receptionist, stepped through.

"Oh. I'm sorry. I thought everyone was gone."

"We're just on our way out," Richard answered.

"You don't have to rush. Take your time. I only needed to make sure things were straightened up in here for a meeting J.D. has first thing in the morning."

She smiled at Richard but he was surprised to see her smile disappear completely by the time she turned to Anna.

Anna didn't seem to miss the sudden disdain in the other woman's eyes. Her shoulders straightened and her chin tilted up slightly but she said nothing.

"We're just leaving," Richard said again.

"Fine." Tina closed the door behind her, leaving behind a sudden awkward silence.

"Look, would you like to go somewhere? Grab an early dinner or something?" Anna asked.

He gazed at her, stunned that some tiny part of him was actually tempted, even though the more rational part of his brain recognized the absurdity of the impulse.

"That's not a good idea, Anna."

Somewhere in the depths of her blue eyes he thought he saw a shadow of vulnerability, just the barest hint of loneliness. But she mustered a brittle-looking smile. "Really? Why not? What could possibly be the harm in it? We're just two old friends catching up over dinner."

"Two old friends who happen to be standing on opposite sides of a corporate battlefield."

"Oh, for heaven's sake. That doesn't mean we can't be civil to each other! You were one of my closest friends, Richard. I told you things no one else in the world knows about me."

You said you loved me and then you walked away when something better came along.

His bitterness again seemed to sweep up out of nowhere, taking him completely by surprise.

He thought he had dealt with all this years ago. He never would have guessed seeing her would dredge up all those feelings and make them fresh and raw all over again.

He chose his words carefully, not at all eager to reveal too much to her. "I'm sorry, Anna. Even if not for the gray area regarding conflict of interest ethics in seeing you socially, I have other plans."

She froze for an instant and color climbed her cheeks. "Some other time then, perhaps. It was…great to see you again."

She headed for the walnut-paneled door. As she reached out to pull it open, he thought she paused slightly. Her gaze met his and if he hadn't known her so well years ago, he probably would have missed the flash of trepidation there.

He wondered at it for only an instant before he realized what must lie beneath her hesitation. Judging by Tina's reaction in the boardroom just now, he was willing to bet Anna wasn't at all popular at Walnut River General Hospital. The antimerger forces were vocal and vociferous in their opposition.

Again that unwanted sympathy surged through him.

He might not agree with her position but he couldn't argue with her convictions. She was only doing her job and she didn't deserve to be mistreated by employees of the hospital who might oppose her mission here.

"I'll walk out with you," he said impulsively.

Her lush, delectable mouth opened a little with surprise, then she rewarded him with a glowing smile that made him far too aware of how the years between them had only added to her loveliness.

Much to his dismay, he suddenly felt a familiar clutch of desire twist his insides. He wanted to reach across the space between them and capture that mouth with his, to see if her skin was as silky as he remembered, if she still tasted heady and sweet.

He had been far too long without a woman. Between Ethan and trying to build his practice, he had little time or inclination left for extracurricular activity.

Maybe he needed to make time—especially since the one woman who stirred his interest in longer than he cared to remember was. Anna Wilder.

It was ridiculous for her to be so grateful Richard was walking beside her. What did she expect, that she would need a bodyguard to help her safely make it through the hospital?

She might be persona non grata around the hospital right now, but she couldn't quite believe anyone would physically assault her to keep NHC at bay.

Still, she couldn't deny she found great comfort from Richard's calm presence as they headed for the elevator. She always had, she remembered now. He had been a source of strength and comfort through high school and college—the one she always turned to for advice, for counsel, for encouragement.

And more.

She pushed the memories away, refusing to dwell on them. She couldn't think about them right now, when he was only a few feet away looking blond and dangerously gorgeous.

They paused at the elevator to wait for a car and stood in silence, watching the numbers rise. She was just about to ask him about his other clients when she heard a commotion down the hall.

"Hold the elevator. The trauma lift isn't working."

Anna sucked in her breath as the familiar voice rang through the hallway. Her insides knotted with dread but she had no choice but to turn her head.

She wasn't at all surprised to see her sister working an oxygen pump as a team of medical personnel pushed a gurney down the hall. Anna had a quick impression that the patient was a middle-aged woman with her face covered in blood.

Ella faltered for just a moment when she saw Anna but she didn't break her stride. "Have the ER hold trauma room one," she told a nurse running beside them. "And alert the surgical team that we've got a femoral compound fracture and possible head trauma."

She snapped out other commands firmly in a crisp, focused tone that reminded Anna painfully of their father, leaving no doubt exactly who was in charge of the situation.

She had never seen her sister in a professional capacity, Anna realized, as a mixture of pride and awe washed through her.

She always knew Ella would kick butt as a doctor. Seeing her in action was all the confirmation she needed. Ella was cool, composed and completely in control—all the things Anna couldn't quite manage during her single year of med school.

Anna and Richard stepped aside to allow the team access to the elevator. Just before the doors slid closed, Anna's gaze met her sister's for only a millisecond.

Everything on the periphery seemed to fade, and for a moment Anna was ten years old again, snuggling in her sleeping bag in a tent in their big backyard next to her sister and best friend while the stars popped out, sharing secrets and popcorn and dreams.

Oh, Ella. I miss you so much, she wanted to whisper, but she could never say the words tangled in her throat, and in an instant, the doors closed and the moment was gone.

She fought back tears, praying her emotions wouldn't betray her in front of Richard.

"Wow," he said after a moment. "Hurricane Ella, as usual."

"Right." She didn't trust herself to say more than that as a thousand different regrets pinched at her.

Their rift was largely her fault, one that had been widening for eight years since she left Walnut River, and it had become an unbreachable chasm these days.

If she had told Ella and their brothers about her job with NHC, her involvement in the merger might not have come as such a shock to the other Wilders. Instead, for two long years she had chosen the coward's way, avoiding their questions when they asked about her work, offering them half-truths and evasions.

She had suspected exactly how they would react.

She supposed that was the reason she had deceived them for so long.

"Not a good time for sisterly conversation, obviously."

She wrenched her mind away from her guilt to Richard, who was watching her with entirely too much perception in his blue eyes.

She forced a smile past her aching heart. "Ella runs a mile a minute. She always has. When we were kids, she was always on the go. You remember what she was like."

"I do. There was never a quiet moment with the two Wilder girls around."

She forced another smile, though she had a feeling it was probably as transparent as it felt. She could only hope he didn't see the hurt washing through her in fierce waves.

"You never asked your question," he said.

She blinked at him. "Sorry. What question was that?"

"I don't know. You said you wanted to ask me something and then we were sidetracked."

She frowned, replaying their conversation of the past few minutes in her mind. Suddenly she remembered the direction of her thoughts and she could feel herself flush.

If not for the encounter with Ella, she might have made some laughing remark and changed the subject. But her emotions were too raw for equivocation and for some strange reason she decided to be blunt.

"I did ask you, but you didn't give me a straight answer. I'm just wondering if it's business or personal."

"What?"

"The…hostility. Coolness, antipathy, whatever you want to call it. I'm just wondering if you're angry because I work for NHC or if there's something else behind it."

A strange light flickered in his eyes for just an instant

before his handsome features became a mask once more. He opened his mouth but before he could say anything, the elevator arrived.

Only after they stepped inside and he pushed the button to return to the main floor did he turn to answer her.

"I suppose a little of both," he said. "We were friends. You said it yourself. And for one night, we were far more than that. I guess I'm trying to figure out how a woman I considered a friend could turn her back on her family and this town."

I didn't, she wanted to cry. But she was already so tired of defending herself and her choices to everyone in Walnut River. Didn't anyone think it was possible—just maybe—that she might have the community's best interests at heart?

Richard certainly didn't. She could see the censure in his eyes. She couldn't argue with him. That was the hell of it. He had the right to his opinions and she suspected nothing she said would convince him her motives were anything other than crass profit.

The elevator arrived at the main floor and the doors sprang open. He walked with her through the lobby, past the censorious eyes and out of the hospital.

She wanted to thank him for providing a buffer, but she couldn't figure out just how to put the words together.

"I'm parked over there," he pointed.

"Oh. I'm on the other side. I guess I'll see you around, then."

"Probably not. I was only filling in temporarily today in the meeting. My partner is usually the one at our firm who represents the hospital. He should be back on the job tomorrow."

She should be relieved, she told herself. The prospect of spending more time with this prickly, distant Richard who had once been so very dear to her was not appealing.

"Well, in that case, it was…good to see you today."

"Right," he answered.

She walked to her car, wondering why she felt worse leaving the hospital than she had going in.

Chapter Three

Twenty minutes later, Anna walked into her duplex apartment and was instantly assaulted by a miniature dynamo.

Her dark mood instantly lifted as if dozens of sunbeams had followed her home.

"There's my Lilli-girl."

Her tiny dog gave one short yip of greeting then did a standing leap on all four legs, jumping almost to Anna's knees. She laughed at the dog's antics and bent to scoop Lilli into her arms, all five pounds of her.

"Did you have a good day, sweetheart? I hope those two big monsters didn't run you ragged."

Lilli—short for Lilliputian—yipped again and wriggled in her arms maneuvering so she could lick eagerly at Anna's chin with her tiny sandpaper tongue.

Anna smiled and cuddled the dog closer. What a blessing this duplex had turned out to be, one of the few bright spots in her life since she had been ordered by the NHC CEO, Alfred Daly to come home to Walnut River to wrap up the hospital merger.

She hadn't been able to find a single hotel in town that would allow pets, but then she'd stumbled on this furnished place near the river that would allow a temporary lease for the short time she expected to be in Walnut River.

The duplex itself wasn't anything fancy, just bare bones lodging with little personality or style. But it had a good-sized backyard for Lilli to play in, and the landlady had two gentle yellow labradors who already adored her little Chihuahua-pug mix and kept her company all day.

Yeah, Anna was paying an arm and a leg above her per diem for the few weeks she expected to be here. But she figured it was worth it if she didn't have to kennel Lilli during her time in Walnut River or confuse her with a temporary placement with one of her friends or coworkers back in Manhattan.

She adored the dog and had from the moment she heard her tiny whimpering squeaks from a Dumpster near her subway stop in the financial district. Anna had been on her way back uptown on a cold dank January evening after working late and only heard the puppy by a fluke when she had paused for a moment to fix a broken heel on her shoe.

Another night, she might have been in too big a rush to investigate the sound. But that night, something had sparked her curiosity and she had dug through the Dumpster until she found Lilli, bedraggled, flea-infested, half-starved. The tiny puppy had looked at her with pleading dark eyes and Anna had been lost.

That had been six months before, just after her father

died. She freely admitted that while dog ownership had been an adjustment, especially with her hectic schedule and the added complications of city life, she had never once regretted her decision to rescue the puppy. Lilli had brought boundless happiness into her world.

Not that her life hadn't been fulfilling before, she reminded herself. She had carved out a comfortable life for herself in New York. She enjoyed her job and found it challenging and interesting. She had good friends in the city, she volunteered at an after-school mentoring program, she enjoyed a full and active social life.

Still, somewhere deep in her heart, she sometimes yearned for the comfortable pace and quiet serenity of Walnut River and she couldn't deny that she missed her family, especially Ella.

She remembered the heated anger that had flashed in her sister's eyes earlier at the hospital and hugged Lilli a little closer to her. She had ruined her chance for any kind of reconciliation with her family by deceiving them for two years.

Understanding and accepting her own culpability in the situation somehow didn't make it any easier to endure.

She sighed. "I need a good ride to clear my head. What do you say, Lilli-girl?"

The dog gave a yip of approval and Anna smiled and set her down, then hurried into her temporary bedroom. The dog followed on her heels, then danced around the room impatiently as Anna changed from her business suit to lycra bike shorts and a matching shirt. The transformation only took a few moments, with a few more needed to change her work chignon to a more practical ponytail.

A short time later, they set off with Lilli in her safety

harness, watching the world pass from her perch inside a custom-made basket on the front of Anna's racing bike.

Almost instantly, Anna felt some of the tension leave her shoulders. Even in the city, this was her escape, riding along her favorite trails in Central Park, exploring new neighborhoods, darting around taxis and buses.

Rediscovering the streets of her hometown had been a particular pleasure these past few days, and she could feel herself relax as the bike's tires hummed along the asphalt.

Early summer had to be her favorite time of year, she decided, when the world was green and lovely. As she rode down one street and then another, she savored the smells and sights, so different from her life the past eight years in Manhattan.

The evening air was thick with the sweet smell of flowers, of meat grilling on a barbecue somewhere, of freshly mowed lawns.

She pushed herself hard, making a wide circuit around the edge of town before circling back. By the time she cut through the park near her duplex, she felt much more centered and better equipped to tackle the mounds of paperwork still awaiting her attention that evening.

The trail through the park took her past a baseball diamond where a game was underway. Because it seemed like such a perfect ending to her ride, a great way to celebrate a June evening, she paused to watch for a moment in the dying rays of the sun.

The players were young. She had never been very good at gauging children's ages but since many of them still had their baby fat and seemed more interested in jabbering to each other than paying attention to the game, she would have guessed them at five or so.

She smiled, watching one eager batter swing at the ball on the tee a half-dozen times before he finally connected. The ball sailed into right field, just past a player who ran after it on stubby little legs.

"Run for it, bud. You can catch it. That's the way."

Anna jerked her head around at the voice ringing from the stands and stood frozen with dismay.

When Richard claimed another commitment, she had assumed he meant a date. Instead, he sat in the bleachers looking gorgeous and casual in jeans and a golf shirt, cheering on the towheaded little outfielder she assumed was his son.

For just an instant, she was tempted to ride away quickly so he didn't think she was stalking him or something, but Lilli chose that inopportune moment to yip from her perch in the basket.

Drawn to the sound, Richard turned his head and she saw his eyes widen with surprise as he recognized her.

For one breathless instant, she thought she saw something else flicker there, something hot. But it was gone so quickly she was certain she must have imagined it.

She raised a hand in greeting and then—mostly because she didn't know what else to do amid the awkwardness of the chance encounter—she climbed from her bicycle, propped it against the metal bleachers then scooped Lilli out of the basket before joining him in the stands.

"That must be Ethan out there," she said.

"It is. We're up one run with one out and just need to hold them through this inning and it will be all over."

He turned his attention back to the game in time to cheer as the next player at bat hit the ball straight at the shortstop, who tossed it to first base. The fielder on first base looked astonished that he actually caught the ball in time to pick off the runner.

"I have to admit, I'm a little surprised to see you here," Richard said after a moment when the crowd's wild cheers subsided. "I wouldn't have expected a T-ball game to be quite up your alley."

Anna gave a rueful smile. "I only stopped on a whim. We live just a block away from here and have ridden through the park several times. This is the first game I've stopped at."

"We?"

She held up Lilli and Richard raised one of his elegant eyebrows. "Is that a dog or a rat with a bad case of indigestion?"

She made a face. "Hey, watch it. This is the queen of my heart. Lilli, this is Richard Green. Say hi."

The dog deigned to lift her paw but Richard only blinked.

"You're kidding."

Anna shook her head, hiding a smile. "I'm afraid not. She'll be offended if you don't shake."

With a sigh, he reached out a hand to take the dog's tiny paw in his, which was all the encouragement Lilli needed to decide he was her new best friend. She wriggled with delight and gazed at him out of adoring eyes.

This wasn't the first time Anna had noticed her dog had a weakness for handsome men.

"So you said the center fielder is your son?"

Richard nodded. "He's the one picking dandelions," he said wryly.

Anna laughed. "Correct me if I'm wrong, but I see three kids picking dandelions out there."

He smiled and she wondered how she could possibly

have forgotten the devastating impact of his smile. "Mine's the one in the middle."

As if on cue, the center fielder began to wave vigorously. "Hi, Daddy! Can you see me?"

Richard nodded. "I see you, buddy," he called out. "Watch the ball, okay?"

Ethan beamed at his father and obeyed, turning his attention back to the game just in time as a pop fly headed straight for him.

"Right there!" Richard exclaimed. "You can do it!"

Ethan held his glove out so far from his face it seemed to dangle from his wrist but the ball somehow miraculously landed right in the sweet spot with a solid thud.

Caught up in the moment, Anna jumped to her feet cheering with delight, along with Richard and the rest of the onlookers on their side of the bleachers.

"That's the game," the umpire called. "Final score, sixteen to fifteen."

Anna held tight to Lilli as the little dog picked up on the excitement of the crowd, yipped with glee and vibrated in her arms, desperate to be part of the action.

"Great game," she said after a moment. "Be sure to tell Ethan congratulations for me."

"I'll do that. Or it looks like you can tell him that yourself. Here he comes."

An instant later, a small figure rushed toward them, his features bright with excitement as he launched himself at his father.

"Did you see that, Dad? I caught the ball right in my glove! Right in my glove! I won the game! Did you see?"

Richard hugged his son with enthusiasm. "Nice work! I'm so proud of you, bud. You're getting better every game."

"I know. I am." He said it with such blatant confidence that Anna couldn't help but smile.

Lilli, never one to sit quietly when hugs were being exchanged and someone else was getting attention she thought rightfully belonged to her, gave another of her love-me yips and the boy quickly turned toward her.

"Wow! Is that your dog?" he exclaimed to Anna, the baseball game apparently forgotten.

Anna set Lilli down, careful to hold on to the retractable leash while Lilli trotted eagerly to the boy. He instantly scooped her into his arms and giggled with delight when the dog licked the little-boy sweat from his cheek.

"What's his name?" Ethan asked eagerly.

"She's a girl and her name is Lilli," Anna answered.

"I like her!"

She smiled, charmed by how much this darling boy resembled his father. "I do, too. She's a great dog."

"My name is Ethan Richard Green. What's yours?"

She sent a swift look toward Richard, not at all sure if he would approve of her engaging in a long conversation with her son. He returned her questioning look with an impassive one of his own, which she took as tacit approval for her to answer.

"My name is Anna. Anna Wilder. Your dad and I knew each other a long time ago."

"Hi." He set Lilli on the ground carefully and held out a polite hand to her, a gesture that charmed her all over again.

She shook it solemnly, tumbling head over heels in love with the little boy.

"I'm very pleased to meet you, Miss Wilder," he said, obviously reciting a lesson drummed into him by someone.

"And I'm very pleased to meet you as well, Mr. Green," she answered in the same vein.

His solemnity didn't last long, apparently, at least not with Lilli around. He knelt to pet the dog, giggling as she tried to lick him again.

"Would you like to hold her leash?" Anna asked.

"Can I?"

"If it's okay with your dad."

Ethan looked at his father, who nodded. "You can take her once around the bleachers but don't go farther than that."

The little boy gripped the leash handle tightly and the two of them headed away.

"I wouldn't have pegged you for a dog person," Richard said after a moment.

"Why not?"

"I don't know. Just seems like a lot of responsibility for a single executive living in the big city."

Though his words echoed her own thoughts of earlier in the evening, she still bristled a little that he apparently doubted she might possess the necessary nurturing abilities.

"It's not always easy, but I make it work," she answered. "What about you? I wouldn't have pegged you for Little League games and car-pool duty. Talk about responsibility, Mr. High-Powered Attorney."

One corner of his mouth quirked into a smile. "Point taken. Just like you, it's not always easy but I make it work."

She didn't doubt it was a major juggling act—nor did she doubt Richard handled it with his typical elegant competence, just as she remembered him doing everything.

Both of them turned to watch Ethan and Lilli make

their way through other onlookers and players back around the bleachers.

Richard sighed as the boy and dog approached. "You know this is going to be one more salvo in our ongoing, occasionally virulent we-need-a-puppy debate."

She laughed at his woeful tone. "Sorry to cause more trouble for you. But Ethan is welcome to borrow Lilli anytime he'd like while I'm still in Walnut River."

He looked less than thrilled at the prospect, which only made her smile widen.

"That was super fun," Ethan exclaimed. "Can I do it again?"

"You'd better give Lilli back to Anna now, bud. Remember what I promised you after the game?"

"Oh yeah!" He handed the leash over to Anna. "We're gonna get a shaved ice," he exclaimed. "My dad promised I could have one if I was a good sport and didn't get mad if I didn't get on base again. Hey, do you and Lilli want a shaved ice, too?"

She slanted a look at Richard, who was again wearing that impassive mask.

Common sense told her to pick up her dog and run. She didn't need to spend more time with either of the Green males, both of whom she found enormously appealing on entirely different levels.

On the other hand, all that awaited her at her place was more paperwork. And she couldn't escape the sudden conviction that Richard wanted her to say no, which conversely made her want to do exactly the opposite.

"I'd love a shaved ice," she proclaimed. "It's thirsty work carrying a huge dog like Lilli around. Wears me right out."

The boy giggled as he eyed the miniscule Chihuahua. "You're super funny, Miss Wilder."

She hadn't heard that particular sentiment in a long, long time. She couldn't remember the last time anyone had thought she was anything other than a boring numbers-cruncher. She decided she liked it.

"You know what? You can call me Anna, as long as I can call you Ethan. Is that okay?"

"Sure."

"Ethan, would you mind holding Lilli's leash while I walk my bike?"

He nodded eagerly. "I won't let go, I promise," he said.

"Okay. I trust you."

She slanted one more look at Richard, who was watching their exchange with only a slight tightening of his mouth showing his displeasure. She almost apologized for forcing herself into a family event but then gave a mental shrug.

They were only sharing shaved ices, not spending the entire evening together.

This was completely unfair.

Richard barely had time to adjust to the idea that she was back in town and here she was again, crowding his space, intruding in his carefully constructed life, making him think about things he had put on the back burner.

A casual observer probably wouldn't be able to imagine that the coolly competent executive he had spent two hours with earlier in the day could be the same woman as this softer, far more approachable, version.

This Anna looked sleek and trim and sexy as hell, with all that gorgeous blond hair pulled back in a ponytail and her skin glowing with vitality.

She looked much like he remembered his old friend from eight years ago—bright and vibrant and so beautiful he couldn't manage to look away for longer than a minute or two at a time.

She seemed completely oblivious to her allure as she walked beside him, pushing her bike. And he would have bet she had no idea how hard it was for him to fight down the surge of pure lust.

The evening was one of those beautiful Walnut River summer evenings and the park was full of families taking advantage of it. He greeted several people he knew on the short walk to the shaved ice stand but didn't stop to talk with any of them.

"Do you know every single person in town?" Anna asked after a few minutes.

"Not quite. There are some new apartment complexes on the other side of town and I believe there one or two tenants there're I haven't managed to meet yet. I'm working on it, though."

He meant it as a joke but she apparently didn't quite catch the humor. "Are you running for mayor or something?"

He gave a rough laugh. "Me? Not quite. I've just lived here most of my life. You can't help but come to know a lot of people when you're part of a community."

"Why did you stick around Walnut River?" she asked him. "You always had such big plans when you were in law school. You were going to head out to the wild frontier somewhere, open your own practice and work on changing the world one client at a time."

He remembered those plans. He had dreamed of heading out West. Colorado, maybe, or Utah. Somewhere with outdoor opportunities like skiing and mountain biking—all the things he didn't have time to do now that he was a single father.

"Things change. Life never quite turns out like we expect when we're twenty-two, does it?"

He didn't think he had ever confided in her the rest of those dreams. He had been desperately in love with Anna Wilder and wanted to bundle her up and take her into the wilderness with him.

She was quiet, her eyes on his son, who was giggling at her little rat-dog. "Maybe not. But sometimes it's better, though, isn't it?"

The fading rays of the sun caught in Ethan's blond hair and Richard's heart twisted with love for his son.

"Absolutely." He paused. "And to answer your question about why I'm still here, mostly it's because this is where my mother lives. She takes Ethan most days when I'm working and they're crazy about each other. She's a godsend."

"Is Ethan's mother in the picture at all?"

He wasn't sure he could honestly say Lynne had ever really been in the picture. Their relationship had been a mistake from the beginning and he suspected they both would have figured that out if not for her accidental pregnancy that had precipitated their marriage.

"Is that the wrong question?" Anna asked quietly and he realized he had been silent for just a hair too long.

"No. It's fine. The short answer is no. The long answer is a bit more...complex."

He wasn't about to go into the long and ugly story with Anna, about how Lynne hadn't wanted children in the first place, how she had become pregnant during their last year of law school together, that she probably would have had an abortion if she hadn't been raised strict Catholic.

Instead, he had talked her into marrying him.

Though she had tried hard for the first few months after Ethan was born, Lynne had been a terrible mother—impatient, easily frustrated, not at all nurturing to an infant who needed so much more.

It had been better all the way around when she accepted a job overseas.

"I'm sorry," Anna said again. "I didn't mean to dredge up something painful."

"It's not. Not really."

She didn't look as if she believed him, but by then they had reached the shaved ice stand. Ethan was waiting for them, jumping around in circles with the same enthusiasm as Anna's little dog as he waited impatiently for them to arrive.

"I want Tiger's Blood, just like I always have," Ethan declared.

Richard shook his head. His son rarely had anything else but the tropical fruit flavor. "You need to try a different kind once in awhile, kiddo."

"I like Tiger's Blood," he insisted.

"Same here," Anna agreed. "You know what's weird? It's Lilli's favorite flavor, too. I think it's the whole dog-cat thing. Makes her feel like a big, bad tough guy."

Though Ethan looked puzzled, Richard felt a laugh bubble out as he looked at her tiny dog prancing around at the end of her leash.

His gaze met Anna's and for just an instant, he felt like he was back in high school, making stupid jokes and watching movies together and wondering if he would ever find the courage to tell the prettiest girl in school he was crazy about her.

They weren't in high school anymore, he reminded himself sternly. She might still be the prettiest girl he had ever seen but he certainly wasn't crazy about her anymore. The years between them had taken care of that, and he wasn't about to change the status quo.

Chapter Four

The line was remarkably short and they had their icy treats only a few moments later.

"I saw a bench over there," Anna said. "Do you want to sit down?"

Richard knew he ought to just gather up his son and head home. But he couldn't quite force himself to sever this fragile connection between them, though he knew damn well it was a mistake to spend more time with her.

He was largely silent while they ate the shaved ice. For that matter, so was Anna, who seemed content to listen to Ethan chatter about his friends in kindergarten, his new two-wheel bike, the kind of puppy he wanted if his dad would ever agree.

Though Richard wondered how he could possibly have time to eat around all the never-ending chatter, Ethan finished his shaved ice in about five minutes flat then begged to play on the playground conveniently located next to the stand.

"Not for long, okay? It's been a long day and you need to get home and into the tub."

Ethan made a face as he handed Lilli's leash back to Anna then raced off toward the slide.

"He seems like a great kid," Anna said after a moment.

"He is. Seeing the world through his eyes helps keep my life in perspective."

"He's lucky to have you for a father."

She paused, her eyes shadowed. "My dad's been gone for six months and I still can't believe it."

Her father's opinion had always been important to Anna. Maybe too important.

He had respected her father—everyone in town had. James Wilder had been a brilliant, compassionate physician who had saved countless lives during his decades of practicing medicine in Walnut River. He doubted there was a family in town that didn't have some member who had been treated by Dr. Wilder.

But he didn't necessarily agree with the way James had treated his children. Even when they were younger Richard had seen how James singled Anna out, how hard he tried to include her in everything and make her feel an integral part of the family.

From an outsider's standpoint, Richard thought James's efforts only seemed to isolate Anna more, reminding her constantly that she was different by virtue of her adoption and fostering resentment and antipathy in her siblings.

"I tried to find you at the funeral to offer my condolences but you must have left early."

She set her plastic spoon back in the cup, her features suddenly tight. "It was a hard day all the way around. My father's death was such a shock to me and I'm afraid I didn't handle things well. I couldn't wait to get out of there and return to New York so I could… could grieve."

He found it inexpressibly sad that she hadn't wanted to turn to her siblings during their moment of shared sorrow.

"Have you seen Peter or David since you've been back?"

"No. Only Ella, today at the hospital." Her brittle smile didn't conceal the hurt in her eyes. "I'm quite sure they're all going out of their way to avoid me."

"They may not even be aware you're back in town."

"You know better than that, Richard. They know I'm here."

She was quiet for a moment, then offered that forced smile again. "It's not exactly a secret that NHC has sent me here to close the merger after six months of problems. I might not have received an angry phone call from holier-than-thou Peter or a snide, sarcastic email from David, but they know I'm here."

He didn't want to feel this soft sympathy for her but he couldn't seem to keep it from welling up, anyway.

She had created the situation, he reminded himself sternly. Why should he feel sorry for her at the estrangement with her siblings when she had done everything possible to stir up their wrath?

She shrugged. "Anyway, I'm sure J.D. spread the word he was meeting with me today."

She rose suddenly and threw her half-eaten shaved ice in the garbage can next to their bench. He had the distinct impression she regretted letting her emotions filter through.

"Which reminds me, I'd better go. I've got a great deal of paperwork to file after today's meeting."

He didn't think the reminder of their adversarial roles in the takeover was at all accidental.

She picked up her little dog and set her in a carrier attached to the handlebars of her bike. In bike shorts that hugged her trim, athletic figure, she looked long and lovely and so delectable she made his mouth water.

"It was nice bumping into you and meeting Ethan. Thank you for letting me share a little of your evening together."

"You're welcome."

She gave him one more small smile then, to his surprise, she stopped at the playground to say goodbye to Ethan. She even went so far as to take the dog out of her carrier one last time so the petite creature could lick at Ethan's face.

Their interaction touched something deep inside him. In his experience, most women either completely ignored his son or went over the top in their attentions, fawning all over Ethan in an effort to convince Richard how maternal they could be.

Anna's interest in Ethan seemed genuine—and it was obvious his son was smitten by her.

Or at least by her little rat-dog.

After a moment she gave Ethan one last high five, settled Lilli in her carrier again and rode away with one last wave to both of them.

He watched her go—as he had watched her go before. He sighed, his mind on that last miserable day when she had left Walnut River.

He still wasn't sure exactly why the hell she had left— or, more importantly, why the memory of it still stung.

They had been good friends through high school and he could admit to himself now that he'd always had a bit of a crush on her, though he hadn't fully realized it until college.

They went to different universities for their undergraduate work. He was at Harvard, but since she had only been a few miles away at Radcliffe, they had seen each other often, but still only as friends.

Though he could sense his feelings for her deepening and growing, they had both been running in opposite directions. He was headed for law school while she was busy preparing for med school.

But one summer night after their first year of graduate work everything had changed.

By a happy coincidence, they had both been home in Walnut River temporarily for the wedding of a friend. Since neither of them had dates, they had decided to go together—again, strictly as friends.

But he had taken one look at her in a sleek, pale-blue dress he could still remember vividly and he hadn't been able to look away.

They had danced every dance together at the wedding reception and by the time the night was over, he'd realized he had been hiding the truth from himself all those years.

He was in love with her

Deeply, ferociously in love.

And she had returned his feelings—or least, she had given a good imitation of it.

After the wedding festivities were over, they had gone to his house for a late-night swim. His parents were gone and he and Anna had stayed up long into the night, sharing confidences and heady kisses, holding hands while they looked at the stars and savored being together.

And then they had made love and he still remembered it as the single most moving experience of his life, except for Ethan's birth. She had given him her innocence and had told him she was falling in love with him.

And then in the morning, everything had changed.

The memory seemed permanently imprinted into his head, of standing on the front porch of her parents' house just hours after he had left her there, those stars still in his eyes.

He'd expected to find the woman he had just realized he loved.

Instead, he'd found chaos. Anna was gone. She must have left soon after he had dropped her at her doorstep, with one, last, long, lingering kiss and the promise of many more.

Both of her brothers were living away from home at the time but Richard clearly remembered the reaction of the three remaining Wilders. Her father had been devastated, her mother baffled and Ella had been crushed.

He couldn't really say she had left without a word. She'd mailed him a letter that had arrived the next day— a terse, emotionless thing.

What kind of fool was he that he could still remember the damn thing word for word?

Dear Richard.

I can't do this with you right now. I'm so sorry. I meant everything I said last night about my feelings for you, but after I've had a few hours to think about it, I realize I can't string you along while I try to figure out my life. It wouldn't be fair to you and to be honest, I'm not sure I have the emotional strength for it. You deserve so much more.

I have to go, Richard. I can't live this lie anymore. Being with you last night only showed me that more clearly. I'm being crushed by the weight of my family's expectations and I don't know any other way to break free of them. I only wish, more than anything, that I didn't have to hurt you in the process.

She had signed it with love and, while he had wanted to believe her, she had made no other effort to contact him.

That had been eight years ago. Another lifetime. Then had come Lynne and Ethan and his world had changed once more.

But his heart had never forgotten her.

He sighed, acknowledging the truth of that rather grim realization.

Some part of him still had feelings for Anna Wilder, feelings he didn't dare take out and examine right now.

It was a damn good thing his partner was representing Walnut River General in the whole NHC matter.

Richard wasn't sure his heart—or his ego—could handle being screwed over by Anna Wilder again.

Two days later, Richard sat in his office rubbing the bridge of his nose and trying to fight back the odd sensation that the walls of his office had suddenly shrunk considerably.

"Say that again. Where are you, Phil?"

His partner gave a heavy sigh, sounding not at all like his normal affable self. "Wyoming, at the Clear Springs Rehab Center. It's supposed to be one of the best in the nation."

"Rehab, Phil? Is this some kind of sick joke?"

"I wish it were that easy."

"I'm stunned!"

"You shouldn't be," the other man said wearily. "You covered for me enough the last six months that you should have seen the clues. Peggy's gone. She moved out two weeks ago and took the kids with her."

Those walls seemed to crowd a few inches closer. "You didn't say a word to me!"

"What was I going to say? I was too ashamed. My wife left me, my kids aren't talking to me. I've only held it together at work by luck and a hell of a good partner."

Okay, Richard had to admit he had suspected something was going on. With all the sick days and missed meetings, he had wondered if Phil was fighting a serious illness he wasn't ready to disclose.

In retrospect, he wondered how the hell he possibly could have missed the signs.

"I'm an alcoholic, Richard. I can't hide it anymore. I've tried to stop a dozen times on my own and I can't. This is the only way I know how to straighten out my life."

All the pieces seemed to fall into place with a hard thunk and again Richard wondered where his own head had been to miss something so glaring in his partner and friend.

Yeah, there had been mistakes the past few months—a couple of serious ones that Richard had been forced to step in and mend. But he had just assumed Phil would tell him what was going on when he was ready. He hadn't minded the clean-up work. Phil had been a mentor and a friend since he came to the practice straight out of law school, green in more than name and a single father of an infant to boot.

"How long will you be there?" he finally asked.

"As long as it takes. I wish I could be more specific

than that but I don't know at this point. The average stay is two months."

Two months? Richard fought down a groan. They had too much work as it was and had discussed adding another partner to the practice to help ease the burden.

"What about your clients?" he asked.

"I'm sorry to dump them on you. But my two junior associates have been basically carrying everything for the last few months, anyway. They can bring you up to speed on the major cases. I'm not worried about anything but the hospital takeover attempt. I'm afraid you'll have to step in and handle that. My files are copious, though. You should find everything you need there."

"I'll take care of everything on this end," Richard assured him. "You just focus on what you're doing there."

"Thanks, man. Entering into a partnership with you was the smartest move I've made in years."

Richard hung up a few moments later and let out a long, slow breath. He was concerned about his friend, first and foremost. But he was also suddenly overwhelmed with the weight of more responsibilities.

The hospital merger had been Phil's project for six months. Richard had helped a little but getting up to speed on all the intricate details was going to take days, if not weeks.

Talk about a complication. Just when he was thinking he wouldn't have to have anything more to do with Anna Wilder, circumstances had to go and change dramatically.

He would have no choice now but to work with her, on a much closer level than he was sure made him completely comfortable, given their shared past.

* * *

Amazing how a day could go from rough to truly miserable in the space of a few moments.

Anna stood in the cafeteria line in the basement of Walnut River General, wondering why she was even bothering to grab a salad when her appetite had abruptly fled and the idea of trying to force down lunch was about as appealing as walking back through the halls of the hospital and encountering another of her testy siblings.

She sighed, moving her tray along the metal track, one step closer to the cashier.

Blast David anyway.

Of all her siblings, she would have expected him to at least be civil to her—not because they had been the best of friends but because she had a tough time thinking he would bother to involve himself in the political side of things at the hospital.

Peter had at least tried to be brotherly to her, but because he was so much older than she, their lives had always seemed on slightly different tracks.

Ella had been closest to her, in age and in their relationship. If not for the distance she herself had placed between them after she dropped out of medical school and moved away from Walnut River, she imagined she and her sister would still have been close.

David, though, had always seemed a challenge. She'd always had the vague sense that he resented her. He had never been deliberately cruel, had just treated her with somewhat chilly indifference, making it overtly obvious he didn't want to be bothered with a whiny little sister who wasn't even really related to him.

She supposed nothing had really changed. Rather

blindly, she pushed her tray one person closer to the cashier, replaying the scene outside the cafeteria doors just a few moments earlier.

After spending all morning going over records the hospital refused to allow her to take off-site, she had been tempted to go somewhere in town for lunch. Maybe Prudy's Menu downtown or a fast-food place somewhere.

But since she was looking at several more hours of analyzing patient accounts, she had decided to save time by eating in the cafeteria.

Big mistake. She should have considered the possibility that she might encounter one of her testy siblings.

Sure enough, when she reached the cafeteria, the first person she had seen had been David, looking relaxed and happier than she'd seen him in a long time.

Becoming engaged and moving back to Walnut River apparently agreed with him. He had lost the edgy restlessness that had seemed so much a part of him for so many years.

She had smiled and opened her mouth to greet him, forgetting for just an instant where things stood between them.

Before she could say anything, he looked straight through her, then turned around and walked out of the cafeteria, leaving his food behind, as if he'd just stumbled into a leper colony.

No, not quite right. David was a compassionate, caring physician. He would rush right in to help anyone who was ill, especially if they suffered from a potentially life-threatening condition.

Apparently, she ranked somewhere well below a colony of lepers in her older brother's estimation. He couldn't even manage to bring himself to say hello to her.

Anna sighed. She had to stop being so maudlin about her siblings. She had made her choice when she had suggested Walnut River General as a possible acquisition target to her superiors at NHC. She had created this situation and she had no business moping about it.

"Looks like you're up," someone said behind her and Anna realized with some chagrin that while she had been sitting brooding, the line had moved forward and she was next to checkout.

She jerked her tray forward along the metal rails then watched with horror as her diet soda toppled sideways from the jolt. In her distraction after the scene with David, she apparently hadn't fastened on the plastic lid securely. As the cup fell, the contents splashed out—directly on the woman standing behind her.

Anna's face burned and she wanted nothing more than to leave her tray there and just escape. Still, she forced herself to turn to the other woman and found an elegant, pretty redhead wearing a pale green Donna Karan suit and a white blouse that now sported a golfball-sized caramel-colored stain on the front.

The woman looked vaguely familiar but Anna was quite certain she had never met her.

"I am so sorry," Anna exclaimed. "I'll give you my card. Please send me the bill for the dry cleaning."

The woman's smile was remarkably gracious. "Don't worry about it. This was my least favorite blouse, anyway."

"I'm sure that's not true."

The woman laughed. "Well, maybe second least-favorite. I've got an orange thing in my closet that's really a disaster."

She narrowed her gaze, her smile slipping just a fraction. "You're Anna, aren't you?"

Anna's stomach clenched. She really wasn't sure she could handle another confrontation right now. The woman was liable to dump her entire lunch all over her.

"Yes," she said warily. "I'm sorry, have we met?"

"No, though I was at your father's funeral. And I've just seen a picture of you in Peter's office."

"You…you have?"

"It was a picture taken at your father's last birthday party and has all four of you together. I've been wanting to meet you for a long time. I'm Bethany Holloway."

Bethany Holloway? *This* was Peter's fiancée?

Here was another stark reminder of the rift between her and her siblings. Her brother was marrying this woman in a few weeks and this was the first time Anna had even met her.

"Your total is six dollars and twenty-three cents," the cashier said pointedly. "You can go ahead and get another soda if you want."

Anna realized abruptly that she was holding up an entire line of hungry people. "Let me at least pay for your lunch," she said to Bethany.

"You don't have to do that."

"I do," Anna insisted. The cashier gave her a new total. Anna handed her a twenty and pocketed the change.

"That was not necessary, but thank you, anyway," Bethany said, moving with her out of the way so others could pay for their lunches.

"You're welcome," Anna replied. "I mean it about the dry cleaning."

Bethany shook her head. "I've got on-the-go stain removal stuff in my office. Soda should come out in a flash. If nothing else, I always keep a spare shirt in my office and I can change into that one after lunch. Please don't worry about it."

Anna had to admit, she was astonished. Bethany Holloway was actually smiling at her. She couldn't quite figure out why. Not only had Anna dumped soda all over her, but Anna would have assumed Peter's fiancée would be firmly on the opposite side of the family divide.

"I was supposed to meet Peter for lunch but he had an emergency. I guess I need to get used to that if I'm marrying a doctor, right? I hate to eat alone, though—are you meeting someone for lunch?"

"Uh, no."

In truth, she had planned to take the tray up to the tiny little hole in the wall office J.D. had begrudged her to go over the accounts.

"Good," Bethany said. "We can sit together and you can tell me all of Peter's secrets."

Her warm friendliness left Anna feeling off kilter, as if one of her heels was two inches shorter than the other, and she didn't know quite how to respond.

"I'm afraid I don't know any. Of Peter's secrets, I mean. I've been away from Walnut River for a long time."

Bethany smiled. "That's all right, then. You can tell me all of your secrets."

Bethany headed for a table without looking to see if Anna followed or not. Anna again fought the urge to flee to the relative safety of her borrowed office.

But she wasn't a coward. For some strange reason, her brother's fiancée wanted to talk to her and Anna didn't see that she had much of a choice but to comply.

Chapter Five

Anna slid into the booth opposite Bethany, wondering how she was possibly going to be able to swallow with these nerves jumping around in her stomach.

It was silly, really.

She had no reason to be apprehensive around Peter's fiancée. By all appearances, Bethany was kind and gracious. Anna didn't know many women of her acquaintance who could handle having a soda slopped all over them with such aplomb—especially when the one doing the slopping was on the outs with her fiancé.

She tried to focus on what she knew about Bethany and remembered that at one point she had been in favor of the merger, identified by NHC as a definite vote for their side. She decided there was no reason to talk around the issue.

"I understand you're an efficiency expert here at the

hospital," she said when they were both settled. "And you've been on the governing board of directors for a little over a year."

Bethany raised a slim auburn eyebrow. "NHC has a good research team. I suppose you have complete dossiers on every board member."

Anna toyed with a piece of lettuce, refusing to feel like a corporate stoolie. "You know how it works. It pays to know the players. At one point you were considered firmly on our side."

"I was. Absolutely."

"But you've gone on record opposing it now," she said. "Is that because of Peter?"

It was a rude question and one she regretted as soon as the words came out. To her vast relief, Bethany only laughed.

"Oh, he would love to hear you say that. No, I didn't change my vote because of my relationship with your brother. From an efficiency standpoint, the merger still makes sense. I won't deny that."

She paused and appeared to be considering her words with delicate care. "From a human standpoint, though, I'm not convinced Northeastern HealthCare has the best interest of our patients at heart."

Just like that, Anna automatically slid back on the defensive. "If you look at the statistics, you'll find we have a great track record at other hospitals of improving patient access to care while saving money at the same time."

"I know all the arguments, Anna. I promise, I've read the reports on NHC. We could debate this endlessly and I'm not sure we would get anywhere. There are compelling arguments on both sides but right now I have to go with my gut, that this deal isn't right for Walnut River General at the moment."

She lifted a slim hand to forestall any further arguments. "Let's talk about something else, okay? I'm sure you get enough arguments from everyone and I'd really like us to be friends."

Anna wasn't sure that was possible, given the current situation, but she found she desperately liked the idea of having Bethany as a friend.

"I hate to be a bridezilla," Bethany continued, "but can we talk about my wedding?"

Anna gulped. She would almost rather stage a public debate on the merger right there in the cafeteria than talk about her brother's wedding. Short of getting up and leaving her food there at the table in her rush to escape, she wasn't sure how to wiggle out of it.

"Okay," she said slowly.

"You're coming, aren't you?" Bethany asked. "Last I checked you hadn't sent an RSVP. You did receive the invitation, right? I sent it to your New York apartment and was hoping it didn't miss you on your way here."

Yes, she had received it. She had pulled out the elegant sheet of calligraphied vellum and had stared at it for a long time, sorrow aching through her at the distance between her and her siblings.

In the end, she had slipped the invitation into her briefcase, though she had absolutely no intention of accepting.

"Yes. I got it," she admitted.

"And? You're coming, aren't you?"

"Does Peter know you sent me an invitation?"

Bethany blinked but not before Anna was certain she

saw a little glimmer of uncertainty in the depths of her green eyes.

"Of course," she answered, but somehow Anna was certain she wasn't telling the whole truth.

The vague suspicion, that tiny hesitation on Bethany's part, was enough to remove any lingering doubt in her mind about whether to attend the wedding.

"I'm really happy for you and Peter," Anna said. "But...I don't think I can make it."

"Why not?" Bethany asked bluntly.

The other woman might look as soft and fragile as puff pastry but that impression was obviously an illusion. She was glad for it, Anna thought. Bethany Holloway appeared more than a match for her oldest brother, who could sometimes be domineering and set in his ways.

"The last thing you need on your wedding day is to have a simmering family feud boil over and explode all over the place. It would be better if I stayed away."

"Oh, don't be ridiculous!"

If Bethany hadn't sounded so sincere, Anna might have taken offense. Instead she merely shook her head.

"It's not ridiculous. None of them are even talking to me right now. I ran into David ten minutes ago just outside and he looked right through me as if I wasn't even there. I got the same treatment from Ella last week when I bumped into her on the fourth floor."

Compassion flickered in the depths of Bethany's green eyes. "That must have hurt."

For half a second, she thought about shrugging off her sympathy but the sincere concern in Bethany's expression warmed somewhere cold and hollow inside her.

"Like crazy," she admitted quietly. "Ella used to be my best friend. Now she won't even talk to me."

"I'm so sorry."

"I knew they would be upset that I'd chosen to work for Northeastern HealthCare. I guess I'd hoped they would at least try to hear my side of things."

"You Wilders all feel passionately for the things you care about," Bethany said.

"I'm not one of them," Anna said quickly.

As far as she was concerned, that was the crux of the problem. She didn't have the Wilder medical gene and she didn't have their dogmatism.

"I'm sure Peter told you I was adopted," she said when Bethany just looked puzzled.

A strange, furtive look flickered in those green eyes. Bethany opened her mouth to respond then closed it again, as if she had suddenly reconsidered her words.

"I've heard the story," she finally said. "Peter told me he was ten years old when your father brought you home and claimed he found you on the steps of Walnut River General. It was a defining moment in his life."

She stared. "In Peter's life or my father's?"

"Well, I'm sure in your father's life as well. But I meant Peter."

"How?"

"As the oldest son he felt responsible for the rest of you, and for your mother's feelings, as well. I know she… wasn't well those few years before you came into the family."

A polite way of saying Alice Wilder had suffered deep depression and had ended up medicated in the years before Anna's adoption.

"Yes," she answered warily. Her relationship with

her mother had always been complicated. She had loved Alice, as every child loves her mother, but their relationship had always felt strained. Cumbersome. Deep in her heart, she had wondered why her mother didn't quite seem to love her as much as she did Peter, David and Ella.

James had more than compensated for any coolness from Alice but the pain still lingered.

"Your father worked a great deal," Bethany said. "As the oldest son, Peter always felt responsible for everyone's happiness. His mother's. David's. And then when you and Ella came along, for yours, as well. I don't know that that has changed much over the years. He loves you very much, Anna. And he misses you. They all do."

She might find it a little easier to believe if she hadn't experienced firsthand the compelling evidence that none of the Wilders was thrilled to have her back in town.

"He might be angry with you right now over the merger," Bethany continued, "but that's because he feels as if your father's legacy is threatened."

Anna's frustration erupted. "It's a hospital! It's walls and a roof and medical equipment! What kind of legacy is that? James's legacy ought to be the children he left behind. Children who have grown into four fairly decent adults who are doing their best to make the world a better place for others. That's a legacy to be proud of, not the hospital where he spent every waking moment he should have been spending with kids who needed their father!"

She was mortified the moment she heard the heat and lingering bitterness behind her own words.

She thought she had gotten over all that when she

walked away from medical school—the secret fear that her father would only love her if she became a doctor like he was, if she devoted all her energy to the hospital where he had rescued her.

How many times had she heard that story about finding her on the hospital steps? Too damn many.

You were the only infant ever left at Walnut River General. I knew the minute I saw you that you belonged in our family. James always used to say that with pride in his eyes—whether for the hospital he loved or for her, she was never quite sure.

She couldn't help wondering what might have happened to her if she had been left somewhere else besides the hospital—an orphanage, a garbage can, even James's and Alice's own doorstep.

Would he have wanted her at all?

"From what I've heard of your father, I know he was very proud of each of his children," Bethany said.

Each of the three physicians in the family, perhaps. As for her, Ella and their brothers wondered why she'd kept her job with NHC a secret for two years. She could just imagine what James's reaction would have been if he had known before his death that she had gone to work for a corporate entity he would have considered the enemy.

The shock alone would have brought on that fatal heart attack.

She forced a smile. "I'm sure you're right," she murmured, though the lie tasted like acid.

"Peter is your brother, despite your current… estrangement. He will feel your absence at the wedding deeply, no matter what he might say. Will you at least think about coming?"

Anna shook her head. "You're a very persistent bride, aren't you?"

Bethany smiled. "That's a polite way to say stubborn as a one-eyed mule, isn't it? I can be, when the situation demands it."

She might not be the woman Anna would have expected her brother to fall for, but she decided she very much liked Bethany Holloway. Somehow she had a feeling they *would* become good friends. It was a comforting thought.

"I'll think about it," she answered. "That's all I can promise right now. The wedding is still three weeks away. A great deal can happen in three weeks."

Bethany opened her mouth to respond, but before the words could escape, Anna's attention was drawn to a trio of men entering the cafeteria—J. D. Sumner, new chief of staff Owen Mayfield, and Richard Green.

Richard spotted her and Bethany at almost the exact same instant. She saw something bright and luminous flash in his eyes for just an instant before it faded.

A moment later, he excused himself from the other men and made his way toward their corner booth.

Anna was aware of several things simultaneously—the funny little dip and shiver of her stomach as he approached, the clean, elegant lines of his summer-weight charcoal suit that made him look as gorgeous as if he had just stepped out of a gentlemen's magazine, the faint lines of fatigue around his blue eyes.

Most of all, she was aware of how her heart seemed to tremble just at the sight of him.

"Good afternoon."

He smiled freely at Bethany, but his light expression faded when he turned his attention to Anna.

She tried to ignore the shaft of hurt piercing through her at the contrast, aware of how very tired she was becoming of fighting battles with everyone she encountered at Walnut River General.

"J.D. was just telling me you were working here this morning," Richard said.

"Yes. The hospital's legal counsel apparently won't give permission for me to take any records off site," she said pointedly.

"All in one more effort to make your life more difficult, I'm sure," Richard said dryly.

She made a face. "It certainly does. But the administration has been kind enough to give me a temporary work space. I suppose I should be grateful they stopped short of blocking access completely."

"Since the municipal council has approved your inquiries, legally there's nothing the hospital can do to stop you."

His hard voice stopped just shy of outright hostility but it was enough to make Bethany blink and Anna bristle.

"No. I don't suppose there is," she said evenly. "Short of tackling me in the parking lot and tying me to a bench somewhere."

Something warm and slightly naughty sparked in his eyes for just an instant, then it was gone. Still, her insides shivered in reaction.

"I was trying to reach Alfred Daly but perhaps you can give him a message for me."

She gazed at him warily, wondering just how many other people from her past would she alienate before NHC succeeded in its efforts to absorb Walnut River General into its family of hospitals.

"All right," she answered.

"Please let him know I will be representing the hospital for the foreseeable future. My partner is taking an indefinite leave of absence."

She thought of the attorney she had met only a few times since coming to Walnut River. He had seemed very nice, if somewhat distracted. Never once had he looked at her with anything resembling scorn, unlike others she could mention.

"Everything's all right, I hope?"

His expression registered surprise at her concern and he hesitated for just a moment before answering. "I'm sure it will be."

He said he was representing the hospital for the forseeable future, which must include the NHC merger negotiations. The jitters in her stomach became a sudden stampede. There was no escaping the grim realization that she would have no choice but to work closely with Richard Green if she wanted to pull off this merger.

"I will let him know," she answered coolly, pleased her voice didn't reveal any of her inner torment. "I should tell you in the interest of disclosure that your partner asked for copies of the reports I'm working on. Our legal team agreed to provide them as a show of good faith to demonstrate our willingness to cooperate as fully as possible. I can have them ready for you first thing in the morning."

He frowned. "No chance they'll be ready before then? I'm going to be in court the rest of the week. Tonight would be the best chance for me to find time to look at them."

She quickly considered her options.

She could be an obstructionist and tell him no, that she couldn't possibly finish the financial study until the next day. But that wasn't exactly true. She was close to being done and with a little accelerated effort, could have things wrapped up in a few hours.

"I can try to finish them tonight and run them over to you at home."

Again, the flicker of surprise in his expression frustrated her. Once they had been close friends. He had known her better than just about anyone in her life, except maybe Ella. Did he really have to register such astonishment when she tried to be cooperative and do something nice?

"That would be perfect. Thank you."

Still annoyed, she gave him a cool, polite smile. "You're welcome. Give me your address and I'll run them by when I'm done."

"You don't need an address. I'm living in my parents' house. It was too much upkeep for my mother so I bought it from her after my father died. She lives in a condo just a few blocks away."

Anna had always liked Diane Green. She had been warm and gracious, always willing to open her home to Richard's friends. His house had been the high-school hangout, with its huge game room and built-in swimming pool.

It would be a lovely place to raise a son, she thought.

"I don't know what time I'll be finished. It might be late."

"That's fine. I'll be up late prepping for court in the morning."

She nodded and managed to hang on to her polite smile when he said a cool goodbye to her and a much warmer one to Bethany before he returned to J.D. and Dr. Mayfield.

She watched his elegant frame walk away for just a moment longer than she should have. She knew it as soon as she turned back to Bethany and found Peter's fiancée watching her with upraised eyebrows.

"I'm sorry. What were we talking about?"

"My wedding." Bethany grinned suddenly. "But that's not important right now. I would much rather hear what's going on with you and sexy Richard Green."

"Going on? Absolutely nothing."

She cursed her fair skin as she felt heat soak her cheeks. She couldn't bluff her way out of a blasted paper bag, the way she turned red at the slightest provocation.

Bethany didn't look at all convinced. "Are you sure about that? There was enough energy buzzing between the two of you to light up the Las Vegas strip."

"We grew up together. His house is just a few blocks away from where we grew up and we were always good friends."

"And?"

She could feel her blush deepen as she remembered that last night together and the kisses and touches she had never been able to forget.

For one shining moment she had held paradise in her hands.

He had offered her everything she'd ever dreamed of. He had told her he was in love with her. She could still remember her giddy joy, how she had wanted nothing more than to hold on tight and never let go.

She had wanted so much to grab hold of what he was offering—but she hadn't been able to figure out a way to break free of her family's expectations while holding tight to Richard at the same time.

Seeing him again, learning more about the man he had become, made her see how immature a response that had been for a girl of twenty-two years.

She had been so certain she had to take all or nothing,

to sever all ties to Walnut River if she wanted to escape the immovable path her family expected her to take.

But Richard had never placed the kind of unrealistic expectations on her that her father had. He had even told her if medical school wasn't for her, she needed to decide earlier, rather than later.

What would have happened if she had decided she could still drop out of medical school and pursue her business career while maintaining a relationship with Richard?

It wasn't at all helpful to speculate on the hypothetical, she reminded herself harshly. The truth was, she had turned her back on Richard when she had turned her back on her family. That ship had sailed, and all that. She would never know, so there was absolutely nothing to be gained by speculating on what might have been.

"There's nothing between us," she assured Bethany. "I haven't seen him in eight years and now we're on opposite sides of the hospital merger."

Which might as well be a twenty-foot high fence topped with another five feet of razor wire for all the chance she had of breaching it.

Chapter Six

"Dad! You shut my door! You know I can't sleep with my door shut all the way!"

Ethan's voice echoed down the hall, drawing nearer with each word, and Richard sighed as he straightened and closed the oven door where he'd just set his dinner to warm.

Here we go, he thought.

He turned and, just as he expected, he found Ethan in the doorway wearing his Buzz Lightyear pajamas, his little mouth set in a disgruntled expression.

"Sorry, bud. I forgot."

"You forgot everything tonight! You forgot to give me an Eskimo kiss and during bathtime you didn't even ask me my five fun things."

Guilt pinched at him and he wished that he could split himself into two or three people to get everything in his life accomplished. His court appearance in the morning weighed heavily on his mind—but his son always had to come first.

"I'm sorry. It's been a long day," he said. "I'll do better tomorrow, okay? Come on, let's get you back into bed and you can tell me your five fun things."

"Okay."

It was a tradition they had started as soon as Ethan learned to talk, where each evening they would share five interesting things they had seen or done that day.

Ethan's list usually consisted of games or toys he and his nana had played with that day. It was sometimes a scramble but Richard usually tried for a little creativity in his own contributions to the game. Today he was afraid he was running on empty.

"You said that yesterday," Ethan exclaimed when Richard tried to use the colorful clown that stood outside the local hamburger joint with a signboard and a pleading expression as one of his five interesting things to report about his day.

"But this time he had on one of those crazy rainbow wigs," Richard said. "I didn't tell you that yesterday."

Much to his relief, his five-year-old accepted his logic and climbed into bed obediently.

They exchanged hugs and the obligatory Eskimo kisses then Richard tucked him in for the second time that evening. "This time I'm spraying glue on your pillow so you can't get out again."

While Ethan giggled he pretended to spray an aerosol can around his son's bed, his hair, behind his back. "There. Now you're stuck. You're not going anywhere."

"Okay. But don't forget to come unstick me in the

morning before you leave. Nana said we can go to the park after breakfast and I don't want to miss it."

He smiled and kissed his son on the nose. "I will. I've got magic un-stick spray just waiting for morning, I promise."

This time, he left Ethan's door slightly ajar and returned to the kitchen. His stomach rumbled at the delicious smells starting to emanate from the oven. A quick check of the timer on the oven revealed he still had twenty minutes before his mother's lasagna would be finished. That should be long enough to go over his opening argument one more time—that is, if he could hang on to his limited concentration long enough to do the job.

He sighed again, all too grimly aware of the reason he had been so distracted all evening.

One word.

Anna.

Since bumping into her at the hospital cafeteria earlier, he hadn't been able to shake her from his mind. The curve of her cheekbones, the little shell of her ear, the fragile vulnerability in the set of her mouth he wondered if anyone else could see.

She said she would drop off her report that night and he felt as if he had spent the entire evening in a state of suspended animation, just waiting for the doorbell to ring.

He knew damn well those feelings swirling through him were entirely inappropriate, but he couldn't seem to move beyond them.

He couldn't wait to see her again, foolish as he knew that was.

He had absolutely no sense when it came to Anna

Wilder. It was a rather depressing thing to acknowledge about himself.

Just how long did he have to carry a torch for her? If someone had asked him a week ago if he still had feelings for Anna, he would have busted up laughing at the very idea. He never even thought of her anymore, he would have answered quite smugly. How could he be foolish enough to think he still had feelings for the woman?

He thought he had done a pretty good job of purging her from his thoughts. Eight years was a long time to burn for a woman who had made it plain she didn't want him.

But now she was back in Walnut River and every single time he saw her, she seemed to become more and more entangled in his thoughts until he had a devil of a time thinking about anything else.

Did he still have feelings for her? He certainly wasn't about to admit something so dangerous, even to himself. Sure, he was still attracted to her. He certainly couldn't deny that, especially since he wasn't able to stop himself looking at his watch every five seconds and had even gone out once to check that the doorbell was working right.

He needed to get out more. He could count on one hand the number of dates he'd had in the years since his marriage imploded.

Richard sighed, wishing again for a clone or two. When, exactly, was he supposed to find time for a social life? Between working to establish his practice and trying to be the best father possible to Ethan, his time was fragmented enough.

What if Anna hadn't blown him off eight years ago and left town? If she weren't here representing NHC? If they didn't have diametrically opposing goals regarding Walnut River General Hospital?

What was the point in wasting time with useless hypotheticals? Richard chided himself. He had too damn much to do tonight to indulge in fantasies of what might have been.

The fact was, she *had* walked away, she *did* work for NHC and he would need to keep all his wits about him to keep her and her corporation from taking over the hospital he cared about.

He would do well to remember all those things, Richard thought as he forced himself to turn back to his laptop, angled on a corner of the kitchen table where he had been working earlier while Ethan played with trucks on the floor.

The screen had just come out of sleep mode when he heard a car engine out front. The swirl of anticipation he'd tried so hard to tamp down became a wild cyclone. So much for the little pregame lecture, he thought ruefully.

A click of the keyboard sent the monitor back to sleep, then he hurried to the front door. He reached it just an instant after she rang the doorbell.

"Oh!" she exclaimed when he opened the door, her hand still half raised to the bell. "Hello."

"Sorry to startle you. I was trying to catch you before you rang the doorbell so you didn't wake Ethan. I have a tough time getting him back down to sleep if something disturbs him."

"I'm so sorry. I didn't even think. I should have knocked."

"No. It's fine. I doubt he's even asleep yet."

The words had barely escaped his mouth when Ethan popped his head out of his bedroom, his hair tousled but his eyes not at all sleepy. They lit up with excitement when he saw Anna.

"Hi!" he exclaimed brightly. "I heard the doorbell but I didn't know it was you."

"Hi, Ethan!"

Richard tried to steel his emotions against the soft delight in her eyes as she looked at his son.

"I thought you were glued to the bed," he said dryly to his son.

Ethan giggled. "I guess the glue must have worn off. When I heard the doorbell, I was able to climb right out. I don't know how."

"What a surprise," he muttered.

Anna sent him a sideways, laughing look that stole his breath.

"Anna, can you read me one more story?" Ethan wheedled. "If you do, I promise, I'll stay in my bed this time for good."

"I guess that's up to your father."

"Daddy, can she?"

He didn't want her to feel obligated, but if the anticipation on her features was any indication, she was excited at the prospect.

"All right. Just one story, and then to bed this time to stay. You have to pinky swear."

Ethan had to hold down his other four fingers with his left hand in order to extend the little finger on his right, but his features were solemn and determined as he interlocked with Richard's pinky.

"I swear. I won't get out again, Daddy, if Anna can read me one story. Oh, and if she can give me one more Eskimo kiss, too."

"Deal," she said quickly, before Richard could even think about negotiating different terms.

She reached for Ethan's hand and the two of them headed for his son's bedroom. Richard followed, unable to resist leaning against the door jamb and watching as they carefully selected the right story.

He wasn't sure what he felt as he watched Anna slip off her heels and sit on the edge of Ethan's bed. His son cuddled up to her as if they were best friends and after a moment, she slipped her arm around him, their blond heads close together.

She read the story, about a worm keeping a diary about his life, with pathos and humor. When she turned the last page, Ethan sighed with satisfaction.

"I sure do wish I could have another one. You're a really good story reader."

"You made a pinky swear, remember," Anna said with a smile. She slipped her shoes back on then leaned in and rubbed her nose against his.

"You smell good," Ethan declared, and Richard wondered how his son had possibly become such a lady killer with the lousy example he had for a father in that department.

Anna laughed. "So do you. Now go to sleep, okay?"

Ethan snuggled down into the covers, his eyelids beginning to droop. "Okay. Will you come to another one of my baseball games? I only have two more."

She glanced at Richard, then back at his son. "Sure," she answered. "I'd love to."

"You have to promise or else I can't go to sleep."

She laughed again. "You're a born negotiator, Ethan, my man."

"What's a go-she-a-tor?"

"Negotiator. It means somebody who works out deals with people. You agree to do something as long as I do something else in return."

"I just want you to come to my baseball game."

"I said I would."

"Is that a promise?"

She shook her head. "All right! I promise."

He grinned with satisfaction. "Thank you for the story, Anna."

"You're very welcome, sir."

"Will you come back and read to me again sometime?"

She paused for just an instant and Richard thought he saw a faint brush of color on her cheeks before she tugged Ethan's covers up to his chin. "We'll have to see about that one. Good night."

"Good night," Richard added. "This time I mean it."

"Okay. 'Night, Dad."

He closed the door behind Anna—remembering just in time to leave it slightly ajar.

"I'm sorry you had to do that."

"I'm not." She smiled softly. "He's darling."

"He's a manipulative scoundrel who's going to end up behind bars someday."

"It's a good thing his father is a lawyer, then."

And his mother, Richard thought. The blunt reminder of Lynne and all the mistakes he had made was like jumping into a mountain stream in January.

Anna picked up her briefcase and rifled through it for a moment, pulling out a slim maroon folder.

"Here's the report I promised you. I'm sorry I didn't get it here earlier. I meant to have it done two hours ago but I, uh, had a bit of a tough time getting some of the information I needed."

Translation: Those who opposed the NHC takeover were making life as difficult as possible for Anna. He didn't need her to spell it out for him when he could see the exhaustion in her eyes and the set of her mouth.

A twinge of pity flickered through him. None of this could be easy for her.

"Have you had dinner?" he asked. The moment the words were out, he regretted them but it was too late to yank them back.

She stared. "Dinner?"

"You know, that meal you traditionally eat at the end of the day?"

"Oh, that one." She smiled. "I guess my answer would have to be no, not yet. That's next on my agenda."

"I've got some of my mom's lasagna in the oven. You're welcome to join me."

Surprise flickered over those lovely features. "It does smell delicious. But I've got Lilli out in the car. Since my place is on the way here, I stopped on the way to check on her and she begged me to bring her along."

He should let her use the excuse as a way to avoid the meal but he found himself reluctant to give up that easily. "She's welcome to come inside while we eat. I don't mind."

"Are you sure? I wouldn't want to provide Ethan more ammunition in the Great Puppy War."

"He'll never know. Besides, maybe having Lilli underfoot during dinner, begging for scraps, will shore up my sagging resolve to wait a few more years before we enter pethood."

She raised an eyebrow. "Excuse me, but my dog is extremely well-behaved. She never begs. She just asks nicely."

Anna was so beautiful when she smiled, he thought, and cursed himself all over again for the impulse to invite her to stay—an impulse, he admitted, that had probably been simmering inside him all evening. Why else would he have thrown an entire lasagna in the oven instead of just grabbing a TV dinner?

He had absolutely no willpower around Anna Wilder and no common sense, either. He had a million things to do before court in the morning. He certainly didn't have time to spend the evening entertaining a woman he had vowed to keep at a distance.

Despite the knowledge, he found he couldn't quite bring himself to regret extending the invitation.

Not yet, anyway.

He wanted her to have dinner with him? Anna wouldn't have been more surprised if Richard had met her at the door doing the hula in a muumuu and lei.

A wise woman would tell him to forget it and get the heck out of there. She had very few defenses left against Richard Green and his adorable son, and she was very much afraid she was in danger of falling hard for him all over again.

"Go and get Lilli and by the time you come back in, the lasagna will be on the table."

She paused for only half a second before surrendering. How could she do anything else, when this was the most amiable and approachable she'd seen Richard since coming back to Walnut River?

"All right," she said. "I'll admit, my mouth has been watering since I walked in the door."

And not just because of the delectable smells of lasagna wafting from the kitchen, she was forced to admit to herself. Richard Green in his charcoal business suit was gorgeous, in a dangerous, formidable kind of way. Richard Green in his stocking feet, faded Levi's and a casual cotton shirt with the sleeves rolled up was completely irresistible.

She quickly collected Lilli from her car and juggled the excited dog and her umbrella as she hurried back up the walkway to his house. He stood in the open doorway waiting for her and her stomach gave a funny little tremble at the sight of him.

"Behave yourself," she ordered as she set Lilli down on the tile of the entryway, the stern reminder intended for her own benefit as much as her dog's.

"I'll do my best," Richard answered dryly. He reached for her umbrella and Anna slipped off her heels, lining them neatly by the door.

Lilli's tail wagged like crazy as she trotted around the house, sniffing in corners and under furniture. With the excuse of keeping a close eye on her inquisitive little dog, Anna managed to assuage her own curiosity about Richard's house.

Their group of friends had spent many hours at his place through high school. With the built-in swimming pool and the huge media and game room in the basement, it was a natural teen hangout. She remembered pool parties and study sessions and movie nights.

Seeing it now after years away was rather disconcerting. Little was as she remembered.

"Your house has changed."

He smiled. "Just a bit. When I bought the place after

my dad died, I had the interior completely redone. New paint, new carpet, took out a wall here or there to open it up. The house had great bones but everything was a little outdated."

"Diane didn't mind?"

"Are you kidding? My mother loved helping oversee the redecorating, as long as it was my own dime."

"It looks great," she assured him as Lilli investigated a cluster of houseplants climbing a matte black ladder in the corner.

The house was elegant but comfortable, with solid furniture that looked as if it would stand up well to a busy five-year-old.

"I'm just going to throw together a salad," Richard said. Do you want to come back to the kitchen?"

"Sure."

With Lilli close on their heels, she followed him down the hall. Here were the most dramatic renovations she had seen in the house. She remembered the kitchen as a rather small, cramped space with dark wood cupboards and a long breakfast bar that took up most of the space.

This must be where he had talked about knocking down walls because it was about twice the size as she remembered. Rain clicked against skylights overhead and in place of the breakfast bar, a huge island with a sink and second stovetop dominated the space.

The colors reminded her of a Tuscan farmhouse, warm red brick floors, mustard yellow walls with white accents. It was a dream of a kitchen, airy and welcoming and vastly different from the tiny sliver of a kitchen in her apartment in Chelsea.

"Would you like a glass of wine?"

"Yes, please," she decided, perching on one of the stools at the island.

He seemed very much at home in his own kitchen and she knew darn well she shouldn't find that so sexy.

She sipped her wine and watched him work while Lilli sniffed the corners of the kitchen. The silence between them was surprisingly comfortable, like slipping into a favorite jacket in the autumn.

"So who was giving you a tough time today?" Richard asked after a moment.

She flashed him a quick look. "How do you know somebody was?"

"You never turned an assignment in late in your life when we were in school. If I remember correctly, you always turned everything in at least a day or two early. I figured the only reason you would be late with anything must have more to do with external forces."

"Clever as always, counselor."

"So who was it?"

She sighed, some of her peace dissipating at the reminder of the hurdles in front of her and their clear demarcation on opposite sides of the NHC front. "No one. Not really. I just had a...difficult time getting some of the information I needed. I don't blame anyone. I completely understand there are mixed feelings at the hospital about the merger."

His laugh was dry. "Mixed feelings is one way to put it."

"Believe it or not, I do understand why not everyone likes the idea of an outside company coming in and messing with the status quo. I understand about tradition and continuity and about safety in the familiar. But I wish people could approach this with an open mind. If people would look beyond their preconceptions, perhaps they might see how Northeastern HealthCare is looking at innovative changes that would benefit both the hospital and the community in general...."

She caught herself just before launching into a passionate argument once more. "I'm sorry. I really don't want to talk about the hospital tonight. After living and breathing this merger from the moment I awoke this morning, I could use a break. Do you mind?"

He stopped mixing the salad, watching her with an unreadable expression for a moment before he suddenly offered a smile she felt clear down to her toes.

"Excellent idea. I wouldn't want to ruin by mother's delicious lasagna by launching into a cross-examination."

He grabbed the salad and carried it through an arched doorway to the dining room.

Out of old habit, she grabbed plates from the cupboard where they had always been stored, finding an odd comfort that they were still there.

The silverware was also still in its familiar spot and she grabbed two settings and carried the utensils into the dining room.

Richard raised an eyebrow but said nothing as she helped him set the table. A moment later, he carried in the lasagna and placed it on the table then took a seat across from her.

Lilli stopped her wandering and curled up, her body a small warm weight on Anna's feet. The next few moments were busy with filling plates and topping wineglasses.

"If we're not going to talk about the hospital, what's a safe topic of conversation, then?" she asked when they were settled. "Baseball? The weather?"

"Who says it has to be safe?" The strangely intent look

in his eyes sent a shiver ripping down her spine. A strange undercurrent tugged and pulled between them.

"All right. Something dangerous, then. Your marriage?"

He gave a short laugh as he added dressing to his salad. "Not what I had in mind, but okay. What would you like to know?"

She had a million questions but one seemed paramount, even though she hardly dared ask it. "What happened?"

He shrugged, his expression pensive. "The grim truth is that it was a mistake from start to finish. I met Lynne at Harvard. She was brilliant, ambitious. Beautiful. In our last year, we started seeing each other, mostly just for fun. Nothing serious. In fact, we both planned to go our separate ways after graduation."

"But?"

He sighed, sudden shadows in his eyes. "A few weeks before we were to take the bar exam, she found out she was pregnant."

She tried to picture a younger version of Richard as she remembered him, perhaps with a few less laugh lines around the corners of his eyes. The Richard she knew always took his responsibilities seriously. She wasn't at all surprised that he would step up to take care of the child he fathered, only that he and Ethan's mother would make things official.

"Marriage is a huge leap of faith for two people who were set to go their separate ways, even with a child on the way."

"I think we both badly wanted to believe we could make it work. On paper, it seemed a good solution. We were both attorneys, we had shared interests, we enjoyed each other's company. I think we both tried to convince ourselves we were in love and could make it work. But

Lynne wasn't ready for a family. She tried, but I could see what a struggle it was for her. She…wasn't really cut out for motherhood. When Ethan was four months old, she received an unbeatable job offer overseas. Her dream position as lead counsel for an international shipping conglomerate. We both decided there was no good reason for her not to take it."

She heard the casual tone he tried to take but she also picked up the subtle sense of failure threading through his words.

He had always been competitive—captain of the debate team, a star on the baseball diamond, school valedictorian. He hated losing at anything and she imagined this particular failure would have hit him hard, especially with the loving example he had of marriage from his own parents.

The urge to touch him, to offer some small degree of comfort, was almost overwhelming. But they didn't have that kind of relationship, not anymore, so she curled one hand in her lap and picked up her wineglass with the other.

"I'm sorry," she murmured. "That couldn't have been an easy situation for you."

"We've done okay. My mother has been a lifesaver. I would have been lost without her."

They were quiet for a moment, the only sound Lilli's soft huffs and the rain clicking against the skylights.

"What about you?" he asked after a moment. "Any relationship mistakes in your past?"

Besides leaving you? The thought whispered through her mind unbidden and she had to shift her gaze away from his so he wouldn't read the truth in her eyes.

"Not really. Nothing serious, anyway."

"Why not?" Richard asked.

She decided to keep quiet about the fact that she hadn't had enthusiasm for dating in a long time, if ever. She had been too focused on her work, in making a success of herself—okay, in proving to her family that she could have a successful life outside medicine.

"I don't know. It hasn't really been a priority for me, I guess."

"I suppose it's a little tough having a long-term relationship when you travel so much."

"Something like that."

She really didn't want to discuss her love life—or decided absence of such a thing—with Richard Green.

"Okay, I just came up with the first dangerous topic of conversation. It's your turn."

"I thought I just asked you about the men you've dated. That's not dangerous enough for you?"

"Not at all. Trust me. The men I date are usually a boring lot. Accountants. Stockbrokers. Mild-mannered, one and all."

Not like you, she thought. Richard radiated a raw masculinity, even during a casual dinner at his home with his five-year-old sleeping only a few dozen feet away.

He studied her for a moment, and she had the vague impression of a lean and hungry wolf moving in for the kill.

"All right. You want dangerous? Why don't we talk about why you broke my heart eight years ago?"

Chapter Seven

Anna stared at Richard across the table, his mother's delicious lasagna congealing into a hard, miserable lump in her stomach.

The noises of the kitchen seemed unnaturally loud in the sudden tense silence, the whir of the refrigerator compressor sounding like a jet airplane taking off.

She wanted to scoop up her dog and race away from the awkwardness of his question and the guilty memories she couldn't escape.

"I didn't break your heart," she mumbled.

He lifted his wineglass in a mocking salute. "Excuse me, but I think I'm a little better judge of that than you are. You haven't seen me or my heart in eight years."

Though his words were light, she saw the barest hint of shadow in his eyes. She thought of all her reasons for leaving. What seemed so compelling eight years ago now seemed like a coward's way out.

"You couldn't have been too heartbroken," she pointed out. "You were married a few years later."

She didn't want to remember how she had holed up in her tiny shared apartment in New York City and wept for an entire day when Ella had called her with the news.

He was quiet for a moment and then he sent her a quizzical look. "Would you like to see a picture of Lynne?"

His question threw her off stride, especially in the context of their discussion. Why would he possibly think she would want to see a picture of his ex-wife right now?

She shrugged, not quite sure how to answer, and he slid away from the table and moved to a mantel in the great room off the kitchen. Through the doorway, she saw him take a picture from a collection on the mantel and a moment later he returned and held it out for her.

A younger, chubbier version of Ethan's winsome face filled most of the frame but just in the background, she could see a stunning woman with blond hair and delicate features. She looked at her son with love, certainly, but also a kind of baffled impatience.

"She's very beautiful."

"You don't see the resemblance?"

"I can't really tell. Ethan certainly has her eyes."

"You don't think she looks at all like you?"

Shocked to the core, she stared at the woman again. Is that the way he saw her? Cool and lovely and...distant?

"Her hair and her eye color, maybe," she protested. "That's all."

"You're absolutely right. That's where the resemblance ends. She's not you. Not at all. But here's the funny part.

I asked her out for the first time because she looked a bit like you. Since I couldn't have the real deal, I tried to convince myself an imitation was just as good. It was an idiotic mindset, one I'm ashamed I even entertained for a minute, but what can I say? I had been abruptly dumped by the only woman I ever loved."

Anna froze, reeling as if she'd just been punched in the stomach.

"Richard—"

"I didn't mean to say that. Withdrawn."

She had no idea what to say, to think. He had said that night he was falling in love with her but she had always attributed it to the heat of their passion.

After a long, awkward moment, he gave a rough laugh. "Dangerous is one thing when it comes to topics of conversation. Excruciatingly embarrassing is quite another."

She had to say something. She knew she did, especially after he stood up and returned his plate of half-eaten lasagna to the kitchen.

She rose, shaky inside. Lilli scampered ahead of her into the kitchen.

"I convinced myself it wasn't real," she finally said quietly when she joined him there. "What we shared that night. It was magical and beautiful and…miraculous. But I tried to tell myself we were just carried away by the night and…everything. You were my friend. Maybe my best friend. I couldn't let myself think of you in any other way or I wouldn't have been able to…to do what I knew I had to."

"Leave medical school and basically cut things off completely with your family."

"Yes," she admitted. "I loved my family. You know

that. But you also know what things were like for me with them. In my father's mind, there was no other possible career for any of his children. He refused to see how I was struggling that first year. How much I hated it. I tried to talk to him—all summer I tried! His advice was only to stick it out, that the second year would be better. *Wilders aren't quitters.* I can remember him telling me that as clearly as if he were sitting right here with us."

"He wanted you to follow in his footsteps."

"That's what *he* wanted. Not what *I* wanted. I was suffocating in med school. I hated it. The blood, the gore. The unending stress. Especially knowing I couldn't help everyone."

She could clearly remember the first time a patient whose care she had been observing had died. It had been a woman in her late fifties with end-stage breast cancer. She could remember the dispassionate attitude of the attending and the residents, in sharp contrast to the vast, overwhelming grief of the woman's husband and teenage daughters.

She had left the hospital that day feeling ill, heavy and ponderous, as if she carried the weight of that grief and the responsibility for their pain. Ridiculous, since she was only a first-year med student who hadn't even really been involved in the woman's care, but she hadn't been able to shake her guilt and the cries of the survivors that haunted her dreams.

"I knew if I made it through the second year, I would be trapped. I had to go, Richard. I didn't see any other choice."

He shrugged. "You could have stayed and stood up for yourself, fought for what you cared about."

Including him, she thought. She should have stayed and fought for what they could have shared.

"I missed you like crazy those first few months in the city," she confessed. "I think I missed you even more than I missed my family."

He leaned against the kitchen counter. "Forgive me if I find that a little hard to believe. At any point that year you could have picked up the phone or sent off an e-mail. But you cut me off completely. What the hell was I supposed to think? I just figured I was crazy and had imagined everything that happened that night."

"You didn't," she whispered, more miserable than she had been those first early days after she left.

"It doesn't matter now. Eight years ought to be long enough to get over a broken heart, don't you think?"

Something shifted between them, a subtle tug of awareness. "Yes," she managed.

"I thought I had done a pretty good job of putting you out of my head. Of course, then you had to ruin everything by coming back and making me remember."

"I'm sorry," she murmured.

His long exhalation stirred the air. "So am I."

Before she realized what he intended, he stepped forward and pulled her into his arms.

She caught her breath, unable to focus on anything but the blazing heat in his eyes as his mouth descended on hers.

The kiss was raw and demanding and she tasted eight years of frustration in it. Despite the undertone, everything inside her seemed to sigh in welcome.

Oh, she had missed this. Missed *him*. No other man had made her blood sing through her veins like Richard.

She knew she shouldn't return his kiss. If she were smart, she would jerk away right now and leave this house that contained so many memories for her.

She couldn't do it, though, not with this heat and wonder fluttering through her.

Her hands were trapped between their bodies and she could feel his heart pound beneath the cotton of his shirt, rapid and strong.

She spread her hands out, marveling at the taut muscles under her fingers. He might be an attorney but Richard still had the lithe athleticism of the baseball player he had been in high school.

His mouth deepened the kiss and she leaned into him, lost to everything but this moment, this man.

She wanted him. Just as she had eight years ago, she wanted him with a wild hunger that stole her breath.

He was the first one to pull away, wrenching his mouth free of hers and stepping away with such abruptness that she could only stare into the blue of his eyes, turned dark by desire.

He studied her for a long moment while she tried to catch her breath and catch hold of her wildly careening thoughts.

"Aren't you going to say anything?" he asked after a moment.

She might, if she could manage to string more than two words together in a brain that suddenly seemed disjointed and chaotic.

"That was...unexpected."

He lifted an eyebrow. "Was it?"

"Richard, I..."

He shook his head with a rough-sounding laugh. "Don't. Just don't. I was trying to remember what you tasted like. My curiosity has been appeased so let's just leave it at that."

That's all it had been? Curiosity? Not the kind of stunned desire that still churned through her body?

"Look, it's late. I'm due in court early tomorrow."

She drew in a shaky breath, mortified at her wild reaction to what had been purely experimentation on his part. "You're absolutely right. I never meant to stay so long."

If she had left fifteen minutes ago, none of this would have happened. She wouldn't have the taste of him on her lips or the scent of him, masculine and sexy, on her skin or the memory of his kiss burned into her brain.

She scooped up Lilli, absurdly grateful for the comfort of the dog's tiny, warm weight in her arms. He walked her to the door and helped her into her jacket, careful not to touch her more than completely necessary. He then held her umbrella while she slipped on her shoes.

"Thank you for dinner," she finally said.

"You're welcome," he answered, as formally as if they were two strangers meeting for coffee instead of lifelong friends who had just shared a moment of stunning passion.

She should say something more, but for the life of her, nothing else came to mind. "Good night, then."

He held the door open for her and she walked out into the night. She didn't bother with her umbrella, hoping the rain might cool her feverish skin and douse the regret that burned through her like a wind-whipped wildfire.

Richard stood at the window of his house watching her taillights gleam on the wet street before they disappeared.

So much for his intention to remain cool and composed around her. He had been about as calm as a blasted typhoon.

What had he been thinking to kiss her? It had been a mistake of epic proportion. Catastrophic.

He should have known he would skate so close to

losing his control. She'd always had that effect on him. What was it about Anna that revved his engine like that?

She was beautiful, yes, with that shimmery blond hair and those luscious blue eyes and skin that begged for his touch....

He jerked his mind away from all of Anna's many attractions. Beautiful as she might be, he had been around lovely women before, but Anna was the only one who ever tempted him to forget every ounce of common sense.

A few more moments of their embrace and he didn't know if he would have been able to stop—and that was with his son sleeping only a few rooms away.

She could break his heart again, if he let her.

Richard sighed. He wasn't about to let her. Not this time. He had learned his lesson well. Anna Wilde wasn't a woman he could count on. She had made that plain eight years ago. His foolishness over her had led him to some fairly disastrous mistakes.

He couldn't afford to lose his head over Anna again— not only for his own sake but for Ethan's.

He couldn't forget his son in this whole situation. Ethan had suffered enough from Richard's poor choices. If Richard had kept his wits around him, he would have known what a disaster his marriage to Lynne would be, that his choices would leave his son without a mother.

Richard's own mother did her best but she was now in her sixties and didn't have all the energy needed to keep up with a busy five-year-old boy.

For Ethan's sake, Richard couldn't afford to risk an involvement with a woman who already had a track record for leaving the things she cared about in pursuit of her career.

Hadn't that been exactly what Lynne had done? She

had tried the whole family and motherhood route but had fled when the responsibility had become too constricting.

Richard just had to use his head when it came to Anna Wilder. He was fiercely attracted to her and apparently that had only intensified over the years, so the only smart course would be to minimize contact with her as much as possible.

He couldn't avoid her completely. The NHC negotiations made that impossible, but he had to do everything he could to make sure their interactions in the future were formal and businesslike and as brief as he could manage.

It was the only way he would get through her temporary stay in Walnut River without hurting himself again.

The resolve managed to last more than a week.

Though he never lost focus of the hospital's fight for autonomy, other clients' legal issues took precedence for the next several days. He was busy, first with a trial date then with several evidentiary hearings.

He might not have seen Anna during that time, but unfortunately she was never far from his thoughts.

At random moments he found himself remembering the silky softness of her hair or the way her mouth trembled when he kissed her or her hands smoothing against his chest, burning through the fabric of his shirt.

He blew out a breath on his way to an appointment with J.D. to discuss strategy for the final board of directors' vote coming up in less than a week.

He supposed he shouldn't have been surprised when he walked into J.D.'s office to find Anna sitting in one of the office chairs, but the sight of her still stopped him in his tracks and he fiercely wished he could just turn around and head back out of the hospital.

She looked prim and proper again in a black jacket and skirt and he was furious at himself for the instant heat that jumped in his stomach.

Her eyes flashed to his and he saw an edge of discomfort, but not surprise. She must have had a little advance warning that he would be joining them.

Lucky her.

J.D. rose from his desk and shook his hand. "Hi, Richard. When I told Anna I was meeting with you this morning, she decided to steal a few minutes of our time so she could ask a couple of questions about our vendor accounting practices, since I told her I couldn't respond without legal counsel present."

J.D. met his gaze with a meaningful look and despite his unease, Richard had to hide a smile. Just the afternoon before, he had lectured the administrator about that very point—to avoid giving any information to NHC they weren't legally obligated to provide under the conditions the municipal council had set forth.

There were three chairs across from J.D.'s desk. As Anna sat in the middle chair, Richard had no choice but to sit beside her, where he was unable to escape her scent, fresh and lovely and sensual, or the heat shimmering off her skin.

"Anna, you're the one with the questions," J.D. said. "Where would you like to start?"

She opened her mouth, but before she could speak, Richard heard voices in the outer office through the open door.

"Hey, Tina," he heard someone greet J.D.'s assistant. "I just need to drop off some paperwork. I won't disturb him for long."

Richard recognized the voice and saw by the way

Anna's features paled that she did as well. A moment later, her oldest brother stuck his head in the doorway.

Dr. Peter Wilder always commanded attention wherever he went, with his dark hair and eyes, handsome features and the undeniable air of authority that seemed to emanate from him. He was very much like his father in that respect.

His gaze sharpened to a laser point when he saw his sister and the room suddenly buzzed with tension.

Richard wondered if Peter had seen the love that leapt into Anna's blue eyes when she had first seen him, before she quickly veiled her expression into cool indifference.

"Sorry. I didn't mean to interrupt."

J.D. rose from his desk and gestured to the vacant chair. "No, it's all right. We were just getting started. Why don't you join us? Anna had some questions about our patient accounting. As the former chief of staff, you might have some insight into that."

Peter looked as if he would rather shove a scalpel down his throat, but after a long, painfully awkward moment, he complied.

"You know I'm always happy to share my insight with NHC. Anything I can do to help," he drawled, and Anna's mouth tightened at his sarcasm.

"And NHC certainly appreciates your cooperation, Peter," she replied sweetly.

J.D. moved to referee before Peter could voice the heated response brewing in his dark eyes.

"So what are your questions?" he asked, interjecting.

She sent another swift look at her brother then seemed to stiffen her shoulders, becoming brisk and focused.

"My analysis of your records shows an unusually high

percentage of patient accounts the hospital deems uncollectible compared to hospitals of similar size and community demographics. Can you explain a reason why that might be the case?"

"I can." Peter broke in before J.D. could answer—or before Richard could vet either man's response.

"We're a local hospital that cares about the community. We refuse to turn anyone away and don't give a damn whether our patients are in the highest tax bracket or not. Our mission is to save lives, not bilk people out of their life savings."

"But according to my analysis, the hospital is losing a hundred thousand dollars a month and most of that is in uncollectible patient accounts," she pointed out. "How long do you think the taxpayers can continue to cover those losses?"

"Some of us care more about our patients' health than going after their wallets," he snapped.

"A noble sentiment, Peter. Exactly what I would have expected you to say. Just what Dad would have said."

Peter bristled. "What's that supposed to mean?"

She sighed and seemed to have forgotten both J.D. and Richard were there. "Nothing. It's all well and good to ride that high horse about focusing on patient care and battling back the evils of HMOs like some kind of league of superheroes with stethoscopes. But what's the alternative, Peter? For the hospital to just keep going deeper and deeper in the hole? Budgets are tightening everywhere. The city council has to do something. What if they decide to close the hospital instead of continuing to try in vain to plug the endless revenue drain?"

"So what you're saying is our patients are screwed either way. Better to get substandard care than none at all."

Anna's blue eyes flared. "NHC is not about substandard care! That's a simplistic argument. Our ultimate goal for all our member hospitals is to find more efficient, cost-effective ways to provide the same level of patient care."

"You really buy that company line? I thought you were supposed to be some hotshot business genius. I would have thought you were smarter than that."

Anna paled a shade lighter and J.D. moved to intervene but she cut him off. "Why can't you at least try to look at what NHC has to offer the hospital with a little rational objectivity?"

"I know what NHC is offering," her brother bit out. "Cut-rate services, increased patient load on physicians. Every day they play money games with people's health care, with their very lives! I can't believe you would pander to these bastards, Anna! What happened to your sense of decency?"

"You're as sanctimonious as ever. There's absolutely no reasoning with you. Yet another way you're just like Dad!"

"Leave him out of this! What do you think Dad would say if he knew you were doing this? Working for the enemy? Doing everything you can to destroy his legacy?"

Her mouth trembled just a bit before she firmly straightened it. While he had to admit he agreed with Peter, Richard still had to fight the urge to comfort her. A hand on her arm, a touch on her shoulder, whatever might ease the pain he couldn't believe her brother missed.

"I'm sure Dad would probably say the same thing you and David and Ella are saying about me. I'm a disgrace to the Wilder name. Isn't that what you all think?"

"Right now, hell, yes," Peter said. "You've always had

a chip on your shoulder but I never dreamed you'd take it this far, by trying to destroy something this family built nearly singlehandedly."

"Why don't we get back to your question." J.D. finally stepped in—about five minutes too late in Richard's opinion—but Anna ignored him.

"I imagine it's a huge comfort to you all that I'm not really a Wilder, then."

Peter's expression changed instantly and something very much like guilt flickered in his eyes.

"You are," he muttered.

"I'm not, Peter. We both know it."

J.D. cleared his throat. "Can you show us the figures that concern you in your report?"

She seemed to drag herself back to the meeting and Richard saw color soak her pale cheeks as she must have realized the detour the conversation had taken.

She took a deep breath and turned back to gaze blankly at the pages in front of her for a moment before she collected herself and rose. "I...yes." She looked flustered and Richard again fought the urge to rest a comforting hand on her arm.

"You'll see I've highlighted several pages in section eight of my report. I would appreciate if you and your legal counsel would formulate a response and get back to me."

"We can discuss it now. Richard's here to make sure I don't speak out of turn."

She twisted her mouth into a facsimile of a smile. "I don't want to take any more of your time, especially since I just remembered I've got a conference call."

She glanced briefly at her brother. "You know. With those bastards I pander to. If you'll all excuse me, gentlemen."

She picked up her briefcase and walked out of the office and Richard wondered if either of the other men saw the way her fingers trembled on the handle—or the determined lift of her chin as she left the office.

Chapter Eight

After Anna left, the three men sat in silence for a long, awkward moment.

J.D. was the first to break it. He gave Peter a long look. "Next time give me some warning when you're going to beat up on your little sister and I'll make sure I have someone from the E.R. standing by to mop up."

Peter shrugged. "Anna gives as good as she gets. She always has."

His nonchalance about the pain that had been radiating from Anna suddenly infuriated Richard. She was vulnerable in ways her family refused to see. She always had been.

As hospital counsel, he knew he ought to stay out of the Wilder family squabbles. It was none of his business. But he cared about Anna—he always had—and he couldn't quite force himself to stay quiet.

"She's only trying to do her job," he finally said. "I know the fact that she has that job infuriates you but you didn't have to make it personal, Peter. You did that, she didn't."

Surprise flickered in Peter's gaze at Richard's defense of Anna, then quickly shifted to guilt. "You're right. You're absolutely right."

"This whole takeover attempt would be much easier to fight if Northeastern HealthCare had sent someone else—anyone else—to do their dirty work," he continued. "Anna's presence makes everything feel personal, like the corporation is waging a war against the whole Wilder family, not just the hospital. I'm afraid I got a little carried away. I'm sorry."

"We're not the ones you need to apologize to," J.D. pointed out to his future brother-in-law quietly.

Peter sighed. "I know. Things are just…complicated with Anna. They have been for a long time. But you're right. She didn't deserve that."

He stood and studied Richard with an odd look in his eyes. After a moment he seemed to come to some decision. "Rich, when you're done here with J.D. would you mind stopping by my office for a moment? I need to talk to you about something."

Still annoyed with him for his casual oblivion when it came to his sister's feelings—and even more annoyed with himself for caring so much about something that wasn't any of his business—Richard wasn't in the mood to be cooperative.

"Sorry. I don't do prenuptial contracts."

Peter gave a bark of surprised laughter. "That's not what I needed. Just stop by if you have time."

* * *

An hour later, his curiosity at fever pitch, Richard made his way through the hospital to Peter's office.

"He's with a patient," the receptionist told him. "Do you mind waiting for a few minutes?"

He had a million things to do but was too curious to leave without some clue as to what Peter could possibly want with him.

Only a few moments passed before Peter joined him. "Thanks for stopping in. I could use some advice."

"You do know I don't handle malpractice cases, either, right?"

Peter laughed. "Wrong again. What I really could use is a little insight from a friend."

Richard raised an eyebrow.

"Specifically, I need advice from a friend of Anna's," Peter added, further confusing him.

He shifted in his seat. "I haven't seen Anna in years, until she came back to town a few weeks ago."

"Neither have I. Not really. But you were friends with her before she left town, right?"

More than friends, but he wasn't about to confide that little detail to her older brother. "Yes," he said warily.

"And Bethany said she saw the two of you together the other day and you still seemed...friendly."

He wracked his brain trying to remember his encounter with Anna the day she had been having lunch with Bethany. "Since she's been back in Walnut River, I've had some interactions with her in an official capacity," he finally said. *Mostly official, anyway.* "I'm not sure how much help I'll be, but I can certainly try."

Peter blew out a breath. "If nothing else, I know I

can at least trust you to keep what I'm about to tell you confidential."

"Of course. What's this about, Peter?"

Peter hesitated for a moment then reached to unlock a desk drawer. He pulled out a slim black folder, from which he extracted a legal-sized white envelope.

"I have a letter to Anna from our father. I received it as executor of his will and I've been trying to figure out what to do with it ever since."

Richard might not have seen Anna until recently, but just from their few interactions, he could tell she still grieved for James. He knew she regretted the stilted relationship and the unresolved business between them before his death.

"Your father has been gone for six months. Why haven't you given it to her before this?"

"When would I have the chance? Anna has done her best to stay away from Walnut River and the family during that six months. Hell, she barely stayed long enough for the funeral. I didn't receive the letter until after she left, and I was still trying to figure out what to do with it when we found out Anna was working for Northeastern HealthCare."

He said the last words like a bitter epithet. Richard remembered how Peter had goaded her earlier in J.D.'s office and the disdain he hadn't bothered to conceal, and his temper heated up a notch.

"What does it matter who she works for? If your father wanted her to read that letter, you have no right to keep it from her, either legally or morally."

"I wish it were that clear-cut. My father didn't make it that easy on me. He left the decision completely up to me. In the cover letter he included with it, he said if I felt she was better off not knowing what it contains, I should burn the letter."

The heat of his temper cooled slightly at Peter's obvious turmoil, though his curiosity ratcheted up another level. "But you haven't burned it, even though Anna works for, in your words, the enemy."

"I haven't burned it. No. Some part of me knows she needs to read it. I just...I don't know how she's going to react. I barely know her anymore, Richard. I wonder if I ever did."

Richard had wondered the same thing about his own relationship with Anna. But he was stunned to realize as he sat in her brother's office that his feelings for her hadn't died. They had only been lying dormant inside him, like spring crocuses, waiting for a chance to break free of the frozen ground.

What the hell was he supposed to do with that? He didn't want to care about her. What possible good would ever come of it, when he was certain she couldn't wait to return to New York and the brilliant business career waiting for her there?

"What's in the letter?" he finally asked.

Peter stared down at the envelope for a long moment and his reluctance was in direct contrast to the vocal, outspoken man who had taken on his sister earlier in J.D.'s office.

"I need your vow of confidentiality first. No matter what, you cannot tell a soul."

"Of course."

"I'll read you the cover letter. That explains everything."

Five minutes later, Richard sat back in his chair, reeling from the information in the letter, from James Wilder's confession that Anna was truly his daughter, conceived during a brief affair with a nurse years ago.

"You have to tell her," he said into the long silence. "You can't keep this from her. She has a right to know."

"You know her, Richard, at least better than I do. How do you think she'll react?"

He thought of Anna and the vulnerability she worked so hard to conceal from the world. "I can't answer that. Stunned, certainly. Overwhelmed. Perhaps angry. Wouldn't you be?"

"Yes. It's a shocker, all right. I've known for six months and I still can't believe it." Peter paused. "I know I probably sound like a cold-hearted bastard here but I have to consider the timing and the possible fallout. In light of the bid to take over the hospital and the vote next week, how do you think this information might impact Anna's role in that bid?"

"I have no idea!"

"What's your best guess? I see things happening one of two ways. Either she might lean more toward our side or, being Anna, she might be more determined than ever to win in some kind of twisted payback against our father for not telling her."

Richard thought of the woman he was coming to know—a woman who could read bedtime stories to a five-year-old with sweetness and affection and then turn shrewdly determined about her career.

She was complex and intriguing, which was a big part of her appeal, he realized.

"I honestly can't answer that, Peter. Why would you think I would have any idea what Anna will do? I told you I barely know her."

"You've got an uncanny knack for gauging people's

behavior. I've seen you in action as you've helped Phil with hospital legal issues. I figured since you and Anna were friends before, you might have a guess."

"Our friendship was over a long time ago. We're both different people now."

"But taking history into account and judging by what you've observed since she's been back, what's your gut telling you?"

"I think none of that matters. It's irrelevant. You need to tell her what's in that letter, regardless of how it might impact the merger. This isn't about the hospital. It's a family matter."

Peter gazed at Richard for a moment then sighed. "I was afraid you would say something like that."

"She deserves to know, Peter. You know she does."

"You're right. I need to tell her as soon as possible. I've put it off too long."

He sighed again, looking not at all thrilled by the prospect. "I don't look forward to it. A hell of a mess my father left, isn't it?"

"Yes. He should have told her himself. This shouldn't be your responsibility."

Peter's laugh was gruff. "An understatement. He took the coward's way out. The only time in his life, I think, that he didn't step up and do what had to be done. I guess my biggest mistake the last six months has been following in his footsteps, at least where Anna is concerned. Thanks, Richard, for the time and for the advice. You have definitely helped put things in perspective for me."

"No problem. Consider it an early wedding gift."

Peter gave a distracted smile and showed him out. As Richard walked through the hospital and to his car he was still stunned by the revelation—and even more stunned by the baffling mix of emotions churning through him toward Anna.

He definitely still had feelings for her. Why else would he be consumed with this warmth and sympathy and something else, something soft and fragile that scared the hell out of him?

Anna was finally back in her rented duplex, wearing her most comfortable jeans and a T-shirt, barefoot, with Lilli curled at her feet, chewing her favorite squeaky toy.

Unfortunately, instead of relaxing, she was getting berated by her boss.

Alfred Daly was hundreds of miles away in Manhattan, probably gazing out the vast window of his office at the peons below who walked the city streets. But despite the distance between them, the man still had the power to make her feel as if she had shrunk several inches since the moment the phone call began.

"Tell me, when are you presenting your report to the hospital board of directors?"

She knew he knew such a significant detail, probably right down to the second, but she played along with him.

"Wednesday at five. They're expected to vote Thursday and give their final recommendation to the mayor and city council later that day."

"And you still believe the vote is too close to call?"

"The board is evenly split, as it has been since we first presented our offer. I believe we're making some progress, though. I think at least one or two of the maybe's have moved toward our camp."

Not without a great deal of wheeling and dealing on her part, but she left that unspoken.

"I certainly hope so. That's why you're there, Miss Wilder."

"Yes, sir."

He didn't mention the threat that had been hanging over her head since the day he had ordered her to come to Walnut River and make the merger happen, though it was uppermost in her mind.

If she failed—if the merger vote did not go their way—Anna knew she would be scrambling to find a new job. Not the end of the world, maybe, but she would find it devastating to start over elsewhere. She had worked too hard at NHC to see it all trickle away because of her stubborn, idealistic family members and their behind-the-scenes opposition.

By the time Daly finished his diatribe fifteen minutes later, Anna realized she had downed half a roll of Tums.

"I want that report no later than noon tomorrow. It's too important to send via e-mail so I want you to upload it directly onto my private server," he snapped.

He gave her a password and username, then hung up with one more dire warning about what would happen if she failed to close the deal.

No pressure, Al. Geez.

Anna hung up the phone and gazed into space, feeling as if she stood at the foot of Mount Everest.

She was on her own here and had been charged with achieving the impossible. Worse, she had just been forcefully reminded that her career hung in the balance if she failed.

Alfred Daly had begun to take the Walnut River General merger personally. She wasn't sure why it was so important to him but she sensed he would not take defeat well. He wanted this hospital and was pulling out all the stops to make it happen.

Suddenly, the doorbell rang, and Lilli bounded to the door, yipping away and jerking Anna from her grim contemplation of an unemployment line in her immediate future. She was not at all in the mood for unexpected company.

After twenty minutes on the phone with her boss, what she really needed was a stiff drink and a long soak in the tub.

Or perhaps both.

The doorbell rang again and Anna jerked the door open, ready to blast away, but the words died in her throat.

Of all the entire population of Walnut River, the last two people she would have expected to find standing on her doorstep on a Friday night were her brother Peter and his fiancée, especially after her altercation with him earlier.

Her day only needed this to go from lousy, straight past miserable, into sheer purgatory.

"Peter...Bethany... What brings you here?"

She could barely even look at her brother. All she could think about was her own immature reaction to him earlier. All her plans to be cool and in control around her family had dissolved with a few harsh words from him. Instead of showing off her logic and business acumen, she had ended up running away like a twelve-year-old girl escaping to the bathroom during gym class to hide her tears.

She wanted to come up with some glib comment, something cool and nonchalant, but the impulse died when she saw his solemn expression.

She instantly forgot about their altercation. "Peter! What is it? What's wrong? Has something happened to David or Ella?"

Peter shook his head. "No. Nothing like that."

"What is it, then?"

For the first time in her memory he appeared to be at a loss for words as he gazed at her mutely.

"May we come in?" Bethany finally asked.

"Oh. Of course. Come in." She held the door open and they walked inside.

Lilli sniffed their ankles for a moment then returned to her chew toy.

"What a darling dog," Bethany said with a smile, and Anna decided she had been right to instinctively like her brother's fiancée. She seemed to have a definite knack for putting people at ease in difficult circumstances.

In fact, right now Anna was quite certain she liked Peter's fiancée more than she liked her brother.

"Come in. Sit down."

"I hope we weren't disturbing you."

"No."

She didn't think Peter would appreciate knowing that she had just finished talking to her boss at NHC so she decided to keep that particular bit of information to herself, especially in light of Peter's obvious unease.

"Can I get you something to drink?" she asked, doing a mental inventory of the meager contents of her larder.

"Nothing for me," Bethany said.

Peter sighed. "I could use a drink right now, but it's probably better if I keep a clear head."

Anna narrowed her gaze at him. "All right, what's going on, Peter? You're freaking me out."

"I'm sorry. I just… Now that I'm here, I don't know how to start."

"I've always found the beginning's as good a place as any," Anna answered.

It was advice they'd all heard from their mother many times and Peter must have recognized one of Alice's familiar axioms. He gave a fleeting smile and she was struck again by his resemblance to their father.

"First of all, I owe you an apology."

She blinked, not at all used to seeing her self-assured oldest brother look so wary.

"I was out of line today at the hospital. Richard Green ripped into me after you left for making things personal and he was exactly right. I said things I shouldn't have today and I apologize. It's just…a little hard for me to watch the little sister I love taking the other side on an issue I care so passionately about."

Warmth soaked through her and Anna didn't know what stunned her more—that Peter said he loved her or that Richard would stand up to defend her.

He had taken her brother to task? She would have liked to have seen it, even though she had a tough time believing it.

"Your apology is not necessary, Peter, but thank you," she said. "You came all the way over here just to tell me you were sorry?"

"Not completely."

He glanced at Bethany and some unspoken signal passed between them, something private and personal that made Anna feel excluded—and envious. She didn't miss the way Bethany slipped her hand in his, or the way Peter seemed to grow a little calmer at the gesture.

"I have something for you," her brother finally said. "Something I should have given you months ago."

He appeared to be empty-handed and Anna gazed at him, baffled. "What is it?"

Peter slid a hand to the inside pocket of his jacket and retrieved an envelope. "Um, Dad left you a letter. It came to me since I'm executor of his estate."

Instantly, joy and anger warred within her—joy that she might have one more message from the father she missed and anger at her brother's high-handedness. "You're just getting around to giving it to me? Dad's been gone for six months!"

"You make it sound so easy. I wish it were. Dad left it up to me whether to give it to you or not, which was a hell of a position to find myself in, especially when you were making yourself scarce."

He held the letter still and she had to fight the urge to snatch it out of his hand and order him out of her house.

"You knew how to find me."

"I did. But you didn't seem to want to have anything to do with us. You couldn't leave fast enough after the funeral. You wouldn't even let me give you a ride some-where. And then we found out you were working for Northeastern HealthCare. You should have told us, Anna."

"Don't make this about me and my choices, Peter. Yes, I should have told you about my job. I was wrong to keep it from the family. But that didn't give you the right to withhold something like this from me."

"No. You're right. I should have given the letter to you long ago. I should have driven to the city and tracked you down at your office if I had to, and I'm sorry I didn't. But I'm here now. Do you want it or not?"

"Peter." Bethany said his name, only that, but it appeared to be enough to center him.

He drew in a deep breath and dragged a hand through his hair in a gesture that again reminded her of their father.

"I'm sorry," he said again. "Here it is. Whatever you want to do. It's out of my hands now."

Chapter Nine

Anna's stomach suddenly clenched with nerves and she wasn't at all sure she wanted to take the letter from Peter's outstretched hand.

What would her father have written in a letter that he couldn't have told her to her face?

Did she really want to know?

The three of them froze in an awkward tableau and the moment dragged out, longer and longer. Finally she drew in a breath and took it from him, though she was still reluctant to open it.

Her name was written on the front in her father's sloping, elegant script. By the weight of the envelope, she guessed it was maybe two or three pages long. No more than that, but it felt oddly heavy, almost burdensome.

She had the strangest premonition that once she read what her father had written in the letter, her life would never be the same. This was one of those before-and-after moments—everything after would be different than it was right at this instant.

She had no idea why she was so certain—maybe the gravity in Peter's eyes.

"Do you know what it's about?" she asked, though she thought she knew the answer.

His mouth tightened and he nodded. "I haven't read it but he included another letter to me explaining what was in it. I think it's safe to say what he has to tell you is…unexpected."

She nodded but still couldn't bring herself to open it.

"We can wait while you read it," Peter said after another moment. "You might have questions. Scratch that. You will have questions. I can't answer many of them but I'll do what I can."

Finally she knew she couldn't sit much longer, putting off the inevitable. She carefully slid a finger under the flap of the sealed envelope and pulled out the sheets of paper.

The lines of her father's handwriting turned wobbly and blurred for a moment. She blinked quickly, horrified that she might cry in front of her brother.

She thought she had come to terms with his death— and the distance between them the last few years. Though she did her best to contain it, a single tear slid past her defenses. She swiped at it, hoping Peter didn't see. But to her surprise, a moment later, he sat next to her on the sofa and Bethany sat on her other side.

"Take your time," Bethany murmured, with a comforting arm around her shoulder. She didn't know what might be in the letter but she was suddenly enormously grateful for their presence and the strength she drew from having them near.

They had taken time from their wedding preparations to be here for her, she realized with some wonder.

She drew in another shaky breath and smoothed a hand down the paper.

"My dearest Anna," her father's letter began.

I have written this letter in my head a hundred times over the years. A thousand. Each time, the words seem to tangle in my mind and eventually I stopped trying. This time I must press forward, no matter how difficult I find the task.

I must first tell you how very proud I am of you for what you have done with your life. I may not have agreed with your decision to leave medical school—I still believe you would have made an excellent physician. You were always so compassionate and loving.

But over the years I have come to accept that you had to chart your own destiny, and I will say now what I should have said eight years ago. I believe you made the right choice to leave medical school. Your heart was never in it, something I refused to see back then. One of my biggest regrets in life is that I was not the sort of father I should have been to you. I should have listened to your worries and fears instead of trying so hard to crowd you onto the path I wanted for you.

I did try to be a good father to you. Perhaps I tried too hard. I wanted so much for you to feel you belonged. I know things were not always easy for you. I could see the lost look in your eyes when you would see one of your siblings on your mother's lap or having a bedtime story with her and I always tried to rush in to fill the void.

My dear, I ask you not to judge Alice too harshly. She was a wonderful woman who endured more than you can ever guess, more than any woman should. I always suspected she had guessed the truth about you, the truth I dared not tell her.

She never said anything and I know she loved you in her way but surely you sensed she treated you differently than Peter or David or Ella.

Neither of us ever spoke of it—afraid, I think, to upset the fragile peace we had achieved. But time is no longer my friend. When a man reaches a certain age, he must come face to face with his own mortality. I don't want this secret to die with me.

I only ask that as you read this, you do not judge me too harshly. Please remember how much I have always loved you.

The truth is, I have lied to you for all these years about how you came to be part of our family. The story about finding you on the steps of the hospital is true. But missing in that tale are certain significant details.

She paused to turn the page, still vaguely aware of Peter and Bethany on either side of her, bolstering her.

I was the one who "found" you, yes, but only because that was the prearranged plan between me and your mother. Your birth mother.

I'm sure it will shock you to find out I knew all

along who she was. It wasn't some unknown mystery woman who left you, but a nurse at Walnut River General. See, Anna, you are my daughter. Not only through adoption but in every other way.

She inhaled sharply and lifted shocked eyes to Peter, who was watching her through her father's solemn eyes. She jerked her gaze away from him and focused on the letter again.

Please, I beg you again, don't judge me too harshly. I had one moment of indiscretion during the depths of Alice's depression, when she had retreated to a dark and terrible place. Monica, your birth mother, showed me great kindness and compassion and in a moment of weakness, I went against every standard I have ever believed in. She was not at fault, the blame was wholly mine. I cannot regret it. I know I should, but without that moment of weakness, I never would have had the great honor and privilege of being your father.

Anna realized she was gripping the letter so hard she was afraid she would tear it. She forced her grasp to relax as she fought back tears. A moment later, a handkerchief appeared in front of her and she took it from Peter but still didn't allow the tears to fall.

I'm sure you're curious about your birth mother and why she would choose to give you up. She was a wonderful woman, kind and generous, but she wasn't at all prepared to be a mother, especially not on her own. I know that leaving you with me was the hardest decision she ever made, but she knew that as a Wilder, you would have opportunities she couldn't provide on her own.

I'm sorry to say she is gone now. She died not long after your birth when the small plane she was flying in crashed, but I am certain her last thoughts were of you.

Our actions were done out of love for you, Anna. Please don't forget that. Even the deception I have maintained over the years was out of love and the enduring hope that you would find acceptance and stability in our family.

I am sorry for the years of deception. I should have told you earlier, I see that now. I only pray that someday you will forgive me for the magnitude of the lie.

I love you, my darling Anna. I have been proud to call you my own every moment of your life.
Your devoted father
James Wilder

She finished the letter and sat stunned for a long moment, the pages dangling from her fingers.

She didn't know what to think, what to feel.

She was not some anonymous orphan, as she had believed for so many years. She was James Wilder's daughter, conceived during a brief affair with a nurse at the hospital.

Her father's daughter, in every possible way.

She felt numb, dazed, and couldn't seem to work her brain around the implications.

"You…knew about this?" she finally said, her jaw so achy and tight the words were hard to get out.

Peter nodded. "I told you, he left me a cover letter explaining everything. I've known for months, I just haven't known how to tell you."

"How could he?"

The words were wrenched from her and she didn't know what she meant—her father's infidelity in the first place or the years of deception upon deception from the man she had always considered the most scrupulously honest she had ever known.

Peter sighed. "You don't remember what Mom went through during those terrible days of her depression, before she found the right combo of meds to control it. I do. I remember it vividly. I was nine and I can remember days when I was afraid to come home from school, because I didn't know what I would find. It was horrible. The medication they gave her made it worse. She was barely there and when she came to herself, she would rage and scream at Dad for hours."

She closed her eyes, feeling battered and achy and still fighting tears. If she let them out, she was afraid she wouldn't be able to stop.

"Do— Do Ella and David know?"

He shook his head. "Bethany knows and I've confided in two others, seeking advice—a social worker and friend at the hospital and more recently, Richard Green."

She stared. "Richard knows? And he said nothing to me?"

"I only told him today after I saw you in J.D.'s office. I swore him to secrecy."

So Richard hadn't betrayed her. She found some solace in that.

"Will you tell them? David and Ella, I mean?"

Peter shook his head. "That's your decision. If you want them to know, I can tell them but perhaps you should be the one to do it. And if you decide to say nothing, I will back you up."

He paused, appearing to choose his words carefully. "Things are difficult between us all right now. I would only ask that if you tell them, you don't do it out of spite or anger."

His words were a blunt reminder of the rift between her and her siblings, of the chasm she had no idea how to cross.

She forced a smile that didn't feel at all genuine. "Always the protector, aren't you, Peter?"

He studied her solemnly. "Of you as well, Anna."

She didn't know how to respond to that and the tears seemed even closer to the surface. Bethany seemed to sense the fissures in her control. She squeezed Anna's arm.

"The wedding rehearsal dinner is next Friday," she said softly. "It would mean a great deal to us if you would be there. Will you come?"

Would she even still be in town? she wondered. The hospital board of directors was set to vote on Thursday and everything would be decided by then.

Still, she was deeply grateful suddenly for Bethany's freely offered friendship.

"I'll try," she managed.

Bethany gave her a hug. "That's all we can ask," she said.

To her shock, Peter hugged her next. "I would say welcome to the family, but it doesn't seem quite appropriate since you've been my sister for thirty years."

Somehow she managed a smile, though it felt watery and thin. "Thank you for bringing this, even though you didn't want to. I understand your hesitation a little better now."

"Dad never should have kept it from you and I shouldn't have either for this long."

He paused, then embraced her again. "When the shock wears off, I hope you will see this as a good thing. You've always been one of us, Anna. Blood or not. But maybe knowing you share our blood will help you see that more clearly."

She nodded and showed them out.

When they left, Lilli gazed at her quizzically. Anna re-read the letter, still fighting tears, while the walls of her bland, boring, temporary home seemed to be closing in on her, crowding her, smothering her.

She suddenly needed to escape from the thick emotions squeezing her chest, stealing her breath, choking her throat.

And she knew exactly where she needed to go.

"Good night, kiddo. You be good for Grandma, okay?"

"Dad!" In that single word, Ethan managed to convey all the disgust of a teenager instead of a five-year-old. "You know I always am!"

Richard smiled into the phone. "Of course you are. I love you, bud."

"I love you, too, Dad."

The sweet, pure words put a lump in his throat, as they always did. "Can you put your grandma on the phone again?"

"Okeydokey."

After a moment's silence, his mother picked up the phone.

"Are you really sure you want to do this, Mom? You've had him all day."

"Absolutely." His mother's voice was firm and not at all as exhausted as he might have expected after she had wrangled Ethan for the past ten hours. "You know we've been planning this sleepover for a week. We're camping out. I've got a tent set up in my living room and the sleeping bags are already up. We're going to roast marshmallows in the gas fireplace after I crank up the air conditioning to compensate and I have all the makings of s'mores ready to go. We're going to have a blast."

That was part of the problem, Richard admitted. He hated being excluded. He hadn't seen Ethan since dropping him off at his grandmother's that morning and he missed his son.

Ethan's absence was part of his restlessness, but not all of it. Some had to do with a particular woman he couldn't get out of his mind.

"Thanks, then," he said. "You two have a great time. I'll pick him up tomorrow morning."

"No hurry. We'll probably sleep in."

"Wishful thinking, Mom. Ethan's idea of sleeping in is waiting to jump out of bed until six-forty-five instead of six-thirty."

His mother laughed. "I'll survive. The question is, what will you do with a night to yourself?"

He was so unused to the idea that he found the prospect of an evening without Ethan rather daunting. "I'm slammed with work right now so I'll probably just take advantage of the chance to catch up."

"Booorrring. Can't you think of something better than work? It's Friday night. Why don't you go out and have some fun? Call up one of those girls on your BlackBerry and head out for a night on the town."

The only females on his BlackBerry were clients or associates, but he decided his mother didn't really need to know that particular piece of information.

"Interesting idea," he murmured. "I doubt it will happen but I'll certainly add it to the list of possibilities."

His mother was quiet for a moment. When she spoke, her voice held a surprising degree of concern. "I worry about you, Richard. You're a wonderful father, but your world has become only about work and about your son. You need to take time for yourself once in awhile. Go have a little fun. Grab a little spontaneity in your life."

Richard frowned. Where was this coming from? Okay, so he didn't have much of a social life. But when, exactly, was he supposed to find the time for one while being a full-time father?

He opened his mouth to answer, but before he could, the doorbell chimed through the empty house.

Relief flooded him at the convenient excuse to end the conversation. "I've gotta go, Mom. Somebody's at the door."

"Oh, good. Maybe it's a hot girl looking for a little action."

A strangled laugh escaped him. "Wouldn't that be an odd twist of fate?"

"Stranger things have happened."

"If I were you, I wouldn't hold my breath. Have fun sleeping on the floor."

He hung up and hurried to answer the door. In light of the conversation with his mother, he couldn't have been more shocked to find Anna Wilder on his doorstep.

"Anna!"

"I...didn't know where else to go."

His initial surprise shifted quickly to concern. Her eyes were hollow and her face looked ashen in the pale glow of his porch light.

She was holding an envelope in her hand and he knew instantly that Peter must have given her James's letter.

He only had about half a second for the thought to register before she launched herself into his arms.

He caught her but the momentum pushed them both back into the room. He heard a strangled gasp and then, like a torrent, she began to weep great, heaving sobs, as if she had been waiting for only this moment to unleash them.

He eased down to the sofa and pulled her onto his lap. He held her for a long time, until the sobs finally began to subside. She was trembling, little shivers that broke his heart, and he tightened his arms. After a moment, she let out a deep breath and struggled to regain control, and he relaxed his hold a little.

"I'm sorry." Her voice sounded raspy. "I'm so sorry. I didn't mean to...I never intended to come here and break down like this. I just...I had to talk to someone and I didn't know where else to go."

"I'm glad you came here."

"I feel so stupid. I don't know what happened. I saw you and suddenly it all just seemed too much."

He was honored and humbled that she trusted him enough to let him see beyond the cool veneer she showed to the world. "Do you want to talk about it?"

"You mean blubbering all over your shirt for twenty minutes isn't enough torture?"

It *was* torture having her in his arms, but not the way she meant. Despite the toll it was taking on his control, he wasn't about to relinquish this chance to hold her, in any capacity.

"I'm guessing you talked to Peter."

She sighed. "Yes. He said he talked to you earlier today and told you about the letter from my father."

"He did."

"Then you know the truth. That James Wilder is my father. My true father, not just my adopted one."

"A bit of a shock, wasn't it?"

She gave a short, bitter laugh. "It changes everything I thought I knew about myself."

"You're still the same person, Anna. Finding out your genetic blueprint doesn't change thirty years of living."

She was silent for a moment, her cheek still pressed against his chest. She didn't seem inclined to leave his lap and he certainly wasn't in any hurry to let her go.

"I have always believed I stood on the outside of the Wilder family circle. My mother—Alice—didn't exactly push me out but I never truly felt welcome, even though James did everything possible to make me feel I belonged. Now I understand why."

"She knew you were his child?"

"My father said in the letter he thought she must have guessed but they never discussed it."

"It must have been terribly difficult for her if she did suspect. To keep her head high while she raised her husband's illegitimate child."

"Yes. It explains so much about...everything."

To his regret, she finally slid from his lap and sat beside him on the couch, her hands tightly folded on her lap.

Though he knew a little distance was probably a wise thing right about now, Richard couldn't prevent himself from reaching out and covering her clasped hands with his. After a moment, she gripped his tightly.

"You know, I think he tried to tell me several times over the years, in an oblique kind of way," she said. "The summer I...left, when I dropped out of med school and everything, I tried to tell him how unhappy I was. I told him straight out that I was afraid I just didn't have the Wilder gene for medicine. I can remember him saying in that sturdy, no-nonsense voice of his, 'Don't let me hear you say that again. You're as much a Wilder as the rest of my children!' I thought it was simply another effort to make me feel I belonged in the family."

"What will you do now?"

She closed her eyes and leaned against the sofa. Her color had returned, he was pleased to see. Despite the crying jag, she was so beautiful he couldn't seem to look away.

"I don't know. Peter says he hasn't told Ella and David. He seems to think I'll blab it to them out of spite over the hospital merger."

Despite her glib tone, he could hear the hurt underscoring her words and his heart ached for her. He couldn't help himself, and he pulled her into his arms again.

"You'll figure it all out, Anna. I know it must feel like an atomic bomb has just dropped into your lap, but when you think about it, what has really changed?"

"Everything!"

"Maybe you found out your father had some human weaknesses after all. But your siblings are still your siblings, just as they've always been. You might all be going through a rough time right now with the hospital merger but they still love you."

She sighed against his chest. "I feel like everything I thought I knew about myself is a lie."

"It's not, Anna. Not at all. What's different right now than it was a few hours ago? You're still a bright beautiful woman who loves her dog and is kind to little boys and who still makes my heart pound."

Her gaze flashed to his for one breathless moment before he surrendered to the inevitable and kissed her.

Chapter Ten

Anna closed her eyes and leaned into Richard, trying to absorb his strength.

She needed him. For comfort, yes, but for so much more. She found a peace in his arms that she had never known anywhere else.

Though she had dated in the eight years she'd been away, she had never cared enough about any of those men to take a relationship beyond the casual to this ultimate step.

This had never felt right with anyone but Richard. He was the only man she had ever made love to.

She wondered what he would say if she told him that and decided to keep the information to herself for now.

She wrapped her arms around his neck with the oddest sensation that this was where she belonged. Right here, with his mouth firm and insistent against hers, his masculine scent filling her senses, his hard strength against her.

Here, in his arms, she didn't feel disconnected or off kilter. It didn't matter whether she was the odd Wilder out or James Wilder's illegitimate daughter. She had nothing to prove here—she knew exactly who she was when Richard Green kissed her. Everything else faded to nothing.

He deepened the kiss, until tiny sparks raced up and down her nerve endings, until her thighs trembled and every inch of her skin ached for his touch.

"You taste exactly like I remember," he murmured.

"How?" Was that breathy, aroused voice hers, she wondered with some amazement. What happened to the brisk and businesslike woman she had always considered herself?

"Like every delicious, decadent, sinful dessert ever created. Sweet and heady and intoxicating. That's you."

His words ignited more heat and she kissed him fiercely, reveling in his sharp intake of breath, in the tremble of his hands on the bare skin above the waistband of her jeans.

He traced designs on the sensitive skin at her waist for long, intoxicating moments, then finally moved to the buttons of her white shirt.

A wild hunger for his touch bubbled and seethed deep inside her and she arched against his hand, needing him with a steady, fiery ache.

He opened the buttons of her shirt and touched her through the lacy fabric of her bra and she found the sight of his sun-browned hand against her pale skin the most erotic thing she'd ever seen.

She arched against him, wanting more. Wanting everything. For long moments, they kissed and touched, until nothing else mattered but this moment.

"I'm going to have to stop." His voice was raspy with

need. "I'm afraid I have no self-control where you're concerned."

"Take it from me. Self-control is overrated," she murmured, her voice a breathy purr.

He closed his eyes for a moment. When he opened them again, they were dark with passion. "I can't take advantage of you, Anna. You're upset. This isn't really what you want."

"You couldn't be more wrong. This is exactly what I want."

He looked torn between desire and his sense of duty and she decided to take the decision out of his hands. She kissed him hard, wrapping her arms around him tightly and savoring the strength against her.

He groaned. "I can't fight you and myself at the same time."

"Then don't," she said.

He kissed her again, fierce and possessive, and her stomach trembled with anticipation. It wouldn't be the same magic she remembered from eight years ago, she warned herself. It couldn't be.

She was only half-right.

It wasn't the same. It was better. Much, much better.

They kissed their way down the hall to his bedroom and she had a vague impression of bold masculine colors and a massive bed before Richard began to undress her with a soft gentleness that nearly made her weep.

She was in love with him.

The realization washed through her, not with the punishing force of a tidal wave, but like a sweet cleansing rain on parched desert soil.

It was terribly difficult not to blurt the words out right then but she choked them back. He didn't want to hear them. Not now. She had hurt him eight years ago, he had said as much. He might let her into his arms and his bed but somehow she knew finding her way back into his heart wouldn't be nearly as easy.

She put the fear away for now as she helped him out of his clothes and then she forgot her fears, lost in the sheer wonder of having all those muscles to explore.

They kissed and touched for a long time, until both of them were breathing raggedly, their hearts pounding.

At last, when she didn't think she could endure another moment, he grabbed a condom from the bedside table and entered her, and she again had to choke back her words of love as sensation after sensation poured over her.

She pressed a hard kiss to his mouth, desperate to show him with her lips and her body how she felt about him, even if she didn't quite feel she could say the words yet.

He gripped her hands tightly as he moved deeply inside her and she cried out his name, stunned at her wild hunger. She arched into him, desperate and achy.

She couldn't wait another second, another instant. Sensing how close she was to the edge, he reached between their bodies and touched her at the apex of her thighs and the world exploded in a wild burst of color and heat and sensation.

While her body still shivered and hummed, he pushed even deeper inside her, deeper than she would have thought possible, then groaned out her name as he found his own release.

He held her while they floated back to earth together and she mouthed the words she couldn't say aloud against his chest.

"What did you say?" he asked softly.

She shook her head, her hair brushing his skin. "Wow," she lied. "Just wow."

He laughed softly and pulled her closer and she wondered how she had ever found the strength—or the stupidity—to walk away from this eight years ago.

He awoke to the pale light of early morning filtering through his window and an odd sense of peace.

The sensation was unfamiliar enough that it compelled him to slide a little further into consciousness. Most mornings, he jumped out of bed ready for the day's many battles—from his regular tussle with Ethan over breakfast cereals to pondering the many things on his to-do list.

This morning, his limbs were loose and relaxed, his thoughts uncharacteristically still.

While he was trying to piece together why that might be, a sexy feminine scent drifted through the air from the pillow beside him, and he saw an unfamiliar indentation with a few long blond hairs against the pillowcase.

The memories came flowing back—of Anna in his arms, her mouth eager, her body soft and responsive.

He closed his eyes, reliving the incredible night they had just shared. It had been more than he would ever have imagined. Much more. He had never known such tenderness, such overwhelming sweetness.

They had made love three times and each time had been more intense than the time before.

And now she was gone.

He opened his eyes, not quite sure why he was so certain of it. Her clothes were gone and some instinct told him he didn't need to search his house to know he wouldn't find her.

He couldn't say he was really surprised. Saddened, maybe, but not really surprised.

The bleak inevitability of it still made him want to throw on a pair of jeans and tear off after her, chase her down at her apartment and confront her, but he checked the impulse. What the hell good would that accomplish, besides making him look like an idiot?

He sat up, his emotions a tight hot tangle in his chest. He was in love with her—a thousand times more now, this morning, than he had been eight years ago. Those had been fledgling, newborn feelings.

This, what he felt right now, was powerful and strong.

Too bad for him, but if their history ran true, Anna was likely to whip out a twenty gauge shotgun and blast his heart right out of the sky.

He didn't learn his lesson very well with her, did he? He was either a masochist or he had no sense of self-preservation whatsoever.

Anna just wasn't emotionally available.

She couldn't make it more clear to him if she took out a damn billboard right outside his office.

Even when they made love, he could sense she held some part of herself back, something she hid away from him. He didn't know whether that was a protective mechanism from a childhood where she struggled to belong, or if it stemmed from her dedication to her career, but even in his arms she wouldn't let him through that last line of defenses.

He sighed. So much for the relaxed state he'd awakened to. His shoulders now ached with tension and regret.

It was still early, just barely daylight. He wasn't going to lay here and brood, he decided. He had survived having his heart broken by Anna Wilder before. He could certainly do it again. The trick was returning to as normal a life as possible, forcing himself to go through the motions until the vicious ache in his heart began to fade.

He was getting to be an expert.

When she had left before, the only thing that had saved him had been law school. He had thrown himself into his final two years, until he didn't have room in his brain to think about anything else but tort reforms and trial transcripts.

At least now he had Ethan to distract him.

A good, hard run before he went to his mother's to collect his son for the day would be an excellent place to start picking up the pieces of his world, he decided. A little physical activity would be just the thing to burn off this restlessness suddenly churning through him.

Ten minutes later, dressed in jogging shorts and a T-shirt, he was heading out the front door when he spotted an envelope on the coffee table in the living room.

He saw her name on the front and realized this must be the letter from her father. His mind flashed to the night before, to her coming through the door and into his arms. She had been holding it then. Sometime during the wild storm of emotion that came after when she had wept in his arms, she must have dropped it on the table.

He was going to have to return it to her, which meant he would have to see her again.

Sooner, rather than later.

He grimaced, gazing malevolently at the envelope. Getting over her again would be a hell of a lot easier if he didn't have to face her every damn time he turned around.

* * *

She was an idiot.

Anna sat in her living room, Lilli curled up at her feet and her laptop humming on the coffee table in front of her as she tried to focus on work instead of the delectable image of Richard, naked and masculine, as she'd left him a few hours earlier.

Walking away from that bedroom and out of his house had been the single hardest thing she had ever done.

She had stood watching him sleep for a long time in the soft light of early morning, trying to force herself to go.

With one arm thrown over his head, his features relaxed and youthful in sleep, he had been so gorgeous that she had wanted nothing more than to climb right back into his bed and never leave.

She sighed, gazing at her computer until the words blurred.

She was in love with him.

It was one thing to face such a thought when she was in his arms, when his body was warm and hard against hers. It was something else entirely in the cold unforgiving light of morning, when she couldn't escape the harsh reality that they had no possible future together.

She had destroyed any chance of that eight years ago, when she made the fatal decision that proving herself to her family was more important than following her heart.

It had been a colossal mistake. She could see that now.

Richard didn't trust her enough to love her. Even when he had been deep inside her, she had seen the doubt shadowing his gaze, the edge of distance he was careful to maintain.

She deserved it. She had hurt him by leaving, more than she had ever imagined.

The night she had shared dinner with him at his house, he had told her with blunt and brutal honesty that he had only dated Ethan's mother because she had reminded him of Anna.

He had offered her his heart eight years ago and she had callously refused it. She supposed it was only right and just, somehow, that now she would be the one to bleed.

She stared at her computer for a long time then glanced at the clock. She had promised Mr. Daly her report would be posted on his private server by noon, which gave her only an hour to finish up.

Compartmentalizing her heartache was almost as hard as walking out of Richard's house, but she forced herself to focus on work with the harsh reminder that she only had a few days left in Walnut River. Either way the board voted, her work here would be done by the end of the week and she could return to the city and the life she had created there.

She quickly input the new numbers from the hospital in her report then went online to access Daly's private server via the instructions he had given her the night before.

It only took a moment to upload her report. Just as she was about to disconnect she spied a folder she had never seen before, labeled WRG/Wilder.

She stared at it for a long moment, a vague foreboding curling through her like ominous wisps of smoke where they didn't belong.

She had no business reading Daly's private files, even if they did have her name on them.

But he had given her the access code to his server,

she reminded herself. Surely he wouldn't have done that if the server contained information he didn't want her to see.

Maybe this was some kind of message to her and he meant for her to see it. Maybe if she didn't read it, he would accuse her of not doing her job somehow. The man could be devious that way.

After another moment of dithering, she surrendered to her curiosity and opened the folder. It contained only one file, she saw, with the initials P.W.

In for a penny, she thought, and clicked to open it....

Ten minutes later, she printed out the document after making her own backup copy. Her hands were shaking so much she could barely move them on the keyboard to disconnect from the server.

She shut down her laptop and folded it closed, then eased back on the sofa. Her stomach roiled as the bagel she'd had that morning seemed to churn around inside her. She pressed a hand to the sudden burning there while her mind whirled with the implications of what she had just read.

She wasn't sure which emotion was stronger inside her right now—outrage at what her superiors planned for the hospital or the deep sense of betrayal that she had been used.

P.W. stood for *Peter Wilder.* That had been abundantly clear the moment she opened the file that turned out to be an internal memo between Daly and his three closest cohorts.

She closed her eyes as snippets of the memo seemed to dance behind her eyelids. *Force out old guard. Bring in cheaper labor. Cut costs and services.*

It was bad enough that NHC planned to do exactly as her siblings claimed, sacrifice patient care for the bottom line. Worse was the way they intended to win this battle, by using her to bring down her siblings, primarily Peter.

Peter Wilder leads the opposition, the memo stated clearly. *Take him out and you'll cut the opponents off at the knees.*

The smear tactics outlined in the memo were brutally ugly, ranging from manufacturing malpractice allegations to planting a patient willing to accuse him of sexual misconduct.

Anna pressed a hand to her mouth, sickened all over again as she remembered her own passionate defense of Northeastern HealthCare, how absolutely certain she had been that the company had the community's needs at heart.

How could she have allowed herself to be so blind?

She thought she had been doing the right thing. For two years, she had bought into the NHC philosophy of providing streamlined medical care to reach the masses. She had wanted to believe in their mission. She had nothing but respect for her direct supervisor, Wallace Jeffers. He had always struck her as a man of integrity and honor.

Not everyone at NHC was like him, she had to admit. Now, as she looked back over two years, she could see times she had turned her head away at practices that might have blurred ethical lines.

She hadn't wanted to see them, she acknowledged now. She had wanted only to focus on her career and climbing as high as she could. Wallace had talked about her succeeding him as vice president of mergers and acquisitions, sometime long in the future, and she had wanted it.

She'd been brought into this project not because of any brilliance on her part, she saw now, but because she was

a Wilder. Alfred Daly seemed to have an almost patho-
logical need to win the NHC merger. He was frustrated
and angry at all the complications and delays the past six
months in what should have been a simple process.

Of course he would use any advantage in front of
him. No doubt he thought her presence would be enough
to distract her family while NHC implemented more nefarious plans.

This memo was dated a few weeks earlier. She read it
again, sick all over again. Were the wheels in motion
already? Was her brother going to be hit any day now with
some kind of trumped-up malpractice suit or an allega-
tion of sexual abuse?

Her honorable upright brother would be devastated by
either option.

"Oh, Lilli. What am I going to do?"

Her dog yapped in response, her head cocked and her
eyes curiously sympathetic.

The dog held her gaze for just an instant before she
suddenly scampered to the door with an excited yip, then
sat vibrating with eagerness, her little body aquiver.

As usual, Lilli was prescient. The doorbell rang an
instant later and Anna groaned, tempted to ignore it and
pretend she wasn't home.

The doorbell rang again, more insistently this time.
Who was she fooling? Her car was in the driveway, and
whoever was out there probably knew she was sitting
here trying to pretend she was invisible.

"Anna?" She heard through the door and closed her
eyes at the sound of Richard's smooth voice.

Who else? She only needed this.

She was even more tempted to ignore the doorbell, but

she just couldn't bring herself to do it. Finally she ramped up her courage and forced herself to wrench open the door.

Sunlight gleamed in his golden hair and he looked gorgeous—sexy and casual in jeans and a polo shirt. She had an instant's image of how she had left him that morning, the sheets tousled at his waist and his muscled chest hard and warm.

Awkwardness at seeing him again temporarily supplanted her dismay over the memo.

A few hours ago, she had been in his arms. She had no experience with this sort of thing and didn't know how to face him.

"Hi," she finally said, her voice throaty.

He nodded, though his stoic expression didn't change.

"Would you...like to come in?"

After a moment, he stepped through the doorway with a reluctance she didn't miss. He stopped for a moment to greet Lilli, who hopped around with infatuated enthusiasm.

"I can't stay," he finally said. "I'm picking Ethan up in an hour. I just wanted to return this. You left it at my house."

He held out a familiar envelope and she stared. She certainly hadn't forgotten the stunning news that she was James's daughter but the letter had completely slipped her mind when she was sneaking away from Richard's bed.

"Oh. Right. Um, thank you."

"You're welcome."

They lapsed into an awkward silence. She wished she could read his expression but he seemed stiff and unapproachable.

"Why did you..."

"Look, I'm sorry I..."

They both spoke to break the silence at the same time and Anna gestured. "You first," she said.

He shrugged. "I just wanted to know why you rushed away this morning without a word. You could have at least nudged me awake to say goodbye."

She flushed, not at all in the mood to talk about this right now after the tumult of the past half hour.

Richard made it sound like she had taken what she wanted from him and then left on her merry way without giving him another thought. It wasn't at all like that, but she could certainly see how he might have been left with that impression.

She couldn't very well tell him she had been terrified by the wild torrent of emotions rushing through her, that she had been almost desperate for the safety of a little distance from him.

"I don't know that I can answer that," she finally said, her voice wary. "I was hoping to avoid this kind of awkwardness. I guess I thought it would be...easier that way."

His mouth hardened. "I wouldn't want you to try something hard."

His words were quiet, which only made them that much more devastating.

"What's that supposed to mean?"

"Nothing. Forget it." He looked toward the door as if he regretted saying anything and wanted to escape.

"No. I'd like to hear what you have to say."

"You sure about that?"

She folded her arms across her chest, though she knew that pitiful gesture would do nothing to protect her heart.

"Yes. Tell me."

"I'm just looking at your track record. You quit medical school because it was too tough for you."

"Not true! I had straight A's my first year. I walked out because I hated it!"

"Fine. You're right. It wasn't tough academically, just emotionally, which for you was even harder. So instead of staying and explaining to your family that you hated it, instead of taking a stand, you chose to run. You were so afraid of your family's reaction that you gave up on *us* before we even had a chance. You've got a track record, at least where I'm concerned, so I guess I wasn't really surprised you walked out this morning. It's what you do. You're good at it."

She managed, just barely, not to sway from the bitter impact of his anger. How dare he? she wanted to say, but the words tangled in her throat. She only had to look at her laptop and that damning memo to know he was right. Absolutely right.

She was a blind, self-absorbed idiot whose actions were threatening her family and her community.

She deserved his condemnation and more. Much more.

Chapter Eleven

He needed to shut the hell up and just leave, pretend the last twelve hours hadn't happened, but Richard couldn't seem to make the words stop coming. "Even as we were making love, I expected you to leave. That doesn't make it hurt any less. That's all I'm saying."

Her features had paled a shade, but in typical Anna fashion, she stiffened her shoulders. "I don't understand. If you have such contempt for me and think I'm such a terrible person, why would you want anything to do with me?"

Though her tone was calm, dispassionate even, he didn't miss the hurt in her eyes, a pain she was trying valiantly to conceal from him.

"I don't think you're a terrible person. Quite the contrary. I wouldn't be—" in love with you, he almost said, but checked himself just in time "—I wouldn't be here if I did. I think you're a brilliant, capable, beautiful woman who doesn't see her own strengths. You don't see yourself as I do, as someone with the ability to cope with anything that comes along. Because you don't see it, you protect yourself by avoiding things you're afraid you can't handle."

She looked as if he had just punched her in the gut and Richard sighed. He needed to just shut the hell up and leave. He tended to forget how vulnerable she was.

He had no business coming here, twisting everything, making it all about her.

"I'd better go. Ethan will be home soon. I just thought you might be looking for your father's letter."

"Thank you."

She didn't meet his gaze and Richard closed his eyes, furious with himself. "Look, I'm sorry. Forget I said anything. I'm just acting like a spoiled brat. I can't have what I want and so I'm blaming everyone in the world but myself."

"What...do you want?"

"Haven't you figured that out yet? I want you. Still. Always."

She blinked those big gorgeous eyes and with a sigh, he stepped forward and pulled her into his arms.

She stood frozen with shock in his arms for just a moment then she seemed to melt against him, her mouth soft and eager against his. Her arms clasped around his neck and he lost himself to the heat that always flared between them.

Was it only because he knew he couldn't have her? he wondered. Was that why each touch, each taste, seemed such a miracle? As if each time might be the last.

He wasn't sure how it happened but she was backed

against the wall, her body wrapped around his, and he was lost in the overwhelming tenderness, unlike anything he had ever known with anyone else.

They kissed for a long time, until finally she sighed against his mouth and he tasted exactly the moment when she started to withdraw.

She slid her mouth away from his and backed away, her eyes wide, slightly dazed, for only a moment before she seemed to blink back to awareness.

"I wish you wouldn't do that."

"What? Kiss you?"

"Confuse me," she said, her voice low. "Distract me. Richard, I can't do this with you. Last night was…"

A mistake. He heard the words, even though she cut off the sentence before she said them.

"I was confused and upset and I—I needed you. I won't deny that. But I shouldn't have stayed. The lines are too blurred. Surely you can see that. You're the hospital attorney and I…"

"And?"

"And things are so complicated right now. I can't even begin to tell you." Her gaze flashed to her laptop behind him. "*Complicated* is an understatement. Right now, I need…I can't afford to be distracted by you. By this."

The words had a painfully familiar ring to them. She was doing it again, damn her.

"I'm sorry," she murmured. "It's just…my life is a mess. The merger. My family. Northeastern HealthCare. Everything."

When would he stop just handing his heart to her and then sit by watching her twist and yank the poor thing into knots?

"You're right. I wouldn't want a little detail like the fact that I'm in love with you distract you from all that other important stuff in your life right now."

He hadn't meant to say that, damn it. The words slipped out of nowhere to hover between them, where they seemed to expand sharply, to grow and morph until they filled the entire room.

"Richard!"

"Forget I said that."

"How can I?"

"I'm sure you'll find a way. Especially since you're so focused on what's really important. The merger. Your family. NHC. Everything."

As he headed for the door, he dislodged some papers from the coffee table. Out of habit, he reached to pick them up to replace them—it wouldn't do to leave a mess, after all, he thought bitterly—then his attention was caught by the top page in his hand.

He shouldn't have read it but a few key phrases leapt out and grabbed his attention. Law school had taught him to read briefs rapidly and digest them just as quickly. It took less than ten seconds to read enough to feel like throwing up.

"What the hell is this?"

She stared at the paper in his hand and he saw the color leach from her face like bones in the sun. She grabbed for the memo. "Nothing. Absolutely nothing."

He held it above his head so she couldn't reach it. Her dog, thinking they were playing some kind of game, yipped besides their feet. "Nothing! You call this nothing?"

Panic twisted her features and she looked like she shared his nausea, so pale and bilious that he might have allowed a twinge of pity if he'd had room for anything else around the disgust.

"It's not what it looks like."

"I hope to hell it's not."

He pulled it down and read it again and had to fight the urge to shove the whole thing down her throat. "Because what it looks like is your master plan to win this merger fight, no matter what the cost. You're planning to sacrifice your own brother for the sake of your damn job!"

"I'm not!"

"What else? *Take Peter Wilder down, any way you can.* That's what the thing says. *With Wilder out of the picture, the opposition will crumble.* How could you? What have you become, Anna?"

If possible, her features paled further but she still lifted her chin. "You're jumping to unfounded conclusions, counselor."

"To hell with that! The proof is right here. How could you?" he asked again. "You're willing to destroy Peter— your own brother—just to win. The job at all costs. Nothing has changed with you, has it?"

She ignored his words, holding out her hand. Her fingers trembled, he realized, but the sight gave him no satisfaction. "Give it to me, Richard. That is an internal Northeastern HealthCare memo. You have no legal access to it. You're an attorney. You know that."

"It was here in plain sight."

"Among my private papers, in a private home. You read it without my permission and now you just need to forget you ever saw it."

She was right, damn it. She was right and there wasn't a thing he could do about it. He handed over the document with bitter reluctance, as all his illusions about her shattered into nothing.

"I don't even know you, do I? I was completely wrong. How could I have been so stupid? You aren't protecting your emotions. You've got none. You're a cold heartless woman who is willing to sell your own family down the river to get your way."

"Richard—"

He shook his head, cutting her off. "I've been in love with an image all these years. You never cared about me. I finally see it. I tried to convince myself you were doing what you thought was best to escape your family's expectations. But the truth is, you left without even a backward glance because I didn't matter. My feelings didn't matter. You don't care about anyone or anything but yourself, do you?"

"Not true. So not true." Her voice was low and cool but she fluttered one hand over her stomach like he'd kicked her. Her dog, sensing the tension, seemed to get more excited, dancing around their feet.

"It is. I can't believe I've been so blind. I've been hanging on to this illusion of the girl you used to be in high school and college. But she has completely disappeared somewhere along the way."

"I'm sorry you had to read that."

"I won't let you and those bastards you work for get away with this," he growled. "No way in hell. I'll go to the media. To your family. To anybody who will listen."

"And say what? You have no proof of anything. Just leave it alone, Richard."

She was right. He was certain the incriminating document would be shredded and the memo purged from the NHC system the moment he walked out the door.

"You would love that, wouldn't you? If I just walked out and forgot everything. It's not going to happen. If I can't go to the media, I can at least do everything I can to protect your brother."

She took a deep breath. "That's not necessary."

His laugh was raw and scraped his throat. "Oh, believe me, Anna, as the hospital attorney and your brother's counsel now by default, I think it damn well is. Northeastern HealthCare is running out of time. I'm sure they're going to move fast. But we'll be ready for them."

He headed for the door but her voice stopped him.

"Richard, I... This is not what you think, I swear. Can you just give me a few days to straighten things out?"

"A few days? In a few days, your brother's life could be devastated. He's getting married in a week, Anna. Did you once think of that? A little accusation of sexual misconduct with a patient would be a hell of a thing to have hanging over his head on his honeymoon."

She drew in a shaky breath. "A few days. That's all I need."

"In a few days, this could be a done deal and your bloodsucking company could win. I am *not* going to let that happen."

She closed her eyes for a moment and the vulnerability on her features gave him the absurd urge to comfort her.

"Fine," she said after a moment. "Do what you have to do. And I will, too. Will you excuse me, then? I have a great deal of work to do."

Without another word, he spun on his heels and headed out the door.

He sat in his SUV for just a moment before turning the key in the ignition. Betrayal tasted like bitter ash in his mouth.

His mind flashed with images. Anna reading to Ethan

with his son snuggled against her and her features soft and affectionate. The way her eyes lit up when he kissed her. Making love with her and the tenderness that wrapped around them like a blanket on a cold winter's day…

All a mirage. He couldn't believe he was so stupid about her. So very, very blind.

He jerked the vehicle in gear and backed out of her driveway, hitting the speed dial on his cell phone as he went.

"Hi, Mom," he said when Diane answered. "I need you to keep Ethan a little longer, if you can."

"Is anything wrong, dear?"

What the hell wasn't wrong? He was in love with a woman willing to sacrifice her family for her career.

"Just a few work complications. I've got to run to the hospital. I'm sorry."

"No problem," his mother answered. "We're having a great time, aren't we, kiddo?"

He could hear Ethan giggling in the background and the pure sound of it centered him. He loved his son. He might feel like his legs had just been ripped out from underneath him but he still had Ethan, his mom, his practice. He had to hold on to the good things in his life. There would be time to mourn his shattered illusions later.

Right now, he needed to find Peter Wilder.

Any more shocks in her life and she was going to need a good cardiologist.

Anna sat numbly in her living room after Richard left. Lilli regarded her quizzically for a long moment then leapt onto her lap. Anna managed to yank herself out of her near-catatonia to pet the dog, while her mind continued to churn.

She felt like she was caught in the throes of a raging tornado for the past eighteen hours. The stunning news about her father, the outrageous discovery about NHC's plans for Walnut River General, making love with Richard and then being forced to face his bitter anger.

Lost somewhere in there had been his stunning declaration that he was in love with her.

I wouldn't want a little detail like the fact that I'm in love with you distract you from all that other important stuff in your life right now.

He couldn't be in love with her. Why would he possibly say such a thing? Still, she couldn't forget the emotion on his face the night before when he had held her, a certain light in his eyes as he kissed her.

I think you're a brilliant, capable, beautiful woman who doesn't see her own strengths. You don't see yourself as I do, as someone with the ability to cope with anything that comes along.

His words seemed etched in her memory, permanently imprinted there, just like the wild pulse of joy that had jumped inside her at his words, only to fade into shock a few moments later when he read that damn memo.

She buried her face in her hands. He couldn't love her. Not really. Obviously his feelings couldn't be very sure if he could tell her in one breath that he was in love with her, then believe her capable of betraying her own brother the next.

She remembered the disgust, the disillusionment in his eyes and wanted to weep. She could have told him everything, that she had just read the memo herself and was as sickened by it as he. The temptation to do just that had been overwhelming.

But she had known even as she opened her mouth that she couldn't do it. Richard had no legal access to an internal NHC memo, just as she had reminded him. But somehow she had a feeling that wouldn't have stopped him from taking on NHC and its powerhouse attorneys single-handedly and potentially endangering his own career.

She hadn't wanted him to take that risk. This was her mess and she was obligated to figure a way out of it herself. She wondered what Richard or her siblings would say if they knew she had been the one to bring Walnut General to the attention of her superiors at Northeastern HealthCare.

She had closed her eyes to some of the more questionable practices at NHC. Fury burned through her at her own negligence, her own gullibility. She should have known better. She should have remembered everything James Wilder tried to instill in his children. Things like character and strength and the awareness of greater good.

She had to fix this, and she had to do it on her own, no matter the cost to her job or her reputation.

She would probably face charges—or at least be sued. She had signed a nondisclosure clause when she took the job at NHC and whistle-blowing about an internal memo was in direct violation of what she had agreed to.

She was going to need a good attorney. Too bad she had just ensured the one man she trusted wanted nothing to do with her.

A sob welled up inside her but she choked it down. She had to keep it together. She had far too much to do right now to waste time sitting here feeling sorry for herself amid the wreckage of the life she had created for herself.

She picked up her cell phone and dialed Peter's number,

programmed there just like Ella's and David's, though she hadn't used any of them for months.

At first, she was frustrated when she was sent directly to voice mail, but then relief flooded her at the temporary reprieve.

Eventually she would have to explain to her older brother how stupid she had been, but at least for now she could escape with only leaving a message.

"Peter, it's Anna." Her voice trailed off as she floundered for words. "Look, this is going to sound really strange but I have a feeling Richard Green will be trying to get in touch with you. When you hear what he has to say, I would...ask you to withhold judgment for now. I have no right to ask you that. To ask you anything, really. But...I promise, I have my reasons. Just don't rush to conclusions, okay?"

She hung up, feeling even more like an idiot. Would he think she was crazy or would he give her a chance to explain?

She drew in a deep fortifying breath, then picked up her phone again. She had to fix this, no matter what might happen to her as a result. For her family's sake—and for her own—she had to make things right.

Chapter Twelve

Richard headed immediately to the hospital, where to his relief he found Peter Wilder's vehicle in his assigned parking space.

After checking Peter's office and the cafeteria, he finally found the man on the fourth floor in the administrative boardroom—along with Ella, David and J. D. Sumner.

Ella looked lovely and competent in surgical scrubs, her dark hair held away from her face with a headband, while her brothers and fiancé wore casual clothes, fitting for a Saturday.

Papers were scattered across the table and they all looked deep in conversation.

He hated what he was about to do to the Wilder family.

Not his fault, he reminded himself. He had done nothing. Anna and the bastards she worked for had created all of this. Acknowledging that didn't make his task any easier, though.

They were so engrossed in conversation that none of them noticed his presence for several moments until Peter finally looked up.

"Richard! Come in. Just the man we need to talk to."

"Oh?" He felt vaguely queasy at their eager smiles.

"We've decided we're not just tossing a white flag up in the air and giving in to Northeastern Health Care without a fight." Animation brightened Peter's features. "We need to come up with another plan for the municipal council to consider. A better alternative."

"Okay," he said slowly.

"What do you think of this? Walnut River wants out of the hospital business. Fine. I understand where they're coming from. With overhead and malpractice insurance costs through the roof, it's tough for public entities to stay viable in today's health-care market. We get it. But what if we could figure out a way to privatize the hospital without a takeover? If we could find local investors with the financial backing to purchase the hospital from the city?"

"That's a big *what if*."

"Absolutely," David Wilder interjected. "But with just a few phone calls we've found several major players who are interested and I think we could get many of the local physicians to join up on a more limited basis."

"I really think we could make it work," Peter said. "This way the city would be out of the hospital business but decision-making control would still remain in local hands instead of some faceless corporate behemoth."

A corporate behemoth that intends to take you down. Richard forced a smile. "Sounds like you've thought it through."

"We're just in the beginning stages." Ella beamed with excitement. "But we need to know what legal hoops we'd have to jump through. That's where you come in."

All three of the Wilders were humming with energy and he hated even more what he had to tell them about their sister. He, conversely, was suddenly exhausted. At the same time, he was filled with a fierce desire to do everything he possibly could to beat Northeastern Health-Care any freaking way possible.

"I'm in," he said promptly. "Whatever you need, I'll help you."

It was the least he could do, especially since they would soon be dealing with Anna's latest betrayal.

"I knew you would help us."

Ella smiled at him and for the first time Richard saw a trace of Anna in her smile. How had he missed the resemblance all these years? Was it simply because he had been acting on the assumption that Anna was adopted and hadn't been looking for it?

What else had he missed about Anna Wilder? he wondered.

"So what brings you here on a Saturday afternoon? Was there something you needed?" Peter asked.

Richard could feel his shoulders tense and he forced himself to relax as much as possible. "I need to speak with you," he finally said. "It's about Anna."

"What about her?" Ella asked, and Richard didn't miss her sudden tension or the disgust dragging down the corners of David's mouth or Peter's weary resignation. Only J.D. looked impartial, but Richard was quite confident that would quickly change.

"Perhaps this would be better in private."

"He'll only tell us what you said after you leave," Ella said.

"Not necessarily," Peter murmured, exchanging a look with Richard.

"You can use my office if you need a place to talk," J.D. offered.

"Thanks," Richard said, then led the way down the hall to the administrator's office.

"What's going on?" Peter asked when Richard closed the door behind the two of them.

Richard let out a long weary breath. This was a miserable thing to have to dump on a man as conscientious and upright as Peter Wilder. "I hate to be the one to tell you this, but you need to know what Northeastern Health-Care is planning."

He briefly outlined the memo he had inadvertently read, including their underhanded strategy to defeat the opposition by taking Peter out through any means necessary.

When he finished, Peter's features were taut with fury. "Sexual misconduct allegations? Malpractice?"

He paused and seemed at a loss for words. "What the hell kind of people does Anna work with?" he finally said.

"We knew they would fight hard and possibly fight dirty to obtain such a potentially lucrative hospital."

"Yes, but I never expected something so underhanded. And you're telling me Anna knew about the memo? About what they planned?"

He hated every moment of this. "I'm sorry. I found it at her place. She told me to stay out of it. That it wasn't any of my business."

Peter raked a hand through his hair, his eyes dark with betrayal. "She called while I was talking to a potential investor earlier but I haven't had time to check my messages."

"I have no proof, Pete. Only what I saw. I couldn't take it from her house since I didn't have any legal right to access the corporation's internal documents. It would have been theft."

"Even if it was there in plain sight?"

"It wasn't. Not really. I wouldn't have even seen it except some papers fell when we were…" Fighting. Kissing. What the hell difference did it make? He caught himself just in time from offering either answer. "When we were talking. I went to pick them up and saw the memo."

"My own sister is willing to throw me to the wolves. How could she be a party to such a thing?"

"I can't answer that," Richard answered.

"I thought after last night, maybe we could manage to salvage some relationship with her. Things seemed… different with her after she read the letter."

"I'm sorry." It was painfully inadequate but he had nothing else to offer.

"This is going to kill Ella. As angry as she's been at Anna, she still misses her sister, especially with all the weddings coming up in the family."

"You have to tell them."

Peter nodded, not looking at all thrilled at the prospect. "If we have no proof of what they're planning, how can we fight it?"

"You're getting married in a week. Any chance you might be willing to take a little personal time, reschedule your appointments, to stay away from the hospital? If you're not seeing patients, they can't entrap you, either through malpractice allegations or anything else."

"I'm not running and hiding! That's not the way my father would handle this and it's not the way I will, either."

He expected exactly that answer. Richard sighed. "I have a few other ideas. None of them easy."

"I don't care," Peter snapped. "I am not going to let them win, no matter what it takes."

Saturday afternoon at Walnut River General brought back a world of memories for Anna: the light slanting through the front doors, the smell inside of cafeteria food, the underlying hint of antiseptic and antibiotics, and the slightly quieter pace.

How many Saturdays of her youth had been spent here waiting for her father while he wrapped up just one more bit of paperwork or attended to one more patient?

Her memories seemed so rich and fresh as she stood in the lobby that she almost expected him to come striding through the halls of the hospital, his stethoscope around his neck, his white coat flapping behind him and that steely determination in his blue eyes.

Oh, she missed her father.

The last eight years had been so strained between them that she couldn't think of him at all without this hollow ache of regret inside her. So much wasted time. She would have given anything if her father had once communicated in person the things he'd written in that letter about being proud of her and supporting her career choices.

Instead, she had always felt the bitter sting of knowing she had disappointed him.

She pushed the familiar pain away and approached the security guard seated behind the information desk.

"I'm looking for my brother, Dr. Peter Wilder. He

wasn't at home and his car is parked in his parking space out front. Can you give me some idea where I might be able to find him?"

"Don't know. Sorry."

His expression was cool, bordering on hostile, and she sighed. She had never met this man in her life. The only reason she could think for his pugnacity was that he belonged to the anti-merger camp and knew she worked for NHC.

She didn't have time to play hospital politics. Not today. "Would you page him for me, then?" she asked briskly.

He went on reading his newspaper as if he hadn't heard her and she nearly growled with frustration.

"It's important," she finally said. "A family emergency."

Though he hesitated, she could see the wheels in his head turning as he wondered whether he might be incurring Peter's wrath by delaying. Finally he picked up the phone and punched in Peter's pager number.

She drummed her fingers on the counter, impatient for her brother to return the page. She was still waiting a few moments later when the elevator doors opened and the absolute last person she wanted to see right now— okay, last five, at least—walked out.

Ella's eyes were swollen and her nose was red, as if she had been crying. Anna had just a moment's advantage since Ella was busy digging through the messenger bag slung diagonally over her shoulder and didn't see her immediately.

Her sister pulled out her cell phone and started to punch in a number when her gaze suddenly caught sight of Anna and her fingers froze on the phone.

Anna was grateful for the tiny window of opportunity

she'd had to prepare herself for the coming confrontation. Otherwise, she was certain Ella's vicious stare would have destroyed her on the spot.

In some corner of her mind, she knew her imagination was running in overdrive but suddenly the previously empty foyer seemed filled with people, all of their attention focused on the two sisters.

Every warning bell inside her was clanging, warning her to escape, that she didn't need this right now. But she couldn't do it. Though it was one of the hardest things she'd ever done, she forced herself to step forward, until she was only a few feet away.

"Ella," she murmured, aching inside, wishing she could make everything right again. After that one word, she had no idea what else to say, but her sister didn't give her a chance, anyway.

Ella glared at her. "If we were kids again, I'd be ripping your hair out right now. Literally. Hank by painful hank, until your eyes watered so much you couldn't see."

Under less dire circumstances, Anna might have smiled at the threat and the way Ella's hands fisted on her messenger bag. She wouldn't have put anything past her feisty little sister. Ella might have been the youngest Wilder but she had always been able to hold her own with the rest of them.

Suddenly Anna missed her sister and the closeness they had once shared, with a fierce hollow yearning. She missed late-night gab sessions and shopping trips to the mall and fighting over their shared bathroom.

While Anna was trying so hard to prove herself, her sister had become a beautiful dedicated physician and she had missed the whole process because of her foolishness.

"Don't believe everything you hear, El."

"Are you calling Richard Green a liar? He knows what he saw in that memo and I believe every word he says."

Anna closed her eyes, hurt all over again that Richard had so quickly allied himself with her siblings against her, that he trusted her integrity so little.

With good reason, she reminded herself. She couldn't blame him for this. She had created the mess through her own stupidity and it was up to her to make it right.

The magnitude of the task ahead of her seemed daunting, terrifying, but she had to do it, for her family's sake and for her own.

"I would never call Richard a liar. He saw exactly what he said he saw."

"So you admit it!" If anything, the shadows under Ella's eyes looked darker, almost bruised. "You're part of Northeastern HealthCare's dirty tactics to destroy Peter's reputation! How could you, Anna?"

"I didn't know about the memo, El."

"That's easy to say now that we know about it."

She couldn't argue with Ella. Nothing she said would convince her sister, and in the meantime, she was wasting valuable time.

"I'm not going to stand here in the hospital foyer and have a shouting match with you. You'll believe what you want to believe. Nothing I say will make any difference."

Ella's mouth drooped and she looked as if she might cry again. "What happened to you, Anna? The sister I loved so much would never have been a party to something like this."

Ella's use of the past tense sent a shaft of pain through her but Anna fought it down. She deserved all of this. How could she blame Ella for thinking the worst of her when she had purposely created so much distance between them that Ella had nothing else to judge her by?

"Can you tell me where to find Peter?"

"Why? Have you come to twist the knife a little harder?" She sighed. "Where is he, El?"

She thought for a moment her sister wasn't going to answer but then she shrugged. "He's in his office with Richard. They're working on strategy."

Great. Not only did she have to face her livid brother but now she had to see Richard again. This was shaping up to be one fabulous day.

"None of us will let you do this to him, Anna," Ella said, her voice fierce and determined. "You need to know that. Whatever friends Northeastern HealthCare has in this hospital won't be on your side for long when word leaks out about these dirty tactics. The entire hospital will mobilize to protect Peter before we let you destroy him."

"Fair enough," Anna murmured.

Knowing any further arguments with Ella were futile and would only deepen the chasm between them, she turned away and headed for the elevator.

As she rode up to the fourth floor, she realized Peter had kept his part of the bargain from the night before. She was certain of it. He was still leaving the choice of telling David and Ella about their father's letter up to Anna. If she had learned about James's indiscretion that had resulted in Anna's conception, Ella would have said something. She would have at least looked at her a little differently.

The last thing any of them probably wanted right now was a closer kinship with her.

The door to Peter's office suite was closed and her hands trembled as she reached to open it.

Forget this and go home.

The thought whispered through her mind and for an instant, she was deeply tempted. Seeing the disillusionment in her brother's eyes would be hard enough. Seeing it all over again in Richard's and knowing she had lost his love forever would be unbearable.

She stood for a long moment, trying to bolster her courage. She had no idea what she would say to Peter but she had to attempt some kind of explanation.

Finally she knocked on the door before she could talk herself out of it.

"Yeah," Peter said gruffly and she took that as all the invitation she was likely to receive.

She pushed the door open and nearly wept with relief to find her brother alone in his office.

"Where's Richard? Ella said he was up here with you." It was the first thing she could think of to say but Peter didn't seem to think it was an odd opening volley.

"He had to leave to pick up Ethan. His son."

"I know who Ethan is. He's a great kid."

She was stalling. She recognized it but this was so excruciatingly hard with Peter watching her out of those eyes that reminded her so much of their father's.

"I guess you're probably surprised to see me."

He shrugged. "I wouldn't have expected you to show your face around here right about now. It's a good thing David had to meet Courtney and Janie downtown or you wouldn't have made it this far."

She laughed bitterly. "Ella threatened to yank my hair out down in the lobby."

"What did you expect?"

The hard edge to his expression made her want to flee but she hardened her resolve and clasped her hands together in her lap.

"I didn't know about the memo, Peter. I swear I didn't. I know you have no reason to believe me, but it's the truth. I found it just minutes before Richard arrived. It was top secret and on a private server I shouldn't have had access to, but my boss gave me his password to upload some documents regarding the merger and it was just...there. I made a backup copy of it for my files and printed it out and was trying to figure out what to do when Richard showed up and saw it."

He was quiet for a long moment, studying her features intently. "And what did you decide to do?" he finally asked, his voice so controlled she couldn't begin to guess whether he believed her or not.

She lifted her chin. "I'm a Wilder. Of course I'm going to do the right thing!"

He smiled with such sudden brilliance she felt a little lightheaded. "Of course you're going to do the right thing."

His certainty washed through her, warm and soothing. He believed her. The rest of the world might think she was a sleazy, sneaky corporate mole but Peter believed her.

To her chagrin, her eyes burned with emotion and a single tear escaped to trickle down her face.

"I'm sorry. I just...I thought you would be as convinced as everyone else that I intended all this from the start."

Peter stepped forward and pulled her into a quick hug. "Richard put forward a convincing argument. But some part of me still couldn't quite believe it."

She leaned against him for only a moment while she struggled to regain her composure.

"I've been a fool. There were other warning signs of NHC's more questionable business practices among the top level of brass but I ignored them. My other boss is a good decent man, so I convinced myself I was imagining things. I was on the fast track there and I convinced myself they were harmless and that I could make a difference when I moved up in management. I never expected these sorts of underhanded tactics, especially not against my own brother. I should have, though. If they make good on any of the strategies outlined in the memo, I'll never forgive myself."

"We're not going to let them get away with it, Anna."

"Neither am I," she said grimly. "It's going to take me some time, though. For a few days, it may seem as if things are continuing normally with the merger negotiations and the board vote Thursday. I know I've given you absolutely no reason, but I have to ask you to trust me, just for a few days."

"Okay."

Just like that.

His faith made her want to weep again but she drew herself together. "In the meantime, listen to Richard. He can help you protect yourself against whatever Alfred Daly and his cohorts might have up their sleeves."

"He wants me to take this week off before the wedding."

"Not a bad idea."

"I won't run. Dad wouldn't have."

She smiled, sensing a ray of light for the first time since she opened that file on Daly's server earlier that day. "No, he wouldn't have."

"You're more like him than you've ever given yourself credit for," Peter said.

"Not yet," she answered with a shaky smile. "But I'm getting there."

Chapter Thirteen

"Hurry up or we're going to be late, Ethan. Where's your baseball glove?"

"Don't know." His son remained remarkably unconcerned that his last T-ball game was supposed to start in forty-five minutes as he continued playing with his Matchbox cars.

Richard drew in a deep breath. Trying for patience was just about the toughest task he faced as a father—especially since Ethan was easily distracted and usually bubbled over with energy.

The process of encouraging him to stay on task was tougher than facing a whole courtroom full of high-powered attorneys.

"Think. Where did you have it last?"

Ethan zoomed one of his trucks along the edge of the carpet where it met the hardwood flooring. "Outside, I guess. Me and Grandma played catch earlier today. I think maybe I left it there."

"So go look for it, or we're not going to make it to your game."

His snappish tone finally captured Ethan's attention. He dropped his car and gave his father a wounded look. "We have to go! It's my last game!"

"Then go find your glove."

Ethan glared at him but headed for the backyard in search of the missing equipment, leaving Richard with only his guilt for company.

He needed to practice a little more patience with his son. His bad mood wasn't Ethan's fault. Richard knew exactly why he had been irritable and out of sorts for the past four days.

Anna Wilder.

He hadn't seen her since Saturday morning at her duplex but she hadn't been far from his thoughts. He had done his best to push away the memory of making love to her but sometimes random images intruded into his mind, usually at the most inopportune moment.

Despite that little glitch, for the most part his whole world had condensed to two clear objectives—protecting Peter Wilder and beating the hell out of NHC in the merger negotiations. Everything he did was aimed at those goals.

So far, Peter appeared to be safe. No malpractice allegations or harassment claims had emerged out of the woodwork. Since the hospital board vote was scheduled for first thing in the morning, he had to look at the relative quiet as a positive indicator that NHC had reconsidered the strategies outlined in that damn memo.

He wasn't letting down his guard, though, and he wasn't allowing Peter to do so, either. He had been fiercely busy wrapping Anna's brother in as many legal safeguards as he could devise.

To his further frustration, Peter seemed remarkably unconcerned about any possible threat to his reputation or his practice, until Richard wanted to shake him out of his complacency.

"See, Dad? I found it! I told you it was in the backyard."

Ethan still looked annoyed at him for the flare of temper so Richard forced himself to smile. "Good job. We'd better get going."

On the way out to the SUV, he closed his eyes and arched his neck one way and then the other, trying to force his shoulders to relax. He couldn't take his grim mood out on his son. Ethan didn't deserve it. The one person who did deserve it was making herself remarkably scarce.

Ethan jabbered all the way to the park where he played T-ball. When they were a few blocks from the baseball field, he suddenly stopped in the middle of a soliloquy about the playdate he had enjoyed with a friend that afternoon.

"Hey, Dad, Anna said she would come to another one of my games. She promised, remember, the night she read me the funny story about the worm and the spider? This is my last one. Do you think she'll be there?"

Apparently, Richard wasn't the only one who couldn't stop thinking about a certain lovely blond double-crosser.

"Anna's really busy right now," he murmured. *Destroying the hospital her father dedicated his life to, and her family in the process.* "She might not make it."

"She promised," Ethan said, his voice brimming with

confidence. "I wonder if she'll bring Lilli. Do you think she'll let me walk her again? I sure like that dog."

He so hated that his son had to learn the lesson early in life that some people couldn't be trusted to remember things like honor and decency and promises made. He wanted Ethan to hang on to his illusions for a little bit longer.

"We'll have to see what happens. Like I said, Anna is really busy right now."

But to his shock, when they arrived at the ball diamond, she was the first person he saw. She sat on the top bench of the bleachers, looking sleek and elegant even in Levi's and a crisp white shirt.

At the sight of her, his heart gave a slow surge of welcome and his body tightened with longing. How was it that when he was away from her, he always managed to forget how her long blond loveliness took his breath away?

"She's here! I knew she would come. Do you see her, Dad?"

"I see her," he answered, his voice gruff. Fast on the heels of his initial pleasure at seeing her was hot hard anger that racketed through him like a pinball.

Why the hell couldn't she leave him alone? This was hard enough for him, knowing how stupid he had been for her.

Even knowing what she was, what she was part of, he couldn't keep himself from wanting her.

"I'm gonna show her how good I am at catching the ball now." Ethan raced ahead of him and climbed like a little howler monkey up the bleachers to talk to Anna. Richard was grateful for the few minutes to gain control of the wild surge of emotions. By the time he reached them, the careening emotions inside him had faded to a dull ache instead of that terrible, piercing pain.

Her blue eyes held wariness and something else— something elusive and tantalizing that he couldn't quite identify.

"Hi." She pitched her voice low.

He nodded, but didn't quite trust himself not to yell at her all over again so he said nothing.

"I promised I would be here," she said. "I didn't want to let Ethan down."

She was willing to crucify her own brother but she didn't want to break a promise to a five-year-old boy? He gave her a skeptical look and she had the grace to flush.

"Where's Lilli?" Ethan asked. "Did you bring her?"

"Not tonight. She hasn't been feeling good the last couple of days. I think she has a cold."

"Dogs get colds?"

"Sometimes. Or maybe it's just allergies."

He looked disappointed for about half a second, then with rapid-fire speed, his mood cycled back to excitement. "Hey, guess what, Anna? Me and my grandma played catch all day today and now I'm super good. I won't miss another fly ball, ever again. Wanna see?"

"Absolutely. Bring it on."

She gripped Ethan's hand and climbed down from the bleachers, smiling at his son with such genuine pleasure that Richard felt as if his heart were being ripped into tiny pieces.

Ethan grinned back and shoved the ball at Richard. "Dad, can you throw it at me so I can show Anna how good I catch?"

"Sure. Let's step away from the bleachers a little so we don't hit anybody if we miss the ball."

"I'm not going to miss, Dad. I told you, I've been practicing."

"It's not you I'm worried about, it's me. I don't even have a glove."

"I won't throw hard, okay?"

Still doing his best not to look at her, he led Ethan to an open stretch of ground between two playing fields. He tossed the ball to his son and was pleased when Ethan easily caught it in his glove.

"Good job!" Anna exclaimed. "You have been practicing."

"Yep. Now watch me throw it back!" He tossed it back to Richard, harder than he expected and a little to the right. Richard managed to snag it with his bare hands, but it was a near thing.

Anna stood watching them both play catch for several minutes, her features revealing little of her thoughts, until Ethan's coach blew a whistle to call his team into the dugout.

Ethan ran off eagerly, leaving Richard alone with her—exactly the position he didn't want to find himself.

They made their way back toward the bleachers in silence. Just before they reached them, Anna touched the bare skin of his forearm to stop him. She dropped her hand quickly but not before the heat of her fingers scorched through him.

"I'm sorry. I'm sure you're wishing me to Hades right about now. But I did promise Ethan."

"I wouldn't want you to break a promise."

That delicate flush coated her cheekbones and he wondered at it. How could she possibly still have the ability to blush?

"Have you talked to Peter?" she asked after a moment.

"Several times. He seems remarkably nonchalant for a man whose sister is trying to destroy him."

"Has anything…happened?"

"You tell me. You're the one with all the inside information."

Her jaw clenched at his bitter tone. "You're going to believe what you want to believe."

"No. I'm going to believe the evidence. I'm an attorney. That's what we do."

"Maybe the evidence isn't as cut-and-dried as you think."

He opened his mouth to offer a scathing rebuke but she cut him off with a shake of her head.

"I didn't come here to fight with you, Richard. I also didn't want to spoil the game for you. I'll just watch an inning or two and then get out of your way. You'll hardly know I'm here."

He was saved from having to respond by Ethan's team taking the field.

The park had two sets of bleachers and she at least had the courtesy to sit on the other bleachers, several dozen feet away from him. That didn't stop his gaze from drifting in her direction entirely too often.

He knew it was crazy but he could almost smell her from here, that feminine, sexy scent of hers.

He didn't miss the way she stood up and cheered when Ethan caught a fly ball to end the inning half and then again a few minutes later when his son hit a two-run single. When his son crossed home plate, sent home by another player's hit, Richard also didn't miss the way Ethan grinned triumphantly first at his father then turned to aim the same grin at Anna.

Damn her. His heart was already shattered. Did she have to do the same thing to his son's?

She lasted all of an inning and a half—long enough to watch Ethan hit another single—before she couldn't bear another minute.

As she slid down the bleachers, the sun was just dipping below the horizon, bathing the baseball diamond in the pale rosy light of dusk. She closed her eyes, wanting to store up this moment.

It had been foolish to come. Foolish and self-indulgent. She had hoped four days of reflection would have had some kind of impact on Richard, that perhaps he might begin to experience a little doubt about her guilt.

She supposed some optimistic corner of her heart had hoped he'd begun to wonder if he might have been wrong about her.

Obviously, that hadn't happened. He was as angry as he had been Saturday morning when he had seen that memo. More so, maybe. Hearing the bitterness in his voice, seeing the cold disdain in those eyes that had once looked at her with such warm tenderness, had been chilling proof that nothing had changed.

She walked back to her car with one hand curled against the crushing pain in her chest.

Nothing had changed and everything had changed. The wheels she had set in motion couldn't be stopped now.

Now she just had to wait and see what happened.

* * *

Richard walked into the hospital the next morning in his best suit and his favorite power tie. He had slept little the night before. After tossing and turning for a couple of hours, he had finally risen well before dawn.

He wanted to think it was diligence to his client that kept him up and not his last glimpse of Anna as she had left the baseball diamond. Unfortunately, he knew otherwise.

He was totally committed to representing the hospital to the best of his ability but the images haunting his fragmented dreams hadn't had anything to do with the hospital. They had everything to do with Anna.

He wanted this hospital board meeting to be over. Though the merger vote was still too close to call, at this point he just wanted a damn decision. Then maybe this sense of impending doom would dissipate. At least Peter would be safe—and maybe Anna would return to New York where she belonged and he wouldn't have to spend a sleepless night every time he happened to bump into her.

He would probably see her this morning at the board meeting. Twisted as he was, he couldn't help the little buzz of anticipation at the prospect.

He sighed as he walked through the lobby. The security guard waved and grinned at him. Richard managed a half-hearted wave, then furrowed his brow when three more staff members beamed at him on his way to the elevator.

Weird.

Though he usually didn't buy into those woo-woo kind of things, he sensed a curious energy in the air. The impression was reinforced when he rode the elevator with Bob Barrett, a physician he knew only casually. The man actually patted him on the back when the elevator stopped at the second floor.

"It's a great day for Walnut River General, isn't it?" he said, before stepping out.

Something definitely odd was going on. He couldn't begin to figure out what.

The first person he met coming out of the elevator on the administrative floor was Ella Wilder. She aimed a thousand-watt smile at him, then went one better, throwing her arms around him.

"Isn't it wonderful?" she exclaimed. "The best news I can imagine. Peter and Bethany's wedding this weekend will truly be a celebration."

Before he could ask her what the hell she was talking about, she released him and jumped into the waiting elevator just before the doors closed, leaving him completely befuddled.

He headed to J.D.'s office, hoping Ella's fiancé could shed a little light on things.

J.D. wasn't alone. Peter Wilder stood in the outer office with him and his assistant, Tina Tremaine, and all of them looked jubilant.

"I knew she would come through for us," Peter exulted when he saw Richard. "She's a Wilder, isn't she?"

He frowned. "Who? Ella?"

"Of course not. Anna!" He grinned at Richard but his smile faded when he took in his confusion. "I'm guessing you haven't read the paper this morning."

"I didn't have a chance. I was too busy prepping for this morning's board meeting." And brooding about Peter's sister. "Why? What did I miss?"

J.D. and Peter exchanged laughing looks. "Maybe

you'd better come into my office and see for yourself," J.D. said. "My staff made sure I received a copy."

He opened the door behind him and Richard was stunned to see every available surface covered with the front page of the *Walnut River Courier.*

The same headline in huge type screamed from all of them: Northeastern HealthCare Drops Hospital Bid.

A subhead read: Municipal Council Considering Options, May Look to Private Investors.

He stared at the headline and then at both men. "They're pulling out? After six months of fighting? Just like that?"

Peter laughed. "No. Not just like that. My brilliant baby sister did it all. In five days, she managed to accomplish what the rest of us have been trying to pull off for months."

He shook his head to clear the fuzziness out, wishing all over again that he'd been able to grab more than a few hours of restless sleep. He grabbed one of the newspapers off the wall and read the first few paragraphs, stopping when he reached the statement released by NHC.

He read,

Upon further study, we have determined that Walnut River General would not be a good fit for NHC. We regret that we will not have the opportunity to bring our winning health-care model to the citizens of Walnut River but wish the community and hospital personnel all the best.

It was definitely a blow-off quote, leaving NHC very little room to reconsider.

"I'm sorry. I'm lost here. You're going to have to back up a step or two for me. What is this? Why did they pull out? And why do you seem to think Anna had anything to do with it? Last I heard, she was the enemy. What about the infamous memo?"

"That memo is the best thing that's ever happened to the merger opposition," J.D. answered.

"How can that be possible?" he growled.

"Because finding it infuriated Anna and mobilized her to our side," Peter answered.

"What do you mean, finding it? She knew about it all along."

Peter shook his head. "No, she didn't."

"So she says." He couldn't keep the bitterness out of his voice, the deep sense of betrayal.

Peter frowned and gestured to the newspaper headlines blaring across the room. "This is evidence she's telling the truth. Do you really think NHC would have dropped their bid for the hospital if Anna hadn't maneuvered things so they had no other choice?"

"How?"

"She's brilliant," J.D. said. "Savvy and smart. She single-handedly orchestrated what amounts to an internal coup to force them out."

"She knew there was an anti-Daly faction at NHC, shareholders and other top-level executives who weren't happy with some of his tactics," Peter added. "Anna has been working like a demon for the last four days, negotiating with them. She agreed to deliver the memo as evidence against Daly to him out if they would consent to drop their bid for the hospital. It all hit the fan yesterday. Daly's out at Northeastern HealthCare, a new guard is in and their first action was to issue the statement withdrawing their bid for the hospital, as promised."

Richard felt as if J.D. and Peter had both taken turns pummeling him with an office chair.

He tried to remember Anna's demeanor Saturday morning when he read the memo at her apartment. She had been shaky and uneasy, he remembered. Pale, nervous, edgy. But he had just attributed it to guilt that he had found out about NHC's nefarious plans for Peter.

Was it possible she hadn't known? When she had faced all his accusations, could she have been withholding evidence that would have exonerated her?

He couldn't seem to wrap his head around it. He had been hard, bordering on cruel. *You're a cold heartless woman who is willing to sell your own family down the river to get your way.*

Those had been his words. And she had stood there absorbing them. Why the hell hadn't she tried to defend herself? She had stood there and let him rip into her without saying a thing.

Not quite true, he remembered with growing self-disgust. She had told him he was jumping to unfounded conclusions. She had asked him to give her a few days to straighten things out but he had assumed she was only trying to delay him from taking action until after the vote.

Just last night, she had told him that maybe the evidence wasn't as cut-and-dried as he wanted to believe.

She had skirted the truth but hadn't told him all of it.

She hadn't trusted him. That's what it all came down to. She had taken his criticism without explaining anything at all of substance to him.

And he deserved her lack of trust. He had jumped to conclusions, had based his entire perceptions of her guilt and innocence on past misdeeds that should have been inadmissible.

Because of what happened eight years before, he had been completely unwilling to give her any benefit of doubt. When he saw that memo, he had taken it as damning evidence against her—proof of her perfidy, he now realized, that he had been looking for all along.

Even if she had tried to defend herself a little more strenuously, he wasn't sure he would have allowed himself to believe her.

He had told her he loved her.

It hadn't been a lie, exactly. He did love her. But love without trust was flimsy and hollow.

"So obviously the board vote this morning has been canceled," Peter interrupted his thoughts. "We're moving ahead with our efforts to privatize the hospital. Is your firm still willing to help us through the legalities?"

"Of course," he answered absently.

"Excellent," J.D. said. "We'd like you to draw up a preliminary partnership agreement as soon as possible so we can present it to the city council. I know this is an imposition, but can you work up a rough draft today?"

"No problem. I allocated most of the day to hospital business, with the merger vote and possible follow-up work. I can have it to you by this afternoon."

"Thanks, Richard," Peter said. "I knew we could count on you."

The other man's words scraped his conscience raw. Anna should have been able to count on him, on the man who claimed he loved her. He should have trusted his own heart, not a stupid piece of paper. Instead, Richard had rushed to convict her without any kind of trial.

He would be lucky if she ever wanted to see him again.

Chapter Fourteen

"We're serious about this, Anna. We want you to stay."

Anna watched Lilli chase her favorite toy, wondering why she couldn't manage to drum up a little more enthusiasm for Wallace Jeffers's unbelievable offer. He wanted her to take over his position as vice president of the mergers and acquisitions division of NHC since he was poised to move into Alfred Daly's newly vacated spot.

This was what she had dreamed about for eight years. Wallace had been her mentor at NHC, the reason she had taken the job there in the first place. He had been one of those at the company who predicted a great future for her there and now that he was taking over for Daly, he appeared to be willing to make those predictions reality.

She should be over the moon. She should be doing cartwheels, sending notice to all the trade papers, ordering new business cards.

Instead, she sat in her rented duplex, watching her dog drool all over a rubber lizard and trying to summon a little excitement. "I appreciate your trust in me, Wallace. I do. But I'm going to have to think about this."

"What's to think about?" He sounded genuinely startled. "It's a no-brainer, Anna. If you take this job, you'll be completely skipping over several rungs in the corporate ladder."

"I know that. It's an incredible offer and I'm grateful. I just need a little time to think about it."

"We need to move fast to reorganize the company if we want to enact the kind of changes some of us have been pushing for a long time. I'm going to need an answer sooner rather than later."

"Can I at least have a few hours?"

She had been thinking for five days that she was going to lose her job and now she was being offered the promotion of her dreams. It was enough to make her head spin.

He sighed. "I want you on board, Anna. Without you having the guts to come forward with that memo we used to push Daly out, none of this would have happened. I want people of integrity and grit on my team. You've earned this promotion. No one in that department works harder than you do or gets my vision more clearly."

She had nothing but respect for Wallace Jeffers and knew that under his leadership, NHC would thrive. She was deeply flattered that he had enough faith in her to believe her capable of replacing him. She ought to just say yes right now and start packing her bags to return to New York, but the words seemed to clog in her throat.

"I appreciate your offer. I'm just…I have to consider my options right now."

"What options?" His voice sharpened. "Have you got another offer I don't know about?"

"No," she assured him. "Nothing like that."

"Then what?"

My heart is here.

She couldn't say the words, not to her boss, a man she respected professionally and personally.

"Give me a few hours, Wallace. I'll call you back by the end of the day, I promise."

"All right. Just make sure you give yourself enough time to pack up and be back here for an 8 a.m. staff meeting so I can introduce the new leadership team of Northeastern HealthCare."

She managed a laugh. "You're so confident I'll say yes?"

"You'd be stupid not to take this promotion, and you are far from a stupid woman, Anna."

Wrong, she thought sadly. She was stupid. A smart woman would walk away from Walnut River and not look back. But these past few weeks had shown her how deeply her life and the person she had become were intertwined with this community and the people who lived here.

She wasn't sure she was ready to leave.

What was her alternative, though? Jobs in her field weren't exactly thick on the ground in Walnut River. And even if she found one, what would she gain by staying? Only more heartache, she was certain.

She sighed. Why delay the inevitable? She couldn't turn down Wallace's offer. She should just pick up the phone right now and tell him yes. What did Walnut River have to offer her?

She even picked up her cell phone, nerves strumming

through her, but Lilli suddenly barked with excitement and raced to the door and Anna's hand froze on the numbers.

Richard?

Her heart jumped along with her little dog as the doorbell rang.

It wouldn't be, she told herself, though she couldn't help the little spasm of hope that faded when she opened the door. Instead of Richard Green, she was instantly assaulted by her entire family. Peter, David, Ella and their significant others—Bethany Holloway, J. D. Sumner and a lovely brown-eyed blonde she assumed was David's fiancée, Courtney Albright.

"There's my baby sister," David announced before she could even greet them.

She opened her mouth to answer but the words were snatched away when he scooped her into his arms and twirled her around her miniscule living room until her head spun while Lilli yipped and danced around their ankles.

"David," she exclaimed. "Put me down before you either step on my dog or make me puke."

"You're still motion sick? I would have thought you outgrew that years ago."

"Not completely," she said as her stomach churned.

"Ew," he said, releasing her so abruptly she almost fell.

Peter was there to catch her, though. Before she could even find her breath, he pulled her into his arms, enveloping her in a tight hug.

"You didn't let us down, Anna."

His voice sounded so much like their father's. "I knew you could do it. If anyone could save Walnut River General Hospital, I knew it would be you. You were amazing. Absolutely amazing."

She allowed herself one quick moment to bask in the warm glow of her siblings' approval before she pulled away. She had to tell them the truth, the one she had been withholding from them for months.

"You know my company wouldn't have even looked at Walnut River General if not for me, don't you? I'm the one who proposed the hospital as a possible acquisition target in the first place."

Peter made a face. "Okay, so you're not completely perfect. But we're still keeping you."

She almost cried then, holding her tears in by sheer force of will as Peter gave her another tight hug then released her.

"My turn," Ella said, stepping forward.

Anna stared at her little sister, overwhelmed, for just a second too long. Ella's expression started to cool, her arms to drop, and Anna's tears broke free.

"El," she murmured, just that, then grabbed her sister tightly.

For so long she had lived with a hole in her heart without even realizing it. She had tried to fill it with work, never realizing it would always be empty until she made her peace with her family.

Now she stood and rocked with her arms around her sister, the tears trickling down her cheeks.

"I have missed you so much," Ella said.

"I'm sorry. I'm so sorry."

"No. I'm the one who's sorry. I said awful things to you."

"I deserved them. All of them. I've been so stupid. Incredibly stupid. When I dropped out of med school, I was sure I had failed everyone. I thought I had to choose between my career and my family. If I wasn't in medicine, I felt like I didn't belong with the rest of you."

"You do," Ella exclaimed. "Of course you do. You always have."

Anna saw that now. She was a Wilder. It didn't matter whether she was their half sister or their adopted sister. Either way, she belonged in this family. She loved them and needed them in her life and she had been so very foolish to believe she could take on the world by herself.

"You're our sister and we love you," Ella said. "We have all missed you."

"Oh, Ella." She sniffled again.

Sometime soon she would tell Ella and David about the letter from their father but not today, she decided.

"Cut it out, you two," David interrupted. "This is supposed to be a party. A celebration of good triumphing over evil. No offense, Anna."

She couldn't help but laugh. "Oh, none taken, I'm sure."

"We even have champagne," Bethany interjected.

"And food," the other woman added. "Hi. I'm Courtney. I'm thrilled to finally meet you. You have to come to dinner sometime soon so you can meet my little girl, Janie. She's thrilled at the prospect of another aunt to add to her growing family."

To Anna's surprise, David's fiancée gave her a warm hug, as did Bethany and even J.D.

"You can't get away from them all now," J.D. murmured in her ear. "You Wilders are relentless. You had your chance to escape but now you're stuck."

Anna had been alone for so long that the prospect of all this family was daunting but wonderful at the same time.

She looked around at her siblings and their loved ones and she had to laugh. "I just have one question. If you're all here, who's left to run the hospital?"

"Nobody. We closed down so we could come and celebrate with you," David deadpanned.

"I've actually got to go back on in an hour," Ella said. "So I'm afraid I'll have to skip the champagne."

"Ha. I'm off rotation for five whole days," David boasted.

"Lucky," Ella muttered.

"Just wait. When you're an attending, you'll be able to flaunt it over all the lowly residents, too," he said with a grin.

Anna smiled at their banter. Once she would have felt excluded when the rest of the Wilders talked shop. It used to bug the heck out of her and she would always bite down frustration when family discussions inevitably turned to medicine. Now she realized her annoyance had been a result of her own insecurities.

If she hadn't wanted to talk medicine, all she would have had to do was change the subject instead of simmering in her separateness.

"Bring on the champagne," Peter said, distracting her from her thoughts.

"I'm afraid I don't have enough glasses."

"No problem." Bethany grinned. "We brought our own. Courtney thought of everything."

Out of a wicker basket, they pulled out plastic champagne flutes along with cheese, crackers, several boxes of gourmet cookies and even Godiva chocolates.

"I raided everything I could think of from the gift shop," Courtney said with a warm smile.

She and Bethany poured champagne for everyone except Ella, who filled her glass with water.

"To Anna," J.D. said and she flushed as everyone lifted their glasses to her.

"And may I add," he continued, "I find it slightly ironic

that the one Wilder who chose a different path than medicine is the one who ended up saving an entire hospital."

"Hear, hear," Peter said, squeezing her arm.

The next hour would live forever in her memory. As she moved around her tiny apartment talking to first one sibling, then the next—and all three of her prospective in-laws—Anna felt eight years of loneliness begin to heal.

"You're coming to the wedding, of course," Bethany proclaimed. "I'm not taking any other answer but an enthusiastic yes."

"Of course," Anna said with a smile. "I wouldn't miss it."

It would be somewhat humiliating to show up alone when all the other Wilder siblings were conveniently paired up. Richard's image flashed in her head but she quickly shunted it aside.

She had no idea where things stood with him and her heart ached as she thought of his anger the day before.

She wanted to share the triumph of this day with him but he had made no effort to contact her. Maybe he wouldn't. After the past five days, he probably wanted nothing to do with her.

"And now on to business," Peter said suddenly, distracting her from the ache in her chest. "J.D., do you want to do the honors?"

Anna frowned, confused, as they both faced her with meaningful looks. "What business?"

"We have a proposition for you," J.D. said.

"What kind of proposition?" she asked warily.

"Obviously, Northeastern HealthCare has pulled out of talks with the hospital or we wouldn't all be here. But we still need to look to the future. It's only a matter of time before another health-care conglomerate sets its sights on the hospital. We want to head that off if we can so we're moving forward with efforts to privatize the hospital to keep it under local control."

"That won't be easy," she warned. "There are very few freestanding hospitals around anymore."

"Exactly," Peter answered. "That's why we need someone smart and savvy to be our chief financial officer and help us make this a viable enterprise. Somebody who knows the business end of things inside and out and who has ideas for making the necessary economies so we can be profitable while not sacrificing patient care."

She blinked at them, stunned at the offer. After all she had nearly done to destroy the hospital, her siblings wanted her here now to help them save it?

"You think I can do that?" she asked.

"We know you can," Peter said. "We want you to be part of this, Anna. Though I guess we should have asked first where things stand for you at NHC now."

Just a few weeks ago, she would have loved to flaunt her job offer to her siblings. Finally, she would have had proof to show her family that she could succeed in her chosen world. How could they look down on her for dropping out of medical school if she were the mergers and acquisitions vice president of a leading health-care company?

That seemed so petty now.

"I'm still considering my options," she said, content to leave it at that.

"Well, add our offer to the mix," Peter said. "We need you in Walnut River. You belong here, Anna. We can't offer you a high-powered corner office in Manhattan or the salary to match. But we can offer an opportunity to genuinely make a difference, to be part of something with the potential to make life better for everyone in this community."

She gazed at her brothers and sister as a hundred thoughts churned through her mind. They wanted her here with them. The Wilder siblings, united in a common effort to save something so important to the community and to their family. They believed in her and seemed convinced she could actually help them pull this off.

She found the idea heady and exhilarating—and terrifying.

Could she do it? She knew she could handle the challenge. Just thinking about the possibilities filled her with excitement. But how could she possibly just take the plunge straight off the steep career ladder she had been climbing at NHC the past eight years, give up all she had worked for, to stay here in Walnut River with her family to rescue one faltering hospital?

"You don't have to decide right this minute," Peter said into the silence. "It's not fair of us to spring this on you all at once. I can see you're feeling overwhelmed."

"A little," she admitted, deeply grateful they didn't expect an immediate answer.

"It's been a crazy day all the way around. Take some time to think about it. The offer will still be open tomorrow, or even after the wedding if you want to take the weekend and get back to us next week."

"I'll think about it," she promised, astonished that the idea of staying in Walnut River could hold so much appeal. Was she genuinely thinking about taking a job as

CFO for a community hospital when she could be a vice president at a major health-care industry player?

"That's all we can ask," J.D. said.

"This has been wonderful but I'm going to have to get back to the hospital," Ella said.

"Of course," Anna said. "Thank you so much for coming. It means the world to me."

"Thank you," Ella said with a hard fierce hug. "I'll call you tonight when my shift ends, okay? I have so much I want to talk to you about."

Anna smiled. "Deal. You know my ear is always here."

It was their secret code. Ear here. Tell me what's on your mind. I'm here to listen.

Ella sniffled again at Anna's words. "I'm so glad to have you back."

"Same, El."

Their sister's departure with J.D. seemed to be the signal to Peter and David and their fiancées to leave as well. In only a few moments, her apartment was quiet once more.

Anna closed the door behind David and Courtney, then slumped against it. She had forgotten how exhausting her family could be, but she wouldn't trade the last hour for anything.

She was still leaning against the door a moment later, marveling at the abrupt change in her life, when the doorbell rang. Assuming someone had left something behind, she hurried to open it then stopped dead.

Richard stood on the other side, looking wildly sexy in charcoal-gray slacks, a white dress shirt with the sleeves rolled up and a red power tie that was just a little off center.

Her heart seemed to thrum out of her chest and she

could do nothing but stare at him, her mind awash in memories of kissing him, touching him, lying in his arms.

"May I come in?" he finally asked, and she realized she must have been standing there staring at him for a full minute or more.

"I...of course," she managed and opened the door for him.

Her duplex apartment had seemed small but still comfortable with her three siblings and their prospective spouses. So why did it seem to shrink immeasurably when Richard walked inside?

She should say something. *Hello. How are you? I love you.*

The words caught in her throat and she couldn't manage to do anything but stare at him.

He was the first to break the silence.

"Why didn't you tell me?" His voice was low and intense, his eyes a heartbreaking shade of blue-green today.

"I tried," she said. Was he still angry at her? She couldn't read anything in those eyes.

"No, you didn't. Not really. You said I was misinterpreting things but you never gave me the full truth. Why didn't you tell me you knew nothing about that memo until right before I found it?"

She chewed her lip. She remembered how desperate she had been to get him out of her apartment after he had kissed her with stunning tenderness and then said such devastatingly cruel things.

"You won't like my answer."

"Try me. It can't be any worse than all the possible scenarios I've been coming up with all morning for why you didn't trust me enough to ask for my help."

She sighed. "It wasn't that. It wasn't that at all, Richard. Of course I would have trusted you if I could. But what would you have done if I'd told you the truth and enlisted your help?"

He shrugged. "I don't know. Maybe go to the media."

"You would have been on extremely shaky legal ground. As I pointed out, you had no right to access internal NHC documents. That was a confidential memo that you shouldn't have seen at all. I was afraid you would be willing to sacrifice your career by going public with what amounted to stolen information."

He stared at her, stunned. She had been trying to protect him? Of all the explanations he had considered, that one wouldn't have even made the top twenty.

"I'm the one who brought Walnut River to their attention," she continued. "I felt like I had to handle the situation on my own. To fix my own mess. If anyone's career was going to be destroyed, I wanted it to be mine, not yours. You could have been disbarred, Richard. I wasn't about to let that happen."

"Was your career destroyed?" he asked carefully.

He knew she had orchestrated the back-door coup but he had no idea where things stood for her with the new management.

She managed a smile. "I wouldn't say exactly that."

She paused. "The new chief executive officer at NHC just offered me his old job as vice president of mergers and acquisitions."

A chill swept over him and Richard thought for sure he could hear the crackle of his heart freezing solid. All the dreams he had dared let himself begin to spin turned to ice along with it.

"Vice president." He forced a laugh that sounded fake and hollow to his ears. Could she tell? he wondered. "That's amazing. Wonderful news. Congratulations."

She looked a little taken aback, as if she expected some other reaction from him. "Right. Wonderful news."

"Is that why the rest of the Wilders were here? To celebrate?" He tried to inject a little more enthusiasm in his tone. "I saw them all leaving when I pulled up. They must be so proud of you. When do you start?"

"They want me there first thing in the morning," she said, somewhat woodenly.

"What about Peter's wedding Saturday?"

"I...haven't figured that out yet."

He gripped his hand into a fist at his side, doing everything he could not to betray his pain. "Make them wait," he suggested. "If they want you badly enough, they'll have a little patience."

"Will they?" she murmured.

Did her words seem double-edged or was that simply his imagination? Richard studied her closely but her lovely features revealed nothing. He knew he was in danger of losing control in a moment so he edged closer to the door.

"Congratulations again on the job offer. I just stopped by to tell you thank you for what you did for Walnut River General. I'm sorry for jumping to the wrong conclusion before and for the things I said. I should have trusted you."

He turned to leave but she stopped him.

"Richard—"

He didn't know what she intended to say. It didn't matter. When he turned back, he thought he saw a misery in her eyes that matched the pain and loss tearing through him.

He didn't give himself time to think it through, driven only by the need to touch her one more time. He crossed the space between them in two steps and pulled her into his arms, crushing her mouth with his.

After one stunned moment, she made a tiny kind of sobbing sound and her arms slid around him, holding him as if she never wanted to let go.

He kissed her fiercely, pouring all his emotions into the embrace, doing his best to leave no doubt in her mind about how much he loved her. If she was going to leave him again, he damn well wasn't going to make it easy for her.

"Anna, don't go."

She blinked at him. "Wh-What?"

His hands were shaking, he realized with chagrin. He should just leave now before he made a bigger ass out of himself. "I shouldn't have said that. I'm sorry."

"You did, though."

"I did. I know I have no right to beg you to stay after the way I've treated you the last five days. But forget that. I'm going to beg anyway. I love you, Anna. It just about killed me when you walked away last time. I don't think I can bear losing you again. Please stay."

She stared at him, saying nothing for a long, painfully drawn-out moment, then joy flared in those beautiful blue eyes and she wrapped her arms around him again and lifted her mouth to his.

He kissed her with all the pent-up frustration and fear and longing inside him, until his insides trembled and his heart threatened to pound out of his chest.

"I love you," she said. "I love you so much. I have been absolutely miserable without you."

He framed her face with his hands, the lovely serene features he had dreamed about nearly all of his life.

"I want to marry you, Anna. I've wanted it for eight years. Longer, if you want the truth. Since we were kids studying for our calculus tests together. You are the only woman I have ever loved."

Anna closed her eyes at the sweetness of his words, at the sheer sense of rightness she found here in his arms. She had almost missed this, she thought with wonder. If she hadn't taken the assignment to return to Walnut River, she would never have found Richard again, would never have realized how very empty her life was without him.

"Yes, I'll marry you!"

"Ethan and I are a package deal. Are you sure you're okay with that?"

She thought of his darling son, with his cowlick and his mischievous smile. "Better than okay. I already love your son as much as I love you."

He kissed her again and for a long time, she forgot everything else.

"I suppose I'll have to start looking to join a firm in New York," Richard said.

She stared, shocked to her core. "But you love Walnut River."

"Not nearly as much as I love you."

The sincerity of his words humbled her. She had no idea what she had ever done to deserve a man like Richard Green but she didn't care. She was keeping him, whether she deserved him or not.

"My family has asked me to stay on and become chief financial officer for the new privately owned Walnut

River General Hospital. I'm going to call them and tell them I'm in."

He looked stunned. "Are you sure? It's a big step down from an NHC vice president."

"I'm positive," she murmured. "I want to stay right here, in Walnut River and in your arms."

He kissed her again while Lilli danced around them, and Anna knew this was one merger that was destined to succeed.

* * * * *

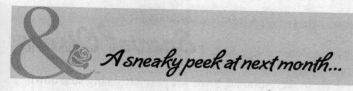

A sneaky peek at next month...

By Request

RELIVE THE ROMANCE WITH THE BEST OF THE BEST

My wish list for next month's titles...

In stores from 19th April 2013:

❏ Billionaires Galore! – Leanne Banks

❏ Bella Rosa Marriages – Fiona Harper, Patricia Thayer & Jennie Adams

In stores from 3rd May 2013:

❏ Hearts of Gold – Meredith Webber

3 stories in each book - only £5.99!

Available at WHSmith, Tesco, Asda, Eason, Amazon and Apple

Just can't wait?

0413/05

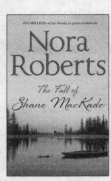

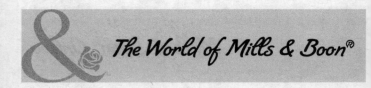